Claiming his mistress!
These rich, hot-blooded Mediterranean males
are ruthless when it comes to seduction!

Mistress to the Mediterranean Male

Three exciting, passionate novels from favourite
authors Carole Mortimer, Diana Hamilton
and Kathryn Ross

9030 00002 8258 4

THE MEDITERRANEAN MILLIONAIRE'S RELUCTANT MISTRESS

BY
CAROLE MORTIMER

Carole Mortimer was born in England, the youngest of three children. She began writing in 1978, and has now written over one hundred and fifty books for Mills & Boon. Carole has four sons, Matthew, Joshua, Timothy and Peter, and a bearded collie called Merlyn. She says, 'I'm happily married to Peter senior; we're best friends as well as lovers, which is probably the best recipe for a successful relationship. We live in a lovely part of England.'

For Peter

CHAPTER ONE

'MR SYMMONDS, would you kindly inform your client that her behaviour when I went to collect Miguel from her home yesterday was unreasonable—'

'Mr Shaw, would you kindly inform your client that I consider his behaviour yesterday worse than un-reasonable—it was positively inhuman!' Brynne's eyes sparkled deeply blue and her cheeks flushed with temper as she glared across the room at the man who stood so tall and broodingly remote in front of the window of his lawyer's office. Alejandro Santiago's swarthily attractive face was half in shadow as he returned her gaze.

Paul Symmonds, her own lawyer, spoke reasonably as he sat beside her. 'I'm afraid, Miss Sullivan, that Señor Santiago really does have the law on his side—'

'Perhaps he does—'

'There is no "perhaps" about it, Miss Sullivan. The judge decreed three weeks ago that, as I am Miguel's father, his place is now with me,' Alejandro informed her glacially. 'But when I called at your home yesterday, as was prearranged, you refused to hand Miguel over to me.'

'Michael is a six-year-old boy,' she said, deliberately using the English version of her nephew's name, 'who recently lost the only parents he has ever known in a car crash. He is not some parcel left at the lost-luggage department for you, as his natural father, to just collect and move on!' She was breathing hard in her agitation, and her hands were clenched at her sides.

What she really wanted to do was scream and shout, to tell this man that, although it might have been proved he was Michael's natural father, and she was only his aunt by marriage, the little boy was staying with her.

Except she knew that wasn't going to happen. The legal battle with this man was already over, a private legal battle—a battle Brynne had lost—that had nevertheless received much publicity in the press.

But she wanted to shout anyway.

Alejandro eyed her coldly, his harsh good looks, from his Spanish heritage, completely unemotional.

He was tall, with slightly long dark hair and the coldest grey eyes Brynne had ever seen, his face was all hard angles, and the tailored business suit he wore added to his air of cool detachment. He was a man Brynne had come to dislike as well as fear over the last few weeks as she fiercely opposed his claim on Michael.

'I am well aware of Miguel's age, Miss Sullivan,' he rasped stiffly in response to Brynne's outburst. 'I am also aware, as I am sure are you, that, as my son, his place is now with me,' he added with determination.

'He doesn't even know you!' she protested.

'I am aware of that too,' the tall Spaniard dismissed abruptly. 'Unfortunately there is nothing I can do about the six years of my son's life that have been lost to me—'

'You could have tried marrying his mother seven years ago!' Brynne scorned.

Alejandro's nostrils flared angrily. 'You have no idea of the circumstances! Do not presume to tell me what I could or could not have done seven years ago!' he amended harshly.

'Damn it.' Brynne choked, deciding to tell him what he should have done more recently instead. 'For the last three weeks, since the judgement was ruled in your favour, I've been waiting in vain for you to use that time to get to know Michael. But you haven't even attempted to see him. In fact, I'm not even sure you've still been in the same country!'

His hard grey gaze narrowed icily. 'Where I have been for the last three weeks is none of your—' He broke off impatiently, turning to the two watching and listening lawyers. 'Mr Symmonds, can you not explain to your client that she has no legal right to keep my son from me? The only reason I agreed to this meeting today in the presence of our respective lawyers was as a courtesy to her—'

'So that you didn't have to go back into court, you mean.' Brynne sneered in disgust.

'I do not fear meeting you again in a court of law, Miss Sullivan,' Alejandro Santiago assured her coolly. 'We both know that you would lose. Again.' His mouth twisted. 'But I accept that you are fond of the boy—'

'Fond of him?' she echoed, outraged. 'I love him. Michael is my nephew—'

'He is not, in fact, related to you by blood at all,' the Spaniard told her harshly. 'Miguel was already four years old when his mother married your brother—'

'His name is Michael!' she bit out tautly.

'Look, Miss Sullivan,' Paul Symmonds cut in smoothly. 'I did advise you before this meeting today that you really have no choice but to—'

'Michael is still deeply distraught by the loss of his parents,' Brynne continued to protest, still upset herself at the death of her older brother and his wife in the car crash that had left Michael orphaned. 'I'm sure, when he made his ruling, that the judge believed Mr Santiago would use this three-week interim period to get to know Michael, not that he would just—just suddenly turn up on my doorstep and expect to take Michael away with him!'

Alejandro raised his dark brows, impatiently wondering why this woman continued to fight him. She had done so now for the last six weeks since it had been revealed that her nephew, through her brother's marriage to the boy's mother, was actually Alejandro's son from a brief relationship he'd had with Joanna seven years ago.

If Brynne Sullivan thought that revelation had left him unmoved then she was mistaken, he thought grimly.

It had been awful to read in the newspapers of the horrific motorway crash that had killed eight people, including Joanna and her husband, Tom.

But the photograph in the newspaper of Joanna's son, the little boy who had miraculously survived the collision, and who bore a startling likeness to Alejandro at that age, had been enough to arouse his suspicions as to the boy's paternity.

He had followed up these suspicions with discreet enquiries about Joanna and Michael, quickly learning that the little boy had been four years old when Joanna had married Tom Sullivan, and that there had never been a father in evidence before that time.

That information had certainly shown that the timing and circumstances seemed right, and together with the child's clear likeness to himself there was a clear possibility that Miguel could be his son.

Alejandro had flown to England immediately in order to make further enquiries, and then eventually make his legal claim, a claim that had resulted in the judge ordering tests to be taken in order to prove or disprove his paternity.

It had been proved beyond doubt!

But this woman, this Brynne Sullivan, the younger sister of Joanna's husband, still continued to fight that decision.

By calling him inhuman amongst other things!

He stepped away from the window impatiently. 'As I have said, this meeting today was a courtesy only, and now it is over.'

'No, it isn't,' Brynne protested firmly.

'Yes, it most assuredly is,' Alejandro insisted in measured tones, very near to the end of his patience with this infuriating woman. 'You will have Miguel's things packed and ready so that he can leave with me by this time tomorrow—'

'No, I won't.' Brynne gave a firm shake of her head. 'I can't let you just take him like this—'

'I'm afraid you have no choice in the matter, Miss Sullivan,' Alejandro's lawyer interjected gently. 'The law really is on Señor Santiago's side.'

He received a glittering blue glare for his trouble as Brynne turned to look at him.

Under different circumstances Alejandro would have thought the woman attractive, with her slender figure, long titian-coloured hair, creamy complexion, sparkling blue eyes and air of youthful confidence. But as the only thing that stood between him and his newly recognized son, he instead found her irritating in the extreme!

'Then the law is an ass!' she bit out angrily in answer to the lawyer's remark.

Under different circumstances, Alejandro would also have found her stubborn determination amusing as he recognized in her a will as indomitable as his own.

But the circumstances were not different, and as such Brynne Sullivan was just an irritant he wanted removed. As soon as possible!

His lawyer looked at her pityingly. 'Whether it's an ass or not, Miss Sullivan, Señor Santiago's claim of paternity has been proven and upheld.'

'He doesn't love Michael as we do!' Brynne said as she glared at Alejandro with undisguised dislike. 'Michael was only four when Joanna and Tom married, and now that they're dead my parents and I are the only family he has left—'

'He has grandparents, an uncle and aunt, and two cousins, in Spain,' Alejandro interrupted derisively.

'He doesn't know them any more than he knows you!' she retorted tartly.

He drew in a deep, controlling breath. 'Miss Sullivan, you have made the same argument for the last six weeks,' he cut in impatiently. 'But as I have already stated, neither you nor your parents are related to Miguel by blood—'

'You really are a monster, aren't you?' Brynne

stood up to accuse heatedly. 'Michael still has night-mares because his mother and the only father he has ever known are now dead. How can you even think about wrenching him away from the people he believes to be his grandparents and his aunt in this callous way?'

'I am merely taking what is mine,' Alejandro ground out coldly, still unsure of how he felt towards Joanna for keeping his son's existence from him all these years.

Admittedly their own relationship had been of short duration, nothing more than a holiday affair, but that didn't alter the fact that Joanna had to have known Miguel was his son, and had chosen not to tell him.

Brynne glared at him in frustration. She knew that it had been medically proven that Michael was this man's natural son. She also knew that legally he now had the right to take Michael wherever he wanted.

She had never really stood a chance of keeping Michael, not once Alejandro Santiago proved his claim as the little boy's father. How could a single woman of twenty-five, a schoolteacher, possibly compete with a man who counted his money in millions of pounds, owned homes all over the world and flew around the world on business in his own private jet? The simple answer was, she couldn't. But that hadn't stopped her from trying!

'I really do not have any more time to waste on this subject,' the arrogant Spaniard turned to tell the lawyers sharply. 'I have business commitments in Majorca that I have already neglected the last twenty-four hours—'

'Heaven forbid ensuring Michael's future happiness

should interrupt your work schedule!' Brynne snapped scathingly.

Cold grey eyes raked over her dismissively before Alejandro turned back to Paul Symmonds. 'Now would be a good time for you to once again advise your client to have Miguel ready to leave for Majorca with me when I call for him at her apartment at ten o'clock tomorrow morning,' he stated briskly. 'Anything else will result in my bringing further legal action against Miss Sullivan,' he added grimly.

He would do it too, Brynne acknowledged in defeat as she looked at the implacability of the man's expression.

It still seemed incredible to her that her beautiful, fun-loving sister-in-law, Joanna, could ever have been involved with a man like Alejandro Santiago. Aged in his mid-thirties, he was just too arrogantly self-assured. Too cold. Too—too immediate, she acknowledged, although she recognized that his height, overlong dark hair and arrogantly chiselled features made him the epitome of tall, dark and handsome.

A fact Brynne, despite her anger and frustration with his claim on Michael, had been all too aware of herself the last six weeks.

Had he been as emotionally aloof seven years ago? Or had something happened during that time to make him this way…?

Not that it mattered; the courts had decided to uphold his rights as Michael's father, and there wasn't a damn thing Brynne could do about it.

She looked challengingly at Alejandro. 'Haven't you forgotten something, Mr Santiago?'

Alejandro's eyebrows raised. 'Have I?'

'Oh, yes,' Brynne Sullivan informed him triumphantly. 'The judge made several other rulings, one of them being that it would be best for Michael to stay with me for a further three weeks so that he could complete the summer school term.'

He eyed her warily. 'Which is now over…'

'But he also ruled that, as my school year is now over for the summer too, that if I wished to do so, I might be allowed to accompany Michael for the first month of his stay with you. In order to ensure Michael's—smooth transition into his new life,' she said, unable to disguise the disgust in her voice.

Alejandro was aware the judge had made that compromise to what was obviously a delicate situation. It just wasn't one that he had ever thought this woman, disliking him as she so obviously did, would ever take up!

Brynne Sullivan, he was sure, would be nothing but a nuisance if she came to Majorca with him and Miguel, and would no doubt disagree with him over every decision he made concerning his son's future.

'That would seem to be the ideal solution to Michael's immediate comfort, don't you think, Señor Santiago?' Paul Symmonds prompted carefully while Alejandro looked at his own lawyer with a frown and received only an acquiescent shrug in reply.

What of his own comfort? Alejandro inwardly fumed. He didn't doubt that if he agreed to this the rebellious Brynne Sullivan would enjoy making life difficult for him for the next four weeks.

Brynne wasn't any happier at the prospect of going to Majorca than Alejandro looked at the idea of taking her there. For one thing she was all too aware of the fact that, despite everything, she actually found the man attractive, nerve-tinglingly so.

But practically she knew her presence would be of help to Michael in learning to accept his change of circumstances. It wouldn't make parting from him at the end of that month any easier for Brynne, but at least she could try and ensure that Michael was reconciled to living with his new father.

She had tried to explain things to Michael, of course, but as a six-year-old he really hadn't been able to understand the complexities of the situation.

'Mr Santiago...' She looked across at him confrontationally, well aware that the wariness she felt towards him was more than reciprocated.

Not surprisingly, really; she had fought this man every inch of the way the last six weeks. A battle Brynne had been destined to lose.

But accepting this man's legal right to his son, and then just walking away while he took Michael from all the people who loved him, were two distinctly different things!

Alejandro gave a dismissive shrug of those broad shoulders. 'It is of little interest to me whether or not you choose to accompany Miguel to Majorca, Miss Sullivan,' he snapped dismissively.

'I'm sure that it isn't,' she replied irritably, her face flushed with resentment.

'But if that is your decision then I advise that you also be ready to leave with Miguel tomorrow morning at ten,' he concluded harshly.

So cold. So intransigent. So damned arrogant!

Only the thought of being with Michael for another

month could ever have persuaded Brynne to spend even another second in the company of this man she should have disliked intensely, but who instead made her legs feel slightly weak just looking at him, and her pulse race!

CHAPTER TWO

'DID you see the swimming pool, Aunty Bry? And the beach as we drove up here? Aunty Bry, did you see the beach?' Michael asked excitedly as he slid open one of the two glass doors that led onto the terrace of the bedroom that Alejandro had informed him was to be his for the duration of their stay here. Alejandro had then stiffly informed Brynne that she could use the bedroom next door. 'I can see the beach from here, Alej—er, Father,' Michael corrected awkwardly as he spoke to the tall, silent man who had accompanied them up the stairs. 'The sea is all bluey-green. And the sand is almost white. And—'

'Don't get too close to the rail, Michael,' Brynne instructed instinctively as she followed him outside, glad of a few seconds' respite from Alejandro's overpowering presence.

The warmth of the late July Majorcan sun instantly beat down on her as she looked at the one-hundred-and-eighty-degree view of the tiered orange groves leading down to the ocean.

It wasn't difficult to understand Michael's enthrallment at his new surroundings. If the two of them had just been here on holiday together then Brynne would have been thrilled by the view and location of Alejandro's villa too, but knowing she would be going alone when she left here in a month's time certainly took the edge off any excitement she might have felt at their luxuriously opulent surroundings.

She should have known that the Spaniard's Majorcan home would be like this.

After being on the private jet that had flown them here, with its twelve seats that were actually like armchairs, and a young man who had supplied them with a lunch that any exclusive London restaurant would have been proud to serve, Brynne didn't think anything was going to surprise her ever again!

This magnificent hillside villa was unbelievable though, she thought. Surrounded by terraces on every level, the marbled interior was wonderfully cool after the hour-long drive from the airport, the white furnishings adding to that feeling of coolness, and the swimming pool was glittering invitingly as an alternative to the tempting beach and cool Mediterranean Sea.

Despite his initial feelings of apprehension Michael had become absolutely captivated with his new surroundings as soon as they had got on the private jet earlier this morning. If he had continued to be a little shy of his new darkly brooding father, who once aboard the jet had ignored them both completely as he had become engrossed in some papers he had taken from his briefcase, then it hadn't been enough to dampen the little boy's enthusiasm once they had been airborne.

Brynne wished she could share his youthful pleasure,

but, unlike Michael, she had been totally aware of Alejandro Santiago's presence for the whole of the flight, and then again as he had sat with them in the back of the limousine that had been waiting to drive them from the airport along the west coast of the island to this incredible villa.

No longer wearing one of the formal suits that were all Brynne had seen him in during their legal battle, he looked tall, overpowering and ruggedly handsome in black tailored trousers and a black short-sleeved shirt that was obviously more suitable attire for the warmer climate they were flying to.

Alejandro's manner had been formally polite when he had arrived at her apartment earlier this morning, and he hadn't shown any sign of emotion when he had seen that Brynne was packed and ready to accompany Michael, after all.

In fact, he hadn't acknowledged her presence at all, she thought. Any remarks he had made had been addressed to 'Miguel'—remarks Michael had completely ignored until he had realized he was the 'Miguel' being referred to!

Seeing the two of them together like this made Brynne achingly aware of exactly why Alejandro had been so sure Michael was his son. Both were dark-haired and grey-eyed, and even Michael's baby face was starting to show some of the harder angles of his father's features. The fact that Michael was also tall for his age indicated that he would probably eventually attain his father's considerable height too.

'I do not believe I have ever given you cause to think that I will be—a strict father to Miguel,' Alejandro said tersely as he saw Brynne's tearful gaze rest indulgently on Miguel as he ran from one side of the terrace to the other in order to look at the amazing views over the valley and sparkling blue sea.

She turned to look at him, her eyes appearing bluer and larger than ever, with tears balanced precariously on the edge of her long, dark lashes. 'So far you haven't given me reason to think you will be any sort of father to him!' she replied tartly.

Perhaps because he still found it difficult to believe he was Miguel's father!

Not that he questioned it for a moment; he knew from the medical tests that there could be no doubt. But it had been a very short journey from having suspicions on seeing Miguel's photograph in the newspapers to having them confirmed so positively. A journey that had been dogged by Brynne's stubborn refusal to relinquish Miguel to his custody.

His mouth tightened. 'I have asked that drinks be served on the terrace beside the pool when you have freshened yourself from the journey.' Turning to open the bedroom door, he called, 'Miguel?'

Like ordering a puppy to heel, Brynne thought resentfully as Michael scampered happily out of the room with the man who was now his father. As expected, her own presence here did seem to be making it much easier for the little boy to accept his change of circumstances.

She sat down heavily on Michael's bed, momentarily burying her face in her hands as the tears that had threatened earlier now fell hotly down her pale cheeks.

Tears that had been long overdue.

Too shocked after the car accident that had killed

Joanna and Tom to do more than try to keep herself emotionally together for her grieving parents and the stunned Michael, Brynne hadn't had the opportunity to release her own grief. But now, in the middle of all the luxury that Alejandro Santiago would be able to give to Michael as his son, seemed as good a time as any.

'I came back for— Why are you crying?' Alejandro rasped harshly as he came to a halt in the bedroom doorway.

Brynne looked up at him, unable not to notice how strong and handsome he looked, despite how she was feeling. She narrowed her eyes. 'Why do you think?' she snapped, resentful that this man, a man who made her pulse race in spite of herself, should witness the grief she was no longer able to contain.

His chin firmed squarely. 'I have no idea,' he said, shaking his head.

'No.' She straightened, her moment of weakness over as if she had been dowsed in icy-cold water. 'You wouldn't,' she scorned. 'What did you come back for?' she prompted quickly, wiping all trace of tears from her cheeks as she stood up to face him.

She had courage, this young woman, Alejandro acknowledged even as he felt discomforted by her crying.

She was very young, of course, ten years younger than his own thirty-five years, and in challenging him she had not chosen her fight wisely; once Alejandro was sure of Miguel's paternity, there had never been any doubt that he would claim the boy as his own.

Nevertheless, he was not completely unmoved by her tears, or the fact that her sadness gave her an air of fragile beauty, with her eyes now almost navy in colour against the pallor of her cheeks. Her red hair was lifted and secured off the long, creamy expanse of her neck to give her an air of vulnerability that had been evident in none of their previous encounters.

His mouth firmed. 'You are upset.' He stated the obvious. 'You perhaps wish for me to arrange for your immediate return to England?'

Her chin rose defiantly. 'You would like that, wouldn't you?'

His nostrils flared impatiently. 'I would like to put an end to these—disagreements, yes.'

'I'll just bet you would!' She gave a humourless laugh. 'No can do, sorry,' she added derisively. 'I intend staying on here for the duration!'

'*Dios mío*!' Alejandro bit out his frustration with her stubbornness, and his hands clenched at his sides. 'Do not try me too far, Brynne,' he warned harshly. 'I make a much better friend than I do an enemy!'

'Friend'? The word echoed incredulously in Brynne's head while she acknowledged that he had used her given name for the first time in their acquaintance. That familiarity aside, there was no way she and this man could ever be friends!

None of her male friends had ever set her senses singing in the way just being in this man's company did.

'I think you'll find, Alejandro, that so do I,' she came back smoothly, her blue eyes dark with challenge as she deliberately made use of his own first name in return.

A nerve pulsed in his tightly clenched jaw. 'You are here on sufferance only—'

'I don't appear to be the one who's suffering, Alejandro,' she taunted mockingly.

His grey eyes narrowed icily as he drew himself up to his full six feet three inches in height. 'Miguel has expressed a wish to swim in the pool. Perhaps you will be so good as to give me his bathing things?'

Michael…

Her anger left her as suddenly as it had erupted as she thought of the only reason she was here. And much as she enjoyed baiting Alejandro Santiago, that wasn't it!

'Of course,' she muttered, moving to unzip the case that contained the clothes she had packed so lovingly late last night when she and Michael had returned from visiting her parents. Several other boxes containing Michael's toys had been put aboard the jet earlier this morning, too, waiting to eventually be forwarded to Alejandro's home in mainland Spain.

In fact, everything that Michael possessed had been brought aboard that plane earlier today…

'Here,' she said as she held out Michael's brightly coloured swimming trunks, tears once again blurring her vision, although she was determined she wouldn't cry in front of Alejandro again. The man obviously only saw it as a weakness he could take advantage of if his offer to have her flown home immediately was anything to go by!

Was she going to cry again? Alejandro wondered, thinking how he never had known how to deal with a woman's tears, not even Francesca's during their brief but wholly unhappy marriage. With Brynne Sullivan he definitely found her anger the easier emotion to respond to.

His impatient gaze remained on Brynne's face as he reached out to take the swimming trunks, slightly missing his objective as his hand brushed lightly against hers.

And instantly received the equivalent of an electric shock up into his fingers and along the length of his arm!

He snatched the swimming trunks before moving his hand back abruptly, his lids half-lowered over his steel-grey eyes as he looked down his nose at her.

He found this woman intensely infuriating.

Irritating.

A nuisance he longed to be rid of.

And yet for that one split second he knew that he had been totally aware of her too, of the pale delicacy of her skin, of the blood flowing so smoothly beneath its surface, of the heat and inner throb of her very being, so much so that he could almost feel that blood pulsing through her veins.

Idiot!

He was hot, he was thirsty, and not a little tired of the verbal fencing that took place every time he was anywhere near this woman.

He stepped back. 'I will sit by the pool with Miguel until you come down to join him,' he said dismissively.

Brynne looked up at Alejandro from beneath her dark lashes. What had happened just now? Some sort of electric shock to add to her increasing awareness of him. It had been a moment, a very brief moment, when everything had seemed clearer, sharper, when it had almost felt as if she could feel and hear the beat of Alejandro's heart.

Which was pretty ridiculous when the man didn't have a heart!

If he did then he wouldn't continue to be so unreasonable where Michael was concerned, and would be as eager as she was to make all of this as painless as possible for his six-year-old son.

Besides, if he did have a heart, it would make her unwanted response to him all the more dangerous!

'I assume my joining you and Michael by the pool will no doubt free you to disappear on some important business or other?' she questioned.

The thinning of his sculpted lips showed his impatience. 'You already know I have business interests here,' he bit out curtly.

'Don't let us keep you from them, then,' Brynne taunted.

His eyes narrowed to silver slithers. 'You are a guest in my home, Brynne, and as such you will be treated with respect and courtesy. But as I warned you once before, do not push me too far, or you may not like the consequences!'

She probably wouldn't, Brynne acknowledged ruefully, having no doubts that Alejandro could make life a lot more uncomfortable for her than she could for him if he chose to do so. She was sure the slightly cruel curl she occasionally saw to his lips could very easily be put into action.

Except she had no intention of being in the least cowed by this man. 'I'll bear that in mind,' she drawled. 'Now, if you wouldn't mind, I would like to go through to my bedroom and unpack a few of my own things before coming down to the pool...' she dismissed.

A dismissal he definitely didn't like, by the look of his glittering eyes and the tensing of his shoulders as he strode forcefully from the room.

She was infuriated by the effect Alejandro Santiago had on her, and never felt in the least relaxed in his company. In fact, her skin seemed to prickle every time she was anywhere near him, almost as if she had been stung by nettles or lots of little insects.

She was also filled, at every opportunity, with a burning desire to shake him out of that cold arrogance with which he seemed to cloak himself.

Unless it wasn't a cloak…

But surely it had to be? Brynne simply couldn't see fun-loving Joanna having fallen for someone who was so cold and remote.

It had to be a shield of some sort, a way of hiding the man he was underneath.

At least, she hoped for Michael's sake that was what it was…

CHAPTER THREE

ALEJANDRO was glad he was wearing dark sunglasses to shield the surprise he felt when Brynne stepped out onto the terrace ten minutes later wearing only a very brief turquoise bikini.

It hadn't been apparent in the tailored trousers and fitted blouses she invariably wore, but, as Alejandro could quite clearly see now, Brynne Sullivan had a spectacularly beautiful body.

Absolutely, perfectly beautiful, with skin a creamy gold colour all over, her legs long and slender, hips curvaceous below her tiny waist, and her breasts pert beneath the clinging turquoise material.

But it was a beauty she seemed completely unaware of as she strolled across to where he sat, her hips swaying gracefully as she walked.

Alejandro, however, was very aware of it as he felt an unexpected throb in his own body!

'You're free to go now,' she told him coolly as she settled herself down on the lounger next to his.

Her scathing tone instantly dampened anything but the anger this woman always aroused in him. 'I intend to,' he snapped as he swung his feet down onto the tiled terrace. 'Dinner will be served at eight-thirty—'

'That's far too late for Michael,' she protested with a firm shake of her head.

It probably was, he acknowledged irritably, not having given too much thought to the changes Miguel was going to make to his daily routine. The fact that he had a son at all was still a source of surprise to him. Not that he thought for a moment that Brynne had even considered this—she seemed to think he was totally without emotions.

His reaction minutes ago to the way she looked in a bikini had told Alejandro quite the contrary!

But he did have several telephone calls to make before this evening's meal—at least one of which would no doubt be lengthy.

'Perhaps I can have a word with the cook so that she can prepare Michael something earlier than that?' Brynne decided to take pity on Alejandro's obvious frustration. 'Michael is usually in bed by eight o'clock.' Although that would no doubt be changed and adapted now that Michael was to take up a Mediterranean lifestyle…

But not tonight, she decided as she watched him swimming in the pool with the agility of a fish. He would be worn out by the early evening, and there had already been enough changes in his young life for one day. Michael needed some of his usual routine in order that everything shouldn't spiral completely out of control.

'That would be best, I think.' Alejandro gave an abrupt inclination of his head as he turned to leave.

'Tell me,' Brynne murmured dryly as she looked up at him, 'who was going to look after Michael if I hadn't been here?' she taunted.

Alejandro's mouth tightened. 'I had arranged for Maria's daughter—Maria is the cook,' he explained dismissively, '—to be with him.'

Brynne grimaced. 'Yet another stranger.'

'Brynne, you do not—' Alejandro broke off, frowning down at her, his jaw once again tight, which emphasized the haughty planes of his face. 'This is—new territory, for all of us,' he finally said quietly. 'I suggest that you give us all time to—adjust.'

'By "us" you presumably mean you,' she dismissed. 'I have been taking care of Michael quite capably for the last two months.'

Alejandro drew in a ragged breath. 'Do you intend arguing with me for the whole of your stay here?'

'Probably,' she replied; after all, Michael's welfare was all she was interested in.

Although she had to say that Alejandro Santiago seemed less—alien, in these surroundings, his dark good looks more suited to this climate. In fact, she was the one, with her red hair and pale complexion, who was out of place. Which was one of the reasons she felt increasingly defensive.

One of them.

The other one was the memory of that brief moment of physical awareness a short time ago between herself and Alejandro…

Alejandro found himself relaxing slightly as he gave a rueful inclination of his head. 'That is honest, anyway,' he drawled dryly.

'Oh, I believe you will invariably find me honest,' Brynne assured him.

'Good.' He nodded, smiling slightly as her raised

brows showed her surprise at his answer. 'Honesty is something I can deal with. It is dishonesty that I find unacceptable.' His mouth tightened grimly as he thought of all Francesca's lies and deceit, and of their marriage that had taught him never to trust a woman ever again. 'If you wish to telephone anyone to let them know of your safe arrival—'

'Anyone?' she echoed with a taunting smile.

'Your parents, possibly,' Alejandro answered slightly impatiently. 'I am sure they would like to know that you and Miguel have arrived here safely.'

Brynne's smile faded as she thought of her mother and father. Her mother had been ill with grief since Tom and Joanna had died so suddenly, and her father was having to deal with that as well as his own agony. The situation with Michael was completely beyond their comprehension at the moment.

A situation this man had created.

'I'm sure they would,' she acknowledged curtly.

Alejandro gave an abrupt nod of his head. 'Please feel free to use the telephone in the villa. I have a separate line in my study for business purposes.'

Brynne roused herself from her melancholy thoughts, her expression once again challenging as she looked up at him. 'Well, of course you do,' she muttered under her breath.

Alejandro's mouth tightened. 'I sincerely hope that this verbal fencing will not continue at mealtimes!'

'Oh, I think it probably will,' she returned wryly.

So the angry frustration Alejandro felt in the company of this woman was now to be accompanied by indigestion after every meal, too!

He thought longingly of his well-ordered life of two months ago. Before he had discovered Miguel was his son. Before the maddeningly outspoken Brynne Sullivan had entered, and then refused to leave, his life.

He nodded abruptly. 'As you wish.'

'Oh, it's not as I wish at all, Alejandro,' she told him derisively. 'You wouldn't be here if wishes really did come true!'

No one had ever spoken to him before in the way that this woman did, Alejandro realized irritably. The honesty he had praised earlier was one thing, but Brynne seemed to have no qualms whatsoever in saying whatever came into her head!

Her beautiful head, he accepted with a frown.

'Brynne—'

'Aunty Bry!' Michael greeted excitedly from the pool as he swam to the side to grin up at them, his dark hair slicked back from his face. 'Are you coming in, Aunty Bry?'

'Of course I am, darling.' With one last mocking lift of her brows in Alejandro's direction, Brynne moved gracefully to her feet, and reached up to pull the clip from her hair to let it fall loosely over her shoulders and down her spine.

Alejandro felt as if time stood still as he watched the wild tumble of titian locks. The sun caught their fiery silkiness, showing gold amongst the red, giving the effect of a living flame.

He knew Brynne was a schoolteacher, but she was unlike any schoolteacher he had ever known during his years of education!

'I will see you both later,' he snapped tersely before turning to stride forcefully back into the villa.

Work, he told himself firmly as he resisted the lure of staying by the swimming pool to watch Brynne and Miguel. He had been away for three days, and had numerous calls and messages waiting to be dealt with.

And that was before he even attempted to placate the other trouble-causing woman in his life—Antonia...!

'Well, isn't this cosy?' Brynne said dryly as she looked down the length of the dinner table to where her host sat in remote solitude at the other end of the twelve-foot-long table.

He looked magnificent, of course, if a little over-dressed for dining with someone he considered an un-welcome guest at best. The black evening suit and crisp snowy-white shirt gave his haughty good looks a rakish appeal she could well have done without.

Not having known whether or not she was supposed to dress for dinner, but having had a feeling that she probably was, Brynne was wearing what she considered her trusty little black dress, a light knee-length sheath of a dress with ribbon shoulder straps that complemented the light tan she had already managed to acquire during her hours beside the pool earlier today.

Michael, at least, was having a wonderful time in the novelty of his new home, and had fallen asleep within minutes of Brynne putting him to bed.

Her gaze narrowed on her host. 'Did you go up and say goodnight to Michael?'

Alejandro gave an inward sigh; dinner really was to

become as much a battleground as every other encounter with this woman!

'He had already fallen asleep by the time I went upstairs,' he said briskly, sure this was yet another black mark against him as far as Brynne Sullivan was concerned. The way her eyes flashed deeply blue told him he was right in his surmise.

'Then perhaps you should have gone upstairs earlier than you did,' she replied disapprovingly.

Critical as well as outspoken; it was not a comfortable combination in a woman!

'Perhaps I should,' he rasped. 'But—' He broke off in frustration as Maria arrived with their first course.

'Thank you,' Brynne said as she turned to smile at the tiny Majorcan woman. She had spent a pleasant hour in the kitchen with Maria earlier as Michael ate his tea, the two of them managing to converse a little in Brynne's schoolgirl Spanish and the small smattering of English the middle-aged woman had acquired from the tourists that flocked to this beautiful island every year.

The language barrier certainly hadn't been an obstacle to Maria's obvious affection for children as she had chatted to and smiled at Michael at every opportunity.

Brynne's smile faded as the tiny woman left the room and she turned to find Alejandro watching her with unreadable grey eyes. 'I'm sure Michael would like to see some of the island while I'm here, so perhaps I could have the use of a car tomorrow?' she suggested in a businesslike manner, having decided earlier that the novelty of the pool would wear off if that was all Michael had to do all day.

Besides, getting out and about on the island also

meant getting away from the unnervingly handsome Alejandro Santiago!

'I will put the limousine and driver at your disposal—'

'That's hardly the same as being able to drive myself about, now, is it?' Brynne protested, having eaten some of her starter of melon and ham and found it delicious.

Alejandro's gaze narrowed as he noted that her red hair was worn up again this evening, the flames tamed into muted fire with only a wispy fringe loose on her smooth brow. There was now a golden tan to her heart-shaped features, a peach gloss on the fullness of her lips, while the gentle arch of her neck was bare and the fragility of her slender body was emphasized by the fitted black dress.

'I would…prefer it if you allowed my driver to take you wherever you wish to go,' he said carefully.

Her blue eyes glittered with mockery. 'Don't you trust me not to disappear back to England with Michael?' she taunted.

Alejandro's mouth tightened. 'I would find you if you did,' he stated with certainty.

A frown creased her brow as she searched his face. 'I'll just bet that you would, too,' she finally murmured disgustedly.

'It is a bet you would win,' Alejandro drawled.

She eyed him in frustration. 'I would prefer to drive my own car so that the two of us are free to explore!'

'I have told you Juan will be happy to take you wherever you wish to go,' Alejandro assured firmly, having no intention of arguing any further with her on this point.

'So Michael and I are to be virtual prisoners while

we're here, is that it?' Brynne snapped as she put her knife and fork down on the plate and pushed it away from her, her appetite quickly disappearing.

Alejandro looked every inch the haughty Spaniard that he undoubtedly was as he gave her a quelling glance. 'It is not a question of making the two of you prisoners—'

'Then what is it a question of?' Brynne demanded as she sat forward, twin spots of angry colour in her cheeks.

He gave a disgruntled snort. 'You are a very difficult woman—'

'Difficult I can live with,' she assured him impatiently. 'It's being treated like a prisoner that I object to!'

Alejandro Santiago looked at her with obvious frustration for several seconds, his mouth in a thin disapproving line, his grey eyes glacial. 'Very well,' he finally said coldly. 'You may take a car and drive wherever you wish, but I cannot allow you to take Miguel about the island unprotected!'

Brynne stared at him incredulously. What on earth—?

'Miguel is my son, Brynne,' Alejandro snapped impatiently.

She frowned. 'Yes, but—'

'I am sure that when we arrived here you noted the electric gates and high fences as we came onto the property…'

'Well, yes…but—'

'There are also several security guards patrolling the property. Do not be so naïve, Brynne!' he bit out tautly as she continued to look puzzled. 'There have been several high-profile kidnappings in Europe in recent years. And my fight for custody of Miguel was very well publicized,' he reminded her quietly.

Brynne felt slightly sick as the full reality of what he was saying hit her. As he was the son of the super-wealthy Alejandro Santiago, there was a possibility that Michael could become a target for kidnappers!

She swallowed hard. 'But—I— Michael has been living with me quite openly for the last two months!'

Alejandro gave an abrupt inclination of his head. 'And he has been protected since I became aware of his existence,' he assured her arrogantly. 'Quietly. Unob-trusively. But, nevertheless, he has been protected.'

Brynne felt her cheeks pale. 'When he was at school…'

'Then too.' Alejandro gave another terse nod.

It was unbelievable. All this time, all those weeks, and she hadn't suspected a thing!

But that was the whole idea, wasn't it? she acknowl-edged. What was the point of being unobtrusively pro-tected if everyone knew about it?

'That's—' She broke off, swallowing down her nausea. 'I had no idea! Why didn't you tell me?' she attacked angrily as her initial shock began to wear off.

Alejandro had been waiting for that, knowing Brynne wouldn't be virtually speechless for very long. 'There was no need for you to know—'

'Oh, and this is on a need-to-know basis, is it?' she retorted furiously. 'Michael could have been in danger any time during the last few weeks and you didn't think I needed to know!' She threw her napkin down on the table before standing up to walk down the length of the table to stand next to him. 'You arrogant…!'

He shrugged without concern, his grey gaze coldly

unyielding as he looked up at her. 'I merely protect what is mine.'

Without telling her there was any need for that protection... How she despised this man!

CHAPTER FOUR

'WOULD you and Miguel like to come for a drive to Deya with me…?'

Brynne glanced up from the magazine she had been looking through while Michael once again frolicked about in the pool, her eyes hidden behind dark sunglasses as she looked up at Alejandro.

If uncovered they would definitely have told Alejandro that her anger towards him hadn't abated in the least since she had stormed out of the dining-room the evening before!

It was an anger she wanted to cling to, finding it a much more comfortable emotion than her physical awareness of this man. Today he was casually dressed again in black trousers and a grey shirt that emphasized his dark colouring.

Her mouth twisted derisively. 'And what's in Deya?'

'Nothing too exciting,' he acknowledged dryly. 'But while I attend a business meeting you and Miguel could have a look around the village, and then perhaps we could all meet up for lunch.'

'What's the catch?' She eyed him suspiciously.

Alejandro was starting to regret making the invitation. 'There is no catch,' he snapped. 'I was merely thinking of your request yesterday to see some of the island.'

'And I suppose Michael and I are to be accompanied by armed guards wearing dark sunglasses and looking totally out of place?' she queried sarcastically.

His mouth tightened. 'They are not armed,' he responded tautly.

'But they will be wearing dark sunglasses and looking out of place!' Brynne scorned as she swung her legs onto the tiled patio, and Alejandro noted she was wearing a black bikini today that suited the golden tan she was quickly acquiring.

Alejandro eyed her impatiently. 'You are being extremely childish about this—'

'Am I?' she challenged. 'Well, I'm terribly sorry about that! But it could be because this is the first time I've ever had to be accompanied anywhere by guards— armed or otherwise!' Although she knew Alejandro saw it as a necessary tool to keep Michael safe, she certainly didn't agree with the way he had gone about it.

He had realized that after their brief conversation on the subject last night, and he had tried to make allowances for it, but at the same time he did not intend fighting this woman over everything.

'I suggest, for the length of your stay here, you get used to it!' he said harshly.

She was arguing for the sake of it, Brynne acknowledged heavily. She still wasn't happy with the idea that Michael would now need to be watched and protected wherever he went, but at the same time she accepted that it was better than Alejandro not caring enough about Michael to keep him safe.

As for herself, she had no intention of getting used to being watched all the time!

She gave Alejandro Santiago one last scathing glance before turning to look at Michael as he swam over to hang on the side of the pool. 'Your father has invited us to go for a drive with him to a place called Deya,' she prompted softly, having no intention of making Michael a part of the tension that seemed to surround his father and herself every time they met; after all, she was here to smooth the way for a relationship between the two, not make the situation any worse than it already was.

Although Michael didn't seem to be having too much trouble adjusting, last night being the first time he hadn't woken up crying for Joanna and Tom.

Her own evening hadn't been quite so untroubled, she thought. Sha had sat out on the balcony of her bedroom still trying to calm down after her argument with Alejandro when she had seen him leave the villa to walk over to the garages, driving a sleek sports car out onto the road minutes later, the red tail-lights quickly disappearing down the winding road as he had accelerated the vehicle away.

She remembered thinking ten o'clock at night seemed an odd time to be going out...

Although it perhaps explained why he had been so formally dressed for dinner earlier. Maybe it hadn't been in her honour at all, but because he'd had another—assignation, later that evening?

She knew from their legal battle over Michael that Alejandro didn't have a wife or a fiancée, but that didn't mean that he didn't have a particular woman in his life.

Not that it was any of her business, she had told herself firmly. No matter what Alejandro might have assumed to the contrary, she intended continuing to be a part of Michael's life even after this month was finished. But at the same time she accepted she had no right, legal or otherwise, to comment on whom Alejandro might possibly one day choose to be Michael's stepmother.

'What do you think?' she prompted Michael brightly now.

'Great!' He grinned, easily levering himself up out of the water to grab a towel and hurry into the villa to dress.

Brynne's heart caught in her throat as she watched him, aware that the sun here was already darkening his skin to the same olive of his natural father, and that Michael seemed to be becoming more and more like Alejandro Santiago with each passing hour.

'I think that's a yes.' Her voice was brittle as she spoke dismissively to Alejandro. 'We'll just change and then join you back down here,' she added before turning to pick up her book and magazine with the intention of joining Michael upstairs.

'I forgot to enquire yesterday evening—your parents were both well when you spoke to them yesterday?' Alejandro asked softly.

She straightened abruptly, her expression tense. 'As well as can be expected, in the circumstances.'

Yes, Alejandro could only imagine his own parents' distress if anything were to happen to himself or his brother.

Or his own distress, even now, if anything should happen to Miguel...

He had only spent a few hours in the little boy's

company, but already he knew him to be strong and independent, his nature naturally cheerful in spite of his recent loss, with none of the spoilt whining that sometimes happened with children.

Miguel was a boy he recognized as being very like himself at the age of six. A boy he was already proud of.

Although no doubt Brynne Sullivan, believing him cold and heartless, would find that hard to believe!

'It must be very difficult for them,' Alejandro recognized.

'Yes,' Brynne agreed. 'Taking Michael to see them the night before we left was—harrowing.'

Alejandro knew this was far from an ideal situation, that the discovery of his son had far-reaching consequences, not least to the couple who considered themselves his grandparents.

But there was no easy solution to this dilemma that Alejandro could see.

'We won't be long,' Brynne told him shortly.

'I am in no particular hurry.' Alejandro shrugged, watching her walk back to the house before sitting down wearily on one of the loungers to wait for them. Allowing his head to fall back on the cushion and his eyes to close, he thought how Antonia had been particularly difficult last night, so much so that in the end he had cut the evening short and driven home much earlier than he had intended.

He accepted that the time he'd had to spend in England the last six weeks had been time spent away from Majorca, but it was a separation that Antonia had felt much more personally than he had. As her displeasure had clearly let him know last night. Even her exotic beauty did not compensate for the air of possessiveness she had started to adopt where he was concerned. A possessiveness she had no right to feel.

Why did women become so highly strung?

Well…women like the possessive Antonia and the faithless Francesca, he conceded ruefully. He somehow couldn't see Brynne Sullivan resorting to hysterics, or tears, in order to get her own way.

He was more likely to feel the sharp edge of her tongue if—he stopped himself quickly.

What was he doing thinking of Brynne in that way, when the chances of the two of them ever indulging in an affair—which was all he had to offer any woman now—were precisely nil?

There had been many affairs since Francesca's death five years ago, brief, transitional relationships that hadn't even dented the air of self-preservation he had adopted after his disastrous marriage.

Alejandro gave a self-derisive shake of his head, knowing that Brynne was the one woman he need never fear he would ever become involved with. She was far too emotional, and since the complete failure of his marriage emotion was something he had avoided like the plague the last five years.

Besides, the two of them disliked each other intensely!

Coming back outside with Michael a few minutes later, Brynne hung back slightly as she took in Alejandro's totally relaxed pose on the lounger.

His face looked younger and more classically handsome when not dominated by those fierce silver-grey eyes, and she was struck once again by how lethally attractive he was.

Or would be—if she didn't dislike him so much!

He did look a little tired this morning though, and after witnessing his nocturnal roaming the night before, she didn't need too many guesses as to the reason why.

He might not have a wife or a fiancée, but after his disappearance the evening before Brynne didn't doubt that he had a 'something'! Nor did she doubt that her own and Michael's presence here made absolutely no difference to the continuance of that relationship.

'I thought we were going out?' she reminded sharply.

Alejandro drew in a deeply controlling breath before raising his eyebrows. One thing it was definitely not possible to do in this woman's company was relax!

Especially when she was wearing a green halter-top that revealed the creamy cleft between her breasts and a pair of brief white shorts that showed the long expanse of her bare legs.

'We are,' he said firmly as he stood up, leaving Brynne to follow behind while he walked over to the garages with Miguel. He was annoyed with himself for even noticing Brynne's leggy beauty, although he dared any red-blooded man not to do so!

He drove them to Deya himself, knowing from Miguel's grinning face in the back of the Mercedes that he was enjoying driving along with the roof down, and having his dark hair blown about by the wind.

It was much more difficult to gauge Brynne's reaction to the magnificent views they encountered on the drive, her eyes once again behind dark sunglasses, and her expression unreadable.

No doubt her thoughts were yet another criticism of himself!

Nothing he did, it seemed, found favour from her,

with his every word and every action viewed with distrust or derision.

It was not a response he was used to in a woman!

Since the age of sixteen, his dark looks had enabled Alejandro to take his pick of women, and with maturity had come the added bonus of being an entrepreneurial multimillionaire. The wealth and power of such a position seemed an added aphrodisiac to many women.

But Brynne Sullivan seemed to detest him for those attributes!

'How do you like the island so far?' he asked, attempting conversation.

'It's very beautiful,' she replied stiltedly.

'Many artists live in Deya. Some good. Some not so good,' he allowed dryly. 'I am sure you will enjoy looking in the galleries there.'

'Maybe,' she conceded with a shrug of her bare shoulders. 'Did you put your guards in the boot of the car?' she enquired derisively.

Alejandro's expression darkened at her deliberate challenge. He was trying to be pleasant, so why couldn't this woman at least attempt to meet him halfway?

'Raul and Rafael are in the car behind,' he muttered softly.

Brynne glanced in the wing mirror of the Mercedes, easily spotting the dark vehicle driving thirty metres or so behind them.

'How nice,' she responded tartly. 'Perhaps we can all have coffee together once we get to Deya!'

'Why do you persist—' Alejandro broke off his angry rebuke, his mouth thinning disapprovingly as he glanced at Miguel in the driver mirror. 'We cannot get there soon enough for me,' he muttered so that only Brynne Sullivan could hear him, her mocking smile his only answer.

Not surprisingly the two of them spent the rest of the journey in silence, although both of them had conversations with Michael as he asked a barrage of questions about his new surroundings.

Thank goodness for Michael, Brynne thought ruefully.

Although, without Michael, she would never have met the nerve-tinglingly handsome Alejandro Santiago in the first place...

There really weren't too many Spanish multimillionaires roaming the streets of Cambridge, she thought wryly.

She had dated on and off over the years, other students, fellow teachers, all of them without exception nice, pleasant men whom she had enjoyed spending time with.

In the six stormy weeks she had known Alejandro Santiago she already knew he was neither nice nor pleasant.

As for enjoying his company...how could she possibly relax enough to do that when just sitting beside him like this made her feel hot all over?

'Deya,' Alejandro announced with a certain amount of relief as he parked the Mercedes outside one of the village's most prestigious hotels, intending to have lunch here with Miguel and Brynne once his business meeting was over.

Although he doubted Brynne would be impressed by the exclusive charms of the hotel, let alone the excellence of the restaurant. She seemed to find little merit to any of the luxurious lifestyle his money provided!

'I will book lunch here for one o'clock,' he told her as he came round to open the car door for her before tilting the seat forward so that Miguel could climb out of the back.

Her head tilted as she looked up at him through her dark shades. 'I'm sure Raul and Rafael will ensure that we don't get lost,' she drawled with a mocking glance in the direction of the two men getting out of the black car parked a short distance away.

Alejandro damped down his rising anger with effort. His meeting was an important one, crucial to the delicate negotiations that brought him to the island at this time, and allowing this constant discord with Brynne Sullivan to sabotage those negotiations by going to his meeting angry and impatient was not an option.

'I am sure that they will,' he acknowledged tautly. 'Take care of your aunt, Miguel,' he added, his hand on his son's shoulders, his expression softening as he looked down at him.

Miguel grinned up at him. 'Aunty Bry usually looks after me.'

Alejandro gave an acknowledging inclination of his head. 'In Spain it is the man who takes care of the woman,' he explained gravely.

'Oh.' Miguel nodded his head understandingly.

Brynne gave an irritated frown. Michael was six years old, for goodness' sake—

'It is as well that Miguel learns the Spanish way,' Alejandro declared.

She raised her chin as her gaze met the challenge in his cold grey eyes. 'I'm sure there's a lot we can all learn from one another's cultures,' she said non-committally, knowing by the way Alejandro's gaze narrowed that the double-edge to her reply wasn't lost on him.

He gave an impatient shrug. 'You will need some euros—'

'I have my own money, thank you,' Brynne cut in sharply as Alejandro would have reached into his trouser pocket.

He raised his dark brows. 'I was talking to Miguel.'

'I have enough for Michael, too,' she assured him, her anger barely contained. She might only be a lowly schoolteacher, but that didn't mean she was going to accept money, even on Michael's behalf, from this man! 'Please don't let us delay you any longer from your meeting,' she added with saccharine sweetness.

Alejandro continued to look at her impatiently for several long seconds before giving a dismissive shake of his head. 'One o'clock,' he bit out tersely before turning away.

Brynne was determined to forget about Alejandro Santiago, and his arrogance for the next couple of hours as she and Michael wandered around the pretty village. The people were so friendly, with men and women alike smiling and talking to Michael in the shops and café they stopped in to have a cool drink.

They were not joined by Raul and Rafael, thank goodness, although the two men were loitering outside waiting for them when they came out of the café half an hour later.

Michael, luckily, seemed completely unaware of the men's presence, holding her hand and skipping along happily at her side as they made their way back.

'Alej—Father is nice, don't you think, Aunty Bry?'

He looked up at her a little anxiously as they walked up the steps to the hotel.

'Nice' was the last thing Alejandro Santiago was!

But Michael's question showed that he wasn't as unaware of the animosity between Brynne and his father as she could have wished. Not surprisingly, really, when that antagonism surfaced every time the two of them were together. But it wasn't good for Michael to have noticed it and so have his loyalties pulled in two different directions in this way.

'Very nice,' she told him brightly.

Michael frowned. 'Did Mummy and Daddy like him, do you think?'

Brynne gave a pained frown. No doubt Joanna had 'liked' Alejandro Santiago seven years ago, but whether or not she would have still liked the man he was today Brynne had no idea. As for Tom, Brynne really had no idea what her brother would have made of this arrogantly assured man who was Michael's real father!

But that wasn't an answer she could give Michael. The little boy's future lay with Alejandro, whether she liked it or not, and loving Michael as she did it was up to her to make this change in his life as easy as possible for him.

If only she didn't find Alejandro so overwhelming physically!

'I'm sure they did,' she told Michael warmly as she gave his hand a reassuring squeeze, hoping Alejandro would appreciate her efforts—against her real feelings on the matter!—on his behalf.

'Good.' Michael sighed his relief.

Obviously Michael, even if he still didn't really understand how it had happened, was nevertheless getting used to the idea of having Alejandro as his father, and that had to be a good thing.

Even if Brynne couldn't share his enthusiasm!

She was even more disconcerted, when they reached the outdoor restaurant, to find that Alejandro wasn't sitting alone at the table they were being shown to. Instead a ravishingly beautiful woman sat beside him, her dark hair long and luxurious, her complexion as olive as his own and her exquisite features dominated by huge dark eyes and a pouting, red-painted mouth…

CHAPTER FIVE

ALEJANDRO'S mouth tightened slightly as he saw Brynne and Miguel being shown to the table where he and Antonia were sitting.

Antonia was not supposed to have been here with her father today, and Alejandro was annoyed that her unexpected presence had changed the meeting from any serious talk of business to yet another social occasion.

Deliberately or accidentally, on the part of Felipe Roig...?

It had been all too easy to flatter Antonia, the daughter of widower Felipe Roig, as a way of charming the older man. But if the way Antonia had begun to actively pursue him was any indication, it was a flattery she had begun to take all too seriously. Which could, in itself, lead to Felipe wanting a much bigger price for the land he had to sell than Alejandro was willing to pay...!

Not that Antonia wasn't beautiful. With a voluptuous figure that indicated a passionate nature she would no doubt more than satisfy the man lucky enough to become her husband—it just wouldn't be Alejandro!

He and Francesca had married for all the wrong reasons, and their union had been painful as well as disastrous; he did not intend repeating the mistake!

It was a problem that Alejandro had had no chance to turn his mind to as Antonia had continued to linger long after her father had departed, but he had managed to avoid inviting Antonia to stay for lunch.

Although now that Brynne and Miguel had actually arrived at the restaurant he might no longer have any other choice!

He stood up as Brynne and Miguel reached the table, his smile less warm than he would have wished. 'Did you have an enjoyable morning?' he enquired politely.

'Oh, it was wonderful,' his son was the one to answer brightly. 'We went to all the shops, and then to a café where the man gave me a biscuit to eat with my juice, and we sat outside and watched as people filled huge water bottles from the stream that runs down from the mountains, and—'

'Slowly, Miguel, slowly.' Alejandro laughed as he halted his son's excited chatter, all the time aware that Brynne was looking at him with those questioning blue eyes before she glanced at Antonia and then back again. 'Miguel, I would like you to meet a friend of mine, Antonia Roig.' He placed his hands on Miguel's shoulders as he turned him to look at the woman sitting at the table. 'Antonia, this is—'

'Your son,' Antonia finished throatily, standing up as she curved her pouting red lips into a smile. 'But of course it is.' She nodded. 'He very much has the look of you, Alejandro.' Her smile warmed intimately as she looked up at him.

Brynne watched the exchange with growing trepidation. It was one thing to acknowledge that Alejandro was Michael's father but the little boy was only just coming to that understanding—surely this arrogant Spaniard wasn't going to introduce him to a stepmother quite so soon?

Antonia Roig was certainly beautiful enough, Brynne recognized as she looked at the tempestuous perfection of the other woman's face. But there was just something about the woman's eyes, a certain lack of warmth when she smiled, that indicated to Brynne that this woman might think 'boarding-school was a good idea' for any child that wasn't her own.

Although with Antonia's curvaceously alluring figure Brynne very much doubted that Alejandro's interest had gone as high as Antonia's eyes!

Antonia's deep brown gaze now narrowed on Brynne. 'How very sensible of you, Alejandro, to have brought Miguel's nanny, too.' She gave Brynne a politely dismissive smile before turning away. 'Alejandro, why do we not—'

'Oh, but Brynne isn't my nanny!' Michael dismissed with a laugh, totally unaware of any tension amongst the three adults. 'She's my aunty. My Aunty Bry,' he added happily.

Yes, very hard eyes, Brynne decided wryly as the other woman's deep brown orbs were turned back on her, with critical assessment this time as Antonia took in her appearance from the top of her red head to the soles of her white flip-flops, before returning to Brynne's make-upless face with its covering of freckles.

'Your…aunt,' Antonia finally murmured speculatively before glancing back at Alejandro, her dark, highly arched, plucked brows raised questioningly. 'The same aunt who…'

Obviously Alejandro hadn't had the chance yet to tell his…this woman that he had brought Michael's troublesome aunt back to Majorca for a visit too.

Oh dear!

'The same aunt,' Brynne told Antonia happily as she held out her hand. 'Brynne Sullivan. Are you joining us for lunch, Miss Roig?' she prompted lightly as the other woman met the gesture with the slightest brush of her slender, scarlet-tipped fingers.

The pouting red mouth tightened slightly. 'I would have, but unfortunately I have another engagement in Palma early this afternoon,' Antonia snapped dismissively. 'You have not forgotten that you are expected for dinner this evening, Alejandro?' she added tartly.

Oh, dear, dear, dear, Brynne mused as she sat down in the seat the other woman had just vacated; poor Alejandro looked as if he might have some explaining to do later!

'Of course I have not forgotten,' he confirmed, a little impatiently, Brynne thought as he brushed his lips lightly against the other woman's cheek in parting.

'What a pity Miss Roig couldn't join us,' Brynne remarked dryly once Antonia had left.

Alejandro turned from watching Antonia's abrupt departure to scowl down at Brynne's bent head as she perused the menu with marked deliberation. 'Yes, a pity,' he bit out tersely as he resumed his seat at the table, knowing by the way Brynne returned his gaze with wide-eyed innocence that she was enjoying what she no doubt sensed was his slight discomfort.

But what could he have done otherwise? To press

Antonia to join them would, with Brynne in this mischievously troublemaking mood, only have resulted in even more embarrassment, he was sure. No, he had done the right thing; he would have plenty of time to explain, and placate Antonia later tonight.

'It all looks delicious. What do you recommend?' Brynne asked as she closed the menu to look at him enquiringly, the mischief still dancing in those deep blue eyes.

She didn't look much older than Miguel with that innocent expression, her face bare of make-up, and her hair pulled back into a green band that matched the colour of her top.

Except that expression was too innocent!

'Everything,' he dismissed impatiently before turning his attention to helping Miguel select his food.

Surprisingly Brynne enjoyed the leisurely lunch. She and Alejandro spent most of the time ignoring each other—which had to be a definite plus as far as her digestion was concerned!—but Michael was starting to relax in his father's company and the food was excellent. The wine Alejandro ordered complemented their lunch perfectly, and the view was spectacular from where they sat high up on one of the terraces that looked down the valley to the sea.

In fact, by the time they left to drive back to the villa she was the most relaxed since arriving in Majorca.

Michael was quite happy to return to the pool in the afternoon, leaving Brynne to laze on one of the loungers as she pondered the merits of the local siesta; she could quite cheerfully have fallen asleep for an hour or so after that lovely meal and wine.

Although Alejandro's presence on the lounger beside her own pretty much assured her that she would never be able to relax enough to do that!

'So you're going out again this evening?' she prompted conversationally as she sat up to rub oil onto her tanning arms and legs.

'Again…?' Alejandro echoed softly as he turned to watch her movements, her fingers long and supple as she smoothed the oil into her shoulders and throat.

Brynne didn't even glance at him as she bent to rub oil on the long length of her legs. 'I saw you go out yesterday evening.' She shrugged.

But she obviously hadn't seen, or heard, him come back again two hours later…

His departure alone had obviously been enough for her to draw her own conclusions. And meeting Antonia today would certainly not have belied that conclusion.

Although why this woman should think she had any right to comment on what he did in his private life was beyond him!

He found his attention caught and held as Brynne pushed her halter-top up to just below her breasts as she now put oil onto her bare midriff. A completely flat midriff, with soft and creamy skin, and just a tanatalizing glimpse of the thrusting swell of her breasts beneath the green top—

What was he doing?

This woman was Miguel's aunt by marriage, his nuisance of an aunt by marriage, not someone whose attractions Alejandro should find in the least arousing.

His mouth tightened. 'You have a comment you wish to make about my dinner engagement?' he rasped hastily, all the time knowing that impatience was aimed at himself more than at Brynne.

She was a constant thorn in his side, an irritant he couldn't wait to be rid of, so what did it matter if she had a lithely beautiful body and that her skin looked like silk? Even the freckles that covered the whole of her body added to her sensuousness as he imagined discovering, and kissing, every single one of them…

'Not at all.' Brynne looked surprised by his question. 'I was just making conversation, Alejandro,' she dismissed lightly.

Like hell she was!

But he was not involved with Antonia in the way that Brynne seemed to think he was. Deliberately so. Flattering and charming Antonia was one thing, but he never, ever mixed business with the sort of pleasure he had been thinking of with Brynne herself a few minutes ago.

Although that slight possessiveness Antonia seemed to be developing where he was concerned told him that he might not have been his usual careful self where relationships were concerned during his distraction over the custody of Miguel. Both Antonia and her father might be expecting something more from the interest he had shown Antonia.

But he had no intention of ever going through the painful process of marrying again. And now that he had an heir in Miguel, he had no need to do so.

But there was still the problem of Felipe Roig's elusiveness…

He stood up quickly. 'I have some calls to make.'

'My, what a busy man you are, Alejandro,' Brynne looked up to taunt, her chin resting on her bent knee.

His gaze was cold as he looked down at her. 'I have business commitments, yes,' he replied coolly.

Brynne raised her eyebrows. 'How pleasant for you when the business is as beautiful as Antonia Roig.'

Alejandro's jaw clenched. 'Not that it is any of your concern, but my only connection with Antonia is business with her father, Felipe.'

'Really?' Brynne derided. 'That wasn't the impression I got!'

'I do not care—' Alejandro broke off his angry retort, breathing deeply as he looked down his arrogant nose at her. 'You really do not have the right to question me in this way, Brynne,' he finally snapped coldly.

'But the two of you are having dinner together this evening,' she challenged, not prepared to let him off that easily. After all, if he was considering making Antonia his wife, and consequently Michael's stepmother, then she did consider it her business!

'I am one of several guests invited for dinner this evening at the home of Antonia's father, yes,' he bit out impatiently.

'Ah...' she murmured speculatively, enjoying seeing this usually perfectly controlled man at a disadvantage for a change.

Alejandro scowled darkly. 'You really are the most— unsettling, of women!'

Brynne smiled. 'I'll take that as a compliment.'

'I would not,' he snarled, his accent becoming more pronounced in his obvious displeasure. 'So far I have not found being with you a restful experience!'

Her smile turned to a chuckle. 'I believe that's the nicest thing you've ever said to me, Alejandro!'

She was infuriating, Alejandro acknowledged, not for the first time. Infuriating, outspoken, and far too familiar.

But at the same time he also knew that he had never found a moment's boredom in this woman's company, either...

For a man who had been soured towards love years ago, his relationships since that time only having ever been on a physical level, it wasn't just unsettling to realize this, it was extremely disturbing!

He shook his head. 'I really do have to go and make some calls. What now?' he questioned in frustration as he saw Brynne's disapproving expression.

She shrugged. 'I was merely wondering if you ever intended to spend any time with Michael?'

Alejandro's frown darkened to a scowl. 'I have just finished having lunch with both of you.'

'Eating together and actually spending time together are two totally different things,' Brynne dismissed evenly.

He drew in a controlling breath. No one, absolutely no one, ever questioned him in this way!

'Tell me, Brynne,' he said tersely, 'have you ever been present at the taming of a wild stallion?'

Brynne gave him a puzzled glance. 'I can't say that I have.'

He nodded abruptly. 'Then if you had you would know that it takes patience. That first you have to let the stallion slowly become accustomed to your presence, to the sound of your voice. Once you have done that, you can begin to touch the stallion as you talk to it. Again this takes time. But once he accepts these things it is time to put on the saddle and bit. Only to put it on, you understand. It will take many more days before you can actually attempt to get up into the saddle. If you try to go too fast, to force these things, then you will break the animal rather than tame it.'

Brynne stared at him incredulously. 'Are you trying to tell me that you're treating getting to know Michael the same as taming a wild stallion?' she gasped disbelievingly.

He shrugged those broad shoulders. 'It is a tried and tested method.'

'You—you—' Her cheeks were flushed, her eyes bright with temper as she stood up to face him. 'Is that how you tame a woman too, Alejandro?' she challenged in disgust. 'Do you talk softly to them? Touch them? Caress them? Before taking them to your bed?' She was breathing hard in her agitation.

His jaw was tightly clenched, his pale grey eyes cold with anger as he glared down at her. 'You have no right—'

'I have every right if that's really the way you think you're going to get close to Michael!' she replied. 'You're incredible, do you know that?' She gave a disbelieving shake of her head. 'Absolutely incredible, if you think you can treat the emotions of a vulnerable little boy as lightly as you would the taming of a wild stallion!'

A nerve pulsed in that tightly clenched jaw. 'And you, Brynne, have never even tried to understand how difficult this situation is for me—'

'Forgive me, Alejandro,' she came back sarcastically. 'But you really aren't my first priority!'

'As well as Miguel,' Alejandro finished angrily. 'In fact, I believe you take delight in thinking the worst of me!' he snapped.

'I would think badly of any man who evaded his responsibilities for six years!' she retorted.

His eyes narrowed dangerously. 'So now we come to the true reason for your obvious contempt for me!'

'I've never even tried to pretend I feel anything else!' Brynne scorned.

He looked at her icily. 'You have no knowledge of what happened between Joanna and myself seven years ago!'

'I know enough,' Brynne assured him scathingly. 'Joanna didn't even trust you enough to tell you of her pregnancy, let alone try to include you in it!'

Alejandro's chest rose and fell rapidly as he tried to control his own temper, and tell himself that Brynne spoke out of ignorance rather than fact. She judged him on what she thought she knew rather than on what had actually happened seven years ago.

It didn't work, his anger not abating in the slightest. 'I advise you not to make judgements on something you do not understand,' he told her coldly.

'Oh, I understand you only too well, Alejandro,' Brynne assured him with a disgusted toss of her head, blue eyes glittering. 'You're cold. You're aloof. And your all-knowing arrogance is just unbelievable!'

He continued to look at her in frustration for several long seconds, his jaw clamped tightly together as he debated whether he wanted to verbally tear Brynne apart, or just pull her into his arms and kiss her until she was senseless.

The latter emotion won!

He reached out to pull her slender body into his and felt the softness of her skin against his own as he held her tightly against him and took possession of the sensuous curve of her lips.

The kiss was so unexpected, so fiercely hot, that Brynne had no chance to do anything other than respond.

It was like drowning! Every part of her seemed to melt into Alejandro, her hands moving up as she clung to the broad width of his shoulders.

And then Alejandro was pushing her away from him, a nerve pulsing in his tightly clenched jaw when he turned back from ensuring that Michael hadn't seen the exchange. He hadn't.

'I have to go,' he finally muttered determinedly before turning on his heel and striding purposefully back to the villa, his back and shoulders rigid.

Brynne watched him go, very much aware of the fact that, instead of repulsing Alejandro's kisses, the ache in her body told her she actually regretted that they had ended so soon…!

CHAPTER SIX

BRYNNE shifted on the bed as she tried to find a comfortable position in which to fall asleep.

Something she had been trying to do for the last hour, feeling too restless to settle down to read the book she had brought away with her, and Alejandro not having returned from his evening out yet.

She had been so angry with him this afternoon, then so surprised and aroused as he had kissed her.

In fact, she had been so distracted, so disturbed, that she had felt relieved when Maria had come out and offered to take Michael for a walk to the village with her.

But the result was that Brynne had been so worn out from puzzling over that kiss, her head so full of the things she should have said to Alejandro and hadn't, that she had eventually fallen into a deep sleep as she had continued to lay on the lounger beside the pool.

Only to wake up an hour later to find her back sunburnt because she had been too agitated earlier to remember to put any oil on it before falling asleep.

Brynne got impatiently out of the bed, the after-sun she had managed to put on her shoulders earlier, and partway up her back, doing absolutely nothing to alleviate the heat or the stinging sensation that continued to keep her from sleeping.

She opened the French doors to stroll out onto the balcony, hearing the distant clanging of a bell around the neck of a goat or sheep, and the clicking sound of the cicadas.

The island really was beautiful, with the brightly coloured bougainvillea that grew in such abundance, the orange and lemon trees that grew on the terraced hillsides and the tiny villages with their wondrous smells of cooking, old-fashioned shops and cafés. Plus it was all surrounded by the most magnificently coloured sea Brynne had ever seen.

But it was all ruined for Brynne by the presence of Alejandro.

What had happened between the two of them earlier today?

She wasn't quite sure…

The conversation had started out so innocently. And ended in that fiercely heated kiss, a kiss that had left such tension and disharmony between them that Brynne had felt restless and disturbed ever since.

Because she was still angry with him, she had told herself after he had left her. It was only when she had come up to bed, and sleep had continued to elude her, that she had allowed her thoughts to become less angry, to try to understand why their conversation had deteriorated in the way that it had, with the result that Alejandro had actually kissed her.

Her conclusion, at least as far as she was concerned, was not a pleasant one!

There had been such intensity between them during that heated exchange, so that when he had kissed her so suddenly her body had given her no choice but to respond. At which point she had been totally aware of the heat of him, of the broadness of his shoulders, of the hard power—and pleasure—that hardness promised—

No!

Brynne closed her eyes to shut out the memory. It would be extremely stupid on her part to allow her sexual awareness of Alejandro to get any deeper than it already was.

But what if it was something she had no control over?

She could hear the sound of a car coming down the narrow, winding road to the villa, and knew it had to be Alejandro returning from his evening out.

There was something slightly undignified about the possibility that Alejandro might see her standing out on the balcony and think she had been waiting here for him to come home.

She hadn't, had she…?

It didn't matter whether she had or not, she decided as she moved quickly back into her bedroom and shut the door behind her; Alejandro wasn't going to see her and jump to any conclusion, erroneous or otherwise.

Sounds carried in the silence of the night, and she heard Alejandro park the car in the garage, then the scrape of his shoes on the terrace as he walked to the villa and let himself in.

Her nerves tensed as she waited for him to ascend the stairs and walk down the hallway as he went to bed.

The light knock on her bedroom door startled her so

much she almost knocked over the vase of lilies that stood on her dressing table.

Alejandro had come to her bedroom, not his own!

Because of that kiss they had shared this afternoon? Had Alejandro realized that part of her anger towards him had been because she had been inexplicably roused by the exchange?

You're being stupid now, Brynne, she instantly rebuked her panicked thoughts. As far as Alejandro was concerned she had told him how much she didn't like him this afternoon.

'Yes?' she called out, lacing her fingers together to stop them from trembling.

The door opened slowly, and Alejandro came quietly into the room. 'I saw the light was still on in your bedroom and wondered if there was a problem…?' He arched his dark brows.

Yes, there was a problem, Brynne realized achingly as she felt her nipples harden beneath her silky pyjamas from just looking at him in his evening suit, the warmth of her body centred between her thighs now.

The darkness of his hair was slightly ruffled by the evening breeze, and the top button of his shirt was undone to reveal the beginning of the dark hair that no doubt covered his chest and went down to his—

She lifted her startled gaze back up to his face and instantly wished that she hadn't as she found her eyes were now held and captured by the intensity of his.

'Brynne…?' he prompted.

She swallowed hard, inwardly chastising herself for her stupidity. 'Er—no, there's no problem,' she answered him determinedly. 'I—just couldn't sleep, that's all. It's—very hot this evening, isn't it?'

Hotter still since Alejandro had entered her bedroom!

What was wrong with her? She wasn't an impressionable teenager but a mature woman of twenty-five, and had been out with a number of men over the last few years—

But none of them had been in the least like Alejandro!

No, they had been nice men, ordinary men, men who had shared her interests, men she had been able to talk to, not a man who filled a room just by walking into it, a man who could command with just a look, a man who had upset and disturbed her life since the moment he had entered it six weeks ago, a man who—

A man who created a moist heat between her thighs just by being in the same room as her!

This was awful.

Terrible.

'Brynne, what—'

'No!' she exclaimed when she saw he was about to walk farther into her bedroom. 'It's late, Alejandro,' she told him abruptly. 'I would like to go back to bed now.'

Alejandro searched her face. Was he being ridiculous? Brynne had looked at him just now as if—well, as if she returned some of the desire he had felt when he had kissed her this afternoon.

It was a feeling he had tried to dismiss as fanciful after he'd left her, and then again this evening as he had sat at the crowded dinner table of the Roigs, Antonia's attempts to tease him out of his reverie completely unsuccessful. In fact, he had felt himself becoming more and more impatient this evening with Antonia's attempts to beguile him with her sultry beauty!

He had seen the light still on in Brynne's bedroom as he had driven down the hill to the villa and had told himself not to knock on her door. It would not be a sensible move on his part after their last encounter, when the emotion had been so heightened between them he had had to walk away from it.

He had told himself to go to his own bedroom, and forget all about Brynne Sullivan. But his feet had seemed to have a different idea of his intentions as he had found himself knocking on her door!

It was there still, a tension, a frisson, that he could feel stretching across the room between them.

Even in pyjamas Brynne looked beautiful, her hair draped across one shoulder and down over her breasts. Firm, uptilting breasts, the nipples of which were outlined against the soft peach-coloured material of her top. Alejandro's lips tingled just at the thought of tasting the rosy tip with his tongue—

'If you are sure you are all right...' He nodded abruptly, knowing he had to leave now or put into practice all the things he was imagining doing with Brynne.

'Yes, of course I—' Brynne broke off, having started to cross the room to encourage his exit before coming to an abrupt halt, wincing slightly as she did so. 'I'm fine,' she told him brightly. 'Just fine.'

Alejandro's brow furrowed. 'Somehow I do not think so...' he murmured slowly, stepping farther into the bedroom.

'Please, Alejandro,' she said in protest, knowing that she shouldn't have moved, because it had caused the material of her top to rub painfully over her red and throbbing back. 'What could possibly be wrong?' she dismissed.

'I do not—' He broke off, standing only inches away from her now as he looked down into her face. 'You look—strained…' he finally murmured.

'Well, that's hardly flattering, Alejandro,' she told him dryly, wishing he would just leave.

She needed him to go now, and not just because she desperately needed to put some more cream on her back!

Alejandro shook his head, not in the least convinced by her attempt at humour. 'I refuse to leave until you tell me what is wrong, Brynne,' he said firmly.

She gave a disbelieving laugh. 'I could just scream,' she warned.

Her humour was still forced, in Alejandro's opinion. 'Is it Michael? Your parents, perhaps? Tell me what is wrong, Brynne,' he repeated sharply.

Her mouth set stubbornly. 'Nothing is—oh, very well,' she snapped impatiently as Alejandro continued to look at her. 'I just stayed out in the sun too long this afternoon, that's all. Are you satisfied? Will you leave my bedroom now?' She glared at him, colour flooding her cheeks.

It was what he should do, Alejandro knew. To do anything else could be dangerous in the extreme.

But he also knew that the Majorcan sun could be fierce in the afternoons, and if Brynne really had stayed out in it too long…

'Show me,' he said impatiently.

Brynne stared up at him with wide eyes. Show him? Take her top off and—

No way! There was absolutely no way she was going

to undress for this man, even though the idea was making her body tingle all over.

'I don't think so,' she told him primly. 'I'm quite capable of dealing with it myself, thank you,' she added defiantly as he still stood looking at her in that arrogant way that said he could be just as stubborn as she could.

'Obviously not if you are still in pain,' Alejandro rasped tersely.

'I've put some after-sun on,' she assured him irritably as she moved across the room to pick the bottle up from the bedside table. 'Here. See.' She held it up.

'On where?' His voice was silkily smooth.

She could feel the heat in her cheeks once again. 'On my back. Now would you please—'

'You cannot possibly reach the whole of your back,' Alejandro told her with maddening accuracy.

Brynne was becoming more and more agitated by the minute.

Wasn't it humiliating enough that he had kissed her earlier, that she had found herself becoming aroused just by his presence in this room, without having to bare her back to him?

'I can reach far enough,' she told him stubbornly.

'I disagree—'

'Do you know something, Alejandro?' she interrupted. 'It's of absolutely no interest to me whether or not you agree or disagree with me! Now please leave my bedroom before I start to scream with rage!'

Alejandro continued to look at her, noting the fire in her eyes, and the flush to her cheeks. But was that with temper? Or something else…?

He shrugged. 'Perhaps that is the answer, after all,'

he murmured as he took the bottle of after-sun from her unresisting fingers and began to unscrew the top. 'If Maria comes in answer to your scream then she can put on the after-sun for you instead of me!' he said in a mocking tone as Brynne frowned.

He was nowhere near as calm and controlled as he wished to appear though. The thought of running his hands across Brynne's back, and feeling her soft skin beneath his fingertips, was playing havoc with his self-control. His hands shook slightly as he tipped some of the after-sun lotion into the palm of his hand.

'Do as I say, Brynne,' he told her, his voice coming out harshly as he acknowledged his deepening arousal. And he hadn't even touched her yet!

Brynne glared at him for several more seconds before letting her breath out in an angry hiss. 'Oh, all right!' she snapped before marching over to the bed and lying down on her stomach, pulling the back of her top up as she did so. At least she could try to protect some of her modesty—

'That will not do, Brynne,' Alejandro said quietly from just behind her. 'I cannot reach your shoulders or the top of your back like that,' he explained patiently as she turned to frown at him.

No, he couldn't, could he? she conceded with an irritated sigh, sitting up to turn away from him as she undid the buttons to her top—mainly so that he shouldn't see the way her hands were shaking!

'Will you please look the other way for a moment?' she told him uncomfortably, waiting until he had done so before dropping her top to the floor and then quickly moving to lie face down on the bed once again, her face burning now rather than her back—with pure embarrassment!

Alejandro sat down on the side of the bed to rub some of the cream onto his hands, then began to caress the lotion into her burning shoulders, relieving some of the soreness but at the same time instantly creating a burning sensation somewhere else in her body.

Brynne's skin felt just as luxuriously silky as Alejandro had imagined it would, and his hands were necessarily gentle as he sensed her discomfort.

As he leant forward he could see the gentle swell of her breasts as they pressed into the cool sheets beneath her, a tantalizing glimpse that made him long to see them fully. He imagined running his hands over her there too, to bring her another sort of relief—

'To lie out in the sun and let yourself get burnt like this was an extremely stupid thing to do,' he declared harshly in an effort to hide his rapidly rising desire.

Brynne lifted her head to glare at him. 'Oh, yes, I just sat out there and got burnt on purpose!' she replied scathingly. 'I fell asleep, okay?' she added as she once again buried her face into the pillow.

Alejandro smiled slightly at her obvious annoyance with herself.

'I hope that isn't a smirk I see on your face, Alejandro Santiago!' Brynne said indignantly, having opened one eye to look at him.

His smile deepened. 'You sound like my mother when she used to chastise me as a child,' he explained as he could see Brynne's exasperation rising. 'Except she always used my full name of Alejandro Miguel Diego Santiago!'

'Perhaps I will too now that I know what it is!' Brynne muttered irritably—at the same time as she realized that one of his middle names was Miguel, the same as Michael.

Had Joanna known that when she had named their son, or was it just a coincidence?

Coincidence or not, it certainly served as a reminder of exactly who and what Alejandro was!

'I'm not sure that Señorina Roig would be too happy if she could see you right now,' she murmured tauntingly.

'Antonia?' She could feel Alejandro's hands tense at her mention of the other woman's name. 'What does Antonia have to do with my helping you deal with your sunburn?' he demanded haughtily.

'In my bedroom helping me deal with my sunburn,' Brynne corrected pointedly. 'In my bedroom helping me deal with my sunburn while I'm only half-dressed,' she added. 'She may just decide to call off the engagement if she knew.'

She felt the bed give slightly as Alejandro stood up abruptly, and Brynne reached out to pick up her top from the floor, holding it protectively against her as she sat up to face him.

To say he looked angry was an understatement. His eyes had turned pale silver, the arrogant planes of his face were enhanced by his tightly clenched jaw and his nostrils flared in the aquiline nose.

'There is no engagement,' he bit out icily. 'There will never be an engagement between myself and Antonia Roig.'

Alejandro was more furious than Brynne had ever seen him—although she had no idea why her teasing should have roused him so intensely…

She gave a shrug. 'Perhaps you haven't made that plain enough to Miss Roig yet, because I'm pretty sure that she was lining up boarding-schools in her head earlier for Michael once the two of you are married.'

Alejandro's eyes glittered coldly. 'You were mistaken,' he said tightly.

She had introduced the subject of Antonia as a means of putting an end to a situation that was becoming far too intimate for her comfort, but she hadn't expected it to succeed quite as well as it had.

She gave a puzzled frown. 'It was just an idea…'

'Once again it is an example of your interference in something that is none of your concern—'

'If she becomes Michael's stepmother it will be my concern—'

'She will not!' His accent was so thick now Brynne thought he was in danger of lapsing into his native tongue completely. 'Miguel will never have a stepmother, Antonia or any other woman, because I never intend to marry again! There, does that satisfy your curiosity?' he rasped harshly.

Again…

Alejandro had said he would never marry 'again'…?

CHAPTER SEVEN

HE HAD said too much, Alejandro realized in disgust as the desire he had been feeling only minutes ago faded as if it had never been.

He had told Brynne Sullivan far too much.

Far more than she needed to know!

She was looking at him now with wide, suspicious eyes, as if the fact that he had once been married somehow made him into a—

'I married precisely three months after my brief relationship with Joanna was over,' he stated forcefully as he guessed the reason for the accusation in Brynne's gaze.

'That was convenient for you,' she replied hollowly, shaking her head slightly. 'No wonder you and Joanna never married—you were probably already married to someone else by the time she realized she was pregnant with Michael!'

'It was not like that at all—'

'Wasn't it?' Brynne scorned. 'Forgive me if I don't believe you!'

'I do not forgive you.' Alejandro was every inch the

wealthy, arrogant Spaniard as he looked down at her with icy grey eyes. 'Once again you speak of things, make accusations, you do not understand—'

'I understand you were married to someone else while Joanna had your baby, completely on her own!'

'I did not know she was pregnant—'

'And what would you have done about it if you had?' Brynne questioned. 'Paid for her to have an abortion? Or confessed all to your wife of only a few months and ruined her life as well? Although the fact that the two of you are no longer married probably shows that she at least had enough sense to leave you!' She was breathing hard in her agitation.

Alejandro had never received such insults to his honour before, from either a man or a woman, and the fact that minutes ago he had ached with wanting this particular woman only seemed to make it all the worse that the insults came from her.

His mouth twisted. 'My wife is dead. And there would have been no question of Joanna having an abortion! If Joanna had told me of her pregnancy, I would have supported both her and my child.'

'It must be nice to be rich enough to be able to salvage your conscience so easily!' Brynne scorned.

'If you were a man I would have knocked you down for the insults you have given me tonight,' Alejandro bit out coldly. 'But as you are not, I instead think it best that I leave you now to give you chance to calm down. We can talk about this again in the morning if that is what you wish.'

What she wished was that she had never met him—and her reasons for that no longer concerned Michael alone!

Minutes ago she had known herself aroused by Alejandro. And not for the first time, either.

What she really wanted to do right now was sit down and have a good cry at her own stupidity in allowing herself to become attracted to this complicated man!

She could so easily have turned over on the bed a few minutes ago and pulled his head down to hers and have him kiss her until she could think of nothing and no one but him. She longed to have him caress her in all the places that ached for his touch.

She was as disturbed by that admission as she was by learning he had been married.

'I don't know what I'll want in the morning,' she said dully.

But she did know. She wanted to go home, back to England, to forget she had ever met this unfathomable man. And instead she had to stay on here, for Michael's sake...

'Please go now,' she told Alejandro flatly.

Alejandro looked at her bowed head, and the beautiful hair that cascaded over the bareness of her delicate shoulders like a living flame. As he stared at her endearing freckles he had longed to kiss such a short time ago some of the anger he was feeling left him.

He had not thought it necessary for Brynne to know the details of his relationship with Joanna or the circumstances of his marriage to Francesca, and, knowing how close he had come tonight to taking her in his arms and making love to her, he believed that more than ever.

Brynne Sullivan was the last woman he should ever make love to!

'Perhaps you are right,' he snapped.

'Yes.' She sighed, reaching up a hand to push back the thickness of her hair to look up at him with pained blue eyes.

Alejandro looked at her for several more seconds before turning sharply on his heel and walking to the door, closing it softly behind him as he left.

He closed his eyes as he leant back against the wall outside in the hallway, fighting the yearning he had to go back into the room, to take Brynne into his arms.

But he had made a decision when Francesca had died five years ago that any relationship he had in future would only ever be of the transient kind, of short duration, with no emotional entanglement, and Brynne Sullivan, he already knew, with her prim morality, and her soul-destroying blue eyes, was not a woman of that type.

Brynne felt gritty-eyed and irritable from lack of sleep the next morning. She'd found it hard to sleep after the things she had learnt about Alejandro.

He had probably been engaged when he and Joanna had met seven years ago and already married by the time Joanna had known she was expecting his baby. Although it appeared that his wife had died some time in the last seven years.

All of these things had gone round and round in her head for hours last night.

One thing she did know was that any growing attraction she might have felt towards Alejandro had to stop.

It should never have happened in the first place after the battle the two of them had had six weeks ago over the custody of Michael!

In fact, the more she came to know about Alejandro Santiago, the stronger her feeling that Michael should have been allowed to stay with her.

The fact that Alejandro was sitting alone at the dining table, calmly reading a newspaper, when she got downstairs for breakfast did nothing to improve her mood!

Alejandro looked up as he sensed Brynne quietly entering the room, his mouth tightening as she avoided meeting his gaze to go over to the side dresser and pour herself some juice.

'Where's Michael?' she asked as she came to sit at the table opposite him.

'He went down to the orchard with Maria to pick some fresh oranges,' Alejandro dismissed, carefully folding his newspaper to place it on the table beside him. 'Is juice all you are having for breakfast?' He frowned.

Brynne shrugged dismissively. 'I'm not hungry.'

'How are you feeling this morning?' he probed softly.

She raised her chin, her blue eyes bright with challenge. 'How should I be feeling?'

He shrugged his broad shoulders. 'I merely wondered if your back was still painful…?'

'Oh.' Her gaze once again avoided his. 'It's much better this morning, thank you.'

She didn't look better, Alejandro noted, seeing that her face was pale and that there were dark shadows beneath her eyes.

He nodded abruptly. 'That is good. I have some business to attend to in Palma today,' he said curtly. 'Will you and Michael be able to amuse yourselves by the pool? With the appropriately applied suntan lotion, of course,' he added ruefully.

'Of course,' Brynne echoed dryly. 'If Michael gets bored I can always take him for a walk to Banyalbufar. Maria says its only just up the coast and—'

'I would rather you did not walk anywhere today,' Alejandro cut in.

'I'm sure the walk will do Raul and Rafael good,' Brynne finished mockingly. 'From their unhealthy pallor they obviously don't get out in the sun enough!'

'But you have,' Alejandro spoke firmly. 'And to go out walking when you are already burnt is not wise.'

Brynne gave him a scathing glance. 'I think I'm old enough to know not to make the same mistake twice!'

Alejandro gave her a searching look. Were they still talking about yesterday's sunburn? Or something else…?

From her guarded response to his earlier enquiry as to how she was feeling this morning he would say it was something else!

Her skin had felt wonderful to the touch last night as he had carefully applied the soothing lotion to her shoulders and the curve of her spine, and he was experienced enough to know that Brynne had enjoyed the caress of his hands. But if she feared he would suggest repeating the process then she was mistaken.

He had paid for his own unsatisfied arousal with a sleepless night, and did not intend repeating the experience!

'I suggest you ask Maria to put some after-sun on your back before you go outside,' he snapped dismissively, throwing his napkin down on the table to stand up. 'I am not sure what time I will get back, so do not—'

'Oh, please don't hurry back on our account,' Brynne assured him derisively, relieved to know that he would probably be out most of the day. 'Michael and I are quite used to entertaining ourselves.'

Alejandro looked down at her coldly before turning on his heel and striding from the room.

Brynne heaved a deep sigh of relief as she relaxed the tension from her shoulders. Painful shoulders, as it happened, with the skin on her back bright red this morning and slightly itchy. No doubt it would start to peel in a couple of days, and then instead of having the appearance of a lobster she would look like a snake shedding its skin. Very attractive!

Although if Alejandro was looking for attractive, he didn't have to look any further than Antonia Roig!

A fact Brynne was made very aware of later that morning when a red sports car roared down the driveway with Antonia sitting behind the wheel as she parked the car beside the villa with an assurance that spoke of familiarity.

Brynne's heart sank as she watched the other woman run her hands through her tumbled dark curls and replenish the red gloss to her lips before sliding out from behind the wheel, the white sundress she wore suiting her smoothly olive complexion and emphasizing the voluptuous curves of her body.

In contrast, Brynne felt at a complete disadvantage, having pulled on a loose white shirt over her bikini after taking a dip with Michael in the pool, her wet hair now slicked back from a face completely bare of make-up.

She stood up as Antonia walked over gracefully on white, high-heeled, designer mules. 'I'm afraid Alejandro isn't here at the moment, Miss Roig,' she began politely.

The other woman gave a gracious inclination of her head. 'He is in Palma today.'

If Alejandro had already told Antonia that, then what was she doing here…?

'Can I offer you some refreshment?' Brynne indicated the jug of fresh orange juice Maria had brought out minutes ago for her and Michael to enjoy, not particularly wanting the other woman to stay any longer than she had to, but at the same time realizing Antonia had other ideas.

'That would be acceptable.' Antonia nodded before sitting down on the lounger next to Brynne's, her eyes hidden behind dark sunglasses as she glanced over to where Michael was throwing euro coins to the bottom of the pool before diving down to collect them. 'He is so like Alejandro, is he not.' It was a statement rather than a question.

'Yes.' What else could Brynne say? The likeness between father and son was indisputable.

'Thank you,' Antonia said as she accepted the glass of juice before placing it down on the table untouched, her long nails still tipped in the red that matched her lipgloss. 'Miguel is the son of your sister…?' she prompted without so much as a polite preliminary.

Brynne's wariness grew at this unexpected visit by the other woman. 'My sister-in-law, actually,' she said.

'Your sister-in-law…?'

Brynne nodded. 'It's a little complicated, but, yes, Joanna was my sister-in-law.'

Anotnia's pouting red lips tightened slightly. 'Alejandro is very anxious that Miguel should…adapt…to his new way of life as quickly as possible,' she declared, obviously deciding not to pursue the subject of Brynne's specific relationship to Michael.

Brynne was starting to like this conversation less and less!

'Yes,' she answered noncommittally.

Antonia gave a shrug of her smoothly bare shoulders. 'As such it would probably be better for Miguel if he were to spend more time with—people of his own kind.'

Meaning what, precisely? Brynne wondered guardedly. Did Antonia mean the people of Majorca and Spain? Or did she mean affluently rich people like her and her father, and Alejandro himself, of course? Something Brynne obviously wasn't!

'Alejandro hasn't said that,' she replied truthfully. He had made it clear he didn't want her here, but not for that reason.

'Alejandro is very much the *caballero*, you know,' Antonia told her with an indulgent smile. 'Always the gentleman,' she explained for Brynne's benefit.

Brynne knew what a '*caballero*' was—she just didn't particularly associate Alejandro with one!

Although perhaps that was being a little unfair. Alejandro was always aware of the social niceties expected of him, was unfailingly polite to his employees, receiving their loyalty, and possibly their affection, in return. It was only with Brynne that he seemed to have trouble maintaining that politeness!

And she certainly didn't appreciate this woman's implication that Brynne had to be aware she wasn't wanted here. Or the fact that Alejandro obviously had to have discussed that subject with Antonia for the other woman to know that!

'I'm sure that if Alejandro wishes to…change our arrangement…he will tell me so,' she told Antonia stiffly, knowing that Alejandro had told her from the start that he didn't want her here, but that she had chosen to ignore it. Obviously by talking to Antonia on the subject he had decided to bring in reinforcements!

'That is a little…difficult…in the circumstances, is it not?' the other woman pointed out. 'Besides, it is so much more…civilized…for the women to talk of these things, yes?' she added sweetly.

Brynne's dislike of this beautiful but venomous woman was growing by the moment. As was her anger towards Alejandro for having discussed this situation with the woman who appeared to be his mistress even if he didn't intend her to be his wife.

'I'm sorry, Miss Roig. I appreciate that you and Alejandro are—friends,' she bit out tensely as she stood up, 'but I really have no intention of discussing something so—so personal, with someone I hardly know.' She glared down at the other woman pointedly as she willed her to leave.

Antonia stood up slowly, completely unruffled as she smoothed the white sundress down over shapely legs. 'I was merely trying to be—kind, Miss Sullivan,' she soothed huskily, smiling slightly. 'As I said earlier, Alejandro is too much the gentleman to be quite so… frank…with you.'

Brynne gave a scornful smile. 'That hasn't been my experience so far!' she dismissed impatiently. 'Now, if you wouldn't mind? Michael and I are going for a walk this morning.'

The other woman gave her a considering look. 'You

must be careful of too much sun, Miss Sullivan,' she advised lightly. 'A golden tan is acceptable, but with your fair colouring you are sure to burn.'

Exactly when had Alejandro spoken to this woman about her? After he had left her bedroom last night? Or had it been first thing this morning?

Well, if he thought telling his girlfriend to come and have a little 'woman to woman' chat with her was going to persuade Brynne into leaving here, then he was going to be sadly disappointed.

It was more likely to have the opposite effect!

CHAPTER EIGHT

'How dare you ask that—that—woman to come here and tell me you want me to leave?'

Alejandro had spent a long day in Palma, locked in further negotiations with Felipe Roig, tired of the cat-and-mouse game Felipe seemed to be having with him as he gave the older man the warning that he might withdraw from the possible deal himself if it wasn't soon settled to his satisfaction. A warning Felipe had obviously taken seriously enough to waste a day of Alejandro's time!

Alejandro would rather have come home once it had become obvious that no deal would be reached today, but the older man had insisted that the two of them had to go out to an early dinner in order to show that they were still friends. As Alejandro still had every intention of buying the tract of land Felipe had for sale, he didn't intend being anything else until he had Felipe's signature on a contract.

But having finally returned to the villa at nine-thirty that evening, he had gone to the pool-house to change into black swimming trunks before diving straight into the refreshing water and swimming half a dozen lengths of the pool before he had felt his temper start to cool. Another argument with Brynne was the last thing he felt in the mood for…

He rested his arms on the edge of the pool as he looked up at her, taking a few seconds to appreciate how sexily attractive she looked in the sky-blue linen dress with her feet bare beneath tanned legs. Her hair was loose about her shoulders and her face beautiful in spite of the angry glitter he could see in her eyes and that becoming flush to her cheeks.

It was an angry beauty he was becoming all too used to where this particular woman was concerned!

'I have no idea what you are talking about, Brynne—and, quite frankly, at this moment I do not think I want to know.' He sighed, holding up a silencing hand. 'I am tired and dusty from my frustrating day in Palma, so if you can wait a few minutes before continuing this tirade, then I would like a glass of cool wine first…' He levered himself quickly out of the water.

Brynne's breath instantly caught in her throat at the sight of all that bare male beauty. Alejandro's skin was dark olive all over, his legs long, his shoulders broad, chest muscled, stomach flat…

She averted her gaze but couldn't resist looking back again as Alejandro strolled over to the pool bar to take a cooled bottle of wine from the refrigerator there, deftly removing the cork before placing two glasses on top of the bar.

God, he really was the most gorgeous—

'Would you like some?' He held up the bottle invitingly. Why not? She wasn't tired and dusty, but she could definitely do with something to soothe her frayed nerves. Waiting for Alejandro to come back to the villa had been tediously long, and on top of that her irritation had grown when he hadn't got back in time to say goodnight to Michael, but she'd had no intention of going to bed herself until after she had spoken to him.

Finding herself in the company of an almost naked Alejandro—those black swimming trunks resting low on lean hips almost didn't count!—was making her senses dance with an altogether different emotion, the dark hair slicked back from those arrogantly handsome features making her mouth go dry.

'Thank you,' she accepted stiltedly as she took the glass of wine he held out to her. 'You—'

'At least let me have one drink before you start again!' Alejandro drawled as he sat down tiredly on one of the loungers, unconcerned by the wetness of his hair and body as he took several sips of the wine before looking up at her enquiringly. 'You may now continue,' he invited mockingly.

Brynne gave him a quelling glance. 'I'm glad you find all of this funny, Alejandro,' she dismissed in disgust, desperately trying to rekindle her earlier anger, but finding it increasing difficult in the company of this compellingly handsome man.

Come on, Brynne, she chided herself impatiently. Alejandro wasn't the first man she had seen in a pair of bathing trunks.

No…but he was the first one to make her want to rip that last remaining garment from that leanly muscled frame so that she could gaze her fill of all of him.

She shook her head in disbelief. 'I, on the other

hand,' she snapped waspishly, 'as the recipient of this "woman-to-woman" so-called advice, don't find any of this in the least funny.'

No, she obviously didn't find it funny, Alejandro acknowledged as he saw that the shadows beneath her eyes had deepened since this morning, her mouth curved down unhappily. Whatever it was!

'Perhaps you are not explaining yourself very well.' He smiled ruefully, leaning back against the cushioned chair and taking another sip of his wine.

The swim had been so cool, so reviving, the wine even more so; after hours of fruitless discussion his throat had felt rough as well as dry.

It was also, he realized, frowning, good to come home and find a beautiful woman waiting for him...

'No—you aren't listening!' Brynne paced restlessly beside the pool on those surprisingly pretty feet. 'And would it have been too much trouble for you to have come home in time to say goodnight to Michael?'

Alejandro closed his eyes briefly before looking up at her. This woman still dared to meddle in things he would accept from no one else. 'I do have a business to run—'

'And was your business any more successful today?' she challenged scathingly.

'As it happens, no.' Alejandro sat forward to replenish his wineglass, his relaxation of a few minutes ago fading as rapidly as the sun now disappearing beneath the horizon. 'Felipe continues to be...elusive...concerning finalizing the deal.' His expression was grim.

'Then perhaps you should become the elusive one,' Brynne dismissed, aware that they were once again veering off the subject—and the more time she spent in

Alejandro's almost-naked company, the less angry and more tinglingly aware of him she was becoming.

Alejandro raised dark brows. 'I beg your pardon?'

Brynne gave a shrug. 'That's the way it usually works with my more disinterested students. The more I ignore them, the more they want me to take notice of them,' she explained at Alejandro's questioning look.

Alejandro continued to look puzzled for several moments, and then he gave a slight smile. 'And do you shout at these students in the way that you shout at me?'

Had she shouted at him? Probably, she realized with a wince.

After all, she had been waiting hours for him to come home, and the first awareness she had had of his arrival had been the sound of him swimming, without any concern, up and down the pool. Not a move that would soothe her temper!

She grimaced. 'No, I don't shout at them.'

Alejandro quirked dark brows. 'Only at me?'

Well…yes.

Despite her red hair, she didn't usually lose her temper with anyone; she was normally cheerfully calm. To shout at one of her students, at anyone, really, was to lose control of the situation, she had always thought.

Unfortunately she had lost control of the situation with Alejandro Santiago from the moment the judge had come down in his favour regarding custody of Michael.

She gave him a frustrated glance. 'You annoy me, yes—'

'And is that all I do to you, Brynne?' he interrupted huskily, putting down his wineglass to get slowly to his feet.

Her eyes widened in alarm as he padded softly towards her. Like a predatory animal approaching its prey, she realized as her pulse started to race.

Alejandro stopped only inches away from where she stood rooted to the spot, not touching her—not needing to…

The sheer height and breadth of him as he stood so close to her blocked out everything but the sight and warmth of him.

'Is it, Brynne?' he encouraged throatily.

She swallowed hard. 'I don't know what you mean.'

'Oh, yes,' he breathed, 'I think you know only too well.'

She could smell the all-male scent of him, making her long to touch him, to caress the hard strength of his shoulders, featherlight across his chest and down that flat, hard stomach. She wanted to reach out and pull his head down to hers even as he moulded her body against his, wanted—needed—to feel the hardness of him against her, to touch and be touched, to—

'You feel it too, do you not?' he murmured huskily.

'Feel what…?' she asked weakly.

But she knew. She knew!

'Did you know…' Alejandro spoke softly, one hand moving up to cup beneath her chin as he tilted her face up to his and looked deeply into her eyes. 'Did you know,' he murmured again, that silver gaze holding her captive, his lips only centimetres away from hers now, 'that you have extremely beautiful feet?'

It was so not what Brynne had been expecting to hear, the very air between them so tense with expectation, that for a moment she could only look up at him blankly.

And then she blinked, once, twice, a frown appearing between dark blue eyes. 'I have beautiful feet...?' she finally repeated huskily with a hint of incredulity.

'You do.' Alejandro breathed softly even as his lips took slow possession of hers.

Brynne swayed weakly against him, her hands at last moving up to those oh-so-strong shoulders, finding them just as muscled and yet warmly sensual to the touch as she had imagined they would be. She groaned low in her throat as Alejandro's tongue parted her lips to deepen the kiss, his hands splayed against her spine as he drew her close against him.

Brynne felt the force of his arousal against her stomach as the kiss became more intense, more intimate. Alejandro's mouth became fierce against hers, the thrust of his tongue creating an answering warmth between her thighs, a heat that was both moist and urgent.

She clung to his shoulders as, his mouth still plundering hers, Alejandro lifted her up in his arms and carried her over to lay her down on the sun-warmed grass, her arms moving up about his shoulders as he lay down beside her.

He lifted his head to look down at her, the last of the sun's red rays turning her hair to fire against the green of the grass, her eyes darkly blue, her mouth poutingingly aroused from his kisses.

His gaze was caught and held by those full lips as he bent his head to draw her lower lip into the heat of his mouth, sucking gently, groaning low in his throat as he felt the quivers of pleasure down the slender length of her body.

Touching and kissing Brynne Sullivan was something he wanted badly, something he had been wanting for a long time.

But, like yesterday, kissing wasn't enough. He wanted more.

His lifted his head, easily holding her gaze with his as he moved one of his hands to undo the buttons down the front of her dress. He smoothed the material aside to reveal completely unrestrained breasts, shifting his gaze to look at those pert, beautiful orbs, the nipples already roused and begging to be kissed.

Brynne gasped, her body arching as she felt the first touch of Alejandro's lips against her bared breasts, his tongue tasting, teeth gently rasping, before he drew that heated tip into the warm cavern of his mouth, suckling, first gently, then harder.

She couldn't think, couldn't see, couldn't feel anything but Alejandro and the pleasure he was giving as his hand moved as surely to her other breast, the pad of his thumb moving there with the same rhythm as his lips sucked and his tongue rasped so erotically.

She moved her hips restlessly against him as she felt her need grow, wanting, aching for, some sort of release from this burning need that was threatening to tear her apart.

Alejandro was suddenly above her, their bodies moulded together from breast to thigh. The movement of his thighs against hers told her of his own pulsing arousal as he looked down at her with fierce silver eyes.

'Tell me what you want, Brynne,' he encouraged gruffly.

'Alejandro—'

'Tell me, Brynne.' he repeated fiercely before his

head lowered, his gaze holding hers as his tongue rasped erotically across her already sensitized nipple.

Brynne trembled even as she arched against him, her hand moving up instinctively as she held his head against her.

It was all the encouragement Alejandro needed. He suckled fiercely, teeth gently biting, tongue caressing, a flush to his cheeks minutes later when he raised his head to look at her. 'Do you want me to make love to you, Brynne?' he prompted forcefully.

Yes...

She had never wanted anything as badly as she wanted Alejandro at that moment, her nails digging into his shoulders, her heart beating so loudly she was sure he must be able to hear it.

She moistened her lips, her breath shallow in her chest as she felt herself held captive by that compelling gaze. 'I—'

'Shh!' He became suddenly still beside her, raising his head, more like the hunter this time than the predator as he tilted his head to listen, eyes narrowing. 'I hear a car.' He rolled onto the grass beside her, his hands moving to the folds of her dress, pulling them back over her nakedness.

He heard a car?

Brynne hadn't been aware of anything but Alejandro, of the touch of his hands, the caress of his lips and tongue, totally lost to the sensuality of the moment, her whole body trembling with the anticipation of this man's possession.

Unlike Alejandro, who heard a car!

CHAPTER NINE

'Who—?'

'The who does not matter,' Alejandro rasped as he stood up impatiently, very aware now of the rapidly approaching car.

And unsure of whether to be annoyed or relieved at the interruption!

Making love to Brynne Sullivan, much as he might have wanted it, was not a good idea. In fact, it was more recklessly stupid than anything he had ever done before!

More stupid than his relationship with Joanna all those years ago.

More stupid than his marriage to a woman he had not loved and who most certainly had not loved him.

His eyes were cold now as he looked down at a still-dazed Brynne, running a hand through the damp length of his hair as he heard the car stopping at the back of the villa. 'As we are about to have company I suggest you cover yourself,' he snapped.

Brynne's shock was starting to fade now, the cool night air on her damp flesh probably contributing to that, she acknowledged self-disgustedly even as she began to do up the buttons on her dress with slightly trembling fingers.

What had happened just now?

What had she allowed to happen?

One minute she and Alejandro had been arguing as they usually did, and the next—

She closed her eyes in embarrassment as she remembered what had happened next!

How on earth had she allowed things to go as far as they had?

Because she had wanted Alejandro with a madness that had driven everything else from her mind and body, had been wanton in his arms, her body still trembling with that need, her breasts still aching, the throbbing warmth between her thighs telling her how near she had come to losing control completely.

God, what must Alejandro think of her?

She didn't even want to think about that now, couldn't think about it, daren't think about it...!

But as she heard the familiar click of high heels on the villa's tiled pathway she knew that the 'who' did matter, after all, sure that their visitor, Alejandro's visitor, was going to be none other than the beautiful Antonia Roig!

Brynne rose quickly to her feet, standing several feet away from Alejandro as Antonia came through the arched gateway at the side of the villa, as sexily alluring as usual in a black fitted dress that left her shoulders bare, its knee-length also revealing her shapely legs.

Was this meeting prearranged? Brynne wondered. Or was Alejandro as surprised at the woman's visit as she was?

His greeting was warm enough as he strolled across to meet the other woman. 'Antonia,' he murmured huskily as he bent to kiss her on both cheeks.

Brynne turned away as she saw the beautiful Antonia reach up to complete the affectionate gesture by placing her red-painted lips against his in the third kiss that confirmed their intimacy with each other.

She had to get away from here.

Now!

Alejandro frowned darkly, slightly annoyed with Antonia for turning up uninvited in this way, but at the same time knowing he should probably be grateful for the interruption, because she had prevented him from making a serious mistake where Brynne Sullivan was concerned.

He was normally a cautious man when it came to his involvement with women, but Brynne had somehow managed to slip beneath his guard, making him forget, however briefly, all of the reasons he had told himself he should not pursue the sexual awareness he had sensed was growing between the two of them.

An awareness he now needed to dispel as quickly as possible!

'How kind of you to come and share your evening with me.' He smiled at Antonia. 'Would you care for a glass of wine?' he invited as they turned.

He couldn't help but notice Antonia's start of surprise as she saw Brynne standing a short distance away—her dress thankfully rebuttoned, although her glorious hair did look slightly wilder than normal.

Antonia's eyes narrowed briefly, losing some of their warmth, before she collected herself enough to resume smiling. 'Miss Sullivan,' she greeted lightly. 'How lovely to see you again,' she added almost questioningly.

'Señorita Roig,' Brynne came back stiffly. 'If you will both excuse me?' she added abruptly, head bent as she moved swiftly towards the villa.

It was what Alejandro had wanted, needing time away from Brynne to collect his scattered wits. For surely they had to have left him for him to have been so reckless as to kiss and touch her in the way that he had?

But as he saw the pallor of Brynne's cheeks, the slight trembling of her lips, the telling glitter to those dark blue eyes, he felt a moment's regret for deliberately hurting her in this way.

'Brynne!' he called after her sharply.

She stopped hesitantly, that tear-wet gaze not quite meeting his as she turned back slightly. 'Yes…?'

'Will you excuse me a moment, Antonia?' He turned back briefly to the woman at his side. 'I—have something I need to tell Brynne before she retires for the evening.' His smile was warmly placating.

'I understand, Alejandro.' Antonia gazed up at him warmly, mouth full and pouting. 'Do not be away too long, hmm?' she added with sensuous invitation as long red-tipped fingers ran caressingly down his cheek.

Brynne watched the intimate exchange between Alejandro and Antonia with mounting humiliation.

She had forgotten, as Alejandro had kissed her, that the reason she had waited so impatiently for his return this evening was because she had wanted to complain of the things this woman had said to her earlier today.

Now, witnessing that warm familiarity between the two of them, the look of triumph in Antonia's gaze as she glanced across at her so dismissively, Brynne thought it too late to make those complaints!

'What do you want, Alejandro?' she muttered impatiently as he reached her side.

His face tightened at her dismissive tone. 'You were the one who wanted to talk to me about something earlier…?' he reminded curtly.

Brynne could have laughed at the ridiculousness of talking about that now; Antonia Roig, despite Alejandro's denials to the contrary, obviously had her red-tipped claws into him so deeply he was unlikely to disapprove of anything the other woman said or did, but especially to Brynne, whom he considered an unwelcome guest in his home, at best.

'It doesn't matter.' She sighed.

His gaze narrowed. 'It mattered enough earlier for you to verbally berate me in the way that you did.'

Brynne gave a humourless laugh. 'I'm always "verbally berating" you, Alejandro—or hadn't you noticed?'

Oh, he had noticed. It was one of the things that made Brynne so different from every other woman he had ever known; none of them, including his wife, Francesca, had ever dared to talk to him in the way that Brynne did.

'Please go back to Miss Roig,' Brynne added with abrupt dismissal. 'I'm sure that she will be only too pleased to…soothe you, after your troubled day!' she added scathingly, that blue gaze raised in challenge to his.

Alejandro regretted even more having deliberately hurt Brynne, after their closeness of earlier, with his implied intimacy of a relationship with Antonia. But he also knew that it was for the best. He had nothing to offer a woman like Brynne—not love, and certainly not permanence.

'I am sure that she will too,' he replied mockingly. 'Goodnight, Brynne,' he added with cool dismissal, turning away to walk back to where Antonia waited for him.

Brynne turned sharply on her heel as she saw Antonia turn to Alejandro, murmuring something softly to him before the two of them laughed companionably.

At her, probably!

Or was she just being paranoid? Oversensitive from her time spent in Alejandro's arms?

Probably, she accepted heavily as she went slowly up the stairs. Alejandro might be many things—fickle obviously being one of them!—but she very much doubted that he was a man who discussed his conquests, especially with a woman who was another one of them.

But at least Antonia's arrival had stopped her making a complete idiot of herself, Brynne acknowledged with clenched jaw and gritted teeth as she heard the other woman's husky laugh several more times as she sat up in her bedroom once again trying to interest herself in the book she had brought away with her.

Again a useless exercise, when her thoughts were tormented with visions of what Alejandro and Antonia would be doing together when the laughter stopped!

She threw the book down on the bed and stood up, deliberately not approaching the window as she paced the room restlessly, having no intention of letting either Alejandro or Antonia think she was actually spying on them.

God, she could do with a plunge into the pool herself, so hot were her memories of her time in Alejandro's arms!

Several of her boyfriends had lasted longer than a couple of dates, but with none of them had she ever felt that mindless need to know their possession, to just forget everything but the moment, to find a release that she had never known.

To still ache, hours later, for that fulfilment!

Her nerves jangled irritably as she once again heard Antonia's husky laughter. She threw herself down on the bed to pull one of the pillows over her head to shut out the sound.

She would get over this ridiculous fascination she seemed to have developed for Alejandro.

She would!

'What do you intend doing today?' Alejandro prompted politely as Brynne joined him at the breakfast table the following morning, his manner deliberately that of a host to a guest.

He had a need, after seriously stepping over a line the evening before, to establish their relationship back to one of formality.

Although Brynne looked less approachable herself this morning as she looked across at him coolly, the white cotton blouse and linen trousers she wore suiting her slenderness, her red hair secured loosely on top of her head.

'You really don't need to even pretend a polite interest in what I'm doing, you know, Alejandro,' she dismissed with a derisive laugh. 'We both know I'm only here on sufferance!'

Alejandro frowned his irritation at Brynne's tone—

that irritation at complete variance with his earlier decision to instigate a distance between them. 'As you are Miguel's aunt, I of course owe you a debt of gratitude for the way in which—'

'Michael's aunt through marriage,' Brynne corrected pointedly as she carefully replaced her coffee cup in the saucer. 'And as anything I may or may not have done for Michael was done out of love for him, I'm sure you know what you can do with your gratitude!' she added forcefully.

Alejandro had let her know quite clearly the night before that he regretted whatever lapse had induced him to make love to her—a lapse that Brynne probably regretted more than he did! He didn't have to treat her like some polite stranger this morning in order to emphasize that point!

He frowned darkly. 'I was merely—'

'I'm really not interested, Alejandro,' Brynne snapped irritably, pushing back her chair with the intention of standing up, but prevented from doing so as Alejandro reached out and grasped her hand. She trembled slightly. 'What are you doing?' She sighed her exasperation with this man's hot-and-cold moods.

He had no idea, Alejandro acknowledged with inward impatience for his own actions; he only felt a need to stop Brynne from leaving with things so strained between them.

He removed his hand, resting his elbows on the table as he steepled his fingers together. 'You wanted to say something to me last night…' he reminded huskily.

Brynne gave him a scathing glance. 'I'm sure that Antonia was only too eager, once I had gone to bed, to tell you all about our little chat yesterday morning!'

Antonia…? What did Antonia have to do with what had been troubling Brynne when he had arrived home yesterday evening?

What was it Brynne had said—attacked him with— last night? Something about that woman telling her he wanted her to leave, he recalled frowningly. He had been too tired and irritable at the time to consider Brynne's anger as anything more than yet another misunderstanding between them. But her mention of Antonia put an altogether different connotation on things.

Antonia had been the woman Brynne referred to…?

Alejandro's gaze became guarded as he looked across at a Brynne, who was obviously angry once again, a flush to her cheeks, her eyes sparkling with the emotion. 'Perhaps I would rather hear it from you…?' he said slowly.

'Well, that's just too bad!' she told him scathingly, standing up to look down at him. 'Because I have no intention of satisfying your curiosity! Suffice to say, I am not leaving here before my month is up, and nothing you can say, or do—or that your girlfriend says or does!— is going to make me leave any sooner. Is that clear enough for you?' she challenged.

'Very clear,' he acknowledged distractedly.

Antonia had come here yesterday while he was out? While she had known he was out in Palma at a meeting with her father?

Exactly what had she said to Brynne…?

Whatever it was he deeply resented Antonia thinking she had the right to come here when he was out and say anything at all of a personal nature to Brynne.

Yes, he had used Antonia's unexpected arrival yesterday evening as a means of ending that tense situation between himself and Brynne, which might or might not have given Antonia completely the wrong idea about their own relationship, but her conversation with Brynne had taken place before that…

'Perhaps you misunderstood Antonia? Her English was perhaps not as fluent—'

'Yes, you would like me to think that, wouldn't you?' Brynne scorned as she gave a rueful shake of her head. 'It hardly fits in with her claim of you "always being the gentleman", does it, to ask your mistress to come here and tell me it would be a good idea if I left?'

Alejandro's expression darkened even more. 'Antonia is not my mistress,' he bit out coldly. 'And I did not ask her to speak to you on this subject—'

'Of course you didn't,' Brynne dismissed wearily.

'Or any other,' Alejandro finished firmly, throwing his napkin down on the table before standing up, tall and forbidding in a black tee shirt and black denims. 'You will forget this conversation with Antonia ever happened,' he instructed arrogantly. 'I will speak to her—'

'In bed or out of it?' Brynne taunted, her anger of yesterday increased by the humiliation she had suffered after being in this man's arms last night.

Alejandro looked every inch the arrogant Spaniard at that moment, his eyes cold, his mouth a thin, angry line. 'You will forget the things Antonia has said to you,' he repeated icily. 'As I will do my best to forget that you have once again insulted my honour with your accusations—'

'Oh, please, Alejandro.' Brynne gave another weary sigh. 'This display of injured Spanish pride may work on some people, but it doesn't work on me!'

Alejandro wanted to make her listen to him. To take hold of her and shake her until her teeth rattled. To take her in his arms and kiss her until she was senselessly compliant…!

He forced himself to do none of those things, instead clenching his hands into fists at his sides. 'Nevertheless, I will ensure that Antonia does not talk to you in this way again,' he assured Brynne coldly. 'And I apologize on her behalf for any misunderstanding that may have arisen between the two of you,' he added stiffly.

'There was no misunderstanding,' Brynne assured him with a derisive shake of her head. 'And I'm sure she wouldn't thank you for implying that there was!'

His mouth tightened. He did not care whether Antonia thanked him or not. He allowed no one, absolutely no one, to act on his behalf in the way that Brynne claimed Antonia Roig had done yesterday.

'I am taking Miguel out with me today,' he informed Brynne distantly. 'Perhaps you would care to get his bathing things together while I ask Maria to pack a picnic lunch for the two of us? You may, if you wish, use one of the cars in the garage to go for the drive you were so keen to go on yesterday,' he added dismissively.

No suggestion of her accompanying the two of them, Brynne noted painfully, knowing that her hurt feelings on being excluded from the outing weren't in the least logical after her comments to Alejandro yesterday about not spending time with his young son, but feeling slightly put out anyway.

Michael, she knew, was still a little nervous of the man who was his father, and would still have welcomed her presence on any outing, so it had to be Alejandro who didn't want her with them…

Not surprisingly, really, she accepted heavily; the two of them were never exactly harmonious when they were together, were they?

Alejandro paused in the doorway. 'I think it best if you put Antonia's comments behind you, Brynne,' he bit out abruptly. 'It is finished. Over,' he assured her before turning sharply on his heel to stride forcefully from the dining-room.

Brynne gazed after him with a frown.

When he said, 'It is finished. Over,' did he mean his relationship with Antonia Roig, or just the other woman's interference in his personal affairs?

And wasn't that yet another thing that Alejandro would consider none of her business…?

CHAPTER TEN

MORE out of defiance than any real wish to go out on her own, Brynne did go for a drive once Michael and Alejandro had gone out in the Mercedes, selecting a car with a soft top she could put down to enjoy the full benefits of the beautifully sunny day.

Whether out of defiance or not, she actually enjoyed her day out, driving down to Palma to park on the seafront and walk along the marina looking at the magnificent yachts moored there, some of them looking bigger inside than the flat she rented at home, and several of them had helicopter pads on the back too.

She bought a baguette for her lunch, finding a park just across from the seafront in which to sit and enjoy it along with lots of other tourists sitting or lying about the wonderful water feature in the park's middle, and then strolling into the city to sit outside a café and have a leisurely cup of coffee before wandering up to look at the cathedral.

Michael, as a six-year-old, would have enjoyed looking at the yachts for a short time, but the cathedral wouldn't have interested him in the slightest, so it felt quite good to take full advantage of this day off.

But lonely too, of course…

And she couldn't help wondering where Alejandro had taken his son for the day, sincerely hoped, for both their sakes, that Alejandro had taken Michael's age into account when he had made his plans.

Not that it was any of her business, of course, but she was aware of the time passing, and would feel happier herself knowing that Michael was going to be happy once she had returned home.

She returned to the villa shortly after five o'clock to find they had only just returned themselves. Her worries seemed completely unnecessary if Michael's enthusiasm about the water park his father had taken him to was any indication!

Although the unlikely picture of the arrogantly aloof Alejandro Santiago in a public water park, full of tourists and children, took a little getting used to!

'Not what you expected?' He quirked dark, mocking brows in Brynne's direction as Michael skipped off happily to the kitchen to ask Maria for a biscuit and some fresh orange juice.

Not exactly, Brynne inwardly acknowledged as she hesitated about joining him at the table where he sat relaxing by the pool; after all, he hadn't wanted her company all day, so there was no reason to suppose that he would want it now, either.

Which was totally childish on her part, she instantly reproved herself impatiently. Whether Alejandro wanted her company or not, he was stuck with it for another three and a half weeks, and she had no intention of making herself scarce every time he was around!

'I'm sure the two of you had a wonderful time,' she said noncommittally as she pulled out one of the chairs to sit down, her legs aching slightly from the amount of walking she had done today.

Alejandro gave a slightly derisive smile. 'I enjoyed myself watching Miguel enjoy himself,' he drawled ruefully, his smile fading slightly as he added huskily, 'He is a charmingly engaging little boy.'

'Yes.' Brynne nodded. 'He is.'

'And that, I know, is due to the way Joanna and your brother brought him up,' Alejandro murmured softly. 'No doubt, your family too.'

'Oh, I don't think we can take too much credit for that,' she denied, a pleased flush to her cheeks nonetheless. 'Joanna had pretty much helped mould him into the happy, unspoilt little boy that he is by the time we all met him.'

'She was a good mother.' It was a statement, not a question, Alejandro knowing just from being with Miguel that this was so.

'The best,' Brynne confirmed unhesitantly. 'She seemed to find no difficulty at all in juggling her career as a very successful lawyer and her role as Migu— Michael's mother.'

Joanna had been twenty-four when Alejandro had met her, had completed her law qualifications and had been taking a year off from her studies to travel the world before commencing her career. It pleased him to know that she had had the success of that career that she had wanted so much.

He nodded. 'She was very determined, very positive, of what she wanted to do with her life.' There was sadness, if not actual grief, in his thoughts that all of that bright determination had been wiped out in a single act. 'I am glad she succeeded.'

'Yes,' Brynne said huskily, slightly uncomfortable with this conversation, in the circumstances.

'You find my interest in Joanna's life—strange?' Alejandro guessed astutely.

She shrugged. 'Well, yes, a little,' she acknowledged ruefully.

Alejandro shrugged broad shoulders, obviously relaxed from his day out with Michael, their own earlier tension seeming to have been put to one side, if not forgotten. 'She was the mother of my son. Of course I am interested in whether or not she was happy.'

'She and Tom were very happy together,' Brynne told him slightly defensively.

'I am aware of that too.' Alejandro gave an acknowledging nod. 'Miguel has talked of "Mummy" and "Daddy" for most of the day!'

Brynne became very still. 'He has?'

'Yes.' Alejandro gave her a quizzical look. 'This surprises you?'

Yes, it did. Apart from those nights when Michael woke up having nightmares, crying for his 'Mummy and Daddy', he never spoke of Joanna and Tom, hadn't openly cried for them, either. Brynne wasn't a psychologist, but she felt it was as if by not talking about them Michael could somehow put it from his mind that they were no longer there, that he could somehow believe they would one day walk back through the door.

The finality of death was very difficult for young children to understand, and only time and a great deal of love, Brynne knew, would help to heal the little boy's deep sense of bewilderment.

And having Alejandro Santiago as his real father…

Because, aged four when Joanna and Tom had married, Michael had obviously always known that Tom wasn't his father.

It was good that Michael felt he could talk to Alejandro about Joanna and Tom. Maybe Michael was already starting to transfer his affection to the other man…?

'I am a stranger, Brynne.' Alejandro broke the silence that had stretched between them. 'Perhaps he feels more comfortable talking of them with someone who he knows…and please do not misunderstand me, but I am someone that Michael knows will not become emotionally upset when he talks of his mother and Tom.'

That was a point.

It was also a point that Alejandro had for once forgotten to call him 'Miguel'…

She managed a rueful smile. 'You're probably right. I'm afraid my parents have been pretty well emotionally demolished by the whole thing, by Joanna's death of course, but Tom's especially. And I can't claim to have been too controlled about it myself.' She grimaced.

'But why should you be?' Alejandro frowned. 'Tom was your older brother, Joanna your sister-in-law. It was—is—a tragedy.'

Brynne gave him a quizzically searching glance. 'But without that tragedy you might never have known Michael was your son—'

'What sort of man do you take me for, Brynne?' he cut in frowningly. 'Do you think I would wish Joanna dead just so that I could claim Miguel?'

Well, she had pretty much put an end to that truce, Brynne guessed with a regretful wince for her inappropriate choice of words.

'Of course I didn't mean that,' she dismissed impatiently. 'I was just pointing out—'

'Brynne, I am very happy to know of Miguel's existence, and I hope that if Joanna had lived I would still have learnt of it one day when he had grown up and possibly asked about his real father.' He was consumed with anger. 'But I certainly do not feel any pleasure in the fact that his mother is dead!'

Brynne gasped breathlessly. 'You're deliberately misunderstanding me—'

'I do not think so!' Alejandro stood up abruptly, his face etched into hard, aristocratic lines. 'No matter what you may have claimed only days ago, Brynne, I am not the inhuman monster you believe me to be,' he bit out between clenched teeth before turning sharply on his heel and striding away.

He had thought Brynne had got to know him better than that in the last few days, felt deeply the knowledge that she still thought of him in that way.

Walking away seemed to be something Alejandro did a lot around her, Brynne acknowledged achingly as she watched him stride off towards the beach, bitterly dismayed at this fresh misunderstanding between them.

She turned sharply back to the villa as she heard the sound of glass breaking, knowing by the look of horror on Michael's white, shocked face as he stood a short distance away on the tiled patio, the broken glass of orange juice at his feet, that he had to have heard at least the tail-end of her exchange with Alejandro, if not all of it!

Brynne got noisily to her feet. 'Michael—' she didn't get any farther as the little boy turned on his heel—much as his father had done seconds ago!—and ran back inside the villa.

She hurried after him, all the time cursing herself for not remembering that as a teacher she was well aware of the fact that children had a way of appearing when you least expected them to—that, in Michael's case, his return hadn't been unexpected.

She should have realized, should have been more circumspect—

It was no good making the excuse that she had been so bemused by Alejandro's almost gentleness as he had spoken of Joanna that she hadn't given Michael's return a second thought—she should have thought!

Michael was her priority. And in this case she and Alejandro were responsible for causing him pain.

'Michael…!' She groaned as she found him in his room face down on the bed, quickly crossing the room to sit on the side of the bed and gather him up into her arms.

Michael clung to her, crying so hard his whole body was racked by the shuddering sobs. 'Mummy and Daddy are never coming back, are they?' he choked as he clung to her. 'I'm never going to see them again, am I?' he cried as he was besieged by fresh sobs.

Brynne was crying too by this time, the salty tears wetting her lips as she held Michael tightly against her.

'Are you going to die too, Aunty Bry?' Michael sobbed. 'And my new daddy?'

'No, Michael,' she gasped at his total desolation. 'Of course we aren't going to die.'

'Don't leave me, Aunty Bry!' Michael clung to her even harder. 'Please don't leave me!'

'Everyone dies one day, my love,' she added huskily, knowing that truth was very important to children; lose their trust once and it was very hard to regain it. And there were no guarantees when it came to life and death… 'But none of us is going to die yet, Michael. You'll be a man yourself, possibly with children of your own, by the time your new daddy or I die.' Surely fate couldn't deal this bereft little boy two such devastating blows…?

'That will be a long time then,' Michael breathed thankfully.

'Yes, a long time, darling,' Brynne confirmed huskily.

'Brynne…?'

She turned to look at Alejandro as he spoke softly to her from the doorway.

They made a desolate picture, Alejandro acknowledged even as he crossed the room to where they sat, both so emotionally wounded by this almost incomprehensible death of Joanna and Tom. 'I heard the breaking of glass and your shout of "Michael",' he explained huskily even as he sat down on the bed beside Brynne. 'I—'

'Daddy!' Michael had turned from his aunt's arms to launch himself into Alejandro's.

Alejandro felt emotion grip his own throat as he held Michael tightly to him, the little boy's arms clinging so pathetically about his neck.

'It is okay, Michael,' he soothed as he stroked that silky dark hair so like his own. 'Aunty Brynne and I will not leave you. You are not alone, Michael,' he assured him firmly. 'I promise you will never be alone.'

He was a man who chose to keep himself separate from

emotion, having decided long ago that it was better that way. But Michael's pain was such that it was impossible to remain unaffected. This was his son. His son! And Michael needed him in a way that no one else ever had.

He was filled with such a tidal wave of love that he found it almost impossible to speak, talking softly in Spanish when he finally found his voice again, reassuring his son of his love for him even as he stroked and held him close.

Not able to speak fluent Spanish, Brynne had no idea what Alejandro was murmuring to Michael, but it only needed one look at the softened arrogance of his face, and to hear the husky emotion in his voice, to know that it was something very personal, something totally private between father and son.

Feeling like an intruder on that emotion, she got quietly to her feet to walk over to the window. Michael had been so brave these last two months, so self-contained, that the release, when it had come, had been heart-shattering.

And when it had come, it had been Alejandro he had turned to for comfort…

She was glad.

For Michael's sake.

But mainly for Alejandro's.

He was a man who held himself so aloof from emotion, even knowing of Michael's existence, bringing him here, not seeming to have shaken Alejandro's well-ordered life too much. But she had seen love in Alejandro's eyes a few minutes ago, and knew that Michael's despair had finally broken through the barrier Alejandro seemed to have placed around his own heart.

Seeing Michael and Alejandro together like this, recognizing the affection, and now love, that was blossoming between the two of them, she could feel the trail of her own tears as they fell hotly down her cheeks.

'He has fallen asleep,' Alejandro murmured softly behind her a few minutes later. 'No doubt exhausted from the release of emotion,' he added huskily as he made his son comfortable on the bed before turning to look at Brynne. 'You and I need to talk,' he bit out grimly as he moved to the door, pointedly holding it open for her to precede him out of the room.

Brynne shot him a nervous glance as she reached his side, not at all sure of him in this mood, the tenderness he had shown towards Michael a few minutes ago having completely disappeared behind a hard mask.

Brynne swallowed hard. 'Perhaps one of us should stay with Michael—'

'You can come back and sit with him in a few minutes,' Alejandro assured her harshly. 'For now you and I have a conversation to finish. Not downstairs,' he instructed tautly as she moved in that direction. 'In here, where we cannot be overheard,' he added determinedly as he pushed open a door farther down the hallway.

'In here' was a room Brynne had never been in before, a huge, sunny room with double French doors leading out onto a large balcony, decorated in muted golds and browns, and dominated by a huge four-poster bed with gauzy drapes that could be pulled at night for complete privacy.

Alejandro's bedroom...

CHAPTER ELEVEN

ALEJANDRO saw the look of panic on Brynne's face as she realized he had brought her to his bedroom, his mouth twisting in derision. 'I am hardly in the mood for seduction at this moment!' He moved to the French doors, throwing them open to breathe in the clean, gentle breeze. He needed the fresh air to help him calm down. That scene with Michael had disturbed him.

'Michael overheard part of our conversation earlier,' Brynne told him unnecessarily.

They should have been more careful, of course, had once again allowed the antagonism that existed between them to spill out unchecked.

Brynne looked pale, her freckles once again standing out against the whiteness of her skin. Her darkly shadowed eyes showed that she was as disturbed by the incident as he was.

Unless finding herself in his bedroom had caused that…?

He gave an impatient shake of his head. 'The distress just caused to Michael has surely shown you that this habit you have of attacking me concerning my past relationship with Joanna has got to stop!'

Brynne gasped. 'You're blaming me—'

'We are both to blame,' Alejandro acknowledged harshly. 'You, for making accusations, judgements, you have no right to make. Me, because I felt the need to defend those judgements.' His eyes glinted angrily. 'My past relationship with Joanna is not your concern—'

'No, I just have to help pick up the pieces seven years later!' Brynne scorned, feeling stung by his words.

She accepted they had been wrong to argue like that in a place where Michael could overhear them. But she didn't accept the argument had been her fault. Alejandro was the one who had reacted to a perfectly innocent remark—

'Is that your only interest, Brynne?' Alejandro challenged, as he looked down his chiselled nose at her. 'Or is it that you feel some—personal curiosity, concerning my relationship with Joanna all those years ago?' he added softly.

Brynne felt the colour warm her cheeks. 'What are you implying now?'

His mouth twisted, there was o humor in his tone. 'There is a saying in your country, is there not, something about people in glass houses should not throw stones…?'

Brynne stared at him blankly for several long seconds, and then her eyes widened as his meaning became clear. 'If you're talking about what happened between us last night—'

'That is exactly what I am talking about, Brynne,' he sneered. 'How do you think that would have ended if we had not been interrupted in the way that we were?'

She had tortured herself with those very same thoughts alone in her bedroom last night…

'Is that why you did it, to prove—'

'We did it, Brynne,' Alejandro cut in harshly. 'I kissed you—certainly not to prove anything!—but once I had kissed you you were a willing participant to what happened next,' he reminded her coldly. 'So,' he clipped. 'What do you think would have happened?' he persisted.

'If your girlfriend hadn't arrived, you mean—'

'Oh, no,' Alejandro cut in softly. 'I am not going to allow you to antagonize me into changing the subject in that way.' He crossed the room to stand just in front of her.

Making Brynne all too aware of him, the heat of his body, that all-male smell, the leashed power that could be released at any second.

She avoided that compelling silver gaze as she moistened suddenly dry lips. 'I like to think—'

'No, Brynne!' Alejandro grasped her arms and shook her slightly. 'No thinking. No wishing. No imagining.' He shook her again. 'Tell me what you think would have happened after I had touched you here.' One of his hands moved to caress lightly across her breast before returning to grasp her arm. 'Kissed you here.' He held her gaze as his head lowered. His lips and tongue grazed lightly across her hardened nipple beneath her cotton top.

'Stop it!' Brynne struggled to pull away from him but was held tight by the strength of his hands on her arms.

'What if we had not stopped—for whatever reason—when we did, Brynne?' he repeated softly. 'What do you think would have happened next?'

She didn't need to think—she knew what would have happened!

She had wanted Alejandro last night, mindlessly, urgently. She had been unable to think of anything but him, of being even closer to him; she hadn't even been aware of the approaching car that had alerted him to Antonia Roig's arrival.

Alejandro could see the pained bewilderment in Brynne's eyes, could guess at the reason for it, knew that he was hurting her, but needed to make her understand the past.

It was this lack of understanding—perhaps of experience?—that caused her to judge him and Joanna as harshly as she did, and while he did not care for himself, Joanna was a different matter.

'We both know what was going to happen next.' He released her abruptly, moving several feet away to thrust his hands into his trouser pockets. 'The two of us would have become lovers—'

'No—'

'But yes, Brynne,' he insisted softly. 'We were almost there already.'

'You're despicable!' she gasped.

'I am honest,' he corrected grimly. 'With myself. And with other people. It is the same honesty that Joanna and I had between us seven years ago. We were not in love with each other, but we liked each other, were attracted to each other. It was an attraction that we acted upon. The same attraction that was between us last night—'

'No—'

'What are you saying, Brynne?' he taunted. 'That what you felt last night was not lust but something else? That you are in love with me?' he added derisively.

Of course she wasn't in love with him!

He was hateful. Arrogant. Mocking. And she despised him for discussing last night in this cold, analytical way.

That completely mindless passion had never happened to her before, with anyone, and it was something she still had trouble accepting, let alone understanding.

'Well, are you?' Alejandro continued remorselessly.

'No, of course not—'

'Of course not,' he echoed scornfully. 'But you allowed me to touch you, to caress you, to kiss you—'

'Stop it!' she cried emotionally. 'Just stop it!' She turned away, shaking.

'Yes, I will stop.' Alejandro sighed heavily. 'But you are a hypocrite, Brynne Sullivan. You are fooling only yourself by believing you are incapable of the same feelings that drew Joanna and I together seven years ago.'

Brynne knew she was fooling herself. She was totally aware of the fact that she wouldn't have been able to pull back from making love with Alejandro last night. She had wanted him completely. She had continued to ache for his possession for hours afterwards.

She still ached for that possession…

'You also blame me for the fact that Joanna went through her pregnancy alone, brought Michael up alone for the first four years of his life,' he continued determinedly. 'My defence to that is it was Joanna's choice—'

'Because you were married—'

'My marriage is immaterial. It was Joanna's choice not to tell me of the pregnancy or of Michael's existence,' Alejandro continued remorselessly. 'If anyone should be angry about that, then it should be me, not you,' he stated flatly. 'I am disappointed not to have known Michael until now, yes, but I do not blame Joanna for the choices she made. They were hers to make, after all.'

He was right. Brynne knew he was right. But it had been far easier to be angry with Alejandro, living, breathing, arrogant Alejandro, rather than Joanna, her feistily independent sister-in-law.

'I do not intend to discuss this subject with you again, Brynne,' Alejandro told her huskily. 'The past is gone. Joanna is gone. And so any further discussion on the subject is pointless. Harbour such thoughts as you want about me—I am sure that others have thought much worse,' he added dryly. 'But do not think those things of Joanna.' He sobered. 'She was a beautiful free spirit when I knew her, a woman who knew her own mind and body, and that is how I will always think of her.'

Joanna had been the same beautiful free spirit when Brynne had known her too, when Tom had fallen in love with her.

And that almost gentle way that Alejandro talked of her seemed to imply that his own emotions had not been as removed in that relationship as he would have liked them to be…

'There is only Michael now,' Alejandro continued briskly. 'He is all that is important.'

'I agree,' she said quietly.

'You do?' Alejandro sounded amused now.

She raised her head to look at him, that amusement also in his eyes. 'Yes, I do,' she confirmed ruefully. 'And I'll try not to be hypocritical again,' she added softly.

Alejandro studied her between narrowed lids, knowing exactly what she meant by that last remark.

Brynne intended to ensure that the opportunity to make love with her did not occur again.

He knew it was the sensible thing to do. The right thing to do. And yet sensibility was not an emotion this young woman aroused in him.

He had wanted her badly last night, had felt her quiver in response a few minutes ago when he had touched her, and knew he could not offer the guarantee, given similar circumstances, that it would not happen again...

'You will "try", Brynne...?' he taunted softly.

Her mouth tightened. 'Yes.'

Alejandro nodded. 'Then I will try also,' he murmured huskily.

'Although this is perhaps not the right room in which to make such an assertion?' He looked around them pointedly.

The sudden vision he had of Brynne lying naked with him on his four-poster bed, those golden limbs entangled with his, the fiery swathe of her hair cascading over his chest, was perhaps not conducive to such a claim either!

'I'll go back and sit with Michael now.' Brynne turned away from him abruptly.

'Brynne...?' Alejandro reached out to lightly grasp her arm. She stared up at him and he looked down into that beautiful but pale face; he saw the guarded emotions in those dark blue eyes.

Alejandro was overwhelmed with a desire to kiss her again, to touch her, caress her!

Instead he spoke harshly. 'I shall be out to dinner again this evening but I will speak to Michael before I leave.'

Brynne didn't need two guesses as to whom Alejandro would be having dinner with again this evening.

Obviously their discussion earlier had made no difference to his continuing a relationship with that other woman. No doubt Antonia Roig was sophisticated enough to deal with the sort of relationship Alejandro was used to, the only sort of relationship he would allow in his life.

The sort of relationship she and Alejandro had almost fallen into themselves last night…

Alejandro had been right to upbraid her on that subject. Her own response to him last night had made a complete nonsense of her assumptions about his casual relationship with Joanna all that time ago.

Last night she had been a victim of her own desire for this man. She knew even now that she could so easily have forgotten everything but Alejandro as his hands and lips had weaved a magic over her body that she had had no thought of denying.

Just the touch of his hand on her arm right now was once again weaving that magic…

'I'm sure Michael would like that,' she bit out.

'And you, Brynne?' Alejandro murmured throatily. 'What would you like?'

She would like him not to go to Antonia Roig! But to stay here with her this evening. For them to talk. To laugh. Before they made slow, leisurely love together.

Madness!

Her chin rose; she was determined to fight these feelings. And to go on fighting them.

'Once Michael is awake I would like to go and have a quick bath before our evening meal,' she dismissed lightly.

The thought of Brynne, those long, golden limbs completely naked, her hair secured loosely on top of her head as she floated in the Jacuzzi bath in the room that adjoined her bedroom, was almost Alejandro's undoing.

Instead he thrust her away from him, his expression harsh and remote. 'Go and bathe now, if you wish,' he rasped, forcing that image firmly from his thoughts. 'I will sit with Michael until you return.'

She looked at him quizzically. 'You've decided to call him Michael, after all…?'

'For the moment, yes.' Alejandro shrugged broad shoulders. 'Perhaps in wanting him to become immediately Spanish, I am expecting too much too soon.'

Brynne gave a rueful smile. 'I think that's very wise.'

'Wise, Brynne?' he echoed mockingly. 'I did not think you believed me capable of such an emotion.'

She believed him capable of many more emotions than she would care to admit, the main one, she realized as she continued to look up at him, being an integrity where the existence of his son was concerned.

Alejandro had remained in ignorance of Michael's existence for over six years, and even once he had seen the newspaper article on Joanna's death, and realized that her son could also be his own son, he could have continued to ignore that existence if he had chosen to. But instead he had claimed his son, had fought a legal battle with her in order to secure that claim. And through all of that he had maintained a respect and affection for Joanna that was unshakeable.

Alejandro Santiago, she acknowledged, was indeed an honourable man.

The fact that he resented her, and her earlier efforts to deny him his son, was perhaps the price she paid for that realization…

Her smile deepened. 'I'm sure that what I think of you is of absolutely no importance to you whatsoever, Alejandro!' she said with certainty.

Was it unimportant? Alejandro wondered. Last night he had made love with this woman, would have taken her completely if Antonia had not arrived so unexpectedly. How would Brynne have behaved towards him today if that had happened?

It would, he knew with sudden clarity, have made it impossible for them to continue to stay here together.

He gave a hard smile. 'None whatsoever,' he confirmed dismissively. 'Go and take your bath,' he instructed curtly before turning away, his back rigid, hands clenched at his sides as he stared out of the window until he heard the bedroom door close softly as Brynne left.

His breath left him in a shaky sigh as he forced the tension from his shoulders and slowly unclenched his fists.

This completely candid conversation with Brynne had been necessary and perhaps long overdue. Even though she didn't appreciate the comparisons he made between his past relationship with Joanna and what had happened between the two of them last night, it had needed to be said. Although it hadn't been deliberate, Brynne now knew that desire was as forceful an emotion as love was reputed to be.

Reputed. Because Alejandro had never loved any woman. Not Joanna. Not Francesca. Certainly none of the now nameless, faceless women he had been involved with over the years.

He wasn't in love with Brynne either, but nevertheless her flame-coloured hair, those candid blue eyes and that delectably arousing body had become a torment to him, a temptation.

It was a temptation he was finding it increasingly difficult to resist…

CHAPTER TWELVE

BRYNNE awoke drowsily as she felt herself being lifted, an arm about her shoulders, another beneath her bent knees. Her lids felt heavy as she looked up and found Alejandro's face only inches from her own, those two cradling arms obviously his.

'What are you doing?' she murmured sleepily.

He looked down at her, eyes dark and unfathomable. 'What does it look like I am doing?' he came back softly.

It looked—and felt—as if he were holding her against that muscled hardness of his chest. Brynne was able to hear the steady beat of his heart beneath the silk material of his shirt.

'I found you asleep on the sofa when I returned home,' he added huskily as he began to walk up the stairs.

Oh, yes, she remembered now. She and Michael had eaten a leisurely dinner together, her own meal accompanied by a couple of glasses of wine. After she had put Michael to bed she had sat in the sitting-room reading—still unable to banish thoughts of Alejandro out with the beautiful Antonia Roig—and must have fallen asleep.

She had been waiting for Alejandro to return, that was

it. She had something she needed to tell him. But cradled close against him like this she couldn't think straight, certainly couldn't remember what that something was!

'Where are you taking me?' She frowned.

Where indeed? Alejandro wondered as he looked down at her, the long red hair feeling like silk as it cascaded over his bare arm, her eyes once again that dark smoky blue, her face slightly flushed from sleep, those slightly parted lips so full and inviting.

It was an invitation, with her silk robe–covered body held so closely against him, the swell of her breast pressed to his chest, that he was fast losing the struggle to resist!

He had gone upstairs to check on Michael when he returned home shortly after eleven o'clock. He hadn't expected to find anyone still up, but the small lamp he had seen still on in the sitting-room when he had let himself in had drawn him back downstairs to investigate.

Finding Brynne there asleep on the sofa had been the last thing he had expected.

Or wanted, after earlier fighting the impulse he'd had to follow her to the bathroom and sit and watch her as she bathed.

She had sat curled up against the cushions, her beautiful face bare of make-up, the rumpled folds of her robe revealing the creamy swell of her breasts, those long, sensitive fingers, that had caressed his back so arousingly the night before, curled loosely about the book she must have been reading when she fell asleep.

Alejandro had looked down at her for several long minutes, drawn between the desire to lie down on the sofa beside her as he kissed and caressed her awake, and the more sensible idea of waking her so that she could get herself off to bed before he gave in to that desire.

In the end he had done neither, instead bending down to lift her easily into his arms with the idea of carrying her up the stairs to her bedroom.

She felt so light in his arms, so soft and silky, that he realized now he had been foolish to think he could simply carry her to her room and just leave her there. The rapidly rising desire in his body clamoured for him to do something quite different...

Brynne, fully awake now, looked up at Alejandro beneath lowered lashes, seeing his tightly clenched jaw, a nerve pulsing in one rigidly set cheek.

He smelt faintly of wine and expensive cigars, of a spicy aftershave, and underlying those scents was the all-male smell that was Alejandro.

And he felt wonderful, she discovered as her arms moved up about his neck and her hands rested lightly on those broad shoulders. He was warm and sensual to the touch, the heat from his body transmitting itself to her much cooler one—that heat seeming to increase as her fingers became entwined in the dark thickness of the hair at his nape.

He looked down at her beneath hooded lids. 'What are you doing, Brynne?' he rasped.

After their earlier conversation about the danger of the two of them being close like this, she wasn't quite sure, only she knew that she wanted to continue touching him. That she wanted more than to touch him. She wanted him to touch her too, to kiss her in the way he had the night before.

'Do not look at me in that way, Brynne,' he ordered, that nerve pulsing more rapidly in his cheek.

'What way is that, Alejandro?' she murmured huskily, slowly moistening her lips with the tip of her tongue, deliberately holding his gaze as she did so.

His mouth firmed impatiently. 'Have you been drinking?'

'Not as much as you have, I'm sure,' she dismissed, knowing it was Alejandro himself that was making her feel so wantonly reckless, not the two glasses of wine she had drunk hours ago and already slept off.

Alejandro came to a halt in the hallway as he looked down at her, knowing he should just take her to her bedroom and leave her there. But his own bedroom was nearer. And at this moment Brynne was so soft and willing in his arms...

His eyes narrowed. 'Are you going to regret this in the morning, Brynne?'

'Probably,' she whispered. 'But I'm trying not to be...hypocritical about it.'

His mouth curved into a smile at this joke directed towards herself.

'You are intoxicated—'

'With you,' she murmured throatily as she turned to where his shirt was unbuttoned, her lips lightly caressing. 'Only with you, Alejandro,' she assured him huskily before her tongue moved to taste him.

Dios Mío, he could perhaps fight his own desire, but he could not fight Brynne's as well.

He hesitated no longer, kicking his bedroom door open and then shut again behind them, before carrying

Brynne over to his bed, laying her down there amongst the cushions.

'I always wanted to sleep in a four-poster bed,' she told him huskily as he moved to release the drapes that enclosed them in their own private world.

Alejandro gave a rueful smile. 'Sleeping was not what I had in mind.'

Brynne returned that smile—if she was still asleep and dreaming, then this was a dream she never wanted to end!

Her arms moved up about his shoulders as she drew his head down towards her, her lips slightly parted as, with a throaty groan, he took fierce possession.

The last twenty-four hours since they had been together like this might never have happened, the desire between them instant, burning, out of control.

Alejandro's mouth continued to plunder hers as he pushed her robe and then her silky top to one side and bared her breasts to the caress of his hands. Brynne's back arched in invitation; she gasped low in her throat as she felt him first cup and then caress those swollen orbs, her nipples hard and sensitive to that touch.

Her hands moved restlessly across his back, nails slightly rasping through the thin material of his shirt, wanting to feel his skin in the way that he was caressing hers. Her fingers shook slightly as she unbuttoned his shirt and slipped it off his shoulders and down his arms.

Alejandro's mouth left hers reluctantly as he raised his head. 'Let me look at you.' He groaned, reaching out to switch on the bedside lamp.

She looked just as wild and wanton as he had imagined she would, her breasts small and perfect, the nipples a deep rose as he slowly lowered his head to suckle, first one and then the other. Drawing those hardened nubs into the moist heat of his mouth as he tasted and sucked, he felt the heat of Brynne's pleasure as her thighs began to move restlessly against him, asking for more, begging for more.

'I want to kiss and touch all of you.' Alejandro groaned as he placed a lingering kiss on each nipple before his hands trailed down across her ribcage to the slender curve of her hips, sliding down the silky material of her pyjama bottoms to reveal the silky auburn triangle between her legs. His hand moved to part and then caress her there.

Brynne had seen the beauty of her body in Alejandro's eyes as he had stripped that last remaining article of clothing from her body, her eyes widening slightly and then closing in ecstasy as he touched between her thighs. She moaned deep in her throat as she felt the touch of his lips against her now, gently seeking, and then finding, the tiny nub of arousal between her thighs. His tongue was a rasp and then a caress as she gasped in rising pleasure, his hand caressing before he entered her, matching that delicate thrust to the increasing caress of his tongue.

She hadn't known—hadn't realized—

And then she couldn't think any more as a pleasure unlike anything she had ever known before tore through her with the force of a tidal wave. Her body convulsed against his hand as he continued to lick that hardened nub until he had given her every last vestige of pleasure.

'So wet,' he murmured huskily as he continued to caress her. 'So hot and wet and ready for me.' He groaned hungrily, lips and tongue kissing and tasting as he moved slowly up her body.

Brynne felt as if she had been taken to heaven and back, had seen the moon and the stars, and Alejandro was the very centre of that universe.

She moved so that she could push him back against the pillows now, instinct taking over as she stripped trousers and boxer shorts from the lean strength of his body before bending down to taste him as he had tasted her, wanting, needing to give him the same pleasure.

Her tongue ran the hard length of him. Feeling empowered, she felt him spasm with pleasure, circling the tip of him before she took him into the moist heat of her mouth, her encircling fingers moving with the same gentle rhythm as her lips and tongue.

'*Dios mío*…!' Alejandro gasped in protest even as his hands reached out to become entangled in her hair and hold her tightly against him. His thighs moved to match those caressing hands and lips, the last twenty-four hours of damping down the release he had craved last night bringing him to the peak of release much quicker than he would have wanted.

'No, Brynne!' He reached down to stop her, lifting her up and on top of him before lowering her down again, the hardness of his shaft pulsing with his need to enter her tight wetness.

Brynne felt Alejandro's silken hardness move against her, reaching down to guide him into her, feeling a moment, a very brief moment, of pain, before he entered and filled her completely.

'You are so tight, Brynne,' he muttered achingly as his hands on her hips controlled her movements above him to the slow thrusts of his body. 'So erotically tight and perfect.' He groaned.

But she was so aroused, so ready for him, that the slickness of her body moved easily against his, taking them to even deeper heights.

'Beautiful, Brynne,' he murmured throatily, eyes dark as he gazed his fill of her breasts. 'You are so, so beautiful.'

She felt beautiful, totally feminine, the pleasure she was giving him, the pleasure they were giving each other, having taken away any shyness she might otherwise have felt at such intimacies.

Alejandro's hands moved up her ribcage to cup the pert swell of her breasts, his thumbs moving lightly across the sensitized tips. 'Let me kiss you again,' he groaned achingly even as he pulled her down to him and his mouth claimed her breast.

Brynne gasped, her hands on his shoulders, her head thrown back as Alejandro suckled the fiery tip of her breast into his mouth, the thrust of his hips against hers, the silken caress of his hardness, taking her to a climax that made her cry out in pleasure, her heat convulsing about him as Alejandro groaned and she felt him pumping his release deep inside her.

Seconds, minutes, hours later, she collapsed weakly down onto his chest, her rasping breathing matched by Alejandro's own as his arms closed about her and held her close against him, their bodies still joined.

'Next time we will go slower,' he promised gruffly. 'Next time I intend driving you to the point of madness before giving you the release you crave.'

Brynne felt so lethargic, so relaxed, so perfectly satiated, she couldn't even think past this moment, couldn't even imagine a next time.

Or could she? she marvelled as Alejandro began to slowly caress down the length of her spine before moving lower, his hands now cupping her bottom, fingers featherlight as he familiarized himself with every silken inch of her.

By next time, did he mean now? she wondered dazedly as she felt him begin to stir inside her. Surely it was too soon? Didn't a man have to rest for some hours before—?

'Ooh!' she gasped breathlessly as she felt his growing hardness against her sensitive inner flesh.

Alejandro grinned up at her wolfishly. 'I hope you are replete from your nap earlier, Brynne—because I really do not intend either of us to sleep tonight.'

Replete or not, Brynne could feel her own desire stirring, eager to know his body as intimately as he knew hers, wanting…

They both looked up as the telephone on the bedside table began to ring. Alejandro frowned. Brynne, in sudden panic, finally remembered exactly what the something was she had waited up to tell Alejandro!

'I forgot to tell you earlier,' she groaned in a rush of guilty apology. 'Your brother telephoned this evening while you were out—' She didn't get any further with her explanation as Alejandro disentangled their two bodies to lie beside her, frowning darkly before he turned to reach out and snatch the receiver from its cradle.

Alejandro's back was towards her as he took the call. He was speaking in Spanish so she had no idea what he was saying, but nonetheless Brynne was able to see the tension that stiffened his shoulders and spine as he listened to his brother's end of the conversation. It just made her feel even more guilty that she had forgotten to tell him of the earlier call. It had to be something important for the other man to have called Alejandro again at—at almost midnight, Brynne realized after a glance at the bedside clock.

How could she have forgotten to tell him? Brynne berated herself as she slid off the bed to push the drapes aside and pull on her robe. She was in the process of tying the belt securely about her waist as Alejandro ended the call, his face turned away from her as he stood up to begin pulling on his clothes.

'What is it?' Brynne frowned as she watched him.

Alejandro sat on the side of the bed to pull on his shoes, once again the arrogant Spaniard she had known for the previous six weeks.

'Alejandro…?' she prompted nervously.

'The chain of hotels we own in Australia are under threat of a takeover. I have to go,' he spoke flatly.

Brynne stared at him, unable to comprehend what he was saying. 'Go where?'

Alejandro shot her an impatient glance as he stood up. 'Australia, of course.'

He received a telephone call from his brother in the middle of the night, and he had to go to Australia?

What of their lovemaking just now?

Did that mean nothing to him at all?

CHAPTER THIRTEEN

BRYNNE stared at Alejandro incomprehensbly as he took a bag from the wardrobe and started to throw things inside it.

The two of them had been to bed together, had made love—wild, abandoned lovemaking on her part—and now Alejandro was just proposing to leave her as if it had never happened?

'Alejandro—'

'I do not have time for this right now, Brynne,' he cut in harshly as he finished packing his bag. 'I have to call my pilot and have him ready the plane for immediate departure.'

Her eyes widened as he picked up the telephone receiver and pressed several buttons. 'You're actually leaving right this minute?' Leaving her now, without any word being spoken between them about what had happened tonight...? 'That doesn't give me very long to wake Michael and pack our bags—'

Alejandro frowned as he turned to look at her. 'And why would you need to do either of those things?'

'So that we can come with you, of course,' she came back sharply.

Take Brynne and Michael to Australia with him after what had just happened? To have her there waiting for him at the hotel whenever he had a spare minute from the lengthy business meetings that would no doubt ensue once he joined his brother in Australia?

No!

He had no idea what had happened between himself and Brynne this evening. She had looked so appealing as she had lain on the sofa, and had felt so soft and warm in his arms as he had carried her up the stairs, that it had been impossible to do anything other than take her to his own bedroom and make love to her.

But Brynne, he knew, was not like the women he had been involved with since Francesca died.

For one thing she was the aunt of his son.

More importantly, he had become aware as they had pulled apart before he had answered Roberto's call—had seen the evidence himself on the sheet she had lain upon—that he had been Brynne's first lover!

He had never been any woman's first, had no experience whatsoever to draw upon to help him deal with that discovery.

His sudden departure might seem cruel to Brynne, but for himself Alejandro knew that he needed this time away from her, if only to consider where their relationship could possibly go after his discovery. If it went anywhere…

'Do not be ridiculous, Brynne.' Alejandro shook his head as he frowned down at her. 'I do not intend to take either you or Michael to Australia with me!'

'But—'

'Consuelo?' Alejandro said into the receiver as his call was finally answered, firing out instructions at a rapid pace before abruptly ending the call to turn and speak to Brynne once again.

Only to discover that she had gone...

Along with all trace of her, he noted with a frown, her pyjamas removed from the bedroom floor, only the rumpled bedclothes to show that he had not been alone in the bed a few minutes ago.

Alejandro drew in a ragged breath as he pushed back the dark swathe of his hair.

Going to bed with Brynne was not how he had envisaged his evening ending, and despite the excitement of their lovemaking he knew he had been less than gentle with her a few minutes ago, the discovery of her innocence having thrown his usually ordered life completely off balance.

For possibly the first time in his life he had not known what to do or say next, the urgency of Roberto's telephone call offering him an escape he had badly needed. Brynne's abrupt departure from his bedroom seemed to imply that she had needed to escape also.

He tidied his room slightly, removing those telling sheets, knowing Brynne would not care for Maria to know of the time she had spent in his bedroom.

Although he couldn't hide his frown when he got downstairs a few minutes later and found Brynne there in the hallway, fully dressed in denims and a body-hugging white top, her hair brushed and tied back from her face. He had not thought he would see her again before he left. In fact, he had hoped that he would not, felt that he needed time away from her to understand what had happened between them tonight before he even tried to discuss it with Brynne.

Brynne saw Alejandro's surprise—displeasure?—at

her presence downstairs, her heart sinking at the realization.

This was the man she had made love with such a short time ago.

The man with whom she had shared intimacies she had never known before with anyone, her body still aching in several places from the unaccustomed lovemaking.

The man who now seemed disinclined to talk about those intimacies.

Thank goodness.

Because one thing she was sure of, Alejandro regretted the lapse, and the worst thing she could think of was actually discussing what for her had been a wondrous time in his arms. For her their lovemaking had been unbelievable, so much more, so much better, than anything she might ever have imagined it could be.

That was due to Alejandro's experience, she knew.

It was that experience that made their encounter just another conquest for Alejandro. Tonight might have been something special to her, something undreamt of, but to Alejandro, if his urgency to get away from her was any indication—and she was sure that it was!—it obviously hadn't meant anything at all.

Sad, but true.

It was also true that a single business telephone call from his brother had been enough to change Alejandro from an ardent lover into the single-minded businessman she had always thought him to be...

The single-minded businessman she didn't doubt that he would always be.

He continued to frown as he drew in a harsh breath. 'I realize you think we need to talk, Brynne—'

'No, I don't think that at all, Alejandro,' she dismissed determinedly. 'In fact, I think the best thing for both of us is to forget tonight ever happened,' she added harshly.

Brynne wanted him to forget it. Alejandro scowled, his own earlier disquiet about the situation briefly forgotten. Forget the mind-blowing perfection of their lovemaking? Forget how beautiful she had been in his arms? Forget how her total arousal had sent him spiralling out of control?

He looked at her searchingly, but found himself unable to read any of her own emotions from her determinedly set features.

Forget it, she said. Would she be able to forget it? Would she just be able to put their lovemaking behind her when the time came for her to return to her life in England? Would she be able to forget him?

Despite his earlier confusion about their relationship, Alejandro found himself intensely displeased at the thought of that!

'And what if it is not possible to just forget it?' he rasped.

Brynne shot him a brief glance. 'I don't—' She broke off, her face seeming to pale as his meaning obviously became clear to her. 'There's absolutely no reason to suppose—'

'There is no reason not to suppose, either,' he snapped, her dismissal of any consequences from their lovemaking annoying him even further. 'Is there?' he pressed forcefully.

Brynne knew Alejandro had to be suggesting she might become pregnant from their completely unplanned lovemaking.

But surely the chances of that happening weren't that high?

After all—

'I obviously didn't use any contraception—did you?' Alejandro persisted with hard determination.

And Brynne wished that he wouldn't because she didn't need that worry to add to all the others she had. Such as how he now thought of her. More to the point, how she now felt about Alejandro!

Because if tonight had shown her anything, it was that any future for her without Alejandro in it—and she was pretty sure after this that he wasn't going to be!—was sure to be a bleak one.

'No,' she answered flatly. 'But that's still no reason to suppose there will be—any repercussions.' She frowned.

'Would you tell me if there were? Or would you be like Joanna and keep my child from me?'

Brynne winced at the bitterness behind the question. She didn't doubt that he respected the decision Joanna had made all those years ago concerning Michael's existence, but the harshness of his tone now implied that he felt angry with her at the same time. As he would be angry with Brynne if she were to do the same thing...

'I think that might be a little difficult, don't you?' she dismissed dryly. 'Michael will continue to be my nephew, a nephew I will expect to be able to visit in future, whether you like it or not,' she explained as she sensed Alejandro's waiting tension. 'I think, in the circumstances, I might find it a little difficult to hide the existence of a child from you!'

As an answer it was not very helpful, Alejandro acknowledged hardly. It certainly told him nothing of the emotions that had brought Brynne willingly into his bed in the first place. And he felt that he needed to know them in order to put what had happened between them tonight into its right perspective.

If there was a right perspective to what had happened between himself and Brynne!

Although Brynne's own reluctance to discuss what had happened seemed to imply that she had no answers, either...

'What will you tell Michael about my sudden departure?' he rasped.

It was a problem Brynne had been trying to find an answer to since the moment she had realized that Alejandro intended going to Australia on his own.

'The truth,' she snapped. 'That you've had to suddenly go away on business. I'm sure that it will be something that Michael will have to get used to in future!' she added disgustedly.

Alejandro sighed his impatience with her deliberate barb. 'Would you rather I didn't go, Brynne? That we continued where we left off?' he added scornfully.

Her cheeks burnt with colour. 'On the contrary,' she bit out hardly, 'I can't wait for you to go.'

His mouth thinned. 'Then on that we are at least agreed.'

'That has to be a first!' Brynne returned challengingly, determined, absolutely determined, that she was not going to break down in front of Alejandro.

That could come later, once she was alone. Alone with only the memories of their time together to haunt her. To taunt her.

Her mouth tightened. 'What do you want me to tell

Antonia if she should call at the villa or telephone?' she deliberately mocked him with the woman who should have shared his bed tonight.

'She will not,' Alejandro dismissed harshly.

'But she might.' Brynne grimaced just at the thought of having to deal with Antonia after the intimacies she and Alejandro had shared such a short time ago.

'Neither Antonia nor her father will call or telephone the villa, Brynne,' Alejandro assured her with such finality the statement couldn't be doubted.

Because, of course, Alejandro would call Antonia himself once he reached Australia, possibly even before that…

'Fine.' She nodded abruptly. 'You'd better go, then, hadn't you?' she added abruptly.

Brynne desperately needed Alejandro to go now, before the tears that threatened started falling down her cheeks and totally embarrassed her!

'Brynne…?' Alejandro's gaze was guardedly searching as he looked down at her.

'Oh, for goodness' sake, will you just go, Alejandro?' she snapped impatiently, her hands clenched so tightly she could feel her nails digging into her palms.

Because if he didn't soon leave she really was going to make a fool of herself!

Now that the time had come to leave her he did not want to go, Alejandro recognized frustratedly.

Which was ridiculous when minutes ago it was what he had wanted more than anything. To get away from her, and the memories of their lovemaking. To try, with many miles separating them, to make sense of what had happened tonight in regard to the relationship—that of father and aunt to Michael—they would have in future.

'Very well,' he bit out grimly. 'Maria knows my telephone number in Australia if you should need to contact me,' he paused to add huskily.

'I doubt the situation will arise,' Brynne dismissed without so much as a glance at him, her expression stony as she obviously couldn't wait for him to leave.

Alejandro gave her one last frowning glance before slamming out of the villa without so much as another glance in her direction, knowing that to do so could be his undoing, that to look at Brynne again, to remember their lovemaking, would result in him gathering her up in his arms and completely forgetting his resolve to put distance between the two of them until he could make sense of what had happened.

What was still happening, from the way his body had stirred with renewed desire when he was just looking at Brynne!

Brynne didn't move after Alejandro left.

Couldn't move.

Because with Alejandro's abrupt departure, she had made a mind-numbing realization.

She had fallen in love—desperately, completely, recklessly—with Alejandro Santiago...

CHAPTER FOURTEEN

'DADDY wants to talk to you, Aunty Bry!' Michael called excitedly even as she heard him running up the stairs to her bedroom.

Brynne straightened abruptly from where she had been packing a bag in readiness for them to go down onto the beach, intending to spend the morning there, already wearing a thigh-length blue cotton shirt over her bikini.

There had been many such telephone calls from Alejandro in the four days since he had flown to Australia so abruptly. One each morning, another each evening, his primary reason for calling to reassure Michael of course, although he always asked to speak to Brynne before ending the call. They were only stilted conversations on Brynne's part though, as she kept to telling Alejandro of the things Michael had done that day.

'Can you tell him I'm too busy at the moment to come to the telephone, please, Michael?' she dismissed lightly, shoving a towel into her bag as she did so, just knowing that Alejandro was on the telephone enough to rattle her nerves.

'Why not tell me that yourself…?' Alejandro spoke huskily from just behind her.

Brynne spun round with a gasp, her eyes wide as she looked at Alejandro standing so tall and powerful in her bedroom doorway.

The last four days had been difficult ones for her as she had tried to come to terms with the love she had realized she felt for this man.

The complete love that had drawn her to him, to his bed, four nights ago…!

But if those four days had been difficult ones for her, one look at the strain etched into that arrogantly assured face showed that—for totally different reasons, of course—they had been just as difficult for Alejandro.

Her heart was beating erratically, loudly, so much so that she felt Alejandro must hear it too. 'Why didn't you warn—er—tell us you were coming back today?' she said awkwardly as she put her hands behind her back so that he shouldn't see they were trembling slightly.

Alejandro's mouth tightened as he heard that correction in her question. Or rather—accusation… Because one look at Brynne's slightly defensive expression, the wariness in her deep blue eyes, was enough to tell him she was not pleased to see him again.

Which was a pity—more than a pity!—when he had wanted nothing else but to see her again the last four days!

He had known almost as soon as he had boarded the plane at Palma airport four days ago that he had made a mistake by leaving Brynne in the way that he had. But to have turned around and come back would have been a mistake too when he had still been uncertain of what he wanted from Brynne. Of what she wanted from him.

So he had flown to Australia as planned, where he and Roberto had dealt successfully with the attempted takeover. Once assured of that, Alejandro had wasted no time in returning to Majorca, needing to reassure Michael by his presence, of course, but personally needing to see Brynne even more.

A sentiment she obviously didn't reciprocate if her guarded expression was anything to go by!

His mouth twisted ruefully. 'It was a sudden decision.' He shrugged. 'I thought to surprise you.'

Oh, he had done that all right, Brynne acknowledged, still breathless from turning to find him standing in her bedroom doorway rather than on the end of the telephone line as she had thought him to be.

'I was surprised, Daddy,' Michael assured him as he beamed up at him, obviously pleased to see his father again.

Brynne was pleased to see Alejandro again, too—she just didn't quite know how she was supposed to behave towards him!

They had become lovers four days ago. But it was something that Alejandro had shown, by his abrupt departure, by his coldness towards her before he had left, that he regretted. She had no reason to suppose that these four days apart had changed that regret…

'Have you come back to stay?' she queried lightly. 'Or is this to be just a flying visit?'

His grey eyes glittered. 'Which would you like it to be?' Alejandro prompted softly.

Brynne felt herself tremble slightly as she recognized the expression of challenge in his eyes. Whichever way she answered that particular question was going to be wrong! If she said the latter, then it would look as if she didn't want him here. And if she said the former, then it made her look desperate for his company.

As Alejandro had been correct in his claim that she would not hear from Antonia Roig or her father while he was away, it had become obvious to Brynne that her assumption he would contact the other woman himself had also been the correct one…

She shrugged. 'I don't think what I want enters into it.'

He smiled without humour. 'Very diplomatic, Brynne,' he taunted. 'Michael tells me the two of you were on your way to the beach…?' He looked pointedly at the cotton shirt she wore over her bikini.

'Yes,' she confirmed huskily.

Alejandro nodded abruptly. 'If you wait five minutes I will come with you.'

'Oh, but—' She broke off her protest as Alejandro raised dark, mocking brows. 'Don't you have—calls to make and—and things you need to do, after being away so long?' she said awkwardly, knowing that the morning on the beach would be far from relaxed if she had to share it with Alejandro.

His mouth thinned. 'No,' he answered flatly, that grey gaze narrowed.

Brynne's heart was still pounding, her palms damp.

She simply had no idea how she was supposed to behave with the man who had become her lover. She didn't know the protocol and just found being with Alejandro again like this totally embarrassing. And the last thing she wanted was to be alone with Alejandro down on the beach, while Michael was snorkelling, and so give Alejandro the opportunity to actually bring up the subject of their time together four days ago…!

'Why don't just you and Michael go to the beach?' she suggested brightly. 'It will give you a chance to spend some time together, and I'm sure I can find plenty of things to do here.'

'Such as…?' Alejandro prompted softly.

Brynne frowned at him in frustration, knowing by his challenging expression that he was fully aware of her reluctance to spend time alone with him—and that he wasn't in any way going to help her to achieve that wish.

She grimaced. 'Well, I could—'

'Never mind, Brynne,' Alejandro rasped. 'Whatever they are I am sure they can wait.'

So was she—she just felt totally panicked at the thought of being with Alejandro again.

Alejandro had no idea what he had thought Brynne's reaction to seeing him again would be, but it certainly had not been this obvious wish to avoid even his company!

Especially when just being near her again like this was enough to tell him that all he wanted to do was take her back to his bed and make love with her once again. As he had ached to do the whole of the time he was away.

A feeling she obviously had not reciprocated!

'You would like Brynne to come to the beach too, would you not, Michael?' he prompted huskily—and then instantly felt guilty for using his son's affection for Brynne, and her affection for Michael—as Michael enthusiastically agreed that he would.

What did Brynne want him to do—beg for her company? Alejandro wondered frustratedly. Perhaps he might even be willing to do that if it would achieve the desired result…

'Then of course I'll come,' she agreed softly. 'I'll meet you both downstairs in five minutes,' she added dismissively, avoiding even looking at Alejandro as she turned to finish packing her bag.

Alejandro looked at her frustratedly. Wanting to shake her. Kiss her. Caress her. Anything that would bring a return of that warmly responsive woman of four nights ago.

Instead he turned abruptly on his heel and walked down the hallway to his own bedroom. Not that it offered any respite from these wild imaginings of Brynne, the four-poster bed a stark reminder of the time they had spent together there, his only consolation—if it could be called that—that Brynne did not seem to realize how deeply he regretted leaving her so suddenly that night. Brynne's own regret for what had happened between them was more than obvious by her lack of enthusiasm for his company.

Finding herself on the beach ten minutes later, Michael already off snorkelling in the shallow water, Alejandro lying on the sand beside her wearing only a pair of brief black swimming trunks that only added to the sheer male power he exuded, did not allay Brynne's feelings of panic in the slightest.

If just looking at him could send her pulse racing, and the heat coursing through her body, what chance did she have of spending the whole morning with him dressed—or, rather, undressed!—like this?

'You seem a little—distracted, this morning?' he prompted huskily as he picked up a handful of sand and watched as the grains fell softly through his fingers.

Distracted?

No, just totally aware of Alejandro…

She shrugged. 'I'm still a little surprised you didn't tell us you were returning, that's all.'

His mouth tightened. 'I told you on the telephone yesterday that the attempted takeover had been successfully blocked.'

Yes, he had, it just hadn't occurred to Brynne that success would mean Alejandro returning to Majorca quite as soon as this. She had thought she still had days before his return.

Not that it really made any difference when he returned—the first meeting between the two of them had been sure to be embarrassing whenever it was!

'You must be pleased that everything went so well,' she said noncommittally.

'Of course.' Alejandro gave an abrupt inclination of his head.

Brynne gave a tight smile. 'I expect you'll need to return to Spain to finalize everything?'

Alejandro's smile was no more humorous. 'You seem very anxious to get rid of me…?'

'Of course not—'

'Do not lie, Brynne,' he rasped coldly. 'You have made no effort to hide the displeasure you feel at my return.'

But that was only because—

Because she loved this man so much she actually ached with the emotion, her joy in seeing him again marred by the danger that he might realize how she felt about him!

Something she would find just too humiliating.

'Don't be silly, Alejandro,' she dismissed lightly.

'This is your villa, after all, and Michael is your son. You were bound to return some time,' she added practically.

'Your enthusiasm is overwhelming!' he drawled hardly.

Brynne turned away, breathing deeply. This was unbearable. This whole situation was unbearable.

'Brynne—'

'If you're going to talk about the other night—then please don't!' She turned to say shakily. 'I have no idea what happened—why it happened. It just did, okay!' she ended forcefully. 'And I really would prefer not to have a post-mortem on the subject!'

Alejandro looked at her searchingly. She looked so beautiful this morning, with her eyes sparkling, a blush to her cheeks and her mouth trembling slightly, that all he wanted to do was lay her down in the sand right now and make love with her.

Again and again…

She had been so responsive the other night, so shyly uninhibited, that he had found himself thinking of her often during the long hours he had sat in business meetings while in Australia.

From feeling irritated at having this woman foisted on him for a month, from not knowing four days ago what he wanted from their new relationship, he now knew that the thought of Brynne simply walking out of his life in a few weeks' time had become totally unacceptable to him!

'As of this morning,' she continued tightly, her gaze not quite meeting his, 'I can safely assure you there will be no unwanted repercussions, either!'

Unwanted?

He had pondered the question of Brynne being

pregnant with his child while he was away too. True, in Michael he already had one child who had been conceived out of marriage, and he would not willingly allow that to happen again. But if it had turned out that Brynne was pregnant it would have meant that she could not just walk out of his life…

'You must feel relieved,' he said softly.

'Of course,' Brynne dismissed lightly. 'As, I'm sure, are you,' she added derisively.

Was he? He was a man who usually had no doubts how he felt about anything, especially when it came to emotional complications, but Brynne Sullivan had slowly eroded all of that certainty over the last ten days, to the point that he was no longer sure of anything except that he wanted her!

'Of course,' he echoed, his mouth tight. 'Michael seems to have coped well since I've been away…?' He glanced over to where his son was now playing in a rock-pool.

Michael had coped with the separation from his father extremely well, Brynne agreed—she was the one who hadn't found it so easy!

Of course the memory of that time in Alejandro's bed wasn't exactly conducive to an easy mind—or emotions—but it was the realization of her love for this man that had caused her the most heartache.

How was she going to feel when she had to leave here? Had to leave Alejandro and Michael?

She nodded, also looking at Michael. 'We were talking about when you expect to return to Spain…?'

'You were talking of it,' he corrected harshly. 'But, yes, I think it is time that Michael was introduced to the rest of his family.'

Brynne swallowed hard. 'When do you expect to leave?' she prompted brittlely.

'Tomorrow,' he came back dismissively.

Tomorrow? So soon? Alejandro would be taking Michael and effectively flying out of her life tomorrow?

He shrugged. 'I have a few calls and business dealings to conclude, but I expect to have them completed by this evening, leaving us free to leave tomorrow morning.'

He certainly didn't intend wasting too much time here, did he?

Her mouth twisted ruefully. 'I'm sure that Miss Roig will be pleased to see you again this evening, even if you are leaving again so soon.'

Alejandro looked at her between narrowed lids. In any other woman he would have seen such a remark as possible jealousy, but in Brynne he saw it was merely a statement of fact.

He sighed. 'It is not my intention to see Antonia before I leave tomorrow.'

Brynne's eyes widened. 'It isn't...?'

'No,' he confirmed harshly, still angry with Antonia for having come here to the villa while he had been out and talking to Brynne in the way that she had.

'But—'

'Brynne, it has been obvious from the first that you have been under some sort of misapprehension where my relationship with Antonia Roig is concerned,' he bit out coldly. 'Considering our own—closeness, the other night, I find the continuance of such a misapprehension highly insulting!'

Brynne looked at him searchingly, remembering all the occasions when she had seen him with the other woman, the amount of time he had spent in the other woman's company, the fact that Antonia had come here and advised her to leave; what else was Brynne supposed to think but that the two of them were romantically involved?

Even though Alejandro had continuously denied such a relationship…

She gave a puzzled shake of her head. 'I'm sorry if I was mistaken—'

'Are you?' he scorned. 'I believe I have said this before, but it seems to me that you take some sort of delight in thinking the worst of me!'

There was no delight involved for Brynne at all in thinking of the woman Alejandro had married seven years ago, of his relationship with Joanna and the dozens of women he had probably been involved with since. Heartache better described her feelings where those women were concerned!

'You're talking nonsense, Alejandro—'

'I do not think so,' he bit out angrily, standing up. 'I will go and spend time with Michael—he, at least, expresses enjoyment in my company!' he added scornfully. 'We will not be returning to Majorca in the next few weeks, so you will need to take everything with you when we leave in the morning—'

'Excuse me?' Brynne cut in frowningly.

Alejandro scowled down at her. 'I am sure I made myself perfectly clear, Brynne,' he clipped impatiently. 'All of us will be flying to Spain in the morning.'

Brynne stared at him disbelievingly. He couldn't seriously expect her to go to his home in Spain with him—

But why couldn't he?

She had told Alejandro at the onset that she intended staying with Michael for this transitional month.

It had just never occurred to her that part of that month would be spent in Spain with Alejandro's family.

Or that by the time that happened she would have fallen in love with him...

CHAPTER FIFTEEN

BRYNNE swallowed hard, knowing it would be a wrench to be parted from Michael so soon, but also aware that she wouldn't feel comfortable being anywhere near Alejandro's family after what had happened between the two of them four days ago, and she wasn't comfortable being with Alejandro again…!

She drew in a deep breath. 'Perhaps when you take Michael with you tomorrow to meet your family would be as good a time as any for me to go back to England—'

'What are you saying, Brynne?' Alejandro cut in harshly.

She looked up at him with guarded eyes. 'That this might be a good time for me to go home—'

'You coward!' he rasped furiously, kneeling down on the sand beside Brynne to grasp her arms. 'How dare you just run away like this—?'

'I'm not the one who ran away!' she came back just as angrily, her pain still very raw. 'Perhaps you've also forgotten that my parents recently lost their only son? That they need me—'

'And perhaps you have forgotten that you agreed to stay with Michael for a month, not eight days,' Alejandro bit out coldly as he glared at her.

Eight days... Was that all it had been? Eight days, when the whole of her life had changed. When falling in love with this man had changed her for ever.

'You're hurting my arms, Alejandro,' she told him huskily.

Alejandro had thought of his abrupt departure four days ago not as the running away Brynne obviously thought it to be, but as a need to be away from her in order to make sense of his own emotions.

His mouth was a thin angry line as he thrust her away from him. 'You are a coward, Brynne—'

'That's the second time you've called me that,' she snapped angrily.

'Because that is what you are,' he said harshly as he glared at her in frustration. 'I do not believe for one moment that you are rushing back to England to be with your parents—'

'Well, I'm not rushing back to England to be with anyone else, either, if that's what you're implying!' Brynne breathed deeply.

It was not what he was implying. He knew Brynne well enough to realize that she would never have allowed their relationship to have developed in the way that it had if she had already been involved with someone in England.

Although she seemed to have had no trouble believing he could go to bed with her while still involved with Antonia Roig...

He stood up once again, aware that if he didn't do so

he might do something they would both regret. 'If you wish to go then you must do so, Brynne,' he told her flatly. 'But you need to tell Michael you are leaving him,' he added abruptly before turning away to stride over to the rock-pool where Michael was playing.

Brynne's eyes were so full of tears that she couldn't even see Alejandro as he walked away from her.

But she was doing the right thing, wasn't she? Putting as much distance between herself and Alejandro as she possibly could?

There was no future for them together. No anything for them together. So to stay, to go to Spain with them, to continue to be with Alejandro and continue to play the part of Michael's aunt, wouldn't help any of them.

Michael was comfortable with his father now, had talked of nothing else the last four days, and the two of them were chatting easily together as Brynne blinked away the tears to look across at them.

Only it seemed she was now uncomfortable being anywhere near Alejandro…

Because she loved him so much she ached with it, couldn't even look at him now without being afraid that love shone in her eyes.

Brynne was not leaving Michael, Alejandro knew even as he helped his son to collect shells, she was leaving him, could not even bear to be anywhere near him after what had happened.

Hadn't he retreated in the same way four nights ago? A decision he now was beginning to regret deeply, as he acknowledged an overwhelming need to keep Brynne beside him. He wanted to know that she would be there for him to talk to, to come home to, to make love to.

But four days of thinking of nothing but her and he had already known that he wanted all of those things with Brynne when he returned to the villa this morning.

And Brynne had made it perfectly clear that she wanted none of them with him.

That she was actually going to leave him tomorrow with the intention of never coming back…

How could he allow that to happen?

Did he have any choice?

'You have telephoned your parents…?'

Brynne looked across the terrace at Alejandro, her breath catching in her throat at how handsome he looked in the black evening suit and snowy white shirt, the darkness of his hair still damp from the shower he had taken before dinner.

A dinner she would much rather not have joined him for, but she'd known he would only call her a coward again if she attempted to excuse herself.

'Yes.' She strolled out onto the terrace to join him, cool and elegant in a fitted cream knee-length dress that showed off the tan she had acquired over the last few days.

Alejandro poured her a glass of white wine before looking up at her. 'They were pleased to hear of your imminent return?' he asked.

'I—didn't tell them,' she answered honestly as she sat down.

It was going to take months, possibly years, for her parents to accept Tom's and Joanna's death, but they had sounded much brighter when she had spoken to them on the telephone earlier, her father assuring her that her mother was off her medication now, and was even thinking of returning to work at the office where she had been a secretary for the last ten years.

It had been such a positive conversation, including her assurances about Michael's blossoming relationship with his father, that she simply hadn't got around to telling them she was returning home tomorrow.

At least, she had told herself that was what had happened.

In reality, she hadn't been able to commit herself to leaving once it had come down to it!

To leaving Alejandro…

Alejandro's gaze narrowed on her searchingly. She looked so cold and distant in her cream dress, her hair secured on top of her head adding to that elegant remoteness. Not at all like the love-tousled woman he had left so abruptly four nights ago!

He shrugged. 'Does that mean you have changed your mind?'

'I—no,' she said firmly before taking a sip of her wine. 'I don't know quite how to broach the subject with Michael, and I thought—I should talk to him about it before mentioning it to my parents.' She grimaced.

Alejandro gave a disgusted snort. 'It seems then that it is only with me that you are reticent!'

Brynne stiffened. 'I thought you would be pleased that I'm leaving—relieved, even—'

'I am not.' His accent was stronger in his anger, his eyes glittering dangerously. 'Brynne, you and I have became lovers—'

'Something that you clearly wanted to forget when you left so abruptly!' she cut in forcefully, colour warming her cheeks.

'But I have not forgotten!' He turned the full force of his attention on her as he sat stiffly in the chair. 'Neither, I believe, have you?' he rasped.

She closed her eyes briefly. 'I've—tried,' she said.

'But have not succeeded?' Alejandro prompted. 'Brynne, it is very important—' He broke off as the sound of a car could be heard coming down the long driveway to the villa. A scowl darkened his face at the possible interruption to this conversation.

Brynne had heard the car too now. And it didn't take two guesses to know who their visitor—who Alejandro's visitor!—was going to be. Obviously Antonia Roig had her own ideas about whether or not Alejandro would see her this evening.

She knew she had guessed the visitor's identity correctly as she heard the car engine switch off and the click of high heeled shoes on the pathway.

'It would seem that you have a visitor this evening,' Brynne murmured mockingly even as she heard Alejandro's muttered comments in Spanish as he slowly stood up, his face dark with anger.

He looked down at Brynne with glittering eyes. 'I assure you, she will not be staying,' he said harshly even as Antonia Roig appeared in the doorway behind a slightly frowning Maria.

Brynne stood up. 'I think I'll make myself scarce—'

'You will stay exactly where you are!' Alejandro's restraining hand on her arm reinforced his words even as he looked unsmilingly across at the beautiful Antonia Roig. 'What are you doing here, Antonia?' he clipped as the other woman strolled smilingly towards Alejandro with the obvious intention of kissing him.

Brynne felt a slight fluttering in her stomach at the coldness of his tone, knowing she would feel like cringing in a corner if Alejandro ever spoke to her like that.

Not that it seemed to deter Antonia Roig in the slightest as she continued to smile, sure of her own beauty and power in the figure-hugging red dress that showed off her olive complexion and her dark eyes. 'I would prefer for us to be alone, Alejandro,' she murmured huskily after giving Brynne a dismissive glance.

Alejandro's hand tightened on Brynne's arm as he felt her poised for flight. 'There is nothing that you have to say to me that Brynne cannot hear,' he assured Antonia, completely out of patience with this woman's machinations.

Antonia gave him a confident smile. 'I am sure that what the two of us have to say to each other can be of no interest to Miss Sullivan, Alejandro—'

'On the contrary,' he bit out scathingly. 'I feel it is very important that Brynne hear exactly what I have to say to you!' His mouth twisted derisively as he glanced at Brynne and saw how uncomfortable she was, those deep blue eyes pleading with him to let her leave.

It was a plea he could not grant. He had many things he wanted to say to Brynne tonight before she left tomorrow, and unwanted as Antonia's presence here was, it would help to dispense with one of those things!

He drew Brynne to his side before turning back to Antonia, those deep brown eyes hardening questioningly as she took in that show of intimacy. 'I have been engaged in a business transaction with your father, Antonia,' he said coldly. 'Nothing else,' he added grimly as she would have spoken. 'There has never been a relationship between the two of us. Nothing beyond a friendship extended to the daughter of a business acquaintance.'

Up to that point Brynne had been squirming with the need to absent herself from another display of the intimacy between Alejandro and Antonia, but Alejandro's apparent determination to establish that he had never been involved in any sort of intimate relationship with Antonia Roig made her stop squirming and look up at him searchingly.

Alejandro spared her a glance before turning back to the other woman, his expression becoming cold. 'But even my business dealings with Felipe were terminated, Antonia, after I learnt of your visit here to talk to Brynne when you knew I was away in Palma at a meeting with your father. A visit during which you took it upon yourself to tell Brynne she was not welcome here,' he added. 'English, Antonia,' he rasped as she began to answer him in Spanish. 'I want Brynne to know exactly what we say to each other.'

'Did she tell you I said that?' Antonia asked, giving a dismissive laugh and shooting Brynne a contemptuous glance. 'Alejandro, I can assure you that—'

'There is no necessity for you to assure me of anything, Antonia,' he replied coldly. 'I had to choose which one of you to believe, and I chose Brynne—'

'She has bewitched you!' Antonia said scornfully, her gaze hardening even more as she turned to glare at Brynne furiously. 'Into her bed, no doubt—'

'You go too far, Antonia!' Alejandro rasped icily.

'Only because I am—concerned, for you, Alejandro.' Antonia's voice softened huskily as she looked up at him. 'I merely suggested to Miss Sullivan that day that she might want to leave, that she is not of our type—'

'I thank God that she is not of your type,' he bit out scathingly. 'You will leave now, Antonia,' he added coldly. 'You will not come here again. You will most certainly never speak to Brynne again in the way that you did.'

Brynne felt a shiver down her spine at the cold anger in Alejandro's voice, knowing by the way Antonia Roig had paled that she was as aware of the implacability of his tone as Brynne was.

But there was only a momentary pause and then Antonia Roig's chin rose challengingly, her expression arrogantly contemptuous as she looked at them both. 'You are a fool, Alejandro,' she told him sneeringly. 'With my father's business connections, and the money I will eventually inherit as his only child, you and I could have been a formidable pair. And instead you choose to consort with this—this—'

'Careful, Antonia,' Alejandro warned softly. 'You are talking of a woman I hold in high regard, a woman of integrity and honesty. Attributes that are obviously completely alien to you!' he added coldly.

Brynne could only stare up at Alejandro in wonder as, after one last sneering glance in Brynne's direction, the other woman turned on her heel and walked briskly away.

Alejandro held her in high regard…? Believed her to be a woman of integrity and honesty…?

Even more confusing, why had he felt a need to make her a witness to all of those things he said to Antonia Roig…?

CHAPTER SIXTEEN

BRYNNE continued to watch Alejandro as he started to pace the terrace, his expression making her hesitate to ask any of the things that hovered on the tip of her tongue.

What if Alejandro had just wanted her to know that, as Michael's father, he was the man of honour he had always claimed to be? That his motives for making her a witness to that conversation with Antonia Roig were that simple? What if—?

'What are you thinking now, Brynne?' Alejandro paused to look at her, his tone rueful. 'Do you still remain unconvinced as to the innocence of my relationship with Antonia?'

Brynne shook her head. 'What I am puzzled about is why you think I needed to hear that…?'

Alejandro looked at her searchingly, wanting to see some sign in her demeanour that his lack of any intimate relationship with Antonia actually meant something to Brynne. But he could read nothing from her expression except that mild curiosity.

But he had gone too far now, was too aware of the danger of Brynne leaving to go back to England tomorrow, to draw back from the decision he had made earlier as he had sat on the terrace waiting for Brynne to join him. He could not let her go without at least telling her something of how he felt. What happened after he had done that was completely up to Brynne.

He was a man used to making decisions, and then acting on them, and it was not a pleasant position to find himself in…

He drew in a ragged breath. 'We need to go back to the beginning again for me to be able to explain that. To my relationship with Joanna,' he said as Brynne continued to look puzzled.

She stiffened. 'Haven't we already discussed that enough—?'

'No!' Alejandro rasped. 'The relationship, yes. Joanna's feelings about that relationship, also yes. But my own motivation behind the relationship? The reason that I was married to another woman only three months after that relationship? No.' He shook his head, his expression grim. 'I do not think we have discussed those at all.'

No, they hadn't—and Brynne wasn't sure she wanted to hear them now, either. Besides, what possible bearing could they have on the here and now…?

Alejandro gave a humourless smile. 'You would prefer to continue thinking of me as a man who uses and discards women, I think,' he muttered huskily.

She felt the warmth in her cheeks. 'I have never said that.'

'Your face has said that,' he assured her dryly.

'The fact that you also believe that I intend to discard you in that way also says that,' he added grimly.

Brynne swallowed hard as she saw his concerned

expression. A concern that he quickly masked as that arrogant pride fell into place once more.

He continued. 'As you have no doubt guessed, I was already engaged to Francesca when Joanna and I met seven years ago. It was an arranged marriage, not a love match. Our parents had decided on it while we were still children. It was to be the marriage of two powerful, rich families rather than Francesca and I.' He shook his head. 'I met Joanna in Australia, at a time when I was trying to decide how best to extricate myself from a situation, an engagement, I no longer wanted.'

'Alejandro—'

'You will do me the courtesy of letting me tell you these things, Brynne!' he rasped. 'You will have plenty of opportunity when I have finished to criticize and chastise!' he added derisively.

What he had already told her was enough to make her revise some of the opinions she had formed before accompanying him and Michael to Majorca.

'Joanna knew of my engagement to Francesca. She and I—talked about it. Joanna could not even begin to imagine marrying someone she did not love. As no longer could I.' He sighed. 'Joanna and I were not in love with each other, either, but she helped me to understand that I had to talk to Francesca, to see if she would release me from the engagement. But before I could do so I received an urgent call from Spain. My father had had a heart attack. To even contemplate causing such a scandal when he was so seriously ill was unthinkable. Can you understand that?' he asked.

Of course she could understand. She knew how binding these arranged engagements could be, that they were usually arranged for the advancement of the family rather than the individuals who ended up married to each other.

'You married Francesca knowing that the two of you didn't love each other.' She nodded. 'I—have to agree with Joanna, I can't imagine anything worse!'

He nodded abruptly. 'It was an unhappy marriage from the first. We both tried—Francesca wanted to be a dutiful daughter, you understand?'

'As you wanted to be a dutiful son,' Brynne acknowledged, unable to stop the slight anger she felt towards the parents who had forced them into such a marriage.

'As I wanted to be a dutiful son.' Alejandro gave an inclination of his head. 'As I tried to be a dutiful husband. Whether you believe it or not, Brynne, I was a faithful husband,' he added.

She grimaced. 'Why shouldn't I believe you, Alejandro?'

'Many reasons,' he sighed. 'I was unfaithful during my engagement when I had my brief relationship with Joanna. I have had many relationships since my marriage ended.'

He wasn't going to spare himself—or her!—any of the hurtful details, was he? Brynne acknowledged ruefully. Although the fact that he was telling her at all, when she knew he wasn't a man who ever opened up about himself, was starting to make her wonder if there wasn't some purpose behind the explanation...

'Unfortunately, Francesca was not a dutiful wife.' He gave a slight shrug. 'Who could blame her? Nineteen years of age, and married to a man she did not even know, let alone love! Within a year of our marriage she had taken a lover. It is not so unusual in such marriages, although it is normal to wait until after the first son is born,' he added. 'To ensure that the husband knows that at least the heir is his!'

'What happened to Francesca, Alejandro?' she prompted huskily.

He looked grim. 'She died while giving birth to her lover's child. The child died, too.'

Brynne gave a pained gasp.

'Are you not going to ask me how I knew the child belonged to her lover?' Alejandro looked down at her.

A pose Brynne was now beginning to realize was as much a defence as anything else. Alejandro might not have loved his wife, but now that Brynne had come to know him better she didn't doubt that once married to Francesca he would have honoured the marriage.

She gave him an encouraging smile. 'Because you weren't her lover…?'

Alejandro felt some of the tension leave him, realizing as he did so just how tense he actually was. But this was important to him. That Brynne believed him was important to him. Much more important than anything else ever had been…

'Because I was not her lover,' he echoed. 'We were lovers—if it can be called that—for only the first three months of our marriage. I do not believe it was something that either of us particularly enjoyed,' he said ruefully, remembering those months when they'd tried to force a feeling of love for each other, an emotion that had never happened. 'Whereas making love with you four nights ago—'

'Alejandro—'

'I was wrong to leave you in the way that I did,' he told her forcefully. 'My only excuse—and it is perhaps not an acceptable one—is that I thought it for the best. I did not understand what was happening between us. But these four days away from you— I have thought of nothing but you, of our time together. Would you like to know why, Brynne?'

Brynne looked at him questioningly, not sure yet what he wanted from her. But she had no doubts that he was being honest; didn't she at least owe him the same?

'Yes,' she answered huskily. 'Yes, Alejandro, I want to know why you have thought of me the last four days.'

'Because our time together was beautiful,' he told her gruffly. 'Making love with you was more beautiful than anything else I have ever experienced.'

Brynne felt a lump form in her throat, hot tears clouding her vision. Because making love with Alejandro had been beautiful for her too.

Alejandro moved to clasp her hands in his as he looked down at her intently. 'It stunned me to learn of your in-experience.' He put up a hand to smooth her hair back from her face as he looked down at her. 'Beautiful, beautiful lovemaking,' he groaned huskily. 'I swore after my disastrous marriage that I would never become involved in that way with anyone ever again. But having got to know you— I am not proud of the way I behaved when I left you so abruptly. My only excuse is that I feared what you made me feel. But please believe me, Brynne, when I tell you I have thought of nothing else but you these last four days, of being in your arms again,' he admitted.

She looked up at him. 'I thought—you seemed so—angry, before you left…?'

He shook his head. 'Not anger, Brynne. Never anger. You had given me a precious gift that night, and I— ungracious swine that I am—did not know how to accept it!'

Brynne hadn't thought of it as a gift at the time, had only wanted to be with Alejandro. To be with the man she loved.

Alejandro's arms tightened about her. 'Brynne, I do not want you to leave me tomorrow.'

Her breath caught in her throat as she looked up at him, at the emotion in those softened dove-grey eyes, an emotion she thought she recognized, but found incredible in this man.

'I suppose I could come with you and Michael to Spain for a couple of weeks—'

'That is not what I mean, Brynne.' His voice hardened. 'I—even now this is difficult for me!' He released her to move away, running a hand through the dark thickness of his hair. 'Try to understand, Brynne, I have never been in love with anyone, was determined that I never would be after my marriage was so painfully unsuccessful—'

'I haven't asked you for love, Alejandro—'

'You do not need to ask!' He turned to her. 'Because the last four days away from you have shown me that I do love you, Brynne. More than life itself. More than anything and anyone,' he said shakily. 'The thought of you leaving me tomorrow, of you ever leaving me, is not something I can even contemplate!'

Brynne stared at him, at the assured, aloof man that she loved with all her heart, at the man who was no longer aloof at all, let alone assured.

Warmth began to course through her, to wipe away all the dread she had felt at the thought of parting from him.

Alejandro loved her.

Alejandro Miguel Diego Santiago loved her.

After the way he had left her four days ago she had never thought—had never even begun to hope—that he could return the feelings she had for him, hadn't understood at the time that what she had seen as his desertion he had seen as a sense of self-protection.

Only to come back today and tell her that he did love her. More than anything or anyone. Challengingly. Defensively. As if he feared the pain she could inflict on him if she chose to do so.

She moved to stand in front of him, their bodies almost touching as she looked up into his face. 'I love you too, Alejandro,' she breathed huskily. 'I love you so much that the thought of leaving you has been impossible for me to contemplate, either—' She got no further as Alejandro swept her up into his arms, her body held against the hardness of his as his mouth claimed and captured hers in a kiss full of the hunger he had felt for the four days of their parting.

It was a need Brynne felt too, holding nothing back as she returned the heat of his kiss, her arms up over his shoulders as her fingers became entangled in the dark thickness of his hair.

Alejandro wanted to devour her, to have her take him so deep inside her body that it would be impossible to tell where Brynne ended and he began.

Brynne was his flame. White-hot. Burning. That heat cleaving him to her side for all time.

He was breathing deeply when at last he raised his

head to look down into her flushed face. 'You do love me...' he said in wonder, knowing that it was true, that his honest Brynne could never be anything but truthful with him, in her emotions as well as her words.

She smiled up at him. 'Of course I love you, Alejandro.' Her fingers moved lightly down the clenched line of his jaw. 'You are everything—everything I could ever want in the man I love. You're a wonderful son. An affectionate and caring father. A man of honour in all things, including your relationships—'

'And you, Brynne?' he cut in searchingly. 'What am I to you, Brynne?'

'That's easy.' She smiled tremulously. 'You're the man I will love all my life.'

His breath caught in his throat at the simple statement that meant everything to him.

He had decided long ago that love and marriage were not for him, that Francesca had married him but had not loved him. The women he had known before her and since her had taken him, and all the things he could give them, but had not given him love.

Brynne gave him love, all her love, without asking for anything in return except that he love her too.

And he wanted to give her so much more than that! Everything that he was. Everything that he would be.

'Will you marry me, Brynne?' he prompted huskily, his arms tightening about her instinctively as she stiffened to look up at him dazedly. 'What did you think, *querida*? That I would tell you I love you, would listen while you tell me you feel the same way, and that I would then dishonour such a love with less than I offered to a woman who did not love me as I did not love her?'

She shook her head. 'I didn't think anything. I never thought, never dreamt, that you would ever love me…'

He frowned darkly. 'If I had never known you, Brynne, I would never have known what it is to love and be loved. Do you honestly think I could ever let such a love escape me by offering you less than marriage, less than everything that I am, that I have to give?'

Brynne hadn't known what to expect after admitting that she returned the love Alejandro told her he felt for her. Perhaps a brief relationship, a brief, beautiful relationship that would have to sustain her for the rest of her life. Marriage was something that she had never dreamt Alejandro would ever offer to any woman again…

She swallowed hard. 'But marriage, Alejandro.' She shook her head. 'You told me you would never marry again.'

'To a woman who did not love me, no!' Alejandro assured her with some of his old arrogance, his arms like steel bands about her. 'But you are different, Brynne. In the short time I have known you you have become the air I breathe, the perfume that warms my pillow, the very essence of my life. I will allow nothing, and no one, to come between us ever again.'

He was talking of Antonia Roig, and other women like her, women who only wanted to take and to use him, not to love him as he so deserved to be loved. As Brynne loved him…

'If you do not agree to marry me for love then I will have to try to tempt you into a marriage with me for Michael's sake.' He raised his eyebrows as he looked down at her.

But Brynne could see the humour lurking in his grey

eyes, the self-derision mixed with a determination that told her he would resort to such methods if all else failed.

'A marriage of convenience, you mean?' she drawled teasingly.

'A marriage that will give me the right to hold you, to love you, to come to your bed every night for the rest of our lives!' he corrected softly.

'Oh, no, Alejandro—'

'Oh, yes, Brynne,' he said firmly.

She shook her head. 'It will give us both the right to hold each other, to love each other, to come to our bed every night for the rest of our lives,' she corrected pointedly. 'If I have one condition to marrying you, Alejandro, then it's that we have a huge four-poster bed to share wherever we might be!'

He tilted his head teasingly. 'That is your only condition…?'

She laughed huskily. 'No conditions, Alejandro!' she assured him happily. 'I would marry you, will always love you, even if I have to live in a shack on the edge of a beach for the rest of my life!' She threw her arms about his neck. 'I love you, Alejandro Miguel Diego Santiago! I love you. I love you!'

Alejandro gathered her even closer into his arms, moulding her against him, knowing her to be the other half of him, the woman who completed him, who made him whole. 'I will love you for our lifetime and beyond, Brynne,' he whispered.

'As I will love you, Alejandro,' she vowed.

'Juanna Mercedes Santiago and Roberta Magdalena Santiago,' Brynne murmured emotionally as she looked up from gazing down at her newly born daughters into the face of the man she loved beyond words or expression.

Alejandro.

Her husband. Her lover. Her best friend. And now, almost a year to the day after their marriage, the father of their twin daughters.

Alejandro fiercely returned that gaze. 'They are truly beautiful, Brynne, but not as beautiful, or courageous, as their mother!' He shook his head. 'I could not bear to see you suffer so ever again!'

Brynne laughed. 'Childbirth isn't suffering, my love,' she assured softly.

A year of marriage had given them a bond of love so deep that it could never, ever be broken, only added to. As the birth of their daughters had done. They had become Michael's parents too, and had been absorbed into Alejandro's loving family as he had been accepted into her own family. They had delighted in each new discovery about each other.

Brynne reached up and touched her husband's cheek, smoothing away the worry and strain he had suffered as he had held her hand through the hours of childbirth. 'I love you, Alejandro,' she told him earnestly. 'Enough and more to have half a dozen babies—'

'Half a dozen!' Alejandro cut in forcefully, his expression only relaxing as he saw how she was teasing him, this beautiful woman he loved to distraction. 'Maybe two more,' he countered.

Brynne laughed softly. 'Maybe three…?'

Maybe three, he conceded achingly, knowing there was nothing he could deny this woman who meant more to him than life itself.

His wife.

The mother of his children. All his children. However many they might have.

The woman who loved him more than he had ever thought it possible to be loved.

But most of all, the woman that he would love, fiercely, passionately, beyond life itself…

* * * * *

THE MEDITERRANEAN
BILLIONAIRE'S
SECRET BABY

BY
DIANA HAMILTON

Diana Hamilton is a true romantic and fell in love with her husband at first sight. They still live in the fairytale Tudor house where they raised their three children. Now the idyll is shared with eight rescued cats and a puppy. But, despite an often chaotic lifestyle, ever since she learned to read and write Diana has had her nose in a book—either reading or writing one—and plans to go on doing just that for a very long time to come.

CHAPTER ONE

DARK brows clenched in irritation above narrowed
smoke-grey eyes, Francesco Mastroianni drove through
the gathering gloom of a chilly March evening. Vicious
rods of rain hit the windscreen of the throatily growling
Ferarri, adding to his already sour mood.

Visiting this part of rural Gloucestershire wasn't his
idea of a picnic—there were too many uncomfortable
memories—but there was no way he could have excused
his way out of it. He was too fond of Silvana even to
think of turning the weekend invitation down and
spoiling her pleasure in showing off her new home.

Trouble was, his cousin Silvana and her husband Guy
had recently moved from their swanky London abode to
a newly renovated manor house in a county that sent a
shiver through him whenever the name was mentioned.

He didn't do cringing, and he found the grossly unwelcome experience infuriating.

Per l'amor del cielo—just get over it! he instructed
himself toughly, gritting his teeth until his jaw resem-
bled something carved out of rock. However painful the
experience, he'd learned a priceless lesson—hadn't he?

Francesco had been cynical where the female sex was concerned since he'd entered his late teens and learned that his family's wealth was a powerful magnet. It was hard to credit that he'd actually been besotted and bewitched into allowing himself to believe that, against all his previous expectations, he'd finally found one woman he could trust. Actually to believe she was the one woman in the world he could trust with his life and his love until the day he died.

His sweet Anna—his mouth curled with cynical derision.

Yeah. Right.

He'd been well and truly suckered! Behaving like a callow youth instead of a mature and worldly-wise hard-nosed thirty-four-year-old!

She'd turned out to be as bad as all the others who'd targeted his personal fortune—worse, even. Pretending—oh, she'd been good at pretending—that she had no idea who he was, pretending she believed he was just a regular guy, earning a crust whichever way he could by fishing, acting as a part-time tour guide, taking casual work wherever he found it. That was the impression she'd seemingly arrived at, and although he hadn't lied he hadn't disabused her, too delighted to have found himself falling for the beautiful, gentle Anna who, so it had seemed, had been in love with him, the man, not with his financial clout.

Expelling a savage hiss of breath between strong white teeth, he slowed down to a crawl at a fork in the narrow lane and peered out through the murk at the signpost.

Left towards his cousin's new home. Right towards the

village where Anna the sneaky gold-digger lived. Rylands. The name of her home was burned into his brain.

He was powerless to prevent his mind flicking back to the last time he'd made this journey.

'Make your way there—I'll tell my folks to expect you and make a bed up. You will stay overnight, won't you?' She'd sounded breathless with excitement when he'd phoned from London to say he was on his way to see her. 'It's a real pain—but I won't be back until around ten. I'll be working this evening. And, no…' a breathy sigh, a sigh that had seemed to his bamboozled self to hold every last ounce of the world's regrets '…I can't cancel—wish I could! Oh, Francesco, I can't wait to see you!'

Replacing the receiver on one of the bank of phones that sat on the gleaming expanse of his desk in the glass and polished teak office of his London headquarters, he'd grinned wryly. He'd already cancelled three scheduled meetings to be with her. But that wouldn't occur to her. Why should it? She hadn't a clue that he headed the vast Mastroianni business empire that ran like well-oiled clockwork from offices in Rome, Brussels, New York and Sydney.

Buzzing through to his senior PA, he'd imparted the information that he was leaving—with a proposal bursting to trip off his tongue and a ring fit for a queen in the breast pocket of his pale grey business suit—reflecting that, though the delay of a few hours in seeing her was more than he could bear, it would at least give him the opportunity to get to know her parents.

Her father had been waiting to greet him. A large,

florid figure in shabby tweeds, he'd bounded down the short flight of stone steps like a boisterous overgrown puppy, hardly giving him time to take in the proportions of the seventeenth-century building constructed of mellow golden Cotswold stone. Or the general look of dilapidation.

'So you are my little girl's fella!' His hands grasped in a knuckle-crushing grip, he'd watched the older man's eyes widen in recognition and then narrow as he as good as licked his lips. 'Welcome to the ancestral home! Anna's told us all about you!'

Led through a huge stone-flagged hall, empty apart from a solitary sorry-looking chair, he'd found himself ushered into a smallish panelled room cluttered with shabby sofas and a scuffed pine table and treated to the most blatant begging spiel he'd ever had to endure.

'Thought I'd get this in before my good lady joins us— you know how it is; they don't understand business matters, bless their pretty little heads! Thing is, old son, I've got this fantastic idea. Can't lose! Great investment opportunity for a man like you. You'd be a fool to turn it down, and from what I've read about you, you're not that!'

Dismissing the crackpot scheme—something to do with wild animals—he'd felt his heart twist with the shock of betrayal, his face stiffen with anger. So Anna had told her father all about her 'fella'? You bet she had! Got him primed and ready to swoop!

No wonder she'd sounded over the moon when he'd phoned to say he was on his way. Congratulating herself that she'd successfully reeled him in!

Had the working excuse been just that? A lie, giving

her father the time and space to wheedle a million pounds from him? Would his sweet Anna have swanned in when the deal was done and dusted, widening those big green eyes and fluttering those thick lashes, exclaiming with a pout of her luscious lips that she didn't understand boring business stuff, confident that fantastic sex would hold him?

His voice like a razor, he'd cut the older man off midflow. 'I've never been begged for money more clumsily.' Then he'd asked for a sheet of paper. Scrawled a message for his 'Sweet Anna', and left. Despising himself. Hating her.

Hating her for turning him into the sort of fool who could be led from the heart instead of the head.

He who prided himself on his cool, calculating brain, his inborn ability to recognise a gold-digger at a hundred yards, had come within a whisker of being taken for the ride of his life.

He was deeply ashamed of himself.

Gunning the engine, he took the left fork and told himself to forget the whole distasteful episode. And hoped with savage impatience that Silvana—an incorrigible matchmaker—hadn't included a wannabe billionaire's wife/mistress in her weekend invitation. He had no interest in the opposite sex. Hadn't had since— oh, forget it!

Her hands pressing against the aching small of her back, Anna Maybury regarded her feet, shod in comfy old black flatties. She was sure her ankles were swelling. One of the penalties of being seven months pregnant.

Her hands slid round to rest lightly on her bump, which was only partially disguised by her voluminous pale green working overall. Despite the discomfort, she loved her coming baby more than she'd ever thought possible.

A termination, as suggested by a couple of her friends, had been completely out of the question, and her parents' nagging on about her right to contact the father and demand financial support had been met with stubborn refusal.

This was her baby, and she loved him or her with every atom of her generous heart. She would manage without any input from its father. The very idea made her seethe. He was an utter cad! He might be more handsome than was good for any man, and, as it had turned out, filthy rotten rich, but he was still a callous, womanising louse!

Annoyed with herself for giving him space in her head, breaking the staunch vow she'd made never to think of him again, she tucked a straying strand of her mane of long blonde hair back beneath the unflattering snood and gave her attention to the makings of dinner for four. The pre-prepared items were waiting in the cool box, and the leg of lamb spiked with garlic and rosemary, for the main course, was sizzling nicely in the oven of the huge old range.

An Italian menu, as stipulated. Anna didn't want to think of anything Italian. Maybe that was why she'd dropped her mental guard and allowed herself to give her baby's father head-room—something she'd successfully avoided ever since she'd discovered she was pregnant.

Apparently her client, Silvana Rosewall, was Italian,

married to some well-heeled English banker. So she'd
have to get herself comfy with that and not give in to
self-pity just because the lady of the house had stipulated
an Italian menu.

She was a professional chef, and her home catering
business was doing OK. More than OK. Though she
could have done with her friend Cissie's help tonight,
to take over the actual serving.

But Cissie had a promising date, and when she'd first
offered to join Maybury Catering in a dogsbody and PR
capacity she'd stressed that she would only be filling in
time until Mr Right and Rich came over her horizon.

She had to hand it to Cissie, though. Her family had
all the right social connections, and a word here and
there had produced some good bookings—like
tonight's—and they were infinitely preferable to the
others that came in—mostly childrens' parties or buffet
lunches for leisured ladies—handed to her like patronising favours because people knew her family and were
sorry for them.

But she was not, *not* going to think about the very real
prospect that Rylands, the family home for over three
hundred years, might be taken from them. It was a scary
thought, because she knew that losing her family's home
would break her mother's already frail heart. And agonising over such scary thoughts would be bad for her
unborn baby. So she wouldn't let herself.

'My guests have just arrived.'

A smile lighting her heart-shaped face, Anna turned
as Mrs Rosewall entered the huge kitchen. Relief that
things would now start moving, occupy a mind that an-

noyingly seemed inclined to brood, flooded through her. The kitchen was way at the back of the rambling manor, so she hadn't been able to hear car tyres crunching on the gravel of the main driveway.

'What do we have?' Silvana Rosewall picked her way over the uneven slate flooring slabs that had been *in situ* since the house was built. A woman in her early thirties, she was beautiful in a blue silk gown, spiky high heels, with a cluster of jewels somehow fixed in her upswept dark hair.

'Tiny hot potato cakes with mozzarella to start, followed by swordfish kebabs, then thin slices of Tuscan-style lamb, with roasted Mediterranean vegetables, and to finish we have zabaglione with caramel oranges,' Anna reeled off confidently. 'And coffee, of course. And I managed to get hold of some of those special Venetian biscuits.'

'*Excellente.*' Silvana nodded her approval. 'We eat in half an hour.' A slight frown marred the perfection of her smooth-as-cream brow as her eyes swept Anna's dumpily pregnant figure. 'You are alone? You can manage—in your condition? I would have thought some other person to wait on the table...'

Someone slim and attractive, not likely to put her guests off their food, Anna translated wryly as her client finally closed the kitchen door behind her. Well, she'd do her best to melt into the background. She had the sort of curves that would have looked great on a six-foot Amazon, but in her own eyes they made her five-two frame decidedly dumpy. Normally she was saved from complete rotundity only by her once tiny waist—although recently that had ballooned with her large and growing larger vigorous baby!

Dismissing her apple-like shape, Anna opened the first of the two large cool boxes which held everything that could have possibly been prepared at home and got on with what she did best. Cooking.

Exactly half an hour later the biggest tray she could find was loaded with four plates of sizzling hot potato cakes topped with melting, slightly browned mozzarella and garnished with fresh basil, and she was on her way, her heart light because all was going as it should. The lamb was resting now, before carving, and the swordfish, tomato and lemon wedge kebabs were ready to put under the grill the moment she was back in the kitchen after unobtrusively serving the *antipasto*. Hopefully the Rosewalls and their two guests would be so knocked out by the delicious food she was serving they wouldn't notice her, and her appearance wouldn't be an embarrassment to her fastidious client.

But her blithe confidence took a shattering nosedive when she entered the panelled room and stared straight into the eyes of…him!

The loaded tray almost followed the abrupt direction of her confidence. Clinging to it for dear life, she felt her face flame. His eyes impaled her. The last time she'd looked into them they'd glimmered between the unfairly long and thick sweep of his dark lashes, smoky with desire. Now they were hard, glitteringly dark and dangerously narrowed.

Gunfighter's eyes, she thought crazily, and swallowed down a cry of outrage. She dropped her transfixed gaze, willed the fiery colour to leave her hot face, and handed the plates around, her hands shaking.

Scuttling out of the room, her dignity long-lost, she made it back to the kitchen. Her heart pounding, Anna leant back against the solid wood of the closed door and tried to pull herself together. Seeing him here—smooth, urbanely handsome, in the sort of beautifully tailored suit that must have cost an arm and a leg, looking at her as if she were something quite unspeakable—had been a cruel shock.

The taunting words he'd scrawled on that note he'd left for her were etched in acid behind her closed eyes.

Nice try. But I've changed my mind. You've a lot to offer, but nothing I can't get in spades elsewhere.

Sex. He'd meant sex.

Her stomach lurched and she thrust a fisted hand against her mouth. Dad must have read the note. Nothing else could have explained his hangdog expression when he'd handed it to her, mumbling that her new fella had only stayed for ten minutes, then left. So her father knew she'd been given the runaround, and that had made her feel even worse, if that were possible.

At first she'd thought that he'd believed she was loaded—hadn't she and Cissie been staying at that ruinously expensive hotel, patronised by the seriously wealthy? He'd thought he was onto a good thing—until he'd faced the reality of Rylands, denuded of anything worth selling, neglect evident everywhere you looked.

That had been before. A few weeks later Cissie had thrust one of the glossy society magazines her mother took under her nose, a scarlet nail jabbing at a photograph.

'That's the guy you hooked up with on Ischia. I thought he looked sort of familiar, but I couldn't place him—it must have been the scruff he was going around in. He must have been incognito—not a minder or a fancy yacht in sight! He's always in the gossip columns of the glossies. He's worth trillions—you lucky cow! Do you keep in touch?'

'No.'

'Pity. Hook him and you'd be set for life! Mind you, to be honest, these holiday flings aren't meant to last, and I guess he'd be a handful—terrible reputation with women!'

Shrugging, she'd turned away, barely glancing at the photographed Francesco Mastroianni, his white dinner jacket contrasting with his fatally attractive dark Latin looks, complete with arm candy. Her mind had felt fried. He hadn't been after her non-existent family money, as she'd first thought.

Just sex.

But in the short time between arriving in London and phoning her he'd met someone who could give him better sex—someone more sophisticated. Creep! Oh, how she hated men who used women as playthings, to be picked up and then chucked away when a more exciting prospect came into view!

So what right had he to look at her now as if she were beneath contempt?

Heaving herself away from the door, she told herself that if anyone deserved contempt it was him, and rushed to turn on the grill.

She was a professional. She would do the job she'd been hired to do, ignore him and, when the evening was over, she'd put him right out of her head again. She would not, *not* 'accidentally' knock his wine glass over into his lap, or drop a loaded plate on his hateful head. She couldn't afford that sort of satisfaction. To get a reputation for gross clumsiness would mean she'd never work in the area again.

But if he dared give her that contemptuous look one more time she'd be sorely tempted!

She was pregnant!

His?

Francesco had to force himself to eat. Force himself to ignore Anna Maybury as she served them. Force out the occasional monosyllable that was his sole contribution to the otherwise animated conversation, oblivious to the come-ons that were steaming his way from the sultry redhead his cousin had produced for his delectation.

Not interested. Not remotely. Grimly sifting facts.

Anna had been a virgin. He hadn't used protection that first time, too blown away to even think of it.

Lost. He'd been lost in a wildly churning maelstrom of unfettered emotion—an experience so new and vivid he'd felt as if the whole of his life up until that moment had been a theatre of shadows.

The child she was carrying could be his. Unless—

Aiming for casual, he leaned back, hooked an arm over the back of his chair and, ignoring the redhead's pouting smile, tossed into the conversation, 'Your caterer? How pregnant is she, do you know?'

Three pairs of taken-aback eyes stared at him. It was Silvana who wanted to know, 'Why do you ask?'

Because I might be about to be a father and not know it. Aloud, he responded with deceptive idleness. 'I wondered if we, collectively, might be required to act as midwives.'

An irritating tinkle of laughter from the redhead—he couldn't remember what she was called—and an apprehensive glance from Guy towards his wife, who answered. 'Seven months, according to Cissie Lansdale. Cissie's a sort of partner on Anna's catering business—a bit feckless, I think the word is. She usually helps out with the waiting—but not tonight, apparently. Guy, darling—our glasses are empty.'

As her husband did the honours with a second bottle of Valpolicella, Silvana confided, 'Personally, I think a woman in her position should be resting, not—' she waved a languid hand over the table '—doing this sort of thing. Of course she doesn't have a husband to lay the law down, and her mother's a feeble thing—not in good health, I hear. Besides, I suppose they need the money. The father's hopeless. He married into that family. They once had real standing in the area. But he squandered everything or lost it.'

'Bad investments followed worse ones, I hear,' Guy put in as he sat down again.

'You seem to know a lot about them,' Francesco commented, reflecting uneasily that seven months was spot-on. The child would be his unless immediately on her return home Anna had jumped into bed with someone else. But that didn't seem likely, given that at that time she'd been banking on reeling him in. She'd been expecting him to follow her to England, so she would not have wanted some other guy hanging around to stir up trouble, he decided forensically.

Making a huge effort to stop a black scowl from forming, and stopping himself from marching straight into the kitchen and demanding to know the truth, he listened to his cousin's answer.

· 'It was necessary when we first came here to introduce ourselves to the better families so they could advise us on local reliable and honest tradespeople. A permanent housekeeper is to arrive next week, but there are others.' She took a sip of her coffee and arched one finely raised brow at him over the central flower arrangement. 'Plumbers, electricians, a man to do the garden, caterers—that sort of person. The pregnant girl came highly recommended.

'Now, why don't we retire to the sitting room while the pregnant one clears away? One Grappa, I think, and then Guy and I will go up and leave you two to relax by the fire and get to know each other properly.' A big smile in Francesco's direction as she got to her feet. 'I know Natalie wants to discuss some charity ball I'm sure you'll be interested in.'

Like hell he would! Deadpan, he met the redhead's over-sugared smile. Introduced by Silvana as 'a friend from London'—an organiser of glittering events for some charity or other—she was certainly a looker. And available. And he was going to have to endure a weekend of having his cousin throwing them together. He would have to let this Natalie know that he was as interested in the female of the species as he was in settling down to read through the telephone directory from cover to cover. And try to be kind about it.

And tomorrow, first thing, he would visit Rylands and demand to know if the child the woman who'd made an idiot of him was carrying was his.

The dishwasher had finished its cycle. Wearily, Anna replaced the contents back in place in the huge Victorian floor-to-ceiling cupboard. Her feet were burning and her back was still aching.

Half an hour earlier Mrs Rosewall had found her re-packing the cool boxes and handed her a cheque.

'The meal was perfect. Are you almost finished?'

'Everything will be back as it was in half an hour or so. I'm just waiting for the dishes to finish. Unless you'd prefer me to leave now?' Said without any real hope.

She'd been longing to get away—well out of the orbit of Francesco and his current woman. But from experience she knew that her clients wanted their kitchens to look as if they'd never been used. That was what they paid her for. And they wanted full value for money.

And this one was no different. 'No hurry. I just wanted to tell you that my husband and I are retiring for the night, but my cousin and his young lady will be in the sitting room and I don't want them to be disturbed. Just let yourself out quietly. And, while I think about it, could you cater for lunch on Sunday? My guests will be driving back to London in the afternoon, so nothing too heavy, I think.'

Anna hadn't even considered saying yes! The fee would be more than welcome, but no way would she put herself anywhere near that womanising creep again!

'Sorry,' she'd declined, resisting the urge to rub her aching back. 'That won't be possible.'

Now, after a final look at the spotless kitchen, she got into her old raincoat, shook her hair free and let herself out. Too tired to hurry, she was drenched when she reached her van and loaded the cool boxes in the back.

It had been a nightmare of a night. The shock of seeing him again had got to her, brought it all back when she hadn't wanted to so much as think about him again. But it was over now, she reminded herself with almost tearful gratitude, and she forced herself to look on the bright side.

Sensibly telling herself that she never need set eyes on him again, she clambered in behind the wheel.

The way that redhead had been positively drooling over him had made her feel nauseous, and the horrible feeling that he must have noticed her pregnant state—how could he miss it?—put two and two together and know that the baby was his had been argued away as she'd grilled the kebabs.

Callously, he wouldn't want to know. What had happened on Ischia was just one in a long line of forgettable flings. He would dismiss the matter, reasoning that if she had fallen pregnant it was her own fault and she could deal with it.

Which was fine by her!

With his heart successfully painted as black as his midnight hair, Anna pushed him roughly out of her mind and turned the key in the ignition.

The engine gave a tortured whine—and died. After the fourth attempt Anna had to concede that the battery was dead. Sternly resisting the temptation to bawl her eyes out, she rooted in her handbag for her mobile. It was entirely her own fault. Nick had advised her to splash out on a new battery, but she had kept putting it off because every spare penny was needed to pay the service bills at Rylands and put food on the table.

The fruitless search for her mobile continued—until Anna had to concede that she must have left it at home. Banging her small fists against the steering wheel, she yelped 'Stupid! *Stupid!*' then slumped in exhaustion in her seat, facing the unpalatable fact that she would have to go and knock them up.

'Them' being Francesco and his current squeeze! The Rosewalls had long since retired for the night. And for all she knew so had Francesco and his lady. The thought galvanised her. It had to be all of eight miles back to Rylands. It was pouring with rain. If she weren't pregnant she would walk it. But as it was—

Francesco permitted himself a small Grappa as the redhead vacated the room. Huffily.

Too edgy to settle, he paced the room, glass held loosely in one hand. Used to fending women off, he usually managed it with finesse. Not tonight. He hadn't been brutal. Just cold, clipped, concise.

Tickets for the charity ball she was organising didn't interest him. Neither did meeting up for lunch when they were back in town. His schedule was too tight to allow room for any socialising in the foreseeable future.

At which point she'd gone to bed. Alone.

So he should be able to relax. But he couldn't. Seeing Anna Maybury again had rekindled all the shaming memories, had brought everything he was doing his damnedest to forget back into unbelievably sharp focus, and her advanced state of pregnancy had deeply unsettled him, raising questions he knew he had to have answered.

The morning, when he could confront her, seemed an unendurably long way away.

Her heart quailing, Anna pressed the doorbell. The rain had turned her hair into dripping rats' tails, and the front of her overall was soaking because the bump meant she couldn't fasten her old waterproof. She felt sick with nerves, and knowing she must look pretty dreadful didn't help.

But she had to contact Nick—ask him to come and collect her—and that meant facing Francesco, speaking to him, asking for the use of the Rosewalls' phone.

The alternative was trudging home along narrow, isolated lanes. The chance of flagging down a passing motorist was a remote one at this time of night, and the likelihood of seeing a light at the windows of one of the scattered cottages or farmsteads was almost non-existent.

As the door swung open in answer to her summons at last she stiffened her spine, barely glanced at Francesco's hard, handsome features and managed to get out, in a disgracefully wobbly voice, 'My van won't start. May I use the phone?'

Silence. Then, above the relentless sound of the rain, she heard his harsh indrawn breath, found her eyes tugged up to his. Hardened grey steel.

And not even the beguiling accent could soften the impact of his rawly savage question. 'Tell the truth, for once in your life. Is the baby mine?'

CHAPTER TWO

Floundering, stunned by such an in-your-face enquiry, Anna decided that it would be more dignified to ignore the question rather than give in to the compulsion to fling *What do you care?* at him.

Woodenly, she elaborated on her request, hammering home the fact that a way out of her present dead van difficulty need be the only point of contact between them.

'I need to call Nick to ask him to fetch me, and for that I obviously need to use a phone.'

Aware of steel-hard eyes boring into her, one sable brow elevated in what looked like disbelief, she squirmed inside. Was he asking himself how he had ever managed to make love—amendment, have sex—with such a creature? Lumpen, hair like wet string, clumpy shoes, old school mac out of which loomed a stomach as big as the Millennium Dome!

Fighting the appalling fizzy upsurge of hysteria, she forced herself to calm down, to forget she loathed and despised him, and to explain, slowly and clearly, flattening dangerous emotions out of her voice. 'Please let the Rosewalls know that Nick and I will collect my van first thing in the morning. All it needs is a new battery.' Fingers crossed! No way could she pay a big repair bill if there was anything more serious amiss.

Shivering now, wet, cold and intensely weary, she felt desperation claw at her as she took a step forward. 'May I come in?'

Glancing up at him when he made no move to allow her entry, she felt her heart twist in alarm. His eyes were grim and his beautiful, sexy mouth was set in a cruel slash. The handsome features were taut, throwing those classical cheekbones and the arrogant blade of his nose into harsh relief.

Was he going to tell her to get lost? Force her to walk back?

He moved then. Towards her. Taking an elbow in a grip of steel, turning her. 'I'll drive you.'

'That's not necessary.' She couldn't hide the note of urgency in her voice, dreading the thought of being cooped up in a car with him, him repeating That Question, getting personal. 'Nick will be more than happy to fetch me.'

His grip tightened. The pace he was setting as he steered her unwilling and yet too exhausted to fight self through the darkness to the far side of the manor house quickened. 'I'm sure he will,' he remarked sardonically. 'However, you need to get out of those wet things and into a hot bath as quickly as possible.' He tugged her to a halt before she could blunder into the parked Ferrari. 'You do not have just your own well-being to consider now.'

He meant the baby, Anna conceded guiltily as she shoehorned herself into the passenger seat. And he was right. The whole evening had been disastrous, and she needed to get dry, warm and relaxed for her baby's sake, but the comparative speed of that operation against the delay of waiting for Nick meant Francesco would have ample opportunity to ask That Question again, and she didn't know how to answer him.

Her spine rigid with apprehension, she felt hot tears of sheer exhaustion flood her eyes, and she bit into the soft underside of her lower lip to stop them falling.

Tell him it was none of his business? Would he accept that? Absent himself smartly, relieved that she wouldn't be making a nuisance of herself, demanding financial support, and—heaven forbid—making herself known to his family and causing him huge embarrassment?

It seemed a definite possibility. As a psychological profile of a guy who would trample a poor girl's heart with as much compunction as he would trample a fallen leaf, it fitted.

Unless she steeled herself to tell a whopping lie and name some other fictional guy as the father? Claim she was just five months pregnant, putting him right out of the frame? But, given the size of her, would he be gormless enough to believe that?

Bracing herself, Anna waited. But the only question he asked was, 'Do you still live with your parents at Rylands?' Receiving a breathless affirmative, he said nothing more until he halted the car at the head of the weedy drive. Then he told her grimly, 'Don't think I've finished. I'll be here first thing in the morning. And if I'm told you're not available I'll wait until you are.'

* * *

Driving back at the sort of speed he had earlier carefully controlled in deference to his passenger, Francesco cursed himself for failing to demand to know the identity of the father of her child.

Once set on a course of action he always pursued it with surgical precision, letting nothing stand in his way. He was single-minded, known to be ruthless when the occasion demanded—he'd had to be. Taking over the almost moribund Mastroianni business empire on the death of his father ten years earlier, he'd dragged it kicking and screaming, into the twenty-first century—not a task for an indecisive weakling.

And as for compassion for fools and knaves—forget it!

So why hadn't he pressed home his advantage when she'd asked to use the Rosewalls' phone? Why had he allowed her to avoid answering the burning question? No one else on the planet would have got away with it!

He should have forced the truth from her. He'd had the ideal opportunity.

Except—

She'd looked so vulnerable. Exhausted. Wet and bedraggled, like a half-drowned kitten. His primary emotion had been rage that a woman in her condition was forced to slave for those too privileged to do anything but issue orders and then sit back and wait for them to be carried out. That had been swiftly followed by the need to transport her to where she could find comfort and rest.

He expelled a harsh breath through his teeth. He had to be getting old, losing his touch!

And who the hell was Nick?

* * *

Clutching her hot water bottle, Anna crawled into bed. The bathwater had been tepid at best and her bedroom was draughty, with damp patches on the ceiling where the venerable roof leaked.

Her throat tightened. She shivered convulsively. She was being threatened. He really did mean to drag the truth from her, against all her earlier expectations he wasn't going to shrug those magnificent, expensively clothed shoulders, discount the fact that he might be about to become a father and leave her to get on with it.

She'd read somewhere that the Latin male was deeply family orientated. The reminder made her shudder.

If only she hadn't accepted the Rosewalls' catering job! They wouldn't have set eyes on each other again. And if only she'd been able to fall in love with Nick and accept the offer of marriage that had been made when her pregnancy had begun to show she'd have been a married woman, and Nick would have sworn blind the child was his. He would do anything for her. The thought depressed her.

She and Nick had been best mates since they were toddlers, and he was the kindest, gentlest person she knew. They were deeply fond of each other—always had been—and that had prompted his proposal, and the vow to care for her and the baby, look on him or her as his own.

He cared for her—she knew that—but he was not in love with her and he deserved better. One day he would meet someone who took his breath away. And she wasn't in love with him either. What she felt for Nick was nothing like what she'd felt when she'd fallen for Francesco—

Oh! Scrub that! Punching the pillow with small, angry fists, she buried her head in it and tried to sleep.

Anna gladly left her rumpled bed at daybreak. Dressing in a fresh maternity smock, she bunched up her hair and pinned it on top of her head. Her eyes looked huge and haunted as they stared back at her from the mirror.

Turning away, disgusted with herself for being scared of the Italian Louse, because he couldn't make her do anything she didn't want to do, she stuffed her feet into a pair of beat-up old running shoes. The comfy flats she'd worn last night were still sodden.

She hunted for her mobile.

Nick sounded sleepy when he answered, and Anna apologised. 'I woke you. Oh, I'm sorry! But listen—'

Briefly she explained what she needed, feeling awful for calling him so early. But Francesco hadn't specified a time—just 'first thing'—and if she and Nick were on their way to the manor with a new battery when Francesco turned up, tough. He would have to kick his heels until she decided to return home. And it wouldn't be running away, she assured herself staunchly. No. It would simply be giving her the upper hand.

'No probs,' Nick was saying. 'Give me half an hour. Didn't I tell you you'd get trouble? How did you get home? You should have called me.'

'I was going to. But one of the Rosewalls' guests insisted on driving me.' She skated over that bit quickly. 'And Nick—thanks.'

'What for?'

'Thanks for coming to the rescue.'

'Any time—you know that. Or should do.'

Ending the call, Anna plodded down to the kitchen, collecting her old waxed jacket on the way. A swift glass of juice, and then she'd set out to meet Nick. Thankfully, last night's rain had stopped, and fitful sunlight illuminated the dire shabbiness of the interior.

No wonder poor old Mum seemed to be permanently depressed as she watched her beloved old family home start on the unstoppable slide into decay. Frustrated too. Beatrice Maybury had always been frail—something to do with having had rheumatic fever as a child—and was unable to do anything practical to change the situation. She'd had to stand by and watch her husband William lose everything through one sure-fire money-making scheme after another, all predictably and disastrously failing.

Sighing, she pushed open the door to the cavernous kitchen—and stopped in her tracks.

'Mum?'

Beatrice Maybury, her slight body encased in an ancient candlewick dressing gown, greying hair braided into a single plait that almost reached her waist, her feet stuffed into rubber boots, lifted the kettle from the hotplate and advanced towards the teapot. 'Tea, dear?'

'You're up early.' She watched, green eyes narrowed, as her mother reached another mug from the dresser. Mum rarely surfaced before ten, on her husband's insistence that she rest. William had always treated his adored wife as if she were made of spun glass. It was a pity, Anna thought in a moment of rare sourness, that he hadn't treated the fortune she'd inherited the same way. 'Is anything wrong?'

'No more than usual.' Beatrice's eyes were red-rimmed and watery in the pallor of her face, her smile small and tired as she put two mugs of steaming tea on the table. 'Your father's worn out. I think that job's too much for him. I insisted he had a little lie-in.'

She sat, cradling her mug in her thin hands. Swallowing a sigh, Anna followed suit, beyond hope now of setting out to meet Nick on his way here and thereby avoiding The Louse if he had literally meant 'first thing'. She couldn't just walk out and leave Mum—not while she was so obviously troubled. As far as Anna could remember her mother had never insisted on anything, meekly allowing others to make all decisions, content to follow, never to lead.

Dad had always been as strong as an ox, but maybe labouring for a firm of local builders was proving to be too much for a man well into his sixties. The wages he earned went to make a token payment to his creditors, while the money she earned paid the household bills—just about. Between them they kept Rylands itself in a type of precarious safety. For the moment.

'I said I'd feed Hetty and Horace and let them out. No egg this morning. I think Hetty's off-colour.'

Anna grinned. It was the first time she'd felt remotely like smiling since she'd clapped eyes on The Louse again. 'She's probably just miffed because you keep taking her eggs. We should let her sit, increase the flock.'

The cockerel and the fat brown hen were the only survivors of a fox raid—the only survivors of Dad's self-sufficiency drive. It had been announced with his unending brio, hazel eyes alight with this new enthusiasm, grin as wide as a barn door. 'Fruit and veg, hens, a pig, a goat. The lot. Keep ourselves like royalty; sell the surplus in the village. Goat cheese, bacon, free-range eggs—you name it! Forget big business—back to nature. That's the life for us!'

The goat had never materialised. The pig had died. A neighbouring farmer's sheep had got in and trampled or eaten the fruit and veg, and the fox had taken the hens.

'And...' Beatrice raised soft blue eyes to her daughter, 'We had a little tiff. He was upset, I'm afraid.'

Anna put her mug down on the pitted table-top. She didn't like the sound of this. Her parents doted on each other. The love they shared was the staunch prop that kept their lives from collapsing around them, becoming a bitter nightmare. Mum had never said a cross word, had never blamed Dad when his bad investments and wacky money-making schemes had gone belly-up. She blamed everyone else instead, always encouraging him in his next, ill-fated 'Big Idea'.

If they were starting to fight, if love and loyalty were slipping away, then what hope was there for them?

Anna loved them both dearly. She felt protective towards her frail mother, and was exasperated by her father, but she loved him for his boundless energy and enthusiasm, his warmth and gruff kindness.

'Well, I'm afraid I'm going to have to put my foot down. Rather firmly.'

'I see,' Anna said gently, astonished by this departure from the norm. But she didn't. 'About...?'

She wasn't going to get an answer, because the clangs of the great doorbell reverberated through the house. She rose. 'That will be Nick. Look, I'm sorry, but I have to go. We'll talk later.' Grabbing her old waxed jacket, wriggling into it, she added automatically, 'Make sure you have breakfast. There's enough bread for toast. I'll pick up another loaf on my way back.'

A detour to the village to pick up a few essential provisions once the new battery was fitted would do nicely. She meant to avoid Francesco Mastroianni for as long as she possibly could, placing herself in a controlling position, hoping she'd be better able to handle the interrogation he obviously intended. Provided, of course, that he didn't emerge from the manor and catch them mid-operation. The thought made her feel vaguely sick as she opened the main door to admit a blast of chilly morning air.

And him.

Francesco swept inside, past her stunned personage. Her tummy flipped. Why did he have to be up and about so early? Couldn't his latest luscious bedmate have kept him glued to her for longer? And this morning he was looking quite unreasonably spectacular.

Six foot two of dominating Italian masculinity— midnight hair superbly styled, midnight lashes narrowed over glinting steel-grey eyes, handsome mouth a sardonic twist as he remarked, 'Going somewhere?'

To her great annoyance Anna felt her face grow hot and pink. To think she had once believed herself fathoms-deep in love with this domineering, sarcastic brute! He'd expertly hidden that side of him from her when he'd set out to seduce her. And dump her.

The immaculately crafted pale grey designer suit emphasised his fantastic physique, his classical features.

The crisp white shirt darkened the tones of his olive skin and the shadowed jawline that remained just that, no matter how often he shaved.

He was an intimidating stranger.

On the island he'd always worn old cut-off denims, canvas deck shoes that had seen better days, and round his neck a fake gold chain that had left green marks on the sleek bronzed skin of his magnificent torso. Those tell-tale stains had made her heart clench with aching tenderness, had made her love him all the more.

Now she didn't love him at all.

She loathed him, and all he stood for.

And she most certainly wasn't about to give him an answer, open the way for any conversation. Leaving the main door open, she sent up a swift and fervent prayer for Nick's speedy arrival and her consequent escape.

'Is there somewhere more comfortable where we can talk?' His tone told her he was running out of patience, and the unnerving steely scrutiny he was subjecting her to told her he didn't like what he saw.

A shabby nobody who might or might not be carrying his child.

'No.' She didn't want to discuss her baby's paternity with him. With anyone. And because she already loved her coming child with all her generous heart she was deeply afraid.

If Francesco knew he was the father he might be more than happy to wash his hands of the whole thing— dismiss it with a shrug. Or—and this was what made her nerves jump—he might come over all macho, wealthy Italian male and demand custody.

And then what would she do? Could she fight him through the courts and win?

'Anna—who is it?' Beatrice appeared from the kitchen region. She stopped dead, clutching the neckline of her shabby robe to her throat. 'I heard voices. It didn't sound like Nick.'

Well, it wouldn't, would it? No one could mistake Francesco's deep, cultured and slightly accented voice for Nick's comforting country burr, Anna thought wearily, wishing her mother had stayed firmly where she was. How was she supposed to introduce him? By the way—this is the man who seduced me, lied to me and dumped me!

It was Francesco who took over, his compressed lips softening into a staggeringly devastating smile as he advanced towards the older woman, his bronzed and far too handsome features relaxing.

'Mrs Maybury. I'm so happy to meet Anna's mother.' He held out a well-shaped hand. After a moment's hesitation, and a swift look at her daughter, Beatrice took it, and went bright pink when it was lifted to the stranger's lips.

'Anna?'

'Francesco Mastroianni,' Anna introduced stiffly. She wanted to shake her mother for simpering and fluttering like a silly schoolgirl, but resignedly forgave her—because no woman alive would be able to stay sensible when bombarded by the charm he could turn on at will when it suited him.

'I met Anna again last night when she catered for my cousin's dinner party,' he was saying. 'I am now here to enquire as to her health.'

Like hell you are! she fumed inwardly, hating him for

his ability to lie and deceive, for looking so sensational, so poised and self-assured, and loathing him for her own helplessness to do anything about it.

Mum had obviously picked up on that word *again*, judging from the way she arched a brow and gave a little moue of a smile. Then, 'How kind of you, *signor*. Won't you come through to the kitchen? It's the only warm room in the house, I'm afraid. And, darling, do close the door. Such a draught!'

Lumbering over the vast expanse of empty hall, Anna was fuming. Mum wouldn't let him over the threshold if she knew the truth. Underneath that fantastic exterior lurked a black devil—a heartless deceiver who would seduce a virgin, tell her he loved her more than his life, ensuring a more than willing bedmate for a couple of weeks to satisfy his massive male libido, his huge conceit, then callously dump her when a new and better prospect shashayed over the horizon.

Preoccupied, it took her several seconds to register that Nick was walking in through the wide open doorway. With his cheerful open face, his mop of untidy nut-brown hair and mild blue eyes, his sturdy body clad in oil-stained jeans and an ancient fleece, he looked so safe and ordinary she could have wept.

'Ready?' His smile encompassed Beatrice. 'Hi, Mrs Maybury!' If he had registered the presence of the superbly groomed stranger he didn't show it. 'Got the van keys?' Assimilating Anna's edgy nod, he supplied, 'Then we'll make tracks. Dad said no need to rush to pay for the battery. It'll wait until it's convenient.'

Anna ground her teeth and felt heated colour flood

her face. Nick's father owned the village garage and he, like everyone else around here, knew of their dire financial situation. His offer of deferred payment was a kind one, but she wished it hadn't been voiced in front of Francesco. She did have *some* pride!

'That won't be necessary,' she put in stiffly, heading for the door, the back of her neck prickling in her need to put as much distance as possible between herself and Francesco whose very presence affected her like an arrow to her heart.

An imperiously drawled, 'Wait!' stopped her.

Exuding sophisticated cool, Francesco stepped forward. 'Nick? I take it you are he?' Receiving a startled glance that he took as an affirmative, he ordered with the sublime confidence of a man who expected to be unquestioningly obeyed, 'There's no need for you to wait. Fix the battery. I'll take Anna to collect her van later.'

'Now, hang on a minute!' Incensed by his assumption that he could call the shots, Anna swung round to face him—and then wished she hadn't. Because just looking at him, at the upward drift of one strongly marked sable brow, the slight querying smile on that wide sensual mouth as he waited for her to expand on her explosive objection, made her heart leap, her mouth feel as parched as desert sand, her pulses race as she remembered—

Smothering a groan, feeling the fight ebbing out of her like water down a drain, she capitulated.

Pointless to avoid the interrogation any longer. The longer she spent dodging That Question, the more uptight and jittery she would become. It couldn't be good for her baby.

Flinging Nick an apologetic smile, she said dully, 'Thanks, pal. I'll see you later. There's stuff I've got to talk over with—him.' And if that sounded rude or ungracious, tough.

She didn't feel even remotely gracious as Francesco ushered her in her mother's wake as the older woman headed back to the kitchen. Just sick to her stomach.

CHAPTER THREE

'I REALLY must go and dress properly. What can you be thinking of me?' Beatrice fluttered as she held the door open for them to pass through and tried to hide her ungainly rubber boots beneath the hem of her dressing gown at the same time—a feat which required considerable contortion. With a sideways curious glance at Francesco's darkly handsome, smoothly polished yet formidable bearing, she added on a breathy rush, 'I won't be a moment, and in the meanwhile—Anna, do offer your guest coffee.'

She did no such thing, forcing herself to stand her ground and not be intimidated by her unwelcome guest's aura of remote and chilling dislike.

So he was appalled by the thought that he might have fathered a child on a nobody who came from a family that was seriously down on its uppers? A nobody who was OK for a brief, easily forgotten holiday fling, but as for anything more meaningful or long term—definitely not.

'Well?' Anna sliced into the stinging silence. She lifted her chin to a proud angle, then winced as her baby gave her a hefty kick to remind her of its sturdy existence. Hopefully her unborn child wasn't picking up on the bad vibes between its parents, she thought worriedly.

Automatically she laid a reassuring hand on the mound of her distended stomach—a gesture which Francesco followed with glittering grey eyes.

'I think you know the answer to that,' he stated, his smooth-as-rich-chocolate voice edged with the harshness of acid. 'And before you tell me whether or not I am the father of your child, be warned. The truthfulness of your answer can be verified, or not, by a simple DNA test.'

He meant it, too! Her half-formed plan to name some fictitious guy and then wait for him to accept it with thankfulness and make a smart exit from her life bit the dust.

As that uncomfortable fact sank in, every scrap of colour leached from her face, leaving her features pinched and her deep green eyes enormous. Since his callous betrayal it had been a relatively simple matter to thrust him out of her head and keep him out, using all her will-power and her instinctive need to protect herself and her precious baby from hurt.

But seeing him again, up close and personal—and what could be more personal than making a baby between them?—was doing terrible things to her emotional equilibrium. Swaying on legs that were no longer strong enough to hold her upright, she pressed her fingertips to suddenly aching temples.

At the speed of a jet plane in a hurry two strong hands were steadying her, easing her down on to a hard kitchen chair.

His starkly explosive expletive brought colour back

to her face as he straightened and stood back a pace, his feet planted apart, his fists bunched into the pockets of his beautifully tailored trousers. Towering above her, he looked darkly menacing, impatience stamped onto each impressive feature.

Stiffening her spine, and dredging up the resolve that had served her so well in the past, refusing to be intimidated, Anna clipped, 'There's no need to swear! And, since you ask—yes, you are the father. You were the first and the last!' She huffed in a deep breath, furious with herself for ever fancying herself in love with such a callous, arrogant creature.

He had the information he had come for now. No way was she going to wait and see which way he ran with it. She said firmly, 'Just understand this: I want nothing from you. Ever. No one will ever hear of your relationship to my baby from me. So you might as well go back to your latest squeeze right now!'

Stark silence greeted her outburst. The strong features were taut, pallor showing beneath the warm olive tones of his skin. Anna tried to guess what he was thinking and couldn't even begin to.

'That is the truth?' Narrowed, penetrating eyes received her mute nod of confirmation and Francesco turned, paced over the uneven flags to stare out of the dingy window.

His child. Flesh of his flesh! His heart clenched.

Dark eyes blazed. His child! Sired on a woman as sneaky as a feral cat. Playing the part of a wide-eyed innocent, pretending she didn't know who he was, enchanting him. And all the while plotting and scheming.

Cleverly manipulating a hardened cynic into the sort of lovelorn idiot that a male over the age of fifteen had no right to be!

And priming her ham-fisted father. How else would he have known that a mere million was peanuts to the man his daughter had ensnared, his for the asking?

Her one mistake.

Besotted, he'd been on the point of asking her to be his wife, offering a lifetime of devoted commitment— something he'd set his face against since he'd been in his late teens. Had she told her father to keep his greedy mouth shut, have patience, then, still besotted, he would have married her, showered gifts on her, secured her family's financial future and lived to bitterly regret it once the scales—as they inevitably would have done— had fallen from his eyes and he'd seen the woman he'd believed to be the love of his life for what she really was.

And as for that vehement statement that she wanted nothing from him—he'd sooner believe the moon was made of cheese! Wait until the child was born, and she'd be there with her demands.

At the sound of the door opening Francesco swung round, his mind assessing the problem he faced like a well-oiled machine, emotions relegated to the area of his brain labelled 'non-productive', fit only to be ignored.

'*Signora.*' Beatrice Maybury's slight frame sported a shabby tweed skirt and a twinset of indeterminate colour. Her long plait was wrapped around her head like a coronet. 'Is your husband in? I would like to speak to you both.' And get this mess sorted out once and for all. No arguments.

'I—' About to chide her daughter for her uncharacteristic lack of manners—for just sitting there like a
block of stone, not providing coffee for her guest or
even asking him to sit, by the look of it—she changed
her mind. Recognising authority, troubled by the sudden
and unwelcome feeling that yet another catastrophe was
about to descend on her weary head, she nodded in mute
obedience and fled.

'There's no need to drag my parents into this.' Anna,
petrified by his now brooding silence, was stung into
speech. 'They don't know you from Adam.'

'I have met your father,' Francesco countered on a
splintered bite. 'Remember?'

How could she forget? He'd dropped by, stayed long
enough to scribble that Dear John note, and left to take
up a more exciting project. 'I'm surprised you reminded
me!' she uttered furiously, scornful of the arrogance of
a man who could calmly introduce the subject of his bad
behaviour without turning a hair.

Some of her abundant crinkly hair had fallen down
into her eyes. She swiped it away and stated, 'I'm trying
to explain—if you'll shut up and listen—that they don't
know who the father of my child is. Nobody does. And
as that's the way it's going to stay, you might as well
leave right now!' she tacked on, incensed by the way he
was looking at her—as if she were a boring child having
a tedious tantrum.

Fully expecting him to swing on the heels of his
handmade shoes and make a swift exit, after yet another
deliberately inelegant slice of rudeness, Anna sagged
back against the chair, feeling dizzy and drained, sting-

ingly aware of the spectacular, darkly narrowed eyes that never left her.

'Just go,' she uttered tiredly—and too late, because her father had made an entrance. Or rather, she amended, crept in, closely followed by her anxious-looking mother.

'Well—this is a surprise!' Two paces into the room and her father had pulled himself together, Anna noted. He was trying to smile now, rubbing his big, work-coarsened hands together in a show of bonhomie.

Only a show, though. She could detect apprehension in his eyes, discomfort in that smile. Sympathising, she put it down to understandable bewilderment following on from that first meeting, when this Italian had breezed in and handed him a note to pass on to his daughter, all those months ago.

'We'll sit.'

Typical! Anna fumed. He Who Must Be Obeyed had spoken! Francesco was taking charge, as if they were in his home, not he the uninvited and as far as she was concerned unwanted guest in theirs—as if they were a clutch of dim-witted underlings about to receive a right royal dressing-down.

It annoyed her to see Dad meekly comply, his head bowed, while Mum dithered, making fluttery noises about the provision of coffee, receiving Francesco's softly spoken rejection of the offer. The faint smile that failed to reach his eyes hid impatience. He must think they were all pathetic!

Taking her time about it, Anna stood, swung her chair around to face the table, impeded by her bulk, and eventually sat.

Across the table her father raised his head just a little. He looked anxious, cowed. Anna couldn't understand it. He was usually so good with people—cheerful and outgoing even when speaking to his creditors, full of his plans, so ebullient. Even the most hard-nosed amongst them had—probably reluctantly, given his track record—believed the energetic William Maybury would get over what he blithely termed a 'temporary blip', and come good.

So what was it about the Italian that made him look as if he was trying to shrink into himself? It should be the other way around, with Dad showing Francesco Mastroianni the door because he knew how he'd treated his daughter.

All those months ago she'd found him pottering about in the greenhouse he'd constructed out of old planks and polythene. 'Dad—while I was on holiday I met this fantastic Italian—Francesco. I'm crazy about him! And it's unbelievable, but he feels the same way about me! He's just phoned. He's in England to see me. He'll arrive this evening. But, listen—I'm catering for a WI meeting in the village hall, so I shan't be here. Until I get back make him comfortable, will you? And don't bore him with all that safari park stuff!'

She hadn't been able to hide the fact that she was almost delirious with happiness, that she was fathoms-deep in love for the first time in her life.

So Dad knew what Francesco done, and yet he couldn't raise a single objection to being bossed around in his own home—much less stick up for his wronged daughter and show the black-hearted devil the door!

So it was up to her! Glancing swiftly at the man who had mangled her heart, who was lording it at the head of the table—where else?—she said flatly, 'Well? If you have something to say, get on with it. Some of us have things to do.'

He ignored her. Leaning forward, long fingers laced on the table-top, he addressed her parents. Anna Maybury, who had once meant all the world to him, now meant nothing except as the carrier of his child. Her wishes in this matter were unimportant, not to be considered.

'Your daughter is carrying my child. We met when she was staying on Ischia.' His mobile mouth hardened as his eyes pinned down William's. 'As of course you know. My point is that as the mother of my child your daughter is now my responsibility.'

'Now, look here!' Incensed by that out-dated assumption, the pointed way he was excluding her from the dialogue, Anna tried to cut him down to size, to point out that she was an adult woman and responsible for herself. But she subsided, red-faced, when he turned his attention to her mother, speaking as if her interjection had no more meaning than the irritating buzz of a fly.

'You must agree, Beatrice—I may call you Beatrice?—that it is not wise for a woman in the latter stages of pregnancy to be working hard all hours of the day, rushing around in hot kitchens until late at night?'

He was turning on that devastating charm now, and her mother was lapping it up, Anna noted sickly. Her eyes bright, her mouth curving with pleasure, no doubt she was enjoying the fact that she now knew the identity of the father of her coming grandchild. 'Don't think I haven't said as much myself, dozens of times!' the older woman concurred quickly. 'She works too hard—and it worries me—but she won't listen. She was always stubborn, even as a baby!'

Thanks a bunch! Anna ground her teeth. So, OK, Mum *had* regularly twittered on about the long hours she worked. But, as Anna had pointed out, they needed the money she earned just to survive. No way was she going to repeat that incontrovertible fact and shame her family, highlight their dire poverty, in front of this brute. He was a stranger to financial problems—would have no idea how it felt to have creditors breathing down his neck.

'So, as I am responsible, Anna will stay at my London home until the birth. I shall not be there, except on the odd occasion, but my excellent housekeeper and her husband will look after her every need,' Francesco stated, with a blithe disregard for any opinion *she* might have. 'She will have every possible care, and the rest she needs for the well-being of the child. Arrangements will be made to have her admitted to a private clinic when the time comes. After the birth—' his eyes swept between her parents '—I will organise a meeting between our respective solicitors to set up a trust to provide for the child's upbringing, schooling and general future welfare.'

'That's very decent of you, old chap.'

Her father was finally showing some signs of life! Anna thought furiously. She scrambled to her feet awkwardly, met the brooding, chilling distance of Francesco's steely eyes and finally got to say her piece.

'Save your breath! I'm going nowhere with you. I

don't want your hand-outs—in fact I never want to see or hear from you again!' And she swept out with as much dignity as her swollen feet and a huge stomach could contrive.

She fumed as she hauled herself up the stairs to her room. How dared he come here and lay the law down? Who did he think he was?

Their brief and to him meaningless holiday fling— which he had already insultingly insinuated the he regretted—had resulted in a new life, but that didn't mean he had any rights. He had forfeited any rights when he'd dumped her!

Indignation kept her going until she reached the chilly sanctuary of her bedroom. Her legs feeling like ill-set jelly, she sank down on the bed and wearily reflected on all she had to do this morning.

Retrieve her van. It would have been accomplished by now if the odious Italian hadn't put his oar in. Pick up provisions in the village. Pay Nick's father for the battery. Phone Kitty Bates to clarify the final number of guests expected at her son's birthday party on Tuesday. Get hold of Cissie and make sure she'd be available to help out. Normally Anna wouldn't turn a hair at catering a kids' party solo, but thanks to the traumatic experience of what had happened over the past dozen or so hours every scrap of energy had left her. And even though Cissie boasted that her culinary expertise went no further than putting bread in the toaster, she was a huge help when it came to fetching and carrying.

Shivering, Anna pulled the quilt over her shoulders and bit back tears of emotional exhaustion. Thinking of

Cissie brought back memories she'd tried and mostly succeeded in wiping from her mind. Memories she didn't want. But…

CHAPTER FOUR

PEACE at last! Anna wriggled her hips further into the warm pebbles and stretched out in the sun. Bliss! All she could hear was the hiss and suck of the clear Italian sea against the shore, and the occasional cry of a seabird.

For the first time since she and Cissie had arrived on Ischia three days ago she felt relaxed and comfortably normal.

To be perfectly honest the hotel they were staying in intimidated her. Silly of her—but it *was* horrendously expensive, with every extravagance laid on for its pampered, seriously wealthy guests. Elegance and sybaritic luxury stretched as far as the eye could see—from the choice of four indoor and outdoor pools, to the coffee shops, formal dining areas, bars, designer boutiques, saunas, right down to the complimentary perfumed essences and soaps in the sumptuous bathroom she and Cissie were sharing.

In her cheap clothes, with her deeply regrettable but entirely understandable air of gobsmacked awe, she stuck out like a sore thumb. She knew she did. It was all right for Cissie, the spoiled and treasured only child of wealthy parents. She dovetailed beautifully with the silk and cashmere set. Cissie, with her sleek, waist-length auburn hair and model figure, her lovely clothes, fitted in. She spoke their language and instinctively knew how to mingle with what the Olds called the jet set. She knew how to have discreet fun on the other side of the tracks!

Only this morning, while covering her micro-bikini with a colourful sarong, Cissie had said, 'Lighten up, Anna. Look—there's no need for you to mope around on your own. I could get Aldo to fix you up, no probs. Just say the word.'

'What word? And who's Aldo?' Anna, glancing up from one of the tasteful complimentary glossies, had wanted to know, and had received an eye-rolling response. 'Aldo—he's serviced our table every evening—even *you* must at least have noticed him!'

A slim Sardinian with coal-black eyes and a dazzling smile. 'You're dating *him*?' Anna made the connection, green eyes widening as her best friend grinned at her.

'Nothing serious—as if! Just a fling—holiday fun! You should try it. It doesn't hurt!' She tossed sunscreen, lipgloss and designer sunglasses into a scarlet cotton beach bag. 'He said he could get you fixed up. Now, I simply must fly. I'm meeting him in the village square— it's strictly against the rules for him to socialise with the guests, apparently. Anyway, think about the offer—you could use some fun.'

'No, thanks.' Anna knew she sounded like a repressive ancient aunt as Cissie left the room, but she wasn't interested in meaningless flings—sex for the sake of it. It made her shudder just to think of it.

Call her old-fashioned, but she equated sex with love. And when she fell in love—and one day she hoped to—it would be for keeps.

Muttering to herself, she got into her plain black one-piece, covered up with a silky shawl Cissie had lent her, and escaped the rarefied atmosphere of the hotel, wishing she had never agreed to come.

'Don't you dare say no!' Cissie had ordered. 'It's a freebie. My parents booked the package—flights, transfers, a fab hotel for three weeks. Only Ma went and broke her leg, didn't she? So they can't go. It's all paid for, and you haven't any bookings on the horizon that you've told me about, so there's nothing to stop you coming along and keeping me company—is there?'

At the time the idea of a free holiday had seemed like a good idea—a chance to escape from what was going on at home. Her dad up to his eyes in debt. Again. There was no more land to sell to keep the creditors at bay. She loved her father to pieces, but wished he was more grounded. His latest 'sure-fire winner' of a scheme was to turn the remaining ten acres of long-neglected gardens into a safari park.

'I just need the right backer,' he'd said when he'd expounded this latest money-spinning plan. 'Can't lose!' When had Anna heard that before? 'Fantastic opportunity for the right investor. We'll get hordes of visitors—rake it in!'

Anna had nightmare visions of mangy old lions eating the giraffes or—heaven forbid—the paying visitors, and tried not to have hysterics.

Of course it wouldn't happen. Dad could charm blood

out of a stone, but not even an out-and-out idiot would put money into such a ridiculous venture.

So they would lose Rylands, Mum's family home, and it would kill her. She had a mental vision of them living in a tiny bungalow, with Dad setting up a chicken farm—or even a pig farm—in a pocket-sized back garden and she shuddered again. Mum would pine for the glory days before she'd married, when her parents had been alive and Rylands had been up there with the very best country houses, complete with indoor and outdoor staff and the comfort of a vast portfolio of stocks and shares. A portfolio Dad had decided to double, but had ended up losing the lot.

Now the hoped-for escape looked like being an uncomfortable experience. Especially as Cissie would be occupied with having fun with her waiter during his off-duty times, leaving Anna to kick her heels around in a hotel where she felt as out of place as a pork pie on a silver dish of caviar.

So she wouldn't stay around—the object of curious stares, the Cinderella in the corner.

Skirting the centre of the village, she stopped to buy fruit and bottled water, and trudged up a rocky incline, wandering through little terraced orchards of fig and lemon trees. She clambered over a low stone wall to a stretch of herb-strewn grassland, alive with butterflies and bees, passing a tiny, lone stone building with its windows open to catch the air, revelling in the uncomplicated, unglitzy rightness of the scents of earth and sea, the warmth of the sun and the endless silent blue arch of the sky.

She came to a narrow track that led down to a secluded cove—a rocky, sheltering headland where deep water lapped with Mediterranean indolence and the pebble beach was devoid of glitterati—of anyone at all.

Perfect.

She wriggled again, relaxed and comfy, on her bed of sun-warmed rounded pebbles, closing her eyes, letting the sun lap her exposed limbs. She could spend all her days here, no problem—eat her fruit lunch, cool off in the sea, catch up with her reading and then join up with Cissie for the evening meal and be entertained—or not—by accounts of the slim Sardinian's sexual expertise, while he served them with smiling obsequiousness.

Drifting between sleep and dreaming, Anna drew her brows together as an alien scraping, rattling noise punctuated by the sound of male voices shattered her solitude. Peering between her tangled lashes she registered the intruders. A shortish, plumpish guy dressed in what were obviously designer casuals stood on the shore, while another dragged a dinghy clear of the water.

The other man was something else, she noted, her eyes widening. Bronzed, at least six foot, clad only in a pair of beat-up old denim cut-offs, he had the type of body—honed, toned, lithe and yet power-packed—that her only experience of was cinematic.

Smiling to herself, she closed her eyes again, waiting for them to go some place else. Voices drifted over on the still, sea-scented air. Italian. She couldn't understand a word of what was being said, of course, but the tone of one of them positively vibrated with authority.

The smartly dressed one thanking the boatman for the trip round the bay, or whatever? The other—the dishy boatman?—was definitely more subservient.

Feet crunched through the pebbles, and curiosity raised her lashes one more time. The smartly dressed one was heading for the zig-zagging path that had brought her down here. Good. The hunk would no doubt be following at a respectful distance.

Silence again. Lovely!

Anna closed her eyes against the glare of the sun and relaxed back into blissful solitude—or tried to. But her skin had started to prickle strangely all over, as if she were plugged into the mains. It couldn't be just the effects of the sun, because there was a weird tingling inside her, too.

'You are on private property.'

Wired as she was, the grating, slightly accented tones made her yelp with shock, sit up, and make a grab for Cissie's silk shawl, her picnic in its tatty plastic bag, her old canvas shoes, her book.

Watching her fumble with the plastic carrier, snatch up the fat paperback and drop it, Francesco regretted the harshness of his tone.

Regret was a stranger to him. His decisions, actions, his tone of voice, tailored to specific situations, were always perfectly judged.

But, standing over her while she'd been supposedly unaware of his presence, he'd taken in the voluptuous contours of a body boldly emphasised by the plain black swimwear, the riotous length of silky sugar-blonde hair, the cute face, the sinfully thick and long lashes, dark but tipped with gold, and had felt his mouth curl with cynicism.

They were everywhere. As he knew from long and tedious experience. They played every trick in the book. They were so predictable. So boring. This particular gold-digger, unable to attract his attention, wangle an introduction, whatever, had decided to drape herself on his private beach. And hope.

And yet...

He'd fully expected her to give him the full works. The sultry look, for starters. That was a given. Then raise her arms above her head, move that sensational body explicitly, lave her lips with the tip of a moist pink tongue and make insincere apologies. Huskily.

Seen it all. Heard it all. He prepared to spell out his uninterest. Brutally, if necessary.

And yet she had squawked like a cat with its tail caught in a door. Scrambled for her scattered belongings without grace or dignity. Or pretence at either. And now she was standing, a good head shorter than he was, clutching a bunch of material in front of her. Hiding, not displaying, with a plastic carrier dangling from the hand that wasn't struggling to arrange the fabric for the best possible concealment.

Maybe, just maybe, he'd made a mistake. There was a first time for everything.

Sable brows drew together as she raised her eyes to his. Green and deep enough to drown in. Part-fascinated, and part-ashamed of his cynical assumptions, he watched as hot colour touched her skin in a wave of mortification as she managed chokily, 'I'm sorry. I had no idea this was private property. I'll go.'

Anna had never felt so disorientated in the whole of

her life. That harsh voice, the condemnatory words, had exploded onto her consciousness when she had believed herself alone. It had really spooked her. So much so that an automatic reflex action had had her practically leaping to her feet and floundering around for her scattered belongs, adrenaline pumping.

And now, actually looking at the guy, she felt a slow, hot fizzle start up inside her. Instinctive—because he really was something else. Too much. Too male, too bronzed, too knock-'em-dead-handsome, with that tousled silky black hair, penetrating smoke-grey eyes, aristocratic nose, razor-sharp cheekbones and a mouth so sensual it made her knees go weak and her breath bunch in her throat.

And as for that physique…

Anna swallowed thickly and dipped her head, ashamed of the heated colour that was burning her face. She turned to go, stumbled, was stayed by a strong, long-fingered hand on her arm. She trembled with the wicked intensity of the sensations that skittered through her entire body at the sizzling contact

'There's no need to go.'

'But you said—' Her voice sounded like a frog with a sore throat. She clamped her mouth shut and shivered again, despite the heat of the sun.

'I know what I said.'

He sounded gently amused now—an improvement on that authoritative bite. Anna flicked a sideways glance, her eyes colliding with the broad expanse of his perfectly honed, bronzed torso, with the 'gold' chain round his neck that left telltale green marks where it touched his so-touchable satin-smooth skin.

No rich playboy, then! No playboy worth the name would be seen dead wearing something that cheap and nasty! Just ordinary—like her! If such a charismatic specimen could ever be classed as ordinary! Emboldened, she raised her eyes, met his. Warm, smoky grey with dancing silver lights. Smiling eyes now.

'But I happen to know the owner is on holiday, and I'm sure he wouldn't want your day to be spoiled.'

Francesco released her arm. He'd made a mistake. Now he had to make amends. In his comprehensive experience of gold-diggers they never blushed. Wouldn't know how. Bold-faced to a woman. As his mother had been. Not content with bleeding his blinkered father dry, she'd broken his heart when she'd taken off with a far better financial prospect after the reality that the cash was drying up had hit.

Not willing to go there, he turned his attention back to the unwitting trespasser, still pink-cheeked and clearly uncomfortable. His sensual mouth quirked. 'I take it you prefer solitude to crowded beaches?'

Anna expelled a long breath and found herself smiling and nodding. Rather inanely, she was afraid.

True, this guy had given her a real fright to begin with—had made her want to scurry for cover before the heavy mob moved in to escort her from someone's private property. But now he seemed nice and ordinary—no, she amended, extraordinary. And despite that initial chilling note of authority he was actually being really gentle as he removed the shawl from her slackened fingers, then the carrier, dropped them to one side and invited, 'Please make yourself comfortable again. Enjoy the day.'

She had a spectacular body. Lush curves, a too-enticing cleavage, a waist he could span with both hands with room to spare. His brow furrowed. 'Look, don't take this personally, but there are some pretty dodgy characters around. A lone attractive woman could be at risk.'

'Attractive' didn't cut it. She was lovely—hair, face and body to die for. Annoyingly, he felt something kick hard in his loins. *Basta!* That was not what he wanted. The women he bedded, when he could be bothered to take up the invitation, knew the score. He had never touched a wide-eyed innocent, and every-thing about the trespasser told him she was exactly that. Which was why he had suddenly become protec-tive, he rationalised. The thought of one of the young men on the prowl latching on to her, all sweet words and empty promises, seducing her, made him meta-phorically clench his fists.

But she'd be safe here. The local Lotharios knew better than to trespass on his property, and visitors tended, sheep-like, to herd together on the public beaches, and in the cafés and shopping areas.

Anna was tempted to take him at his word. She craved solitude, the opportunity to laze around and relax, to clear her head of worries about what was happening back home. It was the only way she could hope to return to England refreshed and able to face the problems, somehow cope with them.

'You're sure the owner—whoever—wouldn't mind?' she pressed. 'You're not just saying that?' She didn't want bother. Bother didn't gel with the bliss of a long unwinding session on a sun-soaked deserted beach.

A slow smile curved his sensual mouth. 'You have my word. I know the owner very well.'

The boat, beached on the shore, seemed to bear this out. He obviously must have permission to use the cove. 'Right. Thanks.' Anna's smile was sunny as she arranged herself back in the comfy nest she'd made in the pebbles, then faded as she saw he was on the point of leaving.

She didn't want him to go. Not giving herself time to analyse how strange that was, she dipped her hand into the carrier and held out a couple of plump peaches. 'Have one? Rowing a boat must be thirsty work.'

There'd been no sound of an engine. Maybe he couldn't afford an outboard? It was the *faux* gold chain that did it, she decided, as her heart flipped. It made her feel all mushy inside. Sort of achingly protective—like a mother who saw a kid of hers trying to keep up with the big boys and failing because he had no street cred. He was unaware that the flashy gold chain left green stains on his skin which shouted out *Brass!* It was crazy, because in every other respect this hunk had everything. Plus.

'*Grazie.*' Mildly surprised at himself, Francesco took a peach and found himself wondering if her skin felt the same—soft, firm, warmly seductive. Just humouring her, he excused himself, and sank down beside her. 'You are English? You are staying here on the island?' he asked.

Nodding her affirmative, peach juice dribbling down her chin, Anna named the hotel and saw his spectacular eyes narrow. She felt immediately uncomfortable.

Being a local, he would know that it cost an arm and a leg just to walk through the doors.

She was about to launch into an explanation of how

she came to be staying there when he said, in a roughened undertone, '*Madre di Dio!* You remind me!' He was on his feet, smiling down at her. 'My—some people are waiting there for me to give them a tour of the island. *Scusi*—' He was walking away, sunlight glistening on those wide bronzed shoulders. 'Enjoy your days here, *signorina*.'

She dreamt of him that night. Which was ridiculous. And woke feeling wired which was quite unlike her normally pragmatic self.

Should she go to the private cove again? Or not?

Would he put in an appearance?

Her tummy flipped alarmingly.

He'd need to collect his boat if he'd found punters wanting a trip out to sea. On the other hand he might again be booked as tour guide and not need to go anywhere near the cove.

Over dinner last night, while Cissie had been regaling her with how she and Aldo had spent the day—going some place on the back of his motor scooter—she hadn't been listening properly at all really. Too busy looking at the other diners and wondering which group had hired the gorgeous Italian to show them round the island.

How stupid was that?

She didn't even know his name.

If they passed in the street he wouldn't recognise her, so she had to stop thinking like a teenager in the throes of a silly crush!

She prodded Cissie awake when Room Service arrived with their breakfast. 'Get up!'

Bleary eyes peered through a tangle of rich auburn hair. 'Why the hurry? Where's the fire?'

No hurry. The whole day and what to do with it stretched out before her. And the fire was here, right inside her, a sort of fiery fever.

'It's another lovely day,' she said inanely, crossing to the side table and pouring coffee into two wide bowls. Passing one to Cissie, forcing her to sit up to take it, ignoring her grumbles, she asked, half hoping the answer would be negative, 'Are you seeing Aldo today?'

If she wasn't then the poser of whether to take off to the cove again would be answered—the decision taken out of her hands. She and Cissie would spend the day sightseeing, lounging by one of the pools—doing nothing in particular except keeping each other company.

'You bet—weren't you listening? I told you over dinner last night, didn't I? His aunt runs a *pensione*—he lives with her during the season—and he's got this room. Said he'd make lunch for me.' The prospect of the day ahead brightened Cissie's eyes as she dumped her coffee bowl on the night-table and swung her endless legs out of bed, heading for the shower.

Shaking her head, a wry smile on her soft mouth, Anna drank her coffee. Cissie's morals were bang up-to-date, twenty-first-century stuff. While she—well, she was so old-fashioned she was in danger of turning into a laughing stock.

So what was she doing, scrambling down to the private cove, her heart banging as if it wanted to jump out of her body, her eyes straining to see if the little row-boat was still beached on the shore?

It was.

Slowing her descent, even more jittery inside, she felt her legs like wobbly jelly. Weak-kneed at the sight of a very ordinary boat!

How sad was that?

Well, the guy was fascinating. No question about that. And people were always fascinated by the exotic, weren't they? And she was no different. It wasn't as if she was wanting to have sex with him. Perish the thought! Her face burned at the very idea. She wasn't Cissie. She was practical, sensible, and very, very moral!

To prove it, she thrust him out of her mind and, not in the mood to lounge around in the sun—because she just knew she'd start thinking about him again—headed over the beach to cool off in the sea…

Sorted. Methodically, efficiently sorted. Without giving himself time to think of anything beyond the practical. Alerting his housekeeper to the imminent arrival of a long-stay house guest. Paying a patiently waiting Nick Whoever for the battery, his time and his trouble. Stopping the objection he saw coming from the younger man with a single downward slash of his hand. Arranging for the return of the van to Rylands. Making his excuses to his cousin, ditto the sex-on-legs offering. And leaving.

The future mother of his child would be waiting. A concise phone call to her mother—Beatrice, nice lady—had elicited her agreement that, yes, Anna would be packed and waiting.

There'd been an unspoken yet firm 'or else' about that

agreement. Despite her wispy appearance there was steel in that backbone. He approved of that. And as for the father—well, he'd seemed happy enough with the financial arrangement. He'd been uncomfortable throughout the entire interview, which pointed to the undeniable fact that Anna had put him up to that attempt to squeeze a sizeable amount of money from her besotted lover. Had she promised that it would be a dead cert?

And as for Sweet Anna—definitely cranky. Spluttering about not wanting anything from him. A plain case of saying one thing and meaning another. Grouchy because perhaps she'd expected, eventually, a bigger pay-off?

Or marriage? His eyes narrowed to dark slits as his jaw clenched. A snowflake in hell just about summed up the chances of that!

Navel-gazing, pulling out buried emotions and putting them under a microscope wasn't his style. What was done was done. Lesson learned. Move on.

Yet as he eased the Ferrari out onto the lane the hypnotic rhythm of the windscreen wipers as they cleared the intermittent rain took him back to where he didn't want to be.

That morning.

He'd seen her walk past his holiday hideaway. The Hovel, his sister called it. The private place he went to when he wanted to unwind, to forget he was one of the wealthiest men in Italy with all the pressures, responsibilities and constant calls on his time that went with that status. The place where interruptions were forbidden.

A rule that had been broken for the first time the day before, when his senior aide had arrived nervously bleating about a problem with the Christou takeover, needing his decision. A decision had been made while rowing out to drop lobster pots on the other side of the headland—a trip not relished by his green-gilled employee. Returning to the cove, he'd found his dishy little trespasser, dismissed the older man and then headed off to tell her to take her scheming little self off his property. A mistake. And he'd ended up assuring her she would be welcome any time, hoping he hadn't scared her off for good.

Obviously he hadn't. That had made him feel good. He wasn't used to making mistakes.

That morning she'd worn her glorious hair piled precariously on top of her white-gold head. Tendrils already escaping. The silky fabric thing had been tied around her waist, fluttering unevenly around her shapely calves, and underneath she'd worn the same black swimsuit as before, which caressed her magnificent breasts like a lover's touch.

Did she realise how gorgeous she was? He had wondered. From their brief encounter yesterday he didn't think so. He would put money on her being that rare creature, a woman in—what?—her early twenties, at a guess, who was innocent, unaware.

After ten minutes he had followed her, telling himself he was merely going to assure her, yet again, that it was OK for her to use the cove. Neglecting, of course to tell her he owned it—owned most of the land on this magical corner of the island, plus the hotel where she was staying.

She had been swimming. A sedate breaststroke.

Without questioning the wisdom of what he was doing he had joined her, his racing crawl powerful, and he had enjoyed the flash of surprise in those wide sea-green eyes before a dazzling smile of recognition had lit her water-spangled lovely face.

From then on, without knowing it, he'd been hooked. By her warmth, her beauty, the artlessness that had made his heart melt. Such a thing had never happened to him before, so he'd had no idea what was happening. Had only known that he didn't want the morning to end. Lazy conversation beneath the lazy sun. Abstract, nothing personal apart from the exchange of names. He had watched, narrow-eyed, for the glitter of recognition as he told her his name—a name regularly turning up in frivolous gossip columns or, more soberly, in the international financial pages in London, where he was based for months at a time.

Nothing. She'd had no idea who he was! He had felt like a six-year-old on Christmas morning. And the feeling had been great!

'Yesterday you gave me fruit. Today I will give you pasta. I will cook for you.' Surprised by that invitation, he waited for her reaction. His hideaway was inviolate, private to him, but her company delighted him and he wasn't about to lose it. How serious was that?

The eyes that had been smiling for him were veiled by the intriguing sweep of her lashes. Finally her glorious hair was down, pale silky tendrils parting over her sun-kissed shoulders, a stray corkscrew lying against a cleavage that was more tempting than she could know.

'I have no ulterior motive,' he vowed softly, guessing

she needed that reassurance. Female English tourists were easy game, or so he'd heard. She wasn't like that. 'Merely I enjoy your company.' That was true, wasn't it?

He wasn't sure at all when he reached out his hand to tip her chin, to let his eyes meet hers and impress upon her his trustworthy intentions. The small chin beneath his fingers, the delicacy of bone beneath the soft skin, the visceral shock of registering that this was the first time he'd touched her, the brilliance of the eyes that met his in unquestioning trust, the way those luscious lips parted as she said, 'I'd like that,' almost proved his undoing.

From then on the outcome was inevitable. Starting with the delight she took in his tiny stone cottage. 'This is just perfect! Do you live here all the time?'

'Not all the time,' he prevaricated, feeling like a cad when she nodded solemnly.

'No, I guess work's hard to find out of season. No call for a tour guide if there are no tourists. You'd have to go to the mainland to find work. But, hey! It must be wonderful to know you've got this place to come back to in the spring.'

Her smile dazzled him. So much so he almost came clean there and then. Selfishly, he supposed, he did no such thing. It was fantastic to find a woman who enjoyed his company, liked him for the man he was rather than his bank balance.

More than liked him? A beat of anticipation slammed through his body at the way that soft veil of colour stole into her cheeks whenever their eyes met. Her breath quickened, and the rise and fall of those magnificent breasts beneath the straining black fabric—

His gruff apologies for their scratch meal, a simple salad and pasta, had brought forth, 'It's delicious! The herby sauce is to die for! And I cook for a living—private dinner parties and stuff—so I should know! Of course bookings slow to a standstill during the summer holiday period, which is why I was able to take a break.'

Cue to delve more deeply into her life, her background. He let it go. The only important thing was that somehow, almost without him knowing it, she had become the most entrancing female on the planet.

Inevitable.

Quite how it happened that first time he would never know. One minute she was on the point of leaving—thanking him, smiling for him, gathering the bits and pieces she seemed unable to go anywhere without—the next his hands were touching her. Her warm silky shoulders. And her hands touched him. Splayed out against his chest, where his heart was beating a furious tattoo.

And then frenzy. A white heat explosion inside his head as he kissed her. Her soft mouth opening for him as their bodies meshed. Her fractured moan of surrender as her hips tilted to meet his urgent arousal. And he knew he was entering paradise as somehow they took the stairs, slowly, one by one, entwined, breath straining, reaching the sanctuary of his bed where he found true heaven, found love, for the first time in his life.

That she had been a virgin, that no thought of using protection had entered his head, he'd accepted without a single qualm. He had found the woman he wanted to spend the rest of his life with.

CHAPTER FIVE

IT WAS well into the afternoon—dull and rainy now, which suited her mood perfectly—when Anna heard the growl of Francesco's arrival. No doubt about it. Trust him to drive that in-your-face piece of costly ego-massaging machinery!

Her stomach feeling like a lead balloon, she picked up her bag of toiletries and followed her father as he carried her suitcase downstairs. She'd been left alone until lunchtime—alone with all that counter-productive backwards-peering stuff—when Mum had walked into her bedroom.

'Time to stop sulking. Lunch first, then you must pack. Francesco will pick you up at around four.'

So when had Mum decided to put on the first brisk act of her life? It would have been a subject of amazement—like watching a house mouse turn round and punch the cat on its nose—if it hadn't been so annoying.

'If you imagine I'm going anywhere with him, you've got rocks in your head!'

'Now, don't be childish! It's not like you, Anna. I know this morning's been a shock—for all of us—but you must have thought he was special once. He is the father of your baby, after all.'

Not something she wanted remotely to be reminded of!

'Your father and I had a long chat with him after you walked out in a huff. He's taking his responsibilities seriously, Anna. He's determined that you have a complete rest before the birth—he does have a vested interest in the well-being of his child, after all—and in that I agree with him entirely. I've been telling you for weeks that running yourself ragged can't be good for you or your baby. In my opinion, and your father's, he's a man of integrity.'

He wouldn't know integrity from a hole in the street!

'He assured us that you would have the best care possible, and that a top-flight obstetrician would be privately engaged at his expense—all the things it would be impossible for us to provide. And to set our minds at rest he'll send a car and driver to pick your father and me up tomorrow, so that we can stay with you for a couple of days and satisfy ourselves that all is as it should be. And while we're there with you he'll have his lawyer draw up some document or other, stating the amount that will be paid into your account each month to provide for the maintenance of the child, which is right and proper. So many unmarried fathers shirk their responsibility.'

Give the devil his due, he knew how to press all the right buttons! He had obviously got her parents right on side. There was no earthly use explaining how he had made a fool of her and then betrayed her. It would only make her folks even more determined to see that he paid for his bad behaviour.

But was she to have no input at all? It was her baby, her body. She was not about to be packed up like a parcel, picked up and plonked down some place she didn't want to be. So—

'Very neat. Very businesslike. But, tell me, how are you and Dad going to manage without my financial contributions?' Not huge, not even middleweight, but they kept the wolf from the door. It wasn't something she had ever rubbed their noses in, but desperate times called for desperate measures.

'That's all taken care of. He's given your father a cheque to cover your loss of income for the next six months. A very generous one, too, if I may say so.'

After more of the same Anna had simply thrown in the towel. Truth was, she had been feeling exhausted for weeks, putting a brave face on her situation and trying not to worry about her baby's well-being. And the unprecedented spat with her mother had left her feeling like yesterday's used teabag.

Taking it easy for the next few weeks could only benefit her unborn child, and she had to admit that she would do almost anything to feel less exhausted and anxious about the prospect of single parenthood. It would be achievable, just about—if Francesco lived up to what he'd said about not being around much himself.

Even so, she wasn't going to give him the satisfaction of letting him know how completely she'd caved in. So she straightened her drooping spine and gave him her coldest glare when she came face to face with him in the vast, echoing hall.

He looked as spectacular as ever, drat him! A

superbly tailored dark grey silk and mohair suit draped those wide shoulders, long legs and narrow hips. It was a perfectly groomed specimen—from his expertly styled dark hair to the pristine white shirt that emphasised the rich olive tones of his skin and the shadowing on his tough jawline. The cool silver eyes were partly veiled by long thick lashes as he registered her appearance, and her steps faltered at the totally unwanted reminder that she knew, intimately, every magnificent inch of that unfairly superb body.

A sting of sexual excitement surged through her, unwelcome and out-of-place, and had her walking out of the open main door, oblivious to the burblings and twitterings of her respective parents. She let herself into his car, with some difficulty because of her bulk, and waited.

The moment he joined her, not even bothering to look at her, much less speak, she levelled at him, 'I'm doing this under protest. As long as you understand that.'

'Really?' He fired the ignition. His classically handsome profile was as arid as his tone had been. 'Protesting about what? The financial arrangements? Your parents seemed satisfied.'

'Well, they would be.' Anna slumped back into her seat as the sleek machine nosed out onto the narrow lane. He would be paying maintenance for his child, and that, in their eyes, would be right and proper. Quite enough. But for her... 'It's not enough.' Unconsciously she voiced her thoughts aloud, uselessly wishing her unborn child could have a proper father—one who loved them both, was there for them on a permanent basis, one who didn't think that money was the only thing that counted.

'I rather thought not.' His tone was dry as dust. 'But there's no more on offer. I made a mistake, and I accept the responsibility that goes with it. I will support the child financially and that's my final offer.'

Too full of loathing to speak, Anna screwed her hands into fists and stared unseeingly through the windscreen, hating him so much she felt physically sick. Vilely, he'd taken it as read that she'd meant she wanted more of his wretched money!

And 'a mistake'! How demeaning was that? He was cynically referring to that first time. When he'd been too overcome by lust to give a thought to contraception, and she'd been too overwhelmed by the awesome sensation of falling in love for the first time in her life to even think of repercussions.

That had been the mistake he now regretted. Hadn't repeated. Oh, no! He'd reined in that animal lust sufficiently to use protection after that.

And his protestations of love had only been made to make sure that he was able to come back for more of the same while she was on the island. Fervent protestations that had fooled her into believing that she had gone to heaven.

Lying louse!

And to think that she had actually been formulating plans to join him in Italy—maybe start a small restaurant together, live hand-to-mouth if necessary. How foolish had that been? That had been before she'd discovered what he'd so carefully hidden—that he was mega-rich. Concealing it from her because he was afraid that she might try to get her hands on some of his wealth!

So let him go on thinking she was miffed because the future maintenance for their child wasn't nearly enough for her. No way would she make an even bigger fool of herself in his eyes and confess that when that unguarded comment had slipped out she'd been wistfully thinking of a proper family—mother, father and child, all loving and caring for each other, all that soppy happy-ever-after stuff! He would laugh until his head fell off!

Men like him—liars and cheats—automatically thought the worst of everyone else. It was beyond a simple, straightforward soul like her to try to change that entrenched view of humankind. So she wouldn't waste her breath trying.

'You need to change your attitude,' he spelt out in a voice as cold as ice. 'You gave it your best shot, but you failed. Accept it and stop acting like a spoiled child who's found out it can't have everything it wants. While you're staying at my London home you will treat my housekeeper Peggy Powell and her husband Arnold with the respect they deserve. I expect to see no more rude and objectionable behaviour.' He gave her a withering glance. 'You can be sweet and charming when you want to be—as I know to my cost.'

Francesco's brow clenched ferociously as he belatedly registered that slip of the tongue. Where had that come from? As far as he was concerned the past was dead—another country he could walk away from and forget—so why refer to it? Yet another mistake, he recognised savagely. Around her he was making too many of them, he castigated.

Then a small explosion came from his side, as she

picked up and repeated, '*To your cost?* That's rich! I doubt you'll even notice the money you pay out for our baby!'

'Our baby.' When had she started bracketing them together as parents? Anna thought. When she'd believed his lies about loving her more than his life she would have joyously accepted that bond, believing they had a future together. Knowing how foolishly gullible she'd been and how much he'd hurt her lowered her even more than his earlier holier-than-thou diatribe had infuriated her.

Receiving that explosive little speech, Francesco let his lean hands relax on the steering wheel. So he hadn't betrayed the hurt she'd dished out, as he'd feared. She'd discounted the emotional cost. It probably hadn't entered her mind. She had homed in on the financial aspect—as she and others of her kind always would.

The relief Anna felt when they finally reached their destination, after a silent journey punctuated only by those early acrimonious exchanges, was tempered by a serious butterfly attack.

She might have known that his home would be an elegant Regency townhouse in a quiet London square, positively oozing discreet wealth and power, but it wasn't that which was making her feel so jittery.

Would the Powells, into whose care she was apparently to be given, treat her like a stray cat their employer had misguidedly picked up from the gutter? Or like a fallen woman, ditto?

In either event she wouldn't be able to stand it, and would be on the first train back home!

'Come.' Impatience spiked the command as Francesco swept past her, carrying her suitcase, and Anna, her soft mouth mutinous, followed. So she was an encumbrance he couldn't wait to rid himself of? So what else was new? It didn't hurt—how could it, when she wanted to see the back of him too?—so why did she suddenly want to cry her eyes out?

The weird hormonal chaos of pregnancy, she sensibly assured herself, blinking the moisture from her eyes as she watched the imposing glossy black-painted door swing open. It revealed a tiny woman wearing a starchy black dress, her iron-grey hair cut as short as a boy's, but the wideness of her greeting smile negated the severities of her appearance.

'Peggy, I'm sorry I'm late. A few hold-ups, I'm afraid.'

His voice was warm, as it once had been for her, and his arm lay easily across his housekeeper's spare shoulders. Anna felt the chill of exclusion shiver through her bones.

He turned, 'Peggy, meet Anna Maybury. As I told you, she is in need of rest and relaxation, and I look to you to provide it.'

She felt quite horribly embarrassed, expecting a sniffy flicker of those button eyes in her direction, and almost sagged with relief when she found herself on the receiving end of a generously warm smile. 'I shall enjoy that! Come in, Anna, do. I've kept dinner back, but I expect you'll want to freshen up first. I'll show you to your room, my dear. Arnold!'

As if her voice had brought him into being, a man as large as his wife was small silently appeared, smiling a greeting for Anna, taking her suitcase from his employer and heading for the imposing staircase.

'Anna will eat in her room when she's settled,' Francesco said. 'I'll just take a sandwich and coffee in my study. I'm leaving for the States first thing in the morning, and I have a raft of work to get through before then. And, Peggy, don't bother packing for me. I'll see to it.'

Not a word for her. Not one, Anna noted as he walked away. She didn't know whether to feel belittled, hurt, or just plain relieved. But what had she expected? A fond farewell? A promise to look in on her later to make sure she was comfortable in strange surroundings, had everything she wanted?

Oh, get real! she grumped at herself as she accepted Peggy's invitation to follow her. This was a man who mightily disliked the situation he found himself in, but who, to prevent any future claims on his wealth, was making sure he could never be accused of shirking his responsibilities regarding the well-being of mother and child. He'd be having some hotshot lawyer draw up a watertight document spelling out exactly what she and the child would be entitled to and what they were not.

Fact.

So him ignoring her existence—leaving for the States and probably not coming near his London home again until he heard from the Powells that his son or daughter had arrived and that mother and child were back at Rylands—was a relief, she assured herself as, feeling impossibly drained, she followed where Peggy led. Being around him was too emotionally traumatic. So his absence would be considerably more beneficial than his presence.

* * *

A week to go—give or take! A quiver of excitement started in the region of her heart and shot down to her toes. Soon she would hold her baby in her arms.

The garden at the rear of the house was a surprising green and floriferous oasis of tranquillity in the heart of the restless city. Arnold looked after it beautifully, and Anna liked to help where she could—dead-heading, mostly, it being the only task the older man thought suitable for a heavily pregnant lady!

She liked to breakfast on the terrace when the weather was fine, and this morning it was spectacularly beautiful.

'Did you sleep well?' Peggy asked as she transferred tea things, orange juice and toast from the tray she carried to the teak table.

'On and off.' Anna smiled. This late in her pregnancy it was almost impossible to get comfortable in bed.

'Not long now.' The tray emptied, the housekeeper held it against her board-flat bosom. 'Sir Willoughby-Burne is very pleased with you, and you'll remember what he said, won't you?'

'That I must tell you the moment the contractions start and Arnold will drive me to the clinic,' she trotted out robotically. Then, catching Peggy's slight frown, she smiled. 'Sorry—of course I'll remember!' She had endured endless tests and proddings at the elegantly urbane obstetrician's instigation—Sir Willoughby-Burne didn't believe in half measures—and had been given a guided tour round a clinic that had left her speechless, because it seemed more like a five-star hotel than a maternity hospital. Which all went to verify the fact that Francesco was sparing no expense in the execution of his duties—as he saw them.

Tears momentarily blinded her as Peggy took her leave. Her baby's father should be the one she went to when the baby decided to make an appearance. He should be the one to drive her to hospital! To stay with her!

Despising herself for that piece of downright mawkishness, she reached for the glass of orange juice. Her teeth chattered against the rim. She put it down again. What was the matter with her? Of course Peggy and Arnold would be the ones she would turn to. Ever since she'd arrived here they'd looked after her, treated her like a cross between a cherished daughter and a valued house guest. While The Louse hadn't shown his face—hadn't even made contact with her. He had only phoned occasionally, apparently, for a progress report from his housekeeper—largely, Anna suspected, to check that she wasn't being 'rude and objectionable'!

Her hand shaking, she poured tea into the pretty china cup.

'Aren't you going to eat your toast?' he said.

The teapot hit the table-top with a clatter. Her breath left her. Lungs starved of oxygen, she twisted round. How long had he been standing there, at the open French windows, watching her? And why did he look so lethally attractive?

A treacherous leap of sexual excitement assaulted her, destroying what was left of her self-esteem. How could her body react that way to the man who had so callously set out to seduce her, make her fall so deeply in love with him she had been in danger of drowning, and then cold-bloodedly dump her?

Riven by emotions she couldn't begin to name, she watched him walk to where she was sitting, her heart-beats going crazy. That glossy dark head, so proudly held, the smoky and unreadable eyes. The impeccable suiting enhancing those broad shoulders, narrow hips and long powerful legs. So effortlessly elegant, so impossibly remote.

But he hadn't always been remote. Angrily, she shook her head. She wouldn't let herself be reminded of the way it had once been, because it had been a lie as far as he was concerned.

A tanned, strongly lean hand pulled out a chair. He sat. 'You don't want me to join you. You shake your head at me.'

'I can't stop you.' She didn't meet his eyes. She couldn't. Her only defence against this awful awareness of his shocking sexuality and the effect it was having on her had to be a façade of dull indifference.

'True.'

He had the gall to sound amused! Anna swiped the top off her egg as if she were biting his head off his shoulders, and almost choked on the first mouthful as he drawled, 'I see your temper hasn't improved. But your appearance has. You look much better—less exhausted. And beautiful, of course.'

'Yeah. Right.' Sarky monster! 'Beautiful' applied to leggy model-types. She could understand that. To wallowing lumps—no way! Giving up all pretence at eating, she glared at him. 'Why are you here?'

'It is my home. Or one of them. And I wanted to know if you'd signed that agreement—if your parents were satisfied that the child's future security was adequately provided for.'

'Perfectly adequately,' she responded, unable to stop a reminiscent grin flickering across her piquant features. And if he thought she looked like the cat that had got at the cream, tough. He would find out soon enough that she'd taken one look at the monthly payment proposed and had had that hotshot lawyer reduce the amount by three-quarters before she agreed to sign. She wanted the security of knowing that if her business failed or even faltered her child's basic needs would be provided for. She didn't want to live in the lap of luxury at his expense!

'Good.' His tone was hard, and he made a visible effort to rein back the cynical comment that he was glad to learn that she'd finally decided to cut her losses and settle for what she could get out of him. Out of deference to her condition he said, 'And did your parents enjoy their brief stay here?'

Anna nodded. She wasn't going to go into that. The way her mother had positively drooled over his beautiful home, over the valuable paintings and lovely antiques—doubtless recalling the things that had once graced Rylands and had had to be sold to repay debts or finance some hare-brained scheme of her father's. Or the way she'd said, 'It's sad, but we have to face it. We can't expect Francesco to do the decent thing and marry you. A man in his position will have the pick of all the independently wealthy society beauties around.'

As Francesco gazed at her profile, at the suddenly vulnerable droop of her mouth, her original question came back to badger him. If he was truthful, he didn't know why he was here. His firm intention had been to steer clear until he received news from Peggy that she had been delivered of the child and that, after a suitable interval, was being driven back to Rylands and the care of her parents. At which point, knowing that he had fulfilled his responsibilities in respect of financial support, he would forget he'd ever met her.

But something unknown had driven him to alter his plans. To be with her for the birth? To support and comfort her? No way! His body tensed in utter repudiation of that idiotic notion.

To satisfy himself that everything was going well because the child she was carrying was his and he needed to know—despite the reassuring updates he'd had from his housekeeper—that she had lost that frightening look of bone-deep tiredness? Quite possibly. More than likely, in fact. Certainly much nearer the truth than that other insane thought. Because he wasn't heartless. Or not completely.

Satisfied with that explanation for his unannounced visit, he relaxed, veiled his eyes. Watched her.

It was true, despite her patent disbelief. She was beautiful. All that glorious silky pale hair framing her lovely face, that peachy skin glowing with health now, the huge sparkling deep green eyes and gold-tipped lashes—even her swollen body had a beauty that touched him deeply. His eyes welded to the sinful curve of that luscious pink mouth—the only feature that belied the impression of angelic innocence, an innocence designed to capture the unwary.

Desire surged through him and he briefly closed his eyes, his teeth clenching. *Dio mio!* He was no longer unwary! He knew what she was—a scheming, avaricious witch, clever enough to use an act of unworldly innocence to get to him. Unlike the other women who threw themselves at him, dollar signs in neon lights deep in their money-grubbing eyes, recognisable at a hundred paces.

When he looked at her again his eyes were cold. 'Finish your breakfast.' Abruptly pushing back his chair, he walked away.

The birth couldn't come soon enough. One of his security men would be delegated to keep a watching brief on the welfare of the child and report back to him. But he need never to have anything to do with the mother again.

The contractions were ten minutes apart. Anna, sitting on the edge of her bed, pleated her brow. Could a first baby come a week early? And how could you tell if they were false labour pains?

Everything she'd been told at the antenatal clinic flew out of her head. She pushed her feet into her slippers, reached her shabby old mac from the massive wardrobe and grabbed the small case that had been packed for days. Dithering about whether or not she should wake Peggy and Arnold was senseless. They wouldn't hold it against her if it was a false alarm.

But out in the dimly lit corridor a contraction so strong it sent her staggering with shock into a delicate table, sending the china bowl of pot-pourri flying, had her deciding that this was happening. This was real.

Almost immediately two doors opened. Francesco was already pulling on a pair of dark trousers, hopping on one leg, his soft black hair a rumpled tangle, and Peggy was pushing her arms into a quilted housecoat.

'I'll take her, Peggy. Go back to bed.' One look at Anna, an awful old coat over a voluminous cotton night-dress, her smooth brow glistening with beads of sweat, told him all he needed to know. To his housekeeper's protest he said, 'It will save time,' and to Anna, 'Stay there. I'll fetch the car.'

Beyond caring who escorted her, Anna watched him fly down the stairs, pulling a dark blue cashmere sweater over his head as he went, and slowly followed, Peggy's hand on her elbow. The anxious father-to-be. A nice thought, but thoroughly erroneous. He just didn't fancy the idea of her giving birth on the priceless hall carpet.

'He's so perfect!' Anna raised love-drenched eyes from her beautiful baby to his father, past wrongs forgotten in this moment of pure joy.

To her eternal surprise and gratitude Francesco hadn't left her side for one moment, encouraging her, praising her, bossing the medical team as if he knew what she needed and they didn't, holding her hand and mopping her brow. So he had earned this moment of blissful truce.

Awestruck, Francesco touched his newborn son's velvety cheek, saw the big, slightly unfocussed eyes open and meet his, and fell irretrievably in love.

His son. Flesh of his flesh. A lump rose painfully in his throat. How could he ever, for one single moment, have believed he could remain at a distance, never see this tiny miracle's first smile, hear his first word, watch him take his first steps, guide him through his childhood and adolescence, see him safely to manhood?

Madre di Dio! He must have been out of his mind if he'd ever imagined he could give his child up.

He wasn't like his father. He would die before he closed his heart to his son just because his son's mother was a deceitful, avaricious witch!

'I will go and phone the good news through to your parents,' he excused himself gruffly, leaving his precious new son with a wrench, his mind already formulating hard and fast rules for the future.

CHAPTER SIX

THREE weeks later Anna replaced the receiver on its wall mount in the showcase kitchen. She'd been helping Peggy prepare lunch when the call had come through.

'Not bad news?' Peggy looked up from the chopping board, her head tipped to one side.

'Not good.' Dismay made her voice thin. 'My mother—it seems our family home is to be sold.'

Mum had sounded so flat as she'd broken the news. 'I've finally got your father to agree that selling up here is the only way to pay off all those debts. He dug his heels in, of course—it's taken me weeks to persuade him, and I hated having to argue with him, but it had to be done. There'll be nothing left over—what the bank doesn't take, the other creditors will. He'll have to keep that labouring job on, unfortunately, and I'll try to find something, too. We'll have to rent a couple of rooms somewhere. They call it downsizing, don't they?'

Her attempt at breezy humour had brought tears to Anna's eyes, but she'd blinked them away as she listened.

'If you hadn't been so awkward over Francesco's monthly allowance you could easily have afforded to rent a nice cottage for you and little Sholto. You'll have to explain your new circumstances and ask for the full amount to be reinstated.'

Anna hadn't argued with that unwelcome, untenable advice. But asking Francesco anything was a distinct impossibility. She hadn't seen or heard from him since the day after their baby's birth when he'd walked in and told her, while sweeping his sleepy son out of his crib and cuddling him close to his broad accommodating chest, that they had to choose a name together. Now.

She'd accepted his odd command, and they'd finally settled on Sholto, just like proper parents. Since then she'd seen or heard nothing. He'd done what he'd always meant to do—left them behind, walked away. She'd told herself over and over that she'd expected it, so why did she feel as if she'd lost something? It didn't make sense.

Removing the apron Peggy insisted she wore—though her shabby maternity dress wasn't worth protecting, and she didn't have anything more suitable to wear because when half-heartedly packing before coming here she'd expected to be taken home on discharge from the clinic—she stated, 'I've been idling around for far too long in the lap of luxury. I must go home and help them through this.'

Her parents would be feeling gutted at the prospect of losing Rylands—her father rightly blaming himself and her mother loyally blaming everyone else and trying very hard, bless her, not to cry. 'I'll look up train times, then pack.'

Aiming a wobbly smile in Peggy's direction, Anna headed for the stairs. The fully equipped nursery had been the first surprising intimation that she and Sholto were expected to remain at Francesco's London address for a week or two after Arnold and Peggy had collected them from the clinic. How long she would have stayed if she hadn't had that phone call she didn't know. Until Francesco eventually returned, unable to drag herself away until she'd seen him again?

Mounting the stairs, she compressed her soft lips, cross with herself for that unbidden and somehow demeaning thought. She would always remember his kindness, his unstinting support while she had been giving birth, but that didn't mean she wanted to see him again. *Ever*, she stressed firmly as she entered the room set aside as a nursery and bent over her sleeping son, her heart swelling with love. She was unaware that the moment she'd closed the kitchen door behind her Peggy had darted to the phone.

Although it was only early afternoon Anna shifted with impatience on the velvet-upholstered chair she'd dragged to the window of the first-floor sitting room.

Watching for Arnold's return.

'Arnold will drive you to your parents' home.' Peggy had popped her head round the nursery door while Anna had been feeding Sholto. 'He's out on an errand at the moment, so you can have lunch before you set out.'

'Oh—if he doesn't mind…' It would be a great relief to be travelling in the comfort of the spacious Lexus kept for the Powells' use rather than having to carry Sholto and all his attendant impedimenta on public transport. Nevertheless, it seemed an imposition.

'Of course not! It will be his pleasure. Mind you, I'll really miss having you and baby around,' she'd added. Then, 'As soon as you've finished here come down for lunch.'

Lunch, helping Peggy clear up afterwards, and then her packing, had passed the time. But now, waiting, it hung heavily. It would be a wrench to have to end this interlude of comfort and luxury, with no care in the world except the sheer pleasure and joy of looking after her baby.

But it had been only a brief interlude, and harsh reality was calling her back.

There would be so much to do. Smartening Rylands for the sale was a no-go area. They would need an army of unaffordable painters and decorators, gardeners and so on. No, she would have to get her business up and running again. Mum, on her meet-your-new grandson visit, had said she'd be more than happy to babysit while she was working. It would be a terrible wrench to leave him, but it would have to be done. And then, of course, she'd have to help find somewhere cheap to rent for them to live—

The sound of a car drawing to a halt below had her on her feet. Expecting Arnold, she felt her heart jerk painfully when she looked down and saw Francesco swing smoothly out of the Ferrari.

Leaping back from the window, Anna put her hand to her breast, where her heart was behaving as if she'd just run a double marathon. Her knees were shaky as she headed across the room. She hated the way he could still affect her—hated him for the way he had lied to her, used her body, shattered her confidence and broken her heart.

Reminding herself that there was nothing between them now but that maintenance contract, sternly telling herself she'd moved on, she opened the door and stepped out onto the soft carpeting of the hushed first-floor corridor, determined to go down and politely explain that she and Sholto would be leaving as soon as Arnold returned. Thank him—but not too fulsomely—for his hospitality.

But he was ahead of her—literally. She watched his broad, elegantly suited back disappear into the nursery next to the bedroom she'd been given. After a sharp intake of breath she followed, and emotional turmoil welled up inside her as she saw him standing over the crib, one hand going out to gently touch the sleeping baby's velvety cheek.

She should be there, at his side. Both of them adoring this precious life they'd created between them, secure in their commitment to each other, their love, their future together. For a bleak moment she felt helplessly excluded.

It wasn't like that. It never could be. They weren't a real family unit, she reminded herself on a spurt of anger. He might find his baby son a transient novelty, but as far as he was concerned his son's mother was just one in a line of discarded bedmates. She was surprised he'd even remembered her name!

'Don't worry—I won't be sponging on your charity much longer. I'll be out of your hair just as soon as Arnold turns up!' The words were low, full of anger, and she didn't know where they'd come from. Propelled from deep inside her on an unstoppable surge of emotional chaos, a light year away from the polite and dignified leavetaking she'd meant to deliver.

Slowly, Francesco straightened, turned. His eyes, she noted uncaringly, were like chips of ice, his lean face was hard, his beautiful mouth stark. So she was being rude and objectionable, as he'd labeled. Something he wouldn't stand for in anyone, and certainly not in an ex-lover he'd discarded like so much trash! So what did she care?

Every nerve-end bristling, she walked further into the room. Mindful of the need not to wake the baby, her words were low but as haughty as she could make them. 'Close the door on your way out. And let me know when Arnold gets back.'

She might have known! One stride brought him to her side. His hand was on her arm and she was with him, out of the door in the time it took to flick an eyelash.

'You don't tell me what to do!' His words stung her as he closed the nursery door quietly behind them. 'From now on I call the shots. I advise you to accept that with grace. Otherwise you will suffer the consequences of my displeasure.'

'I'm shaking already!' she sniped, trying to get her breath back, trying to wrest her arm free of his punitive grip and failing. 'Only remember,' she flung at him as he frog-marched her back into the sitting room, 'I'll be gone as soon as Arnold gets back, so you'll be "calling the shots", as you put it, to thin air!'

'Compose yourself.' He steered her towards the chintz-covered sofa. 'I have something to say to you regarding your future. And my son's.'

What? Suddenly dreadfully nervous, she sat, her mind frantically worrying over what was going on in his mind. She watched him as he was watching her, his savagely handsome features unreadable.

He'd said 'my son', and she'd seen how he'd looked at little Sholto as he'd slept only a few minutes ago, remembering how, during that short time he'd spent with them in the clinic and when he'd insisted on choosing a name, how he had held the tiny shawl-wrapped bundle so tenderly.

Ice clamped her heart. Did he mean to take her baby from her? He couldn't do that, could he? She wouldn't let him! Sounding tougher than she felt, she swept her hair out of her eyes with one hand and lashed, 'Spit it out, then! As soon as Arnold gets here, I'm off. With Sholto,' she stressed.

Francesco held up a lean hand to silence her, and her generously curving mouth closed instinctively while an unwelcome twist of nervous excitement wriggled inside her. She watched dark colour steal over his prominent cheekbones when his eyes, drawn to her mouth, stayed there until, his own mouth suddenly tightening, he stated harshly, 'Peggy phoned me to tell me you were leaving. Arnold won't be taking you anywhere—I suggested he take the opportunity to visit his brother.'

'Then we'll get a train!' Anna said thinly, absorbing that bombshell, deeply hurt because Peggy had fooled her, gone behind her back, lied about Arnold driving her. During her time here she'd really believed the older woman was her friend.

So the train it would have to be. She wouldn't dream of asking her father to fetch her in her van. The state it was in, it probably wouldn't do the distance. Besides, he drove like a lunatic, his head in the clouds. But…

'Nick will collect us!' Why hadn't she thought of him before? He'd do anything for her; he'd always said so.

Leaping to her feet, not looking at Francesco, she started for the door, but his tall frame came between her and her objective, strong hands on her shoulders, staying her.

'You are going nowhere. So you can forget your knight in shining armour,' he stated icily. 'And don't blame Peggy. I've had to be away, but I instructed her to let me know if you showed signs of leaving with my son, and to keep you here until I managed to get back. Fortunately I'd just arrived back from Italy for a board meeting at the London office.'

For a moment their eyes clashed. Hers stormy green, his steel. His words weren't making sense, because physical response flared through her at his touch. Her breath caught in her throat and tears of shame stung the backs of her eyes. She knew what a louse he was beneath that sensationally attractive exterior, so why was he able, with one touch, to make her feel so desperately needy? Needy for him.

She should be immune to all that raw sexuality. Despising herself because she wasn't, she pushed out thickly, 'Why?'

The moment the question was out she knew it was redundant. She knew why. He wanted Sholto. Everything pointed to it. Gently, he pushed her unresisting body back onto the sofa and joined her, angling his virile frame into the corner. Watching her.

Her spine slumping, Anna tried to will away the wave

of weakness that was now swamping her. What would he do? Offer her money to relinquish all rights to her baby? Hire a team of hotshot lawyers to gain custody through the courts if she refused—as she would?

She wouldn't let him! She would fight for her baby until the last breath left her body, she vowed, hysteria rising. Because she knew he was ruthless, an arch manipulator, with the vast financial backing to get what he wanted.

Apprehension ripped through her as she waited for an answer. And waited. Until, on the point of screaming, she risked a direct look.

Emotionless silver eyes looked back at her. One dark brow rose with insulting indolence as he drawled, 'Tantrum over? Willing to listen?'

As unwilling as it was possible to be! But the sooner she knew his intentions the more time she'd have to work out how to fight him. Her hands shook. She twisted her fingers together, not wanting him to see how nervous she was. Her face pale, she nodded.

'I shall marry you.'

Anna's breath snagged in her throat. She caught her lower lip between her teeth, nipping to convince herself she wasn't dreaming. A statement so blandly spoken he might as well have announced that he was going to get a haircut!

She would have laughed in his face if she hadn't felt like crying. It hurt so very much. How often on the island, when he'd assured her he loved her, had she yearned, hoped, believed she would hear those words from him? Lowering her head, hiding behind her untamed mane of hair, she struggled to contain her emotions for long enough to tell him no.

Watching her, watching her colour come and go, the way she hid behind her glorious hair, Francesco twisted his sensual mouth bitterly. Once that proposal had been burning his tongue, the ring burning a hole in his breast pocket, its pale yellow diamond chosen because it had reminded him of her hair. But a few ill-timed words from her hare-brained loser of a father had had him savagely cutting her out of his life, reminded that all women were the same—not to be trusted when a man's wealth and status were dangled in front of their scheming eyes.

And now he was doing what he'd vowed—post-Anna—he would never do. He was asking a woman to marry him.

But it was necessary.

Discovering in himself an unsuspected depth of devotion when he'd first laid eyes on his son, he knew he could never cut him out of his life.

'I want my son.' He voiced his thoughts aloud into the silence, his voice husky with need. 'Ideally, a child needs both parents. Permanently. I had thought it would be enough for me to do the responsible thing and provide financial support. Since holding him I find that it is far from enough. Hence—' harshness now cloaked his words '—the need for us to marry. Because, naturally, he will need his mother, too.'

Still in shock, Anna got out unevenly, 'No. I won't. I couldn't bear it!'

'Such protestations don't cut any ice with me,' Francesco drawled. 'Marriage to wealth was what you aimed for, so why bore me with spurious denials now?'

She did look at him then, green eyes flashing outrage. When she'd wanted to spend the rest of her life with him, had loved him so very much she'd felt she couldn't live without him, she hadn't known he was wealthy beyond the dreams of avarice! Now she knew—and she knew other things too.

'You don't love me—you don't love anyone but yourself,' she gasped, feeling colour flood her face, unprepared for the quietly spoken statement that turned her blood to ice.

'I love my son.'

'We don't have to marry,' she got out before sheer terror could claim her.

Marriage would mean sharing his bed, giving him rights over her body. It would destroy her! She knew herself far too well. Sharing the intimacies of marriage with him, she would go back to being besotted. His shattering sexual attraction was her nemesis—because not even knowing what a heartless bastard he was could cure her of that demeaning weakness.

'If you really want to, you could see him whenever you wanted. I wouldn't stop you,' she offered in desperation.

He was looking at her with disturbing indifference, as if her offer was beneath his notice. Anna shivered and dredged up an argument that would hold water. 'It would never work—marriage, I mean. How could it? We don't love each other, and we both know you'd soon be out of my bed and into one occupied by one of those glitzy model-types you seem to favour. I do read the papers, so I know you do that macho stuff, and are rarely seen without the necessary arm candy!' she huffed. 'We'd end up fighting, hating each other, and I'd start throwing things and you'd probably throw them back—just think what damage that kind of marriage would do to little Sholto!'

She'd made her point—surely she had? she agonised.

But he shot her a look of what she could only describe as amused contempt as he countered, 'I wouldn't *be* in your bed. My needs in that department can be easily catered to.' Though he hadn't been remotely interested since— But he wasn't going to dwell on that.

And he would want to be in her bed, he derided himself with painful honesty. The first time he'd laid eyes on her he'd been tempted, had spent the whole of that first night fantasising about losing himself in that sensationally lush body. And the reality had been beautiful beyond his dreams, putting his fantasies into deep shade.

But he would make sure he was never tempted again. He was strong enough. Hadn't his character been likened to steel? 'Our marriage will be on paper only. A façade to provide our son with two parents.' A frown clefted his brow, his sculpted features hard. 'Immediately after the ceremony—civil, naturally—we will go to my family home in Tuscany, where my son will grow up with the freedom and happiness he needs. He will have the uncomplicated childhood I never enjoyed. You, as his mother, will share my wealth and my status, enjoy the respect that that will bring, and in return you will never complain. Should you attempt to remove my son from my protection, or take a lover, you will be history.'

Raw anger flicked deep inside her. It took gold-plated heartless arrogance to lay down such punitive rules. Colour staining her cheeks, heightening the brilliance of her eyes, she flung at him, 'So I'm to live like a nun in a gilded cage, far away from family and friends? No, thanks. I don't rate feather-bedding that highly!'

'You like money—you like sex. But you can't have both. Get used to it.' His cold intonation fuelled her anger. Who did he think he was?

She got to her feet, unable to sit still a moment longer. 'On Ischia I thought you were the most wonderful, exciting, caring man ever to breathe—now I know you're the dregs!' she told him stormily. 'I won't marry you, and I withdraw the offer to allow you access. Ever! I won't have my son contaminated!'

'Sit down.' Lean fingers fastened around her wrist, tugging her back beside him. Steely grey eyes set a collision course with hers, and her breath came feebly even though her heart was clattering like a runaway train. The force of his personality scared her silly, but she held his gaze, not willing to let him see her weakness.

'You have a regrettable tendency to behave like a drama queen,' he incised, his devastating features set in grim lines. 'You once set your sights on my wealth— you can't deny it. Now it is yours for the taking I suggest you stop behaving like a spoiled brat and face the fact that you can't have me twisted round your pretty fingers, doting putty in your hands. Accept it. Or tell me what you do want from our marriage and I will consider it.'

Anna clamped her mouth shut. What she wanted— would have wanted when she'd thought the sun rose and set with him—she could never have. But she wasn't telling him that. And as for denying that she wanted to get her hands on his wretched money, forget it! Let him think what he liked. She wasn't going to lay her already bleeding heart at his feet and confess that all she'd ever wanted was his love.

'Nothing to say? I thought not.' He dealt her a brooding look from smoky eyes. 'Then I will lay the full details of my proposal in front you of, and you can decide which road you wish to travel.'

Anna stared back at him, twisting her hands on her lap, dry-mouthed with tension as she wondered what he was going to come out with next. If she didn't know better she would have sworn on oath that this wasn't the same man as the exciting, laid-back charmer she'd fallen in love with on Ischia. Talk about Jekyll and Hyde!

'First option: we marry—with the stipulations already spoken of. Furthermore, I have had your father's situation examined, and find he is about to lose your mother her family home.' He leaned back, his eyes contemptuous. 'If we marry I will clear his debts and provide him with employment within one of my companies to help him curb his…shall we say…eccentricities? And that must not be considered an inducement—or a philanthropic gesture on my behalf,' he drawled with cynicism. 'It would not be good for my image were it to become known that my parents-in-law were penniless and homeless.'

She wanted to hit him. 'I hate you!' she said thickly. He obviously looked on her and her family as being beneath contempt—lesser beings who would fall in with his dictates with humiliating gratitude.

Ignoring her interjection, Francesco continued, almost purring now. 'If, however, you refuse my proposal, then

I promise you I will take my son from you. Legally. And don't think that wouldn't happen. It would.'

He got to his feet with the fluid grace that had once mesmerised her. 'I'll leave you to think it over.' Shooting his cuff, he glanced at the face of the slim gold watch that banded his wrist. 'You have an hour to reach a decision.'

CHAPTER SEVEN

SHE'D said she would marry him.

A bad decision? The worst one possible from her point of view! But what choice did she have?

Refuse, as every instinct she possessed counselled, and she'd see her parents lose their home and their dignity. Dad struggling to cope with a job that was far more suitable for a much younger man. Mum mourning the loss of the house that had been in her family for generations and trying not to show it. And she'd have to live with the knowledge that she could have prevented it, all the time having the dark threat of Francesco gaining sole custody of her precious little son hanging over her head, with the totally chilling knowledge that with the help of clever lawyers and a bottomless pit of money he'd do exactly that.

So. No choice at all.

Now, almost twenty-four hours following her graceless acceptance, she remembered Francesco's chilly, 'A wise decision,' and the way his dark head had dipped in terse acknowledgement before he'd swung on his heels and left the room, leaving her struggling to come to terms with what the future held.

Sitting out on the terrace in the late-afternoon sunshine, with her baby on her lap, she remembered, too, waking this morning, before the baby alarm could alert her to the raucous fact that Sholto was ready for his early feed, padding to the nursery and finding Francesco already there, giving his son his bottle.

Resentment that he had denied her the only pleasure now left to her—caring for her baby—had warred with the proof that he meant to be a devoted hands-on father. She'd crept back to her room and hadn't set eyes on him since.

On her lap, Sholto kicked his legs and gurgled, and Anna's heart turned over, bursting with love. In agreeing to a loveless marriage she was doing the right thing. For Sholto and her parents, at least.

Her baby would grow up with all the advantages she, alone, could never hope to provide, secure in the love of both parents. And she would never, *never* give him the slightest hint that his parents' marriage was nothing but an empty sham, that hatred and mistrust lay beneath the smooth surface. Surely it was a price worth paying?

Pausing at the head of the terrace, Francesco felt his heart jolt against his breastbone. He had never seen anything so beautiful. Mother and child in the dappled shade of the overhanging false acacia, her body curved protectively over the gurgling infant.

A beautiful enigma. An innocent, or a clever schemer? Since this afternoon's conversation with his lawyer nothing was quite as clear-cut as it had been.

Intent on giving instructions for a watertight prenuptial agreement, he'd been stunned when the older man had imparted that his bride-to-be had refused to sign the now redundant maintenance contract until the amount stated had been significantly reduced—pared down until it provided just the bare essentials.

The lawyer had excused his lack of communication on the subject. Passing on that information hadn't seemed necessary. If the young lady in question had held out for a larger amount—well, that, of course, would have been very different. His client's instructions on the matter would have been sought at once.

So what was going on? Francesco's brow clenched as he watched his small son grab a fistful of that glorious hair. He had never believed her when she'd protested that she didn't want anything from him, dismissing it as so much bluster and hot air, cloaking her desire to squeeze as much as she could from him, or a forlorn attempt to convince him that when she'd vowed she loved him back on the island, she'd had no knowledge of who he really was. Which didn't hold water. Hadn't she let slip, only yesterday, that she'd seen articles about him—and one of his latest lovers—in the press?

He hadn't been seen with a female since her father—on her advice?—had jumped right in, giving the impression that he recognised him from the financial papers and asking for a huge chunk of investment in some scheme or other. In his book it was clear that she'd lied about not being aware of his financial status.

So what was her long game? Pretend to be uninterested in his wealth—even to the extent of having that contract altered, knowing he would get to hear of it—while all the time banking on the astute belief that having seen his child, held him, he wouldn't want to let him go and would offer a form of marriage as the smoothest way forward? Giving her access to everything that was his.

Clever!

Cynicism bracketing his mouth now, he strode forward, gently scooping his son from her lap, ignoring her startled intake of breath. 'I'll take him. There are people waiting to see you. In your room.'

'People? Who?' The shock of his sudden appearance left her open-mouthed, her breath gone because he was so spectacularly handsome he made her feel dizzy.

Not deigning to answer, he laid a beautifully crafted hand on his son's tummy. '*Ciao, bambino!* Soon, when your tiny feet grow bigger, Papa will teach you to play football—the next day it will be chess!'

Despite herself, and the acid sense of exclusion, Anna felt her mouth quirk. Mental pictures of a large man and a tiny dark-haired boy kicking a ball about in an imagined Tuscan flower-strewn meadow brought a soft sheen of wistfulness to her eyes.

Venting a tiny sigh, because she wanted to stay, be included in the father and son bonding session, she rose, smoothed down her shabby old maternity dress and set out to find out for herself who the people were.

She'd just about gained the garden door at the head of the terrace when Francesco remarked, 'By the way, I visited your parents earlier. They were delighted by the news of our marriage, and almost hysterical when they heard that their debts will be cleared. I got out before I could be drowned in tears of gratitude.'

Anna's steps faltered only a moment on receipt of that flatly delivered statement, then she surged on. She didn't turn to look at him, to acknowledge that she'd heard what he'd said. Her face was flaming with humiliation, and she didn't want him to see her monumental discomfiture and gloat.

He'd sounded dismissive, bored. As if she and her parents were contemptible. Well, what did she expect? He'd said his seemingly mega-generous offer to clear their debts was being made to protect his own precious image—certainly not an altruistic gesture to get a couple of good if slightly eccentric people out of the huge hole they'd dug for themselves.

Trying to put him out of her mind and concentrate on the possible identity of her mystery visitors—Mum and Dad, perhaps?—she swiftly mounted the stairs, headed for her room, pushed open the door and was confronted by two strange women.

Painfully smart women, surrounded by a sea of classy-looking boxes. The older of the two, with the dark hair scraped so tightly back it looked painted on, rose from the chair she'd been occupying.

'Miss Maybury?' Dark eyes swept over her, and Anna could have sworn she heard a wince in her voice. 'Signor Mastroianni instructed us to bring suitable clothes for you to try.'

A slight accent. French? Anna's arched brows drew together. More charity? She didn't want it.

'I'm sorry—you've wasted your time,' she said stiffly, half choking on this new mortification. 'I don't need new clothes.'

A pencil-thin eyebrow rose in repudiation of that mistaken opinion. 'The *signor* was most insistent.'

'No.' She had stuff of her own back at Rylands. Someone could fetch it. She might be a kept woman—courtesy of darling little Sholto—but she didn't aim to look like one. Stepping back, moving as if to show her visitors the door, she saw a look of stark apprehension flicker across the enamelled-looking face, and her soft heart immediately capitulated.

The side of Francesco's character she hadn't dreamt existed when they'd said their passionate farewells on Ischia had told her that anyone who failed to deliver on instruction was in for a tough time. The uneviable situation she found herself in wasn't this woman's fault, so why should she suffer?

So, 'OK. I'll try one or two things.' She felt gratifyingly vindicated for her *volte-face* when both women visibly relaxed, smiling, practically purring, as tops were pulled away from boxes, layers of tissue reverently parted, to reveal costly fabrics in a rainbow of gorgeous colours.

After all, it might be fun to try on the type of designer gear she'd only previously glimpsed on the glossy pages of swanky magazines. And Francesco could buy the lot, but that didn't mean she would ever wear them.

Removing her dress under the pained eyes of the women—maybe they didn't rate chainstore undies?—Anna stamped on the ignoble thought that she would be more than glad to see the back of the maternity tents she'd lived in for what felt like for ever and gradually, very gradually, began to enjoy herself.

Partly because the women made highly flattering

remarks—which no way did Anna take seriously—and partly because she adored the way pure silk, cashmere and linen felt against her body, she went along with what she saw as an amusing game quite willingly. Only blushing furiously when the older of the two, her head on one side, one eyebrow raised to an impossible height remarked, 'The *signor*, he knows the details of your measurements perfectly!'

Intimately! He knew her body so intimately! Her tummy quivered, heat pooling where it shouldn't. She deplored it. She wasn't going to go there!

And suddenly it wasn't fun any more. Her mouth set, she reached for the one remaining garment box. Get it over with. Her eyes sparking with irritation now, over this senseless waste of time, she stood like a wooden doll while the older woman zipped her up and the younger folded away the lovely caramel-coloured linen suit and creamy camisole she'd just stepped out of.

'*Très belle*—look—' Hands on Anna's shoulders turned her towards the pier glass, and her stormy eyes widened as she viewed a self that looked totally unlike herself.

The finest black silk dress moulded her voluptuous breasts, skimmed her back-to-normal tiny waist, caressed the sensuous curve of her hips, then floated down to narrow ankles that just cried out for the high-heeled glittery strappy shoes the younger woman was advancing with. Somehow, her widened eyes registered, the sombre colour made the naked skin of her arms, upper breast and shoulders look like whipped cream and her hair like glossy coils of platinum.

Sexy siren!

It wasn't her—not her at all!

Her cheeks pinkening, adding extra glitter to her stormy green eyes, she was in haste to remove the dress. But the ultra-fine concealed zip was beyond the efforts of her fumbling fingers and turning, looking for assistance, she froze on the spot as Francesco walked in as if he owned the place. Which he did, of course, she grumped at herself.

She swallowed a ragged intake of breath as she found herself unable to look away from his lean, bronzed, classically Italian features, from the searing impact of slightly narrowed eyes that had darkened to unreadable charcoal pools, or the way even in well-worn jeans and a sleeveless black vest he exuded class, natural sophistication and the shattering good-looks that top-flight movie stars would envy.

He was irresistible on an entirely primitive level, she thought despairingly, appalled by her weakness, by her contrariness in lusting after the one man in the world she absolutely hated.

His eyes on Anna, Francesco strode further into the room, his accent more marked than usual as he instructed, 'Madame Laroche, would you and your assistant wait downstairs? My housekeeper will bring coffee. I will join you shortly.'

Periphery movement, smiles and bobbing heads. Anna didn't even note when the women left the room. Francesco was advancing towards her, and she could concentrate on nothing else. There was tension in every line of his unforgettable features, something almost pagan smouldering in his eyes as they swept her, the sexy siren personna that wasn't her at all.

Or was it?

Anna's head spun. It was difficult to breathe and she couldn't think straight—not while there was that wicked throb deep inside her. She trembled, something far too responsive to this devil's erotic magnetism trickling down her spine.

'Madame Laroche chose well.' A scant twelve inches away, he stopped. He was having trouble with his breathing. That dress clung to every lethally voluptuous inch of her body, and the mass of bright hair was inviting him to touch, to run his fingers through the silky coils. His voice thickened. 'That dress is dynamite.'

Anna's insides squirmed. On its own the dress was discreetly revealing, classy. But with her embarrassingly aroused body inside it, it was shocking. She crossed her arms over her chest to hide the way her breasts were straining to escape over the top of the low-cut bodice, as if the fine fabric couldn't contain such bounty. Her nipples were tellingly prominent.

Her voice scratchy with her attempts to control her wretched body's seemingly automatic response to this one man, she pushed at him, 'She can take it all back. You'll waste your money if you buy any of it. I won't wear it!'

'Why not?' Unfazed, he fastened his eyes on the soft fullness of her mouth, and had the forbidden memory of exactly how that mouth had felt in the possession of his, the generous, unquestioning response that had never failed to drive him crazy. He felt his body harden and knew this couldn't go on.

'Because you only want me to wear stuff like this so you aren't ashamed of me—just like you'd hate for anyone to know that your in-laws are sleeping in cardboard boxes—no good for your precious image!'

She slung the reminder at him and rejoiced to see his flush of discomfiture. It lasted a bare second before he countered, with enviable cool, 'No. That is not the case. It would give me pleasure to see the mother of my son wearing lovely things.'

'And I'm supposed to care about your pleasure?' Anna's brows almost hit her hairline. The sheer gall of the man! He had used her and discarded her, and he obviously despised her family—and her. He wouldn't be giving her the time of day if he hadn't discovered he was to be a father. And as sure as night followed day he wouldn't have proposed marriage if he hadn't fallen in love with his son! And yet he expected her to dress in outfits that would give him pleasure! 'I'd rather give you a black eye!' she said, with feeling.

'I don't think so,' Francesco came back with awesome smoothness. 'In fact, there's been a change of plan.'

It took a moment for Anna's seething brain to calm down enough to take that in. 'In what way?' He could only mean he'd rethought the marriage stuff, come to his senses. And that shouldn't make her feel strangely bereft, with the humiliating recognition that she really must have been totally missing from the queue when brains were handed out, but she did feel ridiculously bereft.

'Our marriage is to be a real one.'

Colour flooded her face at that statement. Her arms,

still crossed over her chest, jerked, her fingernails biting into the flesh of her shoulders.

'I find I still want your body,' he confessed, with just a hint of self-derision.

'It's only this dress,' she mumbled, hiding her blushes behind her hair at the crazy thought of being his sex slave, knowing, to her utter shame, that his sexual magnetism could make her do anything he wanted her to do.

'No, it's not,' Francesco said thickly, not telling her he'd still thought her the most beautiful thing he'd ever seen earlier, even dressed in that awful tent thing. Lust, of course. Knowing what he now knew of her, it could be nothing else. 'I've changed my mind about going through simply a form of marriage. It would be—' under her widened gaze he sought an apposite word, felt his heart lurch, and supplied '—uncomfortable. A full marriage would make life easier for both of us.'

Initially he'd thought that having his son would be enough. That he could concentrate on his son and as good as ignore her existence except when necessity—social or business—meant they had to appear as a couple. But being driven half out of his mind by unsatisfied lust, knowing from past experience that he could make her burn with the same desire that burned in him, would make a paper marriage untenable. Ultimately harming his son.

Pent-up emotion had her shaking like a leaf and she stammered, 'S...sex. You mean you'd expect me to have sex with you? You'd—you'd think you'd paid for it!' Her voice rose by several decibels. 'I'd feel like a prostitute!'

'*Calmare*—' He reached for her but she backed away,

arms still crossed protectively over her breasts. He sucked in his breath. *Dio mio!* It would not be like that! He'd had affairs in the past, before he met her, and had been up-front about sex. Beautiful women who knew not to expect anything approaching a long-term commitment, who retired discreetly from the scene with some lavish parting gift when his interest faded.

But with Anna it wouldn't be like that. It was a mystery he wasn't in the mood to try to solve. He only knew. 'It wouldn't be like that,' he verbalised gruffly, then consciously smoothed away an uncharacteristic feeling of walking on quicksand. He advanced until she'd backed herself against a wall. 'We'll have a proper wedding—no downbeat civil service—and our marriage will be consummated.' His voice thickened as he put his hands over hers and drew them slowly down to her sides. 'Whatever our differences, you can't have forgotten how good we once were together.'

How could she ever forget? Anna thought wildly, the intensity of her emotions making her feel spaced out. His eyes slowly travelled her quivering body. Alarm bells were ringing in her head but she couldn't look away.

Her eyes were riveted to the slow smile that curved his sensual mouth as he told her, 'It will be good for us again, I promise.' His hands slid up to her shoulders, detouring tantalisingly over her engorged breasts. She swallowed convulsively. She felt boneless, something hot clenching inside as he imparted huskily, 'Why live in agony through the years of our marriage? Why deny ourselves the release we can give each other?'

'Just sex,' she got out, still trying to fight a battle she

knew she was losing. She wanted him and she couldn't deny that truth. Back on Ischia she had become addicted to him, and he was proving to be an impossible habit to kick.

'Don't knock it!' Smooth as cream, he lowered his dark head and took her mouth with a sensual expertise that made her whimper, whimper some more, then melt and cling to his broad shoulders for support.

Not thinking of what she was doing, not capable of a single rational thought, Anna wriggled her body closer into the hard length of his, felt his deep, responsive shudder as his mouth plundered hers with fierce male urgency. He pressed her back against the wall, firm hands shaping her eager body, the curve of her hips, the mound at the base of her tummy and up to her tingling breasts, long fingers slipping beneath the silky neckline making her gasp with wanton pleasure, wrench her mouth from his and fling her head back in a blatant invitation which he took.

Easing the straps away, he slid the silk from her breasts, dark colour a flash along his angular cheekbones, his eyes heavily lidded as he bent to close his mouth round each taut nipple in turn. Gasping, she dug her fingers into the solid muscle of his shoulders and reality, already a hazy distant thing, slipped entirely away. She was lost again, his again, and her body was screaming demands that only he could meet.

'You are convinced?' He drew away, ran long fingers through his rumpled hair. 'I have proved how good we are together, *si*? Our marriage will be no hardship.' He dealt her a smile that drove the breath out of her lungs before turning. 'Madame Laroche waits. Wear something that will give me pleasure when we dine tonight.'

As the door closed behind him Anna wrapped her arms around her treacherous, unsated body and vented a long, shuddering sob. In his hands she was putty, to be moulded as he pleased. He could seduce her with a look, render her powerless.

He had just proved it. And there was no way out of a marriage that would be full of hot sex and empty of love—not if she wanted to keep her son.

CHAPTER EIGHT

'SOPHIA will arrive on the company jet later this afternoon. Arnold will meet her, and she should be in time to join us for dinner.'

'Sophia?' Anna prompted after a beat of silence. Francesco's statement had been delivered with the first sign of enthusiasm he'd shown all morning.

His sensual mouth was flat, but his dark eyes brooded as they finally turned to her. Had the charade over and done with only a scant five minutes ago brought home with a sickening crunch the reality of the situation they found themselves in?

In the ground-floor drawing room, surrounded by screamingly expensive and beautiful antiques and paintings, Francesco had invited her to make her selection from the fabulous rings displayed in a briefcase that had arrived chained to the wrist of a tall, thin male who looked more like an undertaker than a purveyor of fine gems, accompanied by a hovering stone-faced, flint-eyed bodyguard.

Beneath three pairs of increasingly impatient eyes Anna had only been able to stare at the dazzling array as long awkward moments passed, her throat tightening with every uncomfortable second. She'd felt like an actor who had forgotten her lines and who, if she remembered them, would be reluctant to speak them.

In the end it had been Francesco who had plucked a flashy diamond cluster from its velvet nest without ceremony, and settled it on the third finger of her left hand with about as much romance as a guy would show stuffing loose change back in his pocket.

'My sister,' he now answered on a bite. 'She is flying from Rome and will stay until the wedding to assist you.'

'I didn't know you had a sister.' Anna raised questioning green eyes. She realized she knew very little about him really. Only that he was filthy rich and a womanizer, who liked just now and then to amuse himself by pretending to be dirt-poor and seducing gullible little virgins who wouldn't get ideas about his wealth because he made sure they stayed ignorant. Recalling the cheap brass chain he'd worn the first time she'd set eyes on him, she nearly exploded with the desire to jump up and hit him.

But negative backwards-looking emotions wouldn't get her anywhere in the situation that had been as good as thrust upon her. She took a deep steadying breath and invited, 'Tell me about her.'

Anna's small hands fisted against the pale cotton of the smoothly styled culottes she'd teamed with an emerald camisole top—both garments courtesy of Madame Laroche's good taste and Francesco's bottomless bank account—and did her best to push the other known fact—that he was probably the sexiest guy to walk the planet—right to the back of her mind.

Difficult when he levered his lean, power-packed frame out of the small sofa he'd been occupying and stood looking down at her, feet slightly apart, hands in the trouser pockets of the superbly styled dove-grey suit he was wearing.

He was so breathtakingly handsome he made her feel faint. And so damnably in control that he made her feel so churned up she didn't know where she was half the time. Like after that torrid scene in her bedroom yesterday, when he'd announced his intention to make their marriage a real one and proved, to her private shame, that she'd be a complete push-over. She'd expected him to come to her last night. But he hadn't, and that had left her not knowing whether to be mightily relieved or sick as a parrot!

Now he levelled at her, 'I have wedding arrangements to make. Perhaps you might contact your parents and invite them to stay here for a day or two before the ceremony? I'll let you know the date.' And he was gone, leaving her feeling so aggravated she could explode. The diamond cluster on her finger was like a ton weight, dragging her down.

He couldn't have made his intention to refuse her admission to any part of his life or his family's clearer if he'd written in it red letters a mile high! As the mother of his son he would dress her, feed her, house her in luxury, bed her when he felt like it—but he would give her no part of himself.

Setting her delicate jaw, Anna got to her feet. He was determined to shut her out. What she felt wasn't deep hurt—of course not—it was pique, and, piqued, she would do something about it. After all, he didn't love her, and she as sure as hens were toothless didn't love him, so why should she feel unbearably hurt?

She found Peggy in the kitchen, shelling peas. Pulling a chair out, Anna sat at the table, grabbed a handful of pods and said, as lightly as she could, 'So Sophia arrives later today? Francesco was in a hurry, so he didn't have time to put me properly in the picture. What's she like? Older or younger?' Sneaky, or what? But if she was to learn anything at all about the man who was to be her husband and his family she had to use any means at her disposal.

'Oh, you'll like her,' Peggy promised warmly. 'She's married to a rich Italian banker—Fabio Bocelli—but there's no side to her. Come to think of it, she and her big brother are both like that—they treat everybody as equals. It doesn't matter who they are or what they've got, it's the person inside the skin who counts.'

Really? Despite her best efforts to put on a guileless front, Anna felt one brow shoot towards her hairline.

'Anyway—' Peggy pushed herself to her feet. 'I'll make coffee while you finish that lot. Oh!' Colour washed her narrow cheeks. 'Listen to me! You'll soon be the mistress here, and there's me bossing you around like you were a kitchen maid!'

'Don't be daft!' Anna grinned, grabbing a fresh handful of pods. 'We're friends, right? Make that coffee. I'm gasping!' She'd rapidly forgiven Peggy for the way she'd lied to keep her here until Francesco could put in an appearance. When the boss asked, Peggy would oblige—without question. Not out of fear for her position but from loyalty and respect. He must have treated the Powells much better than he'd treated her to gain such unfailing obedience to his slightest wish, she thought sourly.

As she industriously podded the last of the peas, the diamonds on her finger winked coldly. Grimly, Anna slid the ring off and dug it deep into the pocket of her culottes. Wretched spiky thing! If it had been a thin gold band adorned with a single tiny seed pearl but given with love she would have valued it far more highly than this flashy, eye-wateringly expensive bauble given simply because it was the thing to do.

'There we go—' Peggy slid a coffee mug in front of her and sat down, cradling her own mug, prepared to gossip. 'Now—Sophia. She's six years younger than her brother, so that makes her twenty-eight. She's lively, very pretty, and has a six-year-old daughter—Cristina. Mind you, she'll be leaving her behind with her nanny and Signor Bocelli until nearer the wedding.' She smiled wryly. 'There'll be tantrums there—the little scrap just adores her zio Francesco, and he dotes on her, indulges her rotten! I'm not surprised things have turned out as they have. He's besotted with baby Sholto, but you'll have to watch out he doesn't ruin him with spoiling! Spoil the pair of you, is my guess. You should have seen the look on his face when he broke the news of the wedding—cat got the cream wasn't in it!'

Daddy cat got his kitten, Anna brooded a few hours later. She was just a necessary encumbrance. Necessary to his tiny son's happiness and well-being, not *his*.

Never his.

Wandering around the fabulous ground-floor drawing room, plumping cushions, moving a vase of flowers from one table to another, gave her something to do. She had bathed and fed Sholto, played with him, cuddled him, lunched in solitary splendour, taken her dark-haired little son for an airing in the railed gardens at the heart of the elegant square, and now he slept.

Edgy, unable to settle, she was glad of the interruption when Peggy opened the door and announced impressively, 'A gentleman to see you, madam.'

Still grinning at the formal 'madam', Anna's mouth dropped open when Nick ambled in carrying a huge bouquet of startlingly colourful flowers. 'For you.' He thrust them at her. 'Congrats on the baby, by the way.' His cheerful open face was one big blush. 'So, everything's OK? When I called by your place this morning your mum told me your baby's father's going to marry you. You OK about that?' He shifted his feet, glancing around uneasily. 'Judging by this place he's loaded, but money isn't everything. It didn't take much to work out it must have happened while you were on that holiday— the baby, I mean. And, well, he didn't exactly follow up, did he? Not till he found out by accident he was going to be a dad. Does he want to keep the kid? Is that it? Threatening to take him off you if you don't toe the line? Is that the sort of bloke you want to marry? You can tell me the truth.'

That had been a long speech for Nick. Astute, too. Was he remembering how he'd offered to marry her, care for her baby as if it were his own? Was he feeling hurt and somehow denigrated because he'd been turned down in favour, apparently, of a guy who could offer far more materially?

Her suspicion was confirmed when he stated stiffly, 'Soon as I heard about you getting hitched I had to come and tell you that my offer still stands. If we married quickly no court would grant him custody of the kid. You're his mother, and that gives you a head start, and showing that we would give the lad a stable family background would clinch it. You wouldn't have to worry. I can't give you a fancy lifestyle, but I do care about you.'

He looked so earnest that Anna's throat closed up. Regardless of the personal cost, he was offering her a viable way out, and affection for him made her heart swell.

They were like brother and sister. And they'd always looked out for each other. He wasn't in love with her, but he was looking out for her now. And she couldn't bear him to think she regarded his offer of marriage as second-best, not worth considering.

'I know you care for me—we care for each other. But we're not in love with each other, Nick. We've discussed it before, remember?' She took one of his hands and led him to one of the sofas, placed the flowers at the end and sat down. As he joined her she said, 'You'll make some lucky girl a great husband, Nick. But you see I'm in love with Francesco. I fell in love with him within twenty-four hours of meeting him. I want to be his wife.'

Anna's breath stuck in her throat. She'd said that to make her dear friend feel easier about his rejected proposal. But was it true? Her tummy lurched and she stumbled over her next words. 'You—you deserve to fall in love with a girl who feels the same way.'

Any reservations she might have felt about her claim to be in love with the man she was soon to marry disappeared when Nick grinned, his mild blue eyes washed with relief. 'Then you don't need rescuing? You are happy—not being bullied into doing something you don't want to do?'

'Of course not,' Anna mumbled, her mind in knots over the hardening possibility that she *was* still in love with Francesco—had never really stopped loving him. It made the future seem even bleaker. How would she cope? How could she tread through the years ahead loving a man who saw her only as a necessary encumbrance?

But Nick was blushing again, and telling her, his voice gruff, 'Thing is, if you'd needed me I would have—well, you know—married you, like I suggested. And I wouldn't have taken it any further.'

'Taken what further?'

'Well, there's this girl. Melody. We only met a month ago, and—well, it's early days—only I think—' Unable to articulate further, he spread his big hands, his grin wide enough to split his face.

Anna, overwhelmed with affection for this good, uncomplicated man, this lifelong friend who would have swallowed his feelings for this girl Melody and dedicated himself to caring for her and her child had she needed him, flung her arms around him and cried, 'Didn't I tell you the real thing would happen for you one day? I'm so happy for you! If she's the one, don't you dare let her get away!'

'I won't!' Nick got to his feet, pulling her with him. 'Better make tracks. Get the train back.'

'So soon? Peggy could make us some tea,' Anna offered. Her old and valued friend, uncomplicated and steady, was easier to be around than the tricky enigma that was her future husband.

'Thanks, but I'll pass. Now I know you're OK and everything I'll head home, be in time to phone Melody and fix a date for tonight.'

'Then I'll see you out. And Nick?' She smiled up at him as they headed for the hallway. 'I'm really happy for you. Remember to send me an invitation to the wedding!'

'Will do—and that goes for you, too.' His arm went around her, holding her close, and Anna felt tears clog her throat at the thought of her wedding. She would make her vows and, more fool her, would mean them. While Francesco would just go through the motions.

For a moment Anna closed her eyes, blocking tears. When she opened them again Francesco was walking in through the main door they'd been heading for. Tall and strikingly handsome, so elegant, he made Nick in his cheap brown suit look like a peasant, and his voice was dark menace as he observed, 'How touching. But I would prefer not to see my fiancée being pawed by a garage mechanic whose services are not required here.'

Anna's gasp of outrage was smothered by Nick's grinning, 'On my way, mate. Just called in to check if my services *were* required. And as they're not—' He dropped a light kiss on Anna's cheek and headed swiftly for the door, which Francesco was holding ostentatiously open. Obviously fully aware of six feet plus of intimidating, fist-clenching male, he made a rapid exit, leaving a sizzling silence.

'You're jealous!' Anna's amazement made her feel light-headed. Nick must have picked that up too—hence his unstoppable grin, his tongue-in-cheek riposte in the face of the furious male.

She had never, *ever* seen the so arrogantly in control Francesco look so discomfited as he closed the door with unnecessary force then turned to her. 'I? Jealous?' As if such a concept was beyond human imagining.

Dark colour stained his classically moulded cheek-bones as she pointed out, 'Then why were you so rude to him?' Only searing jealousy could have made him lose his famous cool urbanity, and the implications of that made her bones go weak.

His handsome mouth hardened, but there was a febrile glitter in his charcoal-dark eyes as Anna went on, 'The poor guy only called by to say hello and bring me flowers,' knowing that would further rattle his cage. Because Francesco didn't do romantic gestures. Except for when she had first met him, when he had picked wild flowers and tucked them in her hair. But she rapidly thrust that memory aside, concentrating only on the here and now.

'The *poor guy*—' he parodied her tone '—was lucky not to have his jaw broken.' His body tensed and burned at the recollection of wanting to tear the other man limb from limb, because looking at her, at that glorious hair framing her flushed features, that lethally luscious body clothed in silky tones of green that brought out the emerald depths of her lovely eyes, confirmed what he already knew. That no man could look at her and not want to bed her.

'You are to be my wife. You are the mother of my

child,' Francesco pointed out with suppressed fury. 'I take exception to coming home and finding my future wife and some oaf wrapped around each other.'

He caught her raised hand before it could connect, and received an irate shriek. 'Nick is not an oaf! You horrible snob! He's the nicest, kindest friend anyone could have—he's worth a dozen of you!'

'How many times have you slept with him?' he enquired with crushing cool, his eyes like daggers of ice.

'Never!' Anna tried, and failed, to release her wrist from his punitive grasp. 'I don't sleep around—I was a virgin when we met—you know that!'

'And later? After we split?' He was breathing raggedly, suppressing the wave of lust that always washed over him around her, forcing him to voice the cynical doubts that plagued him. 'When you discovered you were pregnant, perhaps? Did you get him on your hook as back-up, in case any plans you might have had to present me with a flesh-and-blood child and demand a handsome settlement from me failed?'

Anna paled. She didn't know how she could still love him, but she did. And he thought she was a scheming monster. The future was a nightmare. Tears she couldn't fight glittered in her eyes, and her voice was thin as she protested, 'How could you think that of me?'

'It's not something that fills me with joy,' he gritted, frowning as his gaze hit her wobbling mouth. 'But I have to face facts. You discovered my private beach, draped yourself alluringly, and waited until I showed up—hoping I'd find you as irresistible as indeed I did.'

So that was what he'd decided, and he was sticking

to it. Nothing she said would make him change his mind. Her slim shoulders shook as tears fell.

Shock made her gasp as, uttering a low expletive, he scooped her up into his arms. 'I can't bear to see you cry. There's no need.'

There was *every* need! Beyond explaining her horrible inner turmoil, Anna sagged in his arms as he carried her upstairs, not even breathless as he told her with infuriating complacency, 'You shouldn't make scenes. They upset you.'

To counter that he had started it would be too childish for words, so she kept her mouth shut. His arrogance, his conviction that he was never in the wrong, inexplicably made her want to giggle—but all desire to give way to hysterical hilarity vanished when he shouldered her bedroom door shut behind them and lowered her to her feet, down the length of his taut, beautifully made body, his hands still holding her against him.

Her tummy muscles tightened. Heat pooled deep inside her. She could feel his arousal. Her breath caught as he used the pads of his thumbs to stroke away the signs of recent tears, and she was powerless to stop the urgent peaking of her breasts against the thin fabric of her camisole top. And he registered the invitation—of course he did—and his hands lifted to tangle in her hair as he took possession of her lush mouth. She gave herself up to sweetly intense sensation, desperate for him as she always would be, she recognised weakly as a stormy river of response raged through her.

Breaking the kiss, Francesco held her eyes as his supple hands dropped to shape her bountiful breasts. He felt her quiver as she wound slender arms around his neck, nuzzling her pelvis into the hardness of his, and he knew he had a monumental fight on his hands.

A fight with himself and with the torrent of male need that told him they were only paces from the bed, murmured far too temptingly that a few deft movements were all that were needed to remove the thin silky fabric that clothed her to-die-for body, scarcely more to jettison his own constricting garments and, lie with her, flesh to eager flesh, skin to burning skin. A fight against the conventional necessities that awaited him.

His breath scorching his lungs, he ground out huskily, 'You want me; I want you. We must put the past way behind us and for Sholto's sake make our marriage work. Be civilised, build on what we have.'

'You mean sex,' Anna whimpered, trembling with need, ravaged by knowing that all he wanted from her was a civilised front and animal lust in the marriage bed. She wanted so much more, but was besotted enough to settle for what she could get.

'What else?' To her shamed humiliation his hand dipped to the waistband of the culottes and dealt with the buttons with a practised ease that excited and further shamed her, dipping his fingers and languuorously exploring the slickness between her thighs. 'Don't knock it. Apart from our son, it is all we have.' Silvery eyes mocked her. 'And it is good. Admit it.'

He released her. 'To my regret, I am unable to give the decisive demonstration.' He straightened his wide shoulders. 'Sophia will be arriving at any moment. I must greet her. You will meet at dinner.'

And he was gone in a handful of smooth strides, leaving Anna to wrap her arms around her tormented body and wish she'd never set eyes on him.

He would have his son and heir—with her thrown in as a bonus. A sex slave. A *willing* sex slave, she admitted with an inner cringe of shame. He lusted after her. But lust died. And when it did he would satisfy his needs elsewhere.

She didn't know how she would cope with that!

CHAPTER NINE

FRANCESCO had been closeted with the hired wedding organiser since eight that morning—a cool, smooth blonde, with efficiency dripping from her beautifully manicured scarlet-tipped fingers.

Anna had done as she'd been asked and written her list of wedding guests, which she had handed over horribly conscious of the manic state of her hair—courtesy of Sholto's desire to explore every crinkly strand—and the baby dribble on the shoulder of her designer shirt.

Fancy labels didn't go with child-minding, and, regardless of what Francesco had to say on the matter, she was going to have to acquire a few bog-standard jeans and T-shirts.

The cool blonde had placed her list, together with the one faxed through from his cousin Silvana and, presumably, the one Francesco had supplied, into a slim leather briefcase and departed.

Musing on the unpalatable fact that she was being allowed very little input towards her own wedding, she gave a little leap of surprise when Sophia tucked her hand beneath her elbow and crowed, 'The wedding organiser has gone. Now for the fun part!'

Turning startled eyes on the pretty brunette, Anna visibly relaxed. 'I didn't see you coming—you made me jump!'

Meeting Francesco's sister at dinner last night, she had immediately taken to her. Lovely to look at, with sleek dark hair flowing down to the middle of her narrow back, dancing black eyes and a ready smile, she possessed a warm, outgoing personality that had made Anna able to endure ploughing through three of Peggy's excellent courses beneath Francesco's brooding gaze, under the explicit curve of his handsome mouth that reminded her so forcibly of her soon-to-be sex slave status.

A shudder of awareness rippled down her spine at that reminder, and Sophia soothed her. 'Every bride-to-be gets the nervous attack. I was dreadful before my wedding—I couldn't stay still for one small moment! Here—' she tucked an oblong of smooth plastic into Anna's hand '—Francesco said to give this to you. He has opened an account—all you have to do is sign.'

'Where is he now?' The credit card was burning a hole in he palm of her hand. She wanted to drop it! Her throat tightened. She wanted to toss it on the ground in front of his feet and loudly restate that she didn't want his wretched money!

'He was going to look in on the baby, then shut himself in his study to work, so forget him if you can. I know you can't take your eyes off each other—probably can't keep your hands off each other, either!' She giggled. 'I have seen this—but this morning we are going make the plastic work very hard, so hurry and get ready. We shop for your trousseau, silly!' she stated, when faced with Anna's blank stare. 'And Francesco tells me he is having a choice of wedding gowns flown over from Milan. We will have a hard time choosing—they will all be beautiful!'

Three hectic hours later Anna collapsed with thankfulness at a table outside a fashionable bistro, fanning her perspiring face and surreptitiously slipping her aching feet out of her shoes.

The sun was unseasonably hot, and Sophia had dragged her in and out of so many classy boutiques she'd lost count. At least she had acquired a couple of serviceable cotton skirts and cheap T-shirts—but the dreadfully expensive nightgown and matching negligee, not to mention a whole raft of wickedly sexy underwear that Sophia had proclaimed impossible to leave behind, threatened to give her terminal indigestion.

'There—this is good!' Sophia seated herself, the sea of carriers—some classy, one or two definitely down-market—flowing around her feet. 'We have an hour before Arnold arrives to collect us.' She picked up the menu. 'What shall we eat?'

In the end they chose herb omelettes with a simple green salad, and a glass of chablis. Sophia tipped her head on one side and said, 'I never thought the day would come when Francesco married. It is a joy to me to know I was wrong!' Her smile was mega-watt and full of warmth. 'He chose well—you will make him so happy!'

Anna gave her attention to the omelette to hide her bleak expression. Happy? It wasn't in her gift to make him happy. Satisfying him in bed until he tired of her was as good as it could get.

Anything to get her mind off that miserable track, she laid down her fork and asked as lightly as she could, 'So why didn't you think he'd marry? After all, he's got to be every girl's dream.' Breathtakingly handsome, fabulously wealthy, able to charm the birds out of the trees when the mood took him—what woman wouldn't go weak at the knees in his vicinity?

'Yes, and that's the problem.'

Sophia's serious response drew Anna's brows together in a puzzled frown. As far as she could tell there would be no problem as far as Francesco was concerned. Arm candy came with his status.

'It is not something we talk about.' Sophia sighed. 'But you are family now, and you have given him the blessing of a child.' She drained her wine glass. 'My brother never talks of it—he refuses to speak of it—but there should be no secrets in a family.'

Her dark eyes misted, and Anna saw that if Francesco refused to talk about whatever it was, then his sister was also finding it difficult.

'You see, a bad thing happened when we were children,' Sophia continued quietly. 'It saddens me to say this, but our mother had no heart, no love in her. She was a great beauty, a society darling, and to our father she was a great passion—an obsession, I suppose you could call it. When she left us he was a broken man. He changed overnight from being a normal sort of father to being cold and distant—he seemed to hate having his children around him.'

'She left you?' Anna couldn't make sense of that. 'She had two beautiful children who both needed her and a husband who adored her. Why leave? Did she fall in love with someone else?' How terrible!

'No. Now I am older I have put the picture together—with the help of people who knew the family at that time. I was barely four years old when she left, and I don't really remember her. But Francesco was ten, and her leaving hit him hard. He adored her. And of course Papa was a changed man. He took to drinking too much and not wanting his children around. Francesco had to be like both parents rolled into one. He looked after me.'

She fiddled with the stem of her glass and turned to ask a passing waiter for a refill. 'What happened was that Papa's business had hit a rough patch. He could no longer give our mother the magnificent lifestyle she demanded. She went away with someone who could. Falling in love had nothing to do with it. Francesco and I discovered that from the note she left Papa when we were going through his things after he died.'

She spread expressive hands. 'Francesco was twenty at that time, and already had females swarming all over him like bees at a honeypot. You wouldn't believe some of the lengths they went to—one had herself delivered in a big pretend cake, another got into his bed quite naked for him to find! But he ignored them all. He chose the occasional mistress with care, making sure they knew he wasn't asking for or giving any commitment,

and spent all his energies on getting the family busi-
nesses more profitable than they'd ever been.'

'So he saw all women as clones of your mother?
Only interested in his wealth?' Anna intuited, her heart
aching for the ten-year-old Francesco, whose beautiful,
adored mother had deserted him and his little sister with
no more thought than as to where her next suite of
diamonds would come from. No wonder he found it impossible to believe he could be loved for himself.

'*Precisamente!* He saw what loving such a self-
seeking woman had done to his father, decided it would
never happen to him, and became unable to trust any of
the female sex. A great big cynic!' She smiled widely.
'But no more!' She put her hand over Anna's as it lay
on the table, patted it. 'You have taught him how to trust
and how to love! And you can't know how grateful I am
to you for that—he so deserves to love and be loved!'

Unable to sleep, despite the two large glasses of wine
with dinner, which she and Sophia had companionably
lingered over, Anna stared into the darkness.

It should have been a relaxing evening. She and
Sophia had had fun bathing Sholto, and Sophia had
chattered non-stop throughout dinner. Francesco hadn't
put in an appearance—Peggy delivering a message that
he'd been called in to head office and would be delayed
until late.

It should have been relaxing. But it hadn't been.
Shocking herself, she'd found she'd really missed him,
and when Sophia had opined, 'When you are married
and living in his beautiful *palazzo* in Toscana it will be

different. My brother will not want to work so hard, be away from you and the gorgeous *bambino* for the smallest moment!' Anna had had to bite her tongue to stop herself blurting that it wouldn't be like that.

Somehow she had to maintain the façade that her marriage to Francesco would be the love-match that so obviously delighted his sister.

But pretending was hard.

When at half past ten Sophia had yawned and confessed that the excitement of trousseau-shopping had tired her out, and she couldn't wait for the morning when the wedding dresses would be arriving from Milan, Anna had gone to bed, too, not wanting to hang around waiting for a glimpse of Francesco because that would make her look needy.

She'd heard him return just after midnight. Acutely attuned to every move he made, she'd listened to his quiet footsteps, first visiting the nursery and then going to his room at the far end of the corridor.

Now, her eyes aching with the strain of staring into the darkness, she knew she had to go to him. What Sophia had told her had made a deep impression. It had explained much. Starting with his entrenched view that she, like the rest of the female sex, wanted only to get her hands on his wealth, to enjoy the kind of lifestyle that could be provided by a man with millions behind him.

Apparently he'd been targeted by gold-diggers since he'd hit his late teens—including the one who'd had herself delivered in a cake, and the other planting herself in his bed. The trauma of his mother's desertion, and the reason for it, etched on his heart, he'd become wary, distrustful of all females under ninety!

Hadn't he accused her of draping herself 'alluringly' on his private beach, hoping he'd happen along? Echoes of other distasteful attempts to snare him?

And hadn't he also said, quite unequivocally, that they had to put the past behind them and be civilized? Enter marriage for the sake of their child, with great sex the only thing going for them?

She slipped out of bed, snatching up the summerweight coverlet and draping it around her because her nightie, courtesy of Madame Laroche's excellent taste, was too revealing for a woman who was set on putting the record straight, not on seduction.

Put the past behind them, indeed! They could try, but it wouldn't go there!

His misconceptions about her were one huge stumbling block, and she was going to get rid of it!

Pushing his bedroom door open before her courage deserted her, she heard the shower in the *en suite* bathroom. Firmly she told herself she was not going to bottle out, turn tail and scurry back in wimpish haste to her own room. This had to be done if their future relationship was to have any meaning at all.

So, OK, he had seduced her, used her, dumped her—and had only offered marriage because she had given him the child he openly adored. He certainly didn't love her—never would. She would have to live with that. What she wouldn't live with was his jaundiced impression that she was nothing but a greedy schemer.

The shower stopped. Every last muscle in Anna's

body tensed to screaming point, and her bare toes dug into the pile of the plain fawn carpet. Unlike the room she occupied, this was severely masculine—that was her edgy thought just as a severely masculine male appeared in the doorway.

Stark naked.

In a ridiculous reflex action Anna snatched at the edges of the coverlet and enclosed her suddenly quivering body even more tightly. He was shatteringly beautiful. A magnificent torso, smooth and tanned, a stomach taut and flat as a board, a silky line of dark hair running down to cradle his manhood, long lower limbs in perfect proportion to his height.

She should look away.

She couldn't.

Her throat was too thick to get out the words that would explain her presence here in his room late at night, and they fled her brain completely when he strode towards her, his handsome mouth sardonically amused as he placed firm hands on her narrow shoulders and delivered, 'We must start on equal terms, *cara*.' And he removed the light coverlet from her oddly unresisting hands.

Hot colour flushed her face. She felt horribly exposed in the thin oyster-hued silk that skimmed her body to display barely concealed bountiful curves that sent dark colour flaring over his hard cheekbones and turned his eyes to smoke.

'What—what are you doing?' Anna gasped as he slid the thin ribbon straps down over her shoulders, not stopping until the creamy, rose-tipped mounds of her peaking breasts were exposed.

'What do you think?' Eyes shimmeringly intent, Francesco snatched a ragged breath. 'I am obliging my eager bride-to-be by taking what she is so enticingly offering.'

'But—' The vehement denial she'd been about to make was forgotten in a white-hot wash of addictive need as she felt the nightdress slip down over her hips and he took her mouth with ravishing hunger, plundering the sweet interior.

All control was lost.

Just as it had been that very first time. That was her helpless thought as honesty belatedly compelled her to admit that maybe this was what she had really come for. Maybe she had cloaked her need with the cover of setting him straight about her ignorance of his high financial status. That surely could have been more sensibly embarked upon in the cool, sober light of morning.

Her knees shaking beneath her, she deepened her response to his plundering mouth and lifted her arms, her fingers digging into his thick, still-damp hair. She was hot as a furnace all over, wanting to tell him she had never stopped loving him but not daring because he wouldn't believe her, gasping convulsively as she felt the burning strength of his arousal against her quivering tummy. She heard him give a raw growl low in his throat as he broke the kiss and swept her up in his arms, to come down beside her on the massive bed.

He spread the bright shimmer of her hair against the dark cover, his lips on her forehead, on the tip of her small nose, his eyelids lowered over gleaming, sensual silver.

'When I look at you, I want you. I hunger,' he

murmured roughly. He lowered his head to take a pouting nipple between his lips, expert hands shaping her body.

The sensation made her squirm beneath him, whimpering as his mouth roved from one sensitively peaking tip to the other, until she was driven to plead, with aching desperation, 'Make love to me, Francesco!'

CHAPTER TEN

In a tangle of limbs and rumpled sheets Francesco slept, while Anna, her cheek against the warm satin of his impressive chest, listened to the steady beat of his heart, breathed in the intoxicating male scent of him and tried to hold onto the magic.

The magic of pretending they were back where they once had been, in those lost enchanted days beneath the hot Italian sun, when she'd been so ecstatically happy, believing he meant it when he vowed he loved her as much as she loved him.

She'd known he was a fantastic lover—had first-hand unforgettable experience—but tonight had been something else. Something driven. He had dominated her, thoroughly possessed her, and the ecstasy he had given her had been so intense she'd thought she might die of it.

Sex slave.

Reality hit hard. Made her eyes well with tears, her throat tighten. She'd once told herself she hated him. But she didn't. For her sins, she couldn't stop loving him, but that didn't mean she had to leap into bed with him with shamefully eager wantonness. Especially as she knew darn well that he didn't love her, actually despised her for what he thought she was.

'What is wrong, *amante*?'

So he hadn't been asleep! His voice shook her rigid—purring with contentment, his accent more pronounced than usual, reeking with the dominant male satisfaction of knowing his sex slave was his for the merest crook of his little finger!

'Your beautiful body has gone quite tense,' he drawled, with a lacing of amusement. He rolled over onto his side, his long, muscular, shatteringly sexy body partly covering her. 'I shall relax you,' he stated, with indolently sensual intent, a long-fingered hand sliding over her tummy, where the muscles tensed, down to the apex of her thighs.

Something fierce and hot shot through her responsive body, melting her bones. He could always make that happen. And she was always helpless, the fire in her greedily leaping to reach the fire in him.

'No!' Desperate to save herself from once more shaming herself by demonstrating what a complete and utter pushover she was—his for the taking whenever he wanted her—Anna shot up against the heaped pillows. 'You just don't get it, do you?'

'Get what?' Vibrant amusement still glimmered in his hooded eyes. He was still looming over her. She flattened her palms against the solid wall of his chest, pushed with all her might—and didn't budge him an inch.

Emotionally all over the place, she blurted, not caring how much of herself she was revealing, 'I love you!'

Stinging silence met her self-betrayal. Then, eyes

suddenly hostile, Francesco pulled away from her, clipping, 'There's no need to say that. What we just shared was great sex. Don't spoil it by lying.'

Infuriated, she slid off the bed in haste, to put distance between them, her heartfelt but probably misguided confession embarrassing her. 'Lying's your territory, not mine!' she charged heatedly, humiliation washing over her—because she'd bared her soul to him and he'd unforgivably accused her of lying, of putting a pretty gloss on their troubled relationship. A gloss he found distasteful because he judged it to be insincere.

'Meaning?' His voice was black ice.

'Pretending to be a practically penniless peasant, not coming clean about who you were.' She confronted him, snatching the coverlet from the floor, where he'd dropped it, and wrapping it with savagery around her nakedness. Voice spiked with bitterness, she put in with derision, 'The cheap and nasty chain you wore was a nice touch! A very convincing stage prop! Does deceit come naturally to you, or did you have lessons? Don't you dare accuse *me* of lying!'

Heading for the door as fast as her feet would carry her, she paused, dragged in a giant breath and imparted, 'I came here to make you understand that I'm *not* one of the gold-diggers you're so wary of. I had no idea you could pay off the national debt and still have change!' she exaggerated wildly, and gave a 'so there!' flounce as she turned again for the door.

She was stopped in her tracks when he launched at her, 'You knew. You'd seen photographs of me in the press. You admitted it, if you remember. And if your father was expecting to entertain your new "penniless peasant" of a lover, why did he ask me for a million sterling five minutes after I crossed the threshold? Your big mistake was in not advising him to wait patiently for the plums to fall into his lap.'

Absolutely stunned, Anna could only stare as he leant over and switched off the bedside light, plunging the room into darkness. Sounding ice-cool, he advised, 'Face up to what you are. I have. After all,' he added, dry as dust, 'you've got what you set out to get. Cut the histrionics and we might make a reasonable attempt at a future life together. Go to bed.'

Anna headed for the nursery next morning feeling as if she were sleepwalking. Her head was pounding and her puffy eyes bore witness to a prolonged crying jag.

She'd spent the rest of the night after Francesco had so calmly dismissed her wondering if it could possibly be true. Had Dad really brazenly asked him for a million pounds? The very idea made her stomach roll over.

Remembering his crazy idea of starting a safari park, in yet another ridiculous scheme to recoup the money he'd lost, she had sickly acknowledged that it could be so.

She had no idea how he'd known the Italian owned much more than the shirt on his back. *She* certainly hadn't. But, he had as good as accused her of putting her father up to asking for such a massive amount, and no amount of denials on her part would make him believe her.

Her last hope of gaining his respect, if not his love, had vanished. And she didn't know how she could spend the rest of her life with him, loving him, needing him, knowing he thought so badly of her.

He was right about one thing. The sex was out of this world. And at the moment everything in that department was fine for him. But he didn't love her, never would, and the time would inevitably come when he looked for new challenges. And then she would have nothing of him. They would be just two strangers with nothing to bind them but their child. And when their child was grown, setting out on his own, she would have nothing. She really didn't think she could face such a future.

Yet how could she deprive darling Sholto of two parents who loved him to bits. Not to mention all the massive advantages of being the son of Francesco Mastroianni? How could she refuse to go through with the marriage and then live with the dreadful and pressing fear that her baby's father would do all within his limitless power to claim him?

Not forgetting her parents. Despite Mum being too feeble to put her foot down, to take control of the family finances before things had got so way out of hand, and despite Dad being so ebulliently sure that he knew better than a coachload of financial advisors, she loved them both. Refuse to marry Francesco and the years that were left to them would be lived in grinding poverty.

Her headache was getting worse by the second. Determined to stop going over and over her dreadful situation, at least for as long as it took to bath and feed little Sholto, she put a pallid smile on her face and opened the door.

'For once I beat you to it.' Francesco's lithe lean body

dwarfed the nursing chair. Sholto, wearing a fresh white sleeper suit, was cradled in his arms, blissfully asleep. 'I changed and fed him,' he claimed proudly. 'It is not so difficult.'

'So I see,' Anna mumbled, through lips that felt as stiff as cement. Last night might not have happened, she registered. Things had been said by both of them, accusations hurled like bricks. And now they had to be forgotten. He was being civilised!

Sex was the only level on which she could fleetingly reach him. She couldn't touch him on any emotional level. He had put his distaste for what he thought she was to one side for the sake of Sholto's future well-being. All his emotions were centred on his tiny son, as he now demonstrated as he ran the back of a forefinger softly over the baby's downy cheek and imparted, 'After the marriage we will spend most of our time at my home in Tuscany, where he will have all the freedom and space to run and play in air that is not polluted. I will teach him to fish and ride, and he will grow tall and strong.'

Easing himself from the low chair, he laid the contented baby back in his cot, straightened and announced, 'We will have a nanny.'

Just like that! Rebellion sparked inside her, but she was careful to keep her voice low and level as she asked, 'Don't I have a say in that? I don't need a nanny to look after him.'

Already she was feeling dreadfully deprived of the only time she now found anything approaching real happiness. That precious early-morning hour spent bathing, dressing, playing with and feeding her baby.

How intolerable it would be to have a hired nanny—no matter how good her references, how kind she was—taking over!

Was he intending to completely sideline her? Turn her into a cipher, a creature of no importance, only useful in his bed—until he tired of her?

'Perhaps not,' he conceded. 'But consider—when you are pregnant again you will be grateful for just a little help. Especially when you have a newborn and an energetic toddler to entertain. And maybe another on the way in the blink of an eye?'

'I can't believe you actually said that,' Anna told him in a strangled tone. Shut away in the back of beyond, unable to speak the language, with no friends or family to support her, producing one baby after another—like on a conveyor belt! The mental image alone was enough to give her hysterics! 'You want loads more children?'

His narrowed-eyes appraisal was full of amusement as he said, 'Given our track record, *amante*, it's a foregone conclusion. Swept away by lust just about covers it, wouldn't you say?'

An unsubtle reminder of her wanton behaviour last night, when the thought of precautions had not entered her head. Or his. On purpose? Did he intend to keep her permanently pregnant, surrounded by so many children she wouldn't have the time or energy to notice when he strayed?

Her ashen face did the impossible and turned even whiter. As if properly seeing her for the first time, he gave an impatient click of his tongue, swept his hand beneath her elbow and escorted her to the door. 'You look terrible. Go back to bed and rest for a couple of hours. Peggy will bring breakfast to you at ten.'

Opening the door to her room, he placed a hand in the small of her back, eased her over the threshold and drawled, 'And, by the way, if wearing those ugly things is your idea of shaming me, of paying me back for seeing through your attempt to bamboozle me last night, you've failed.'

He meant the baggy T-shirt and undeniably cheap and badly cut jeans she'd bought from the market around which she'd dragged a disapproving and reluctant Sophia on that shopping trip.

Rallying as he began to close her into her bedroom, furious that he should automatically assume that her emotionally riven declaration of love was a pack of lies, she rounded on him, faint colour brushing her pale cheeks.

'You are the most self-centred male I have ever met! Everything I do or say has to be meant for you, doesn't it? Well, listen up—every thought I have *doesn't* revolve round you. I bought this cheap gear to wear to save that fancy stuff you've lumbered me with!' She was getting into her stride, almost enjoying herself—and the startled light in those smoke-grey eyes. 'Sholto loves his morning bath, which means he squirms and wriggles and soaks me. And he dribbles when I burp him. So, no, you didn't even enter my head when I dressed this morning!'

And she closed the door on his astonishment.

CHAPTER ELEVEN

FRANCESCO tossed his suit jacket over the fax machine, loosened his tie. The room he used as his home office was his only oasis of peace.

Returning after an absence of more than two weeks, he had found the large London house uncomfortably full of relatives. Anna's parents had been fussing over the wedding gifts that had, apparently, been arriving by the truck-load. Declining to join them in the general oohs and aahs, he had been almost knocked off his feet by his niece's exuberant greetings, and had only been able to extricate himself from her stranglehold around his neck with the arrival of Fabio, his brother-in-law.

'Cristina—let Zio Francesco breathe!' He had grabbed the squirming six-year-old by the waist and un-plastered her from her uncle's chest. 'He will admire your bridesmaid's dress later, at a time of his convenience! Right now he has things to do.'

After exchanging a wry grin with the older man, he had found the wedding organiser holding court with her usual brisk efficiency in the ground-floor sitting room with Sophia, as he would have expected, nodding, agreeing and exclaiming excitedly. Anna had been sitting mute, with a face like stone.

The wedding was two days away. He wanted it over. Although he'd been back for a scant twenty minutes he was already finding the preliminaries irritating, making him edgy. He had never thought the day would dawn when he'd actually embrace the notion of marriage to a proven gold-digger without running the proverbial mile, when he'd be positively aching to be alone with his family. His wife. His baby son.

But it had. And that state of affairs surely meant his mental faculties had been severely impaired! Or was he a sensible guy, sure of his ability to handle the future, doing what was right for all concerned?

His hard, sensual mouth twisted wryly. What was that old saying? Never make a wish, it might come true.

Once entranced, besotted, eager as a callow youth— his dearest wish had been to make Anna his wife. Now that wish was about to come true. But how different from the wedded bliss he had envisaged!

And Anna? Her wish to marry into great wealth was about to be granted. But she acted as if she were about to keep an appointment to have her limbs severed from her torso without benefit of anaesthetic rather than go through the ceremony that would see the fulfilment of her avaricious dreams.

Had she, too, painted a rosy mind-picture of their glittering future together? Spoiled and pampered, with an adoring, blinkered husband dancing attendance on her slightest whim?

If so, tough! He wasn't his father!

Impatiently, Francesco ran a finger round the inside of his shirt collar and undid the top button. Something had to be sorted out. Now. They couldn't spend the rest of their lives together indulging in not so lightly veiled warfare.

The past two weeks or so had been spent visiting his company head offices across the world. Promoting, demoting, putting the most able and trustworthy managers in place to take the burden of day-to-day decisions off his shoulders in order to leave him free to spend much more time with his son. Little Sholto would grow to manhood knowing that his father loved him, wanted to be around him, spent quality time with him, would be there for him whatever happened.

Now all that had to be done was to reach an understanding with his bride-to-be.

He found her in the garden. Sholto lay on a rug in the dappled shade. His rounded limbs were bare, punching joyfully energetic holes in the warm late-afternoon air, and Anna was beside him, propped up on one elbow, gently tickling his tummy, her lovely face softened and glowing, her abundant hair precariously massed on the top of her head.

For long moments he stayed where he was, his heart so full he thought it might burst. Love for his tiny son, he rationalized. Nothing else. This overwhelming emotion could be nothing else.

He had loved Anna once—loved her beyond reason. But that had died at the exact and damning moment when her father had tried to part him from a hefty wad of the folding stuff. He still lusted after her. He only had to look at her and his whole body went into overdrive, aching to possess her. Lust wasn't pretty, but it was reality. And he always faced reality.

His impressive shoulders squared, he strolled forward. 'In two weeks he has grown,' he observed, annoyed by the definitely husky quality of his voice. His annoyance intensified by a thousand per cent when he noted how she stiffened at his arrival on the idyllic scene.

Stifling the desire to make the cynical observation that she didn't go as rigid as a plank of toughened steel when he touched her, but melted into his arms like warm honey, he lifted his son and held him aloft in his arms, grinning like the besotted fool he was, exulting as his action produced crowing sounds in the precious infant.

'He smiled at me!' he enthused, forgetting his future bride's less than welcoming body language for the moment, revelling in the bubbly, crinkly movement of the tiny mouth. 'I swear it wasn't just wind!'

In this mood her son's father was irresistible, Anna thought sourly. But no way was she about to succumb, give way, let her heart reach out to him with love and then wait for the inevitable cruel accusation or unpleasant revelation to hit her. She would not live her life seesawing from one violent emotion to another.

She stood, brushing non-existent creases from the fine cotton skirt she was wearing with a matching jade green sleeveless top, and Francesco said, with a touch of dryness that made her ears sting, 'Don't let me drive you away! It is good for our son to have the company of both parents.'

'Don't flatter yourself! It's time for his evening bath and feed,' Anna countered matter-of-factly, refusing to let him get to her on any level. No way would she allow him to think his presence had her scuttling away like a frightened rabbit. She wouldn't give him the ego-trip of thinking he could affect her behaviour. 'You can carry him up to the nursery and hang around if you want to,' she conceded calmly, and set off towards the house.

Even though her heart was pattering like mad, she was proud of the way she'd managed to let him know she could take his presence or leave it. She nearly fell over her feet when he, following with Sholto, confirmed warmly, 'I would like that. And tonight we dine out. It is arranged. Sophia will take the monitor—she is looking forward to babysitting. You and I need to talk away from the eyes and ears of our assembled family members.'

Taking her seat at the pricily secluded and intimate table in one of London's most fashionable restaurants, Anna felt, ridiculously, like a fluttery girl embarking on her first date.

Her escort, eye-swivellingly handsome in his white dinner jacket, had turned all female heads as they'd been shown to their table, and Anna couldn't blame them. Francesco Mastroianni was one class act. She was probably the envy of every female in the place. But she wasn't going to let that go to her head, because she knew that nothing was what it seemed. Very far from it.

And she wasn't going to get flustered because those silvery grey eyes of his were quite definitely appreciative and amazingly proprietorial, nor react when he remarked softly, his accent pronounced, 'You are very beautiful. The dress suits you. But, like me, every man in the room is probably wanting to remove it from you.'

She would not blush. She would *not*! Neither would she give way to the silly impulse to pluck at the dipping neckline of the understatedly sexy red dress and simper, Oh, this old rag!

Instead, she laid aside the menu she'd been given and said, 'This is your idea. You order for me. You said you wanted to talk. Well, I've got something I want to say to you.'

'And that is?' One sable brow arched lazily, his gorgeous mouth taking on the slow half-smile that infuriated her because it usually meant he was patronising her.

So she said, 'My parents tell me they are to live at your London address. Permanently. Everything thrown in—even a part-time job of sorts at your London office for Dad.'

'And they are not pleased?'

'You know damn well they are!' It was a dreadful struggle to keep her voice down, to button her lip as Francesco gave their order, indicated that the wine waiter should open the bottle of champagne that had been waiting on ice for their arrival.

Since their arrival two days ago her parents had hardly stopping singing the praises of their so-generous future son-in-law—going on and on about how much they were looking forward to living here, being able to go to the theatre whenever they wanted to, wander round the shops and galleries when the mood took them, take in all the sights, and wasn't it a blessing that they both got on so well with Peggy and Arnold, who were to be kept on to look after them? It had been the first she had heard of it, and it rankled.

'So? Your point is?'

'That you arranged all that without telling me. You really know how to make sure I know just how unimportant I am.' Her sense of exclusion had been shockingly painful. Her eyes sparked emerald fire, wild rose colour flooding her cheeks as she accused, 'And my wedding—*you* briefed the blonde iceberg. I wasn't consulted about anything!'

'But she kept you up to speed?' He was fingering the stem of his glass, and though she was doubting her own eyes, was he really looking just slightly discomfited?

'I was *told* what flowers I would have, what food and wine would be served at the reception and so on, if that's what you mean. All done and dusted—with the distinct impression that if I wanted the slightest change I'd be told to go and sit in a corner, and not speak until spoken to!'

Not that she cared what arrangements were made, because as far as she was concerned the ceremony would be the equivalent of being handed a life sentence, bound to a man who viewed her as a necessary evil.

Francesco leaned forward, his laid-back façade showing signs of cracking, 'If there is something you're not happy with then it's not too late to change it,' he assured her rapidly, taking the wind out of her sails. 'She is, I am told, the best wedding organiser around, but—'

'No,' Anna put in with deflated honesty. 'There's nothing I or anyone could object to.' So he was willing to take her concerns on board? It was news to her! 'It was the principle of the thing.'

'Of course. I'm—' He broke off impatiently as the deferential waiter served their first course, and as soon as they were alone again resumed. 'I'm sorry you haven't been consulted. My fault. Truth is, the last few weeks have been hectic. There were decisions to be made. I made them, acted on them. That's how I operate. But—' he smiled at her, making her defenceless heart flip '—I shall teach myself to think twice where you have concerns. You won't be kept in the dark in future. Starting now.'

His eyes held hers, reaching her, and for a moment she felt as if she were floating out of her body. She despised herself for still craving this man she loved to bits, even though she knew he saw her as a greedy liar, but her flesh trembled in reaction to the rough velvet of his voice as he told her, 'As you know, your father's debts have been cleared, and I now own Rylands. They were happy to sell to me. Apparently your mother has long wanted to move to somewhere more easily managed. And it seemed like a good idea to offer them the permanent use of my London home. Besides,' he intoned flatly, as if what he had to say was distasteful to him, 'I thought a token position on the board might stop your father from filling my garden with wild animals.'

Mutely, Anna nodded, resolutely ignoring the jibe about wild animals because it made her feel ill, concentrating on her mother's astounding confession.

When her parents had broken the news that they'd be living permanently at Francesco's London address she'd asked Mum if she would miss her family home, and she'd confessed no, not at all. She'd suggested selling up and cutting their losses to Dad many times, but he'd always flatly refused to entertain the idea. It was her family home and he wasn't going to see her lose it because of a few business setbacks. He would never forgive himself. In the end she had had to put her foot down—they'd almost quarrelled—and then their saviour, in the form of the generous Francesco, had happened along.

His smile was back as he explained, 'Major renovation work is soon to start on the house and grounds. And, if you agree, I'd like it to be kept in the family. In the normal course of events the house would have been part of our son's heritage. As you know, we will spend most of our time in Tuscany, but Sholto needs to learn something of his English roots. Rylands would be ideal for summer holidays—a traditional British Christmas, maybe. What do you think?'

He was actually asking her opinion instead of letting her know through a third party after the decision had been made! The fact that his prime concern was what was right for his son was something she would have to learn to live with. Her needs and wants didn't come into it. The knowledge was chilling.

'You're right.' He always was—or thought he was! But in this instance she agreed with him. 'Having a base in the English countryside will be good for Sholto.' And all the dozens of other children he expected her to give him!

She laid down her fork, her appetite disappearing like dew in hot summer sun, as Francesco said, 'I wanted to talk to you, discuss our future.' His beautiful mouth twisted wryly, 'To date we have been like duellists, circling each other, waiting for the opening to strike—apart from that one unforgettable night when you came to my bed, and that ended sourly, too. It mustn't go on,' he stated, with a sincerity that sent shivers up her spine. 'We are to be married. We have a son. The only sensible thing to do is to forget everything that has gone before, and go forward together in harmony.'

He raised his champagne flute and gave her the smile that always managed to splinter her heart. 'A toast to our future. Let it be calm. No more fighting! I give you peace in our time!' His eyes were wicked, sexy, warm, reminding her forcibly of the time on the island when happiness for her had been his glance, his smile, his touch, drenching her in the sadness of loss.

Make the best of a bad job, she translated with an inner shudder. Hardly the best recipe for wedded bliss. But then she hadn't expected that, had she?

She stared at the glass, at the straw-coloured liquid alive with diamond-bright bubbles, and her throat closed up. With inner reluctance she slowly raised her glass to his. No more fighting. Sweep the past—the hurt—under the carpet. Take whatever the future held with calm stoicism. Never complain, never look into the past, never be seen without a serene smile on her face.

A marriage like tramlines. Running parallel, never meeting except on the most basic physical level. Wham-bam, thank you, ma'am! Always being careful. Careful not to say or imply anything that might bring up things that had been said or done, nasty accusations that had to stay hidden under that carpet.

She didn't know if she was going to be able to live like

that. She owed it to herself to try—again—to make him believe her. Remembering how he had met her earlier attempts with cringe-making cynicism, she shivered.

After recklessly draining her glass, she watched him refill it as pork roulades and individual dishes of beautifully cooked vegetables were placed on the table. She didn't think she could eat any of it, and told him flatly, 'I might be about to break this peace you suddenly seem to find less taxing than sniping at each other, but—and this is important to me—you have to know that I had no idea of who you were or what you were worth until weeks after you dumped me.'

She bit her lip. His eyes were cold, his mouth tight. He was determined not to believe her! But she'd started this, so she would finish it.

Her voice firm, belying the quaking going on inside her, she said, 'Cissie showed me an old magazine. There was an article about you—your successes in the financial field.' Pointless to mention the simpering arm candy. 'Know this about me—I am *not* the same as your mother.'

Silence. Just the muted chatter of the other diners.

'Sophia has been talking,' he said, with nerve-shredding quietness. Dull colour laid a path over his angular cheekbones and his mouth was tight with displeasure.

But all Anna could see was a bewildered ten-year-old boy whose adored mother had suddenly disappeared from his life. And whose father, just when he needed him most, had turned his back on him and the tiny sister he found himself responsible for. He would have played with Sophia, who'd been little more than a baby, given her the love she wasn't getting from any other quarter, tried to take the place of both parents, growing up with responsibility, a strong sense of duty deeply ingrained.

Hence his decision to marry the mother of his own son—despite her being, in his eyes, just another greedy woman on the make. No matter what she said in her own defence, circumstances had conspired to make any belief in her impossible. But she could, and would, defend his sister.

Leaning forward, her eyes brimming with compassion, she told him softly, 'Don't be cross with Sophia. She's so pleased about the wedding—she just came out with it, said she'd never thought she'd live to see the day. I asked why, naturally, and she told me about your mother only marrying your father for the money that could buy her the glittering lifestyle she wanted. Then leaving him for some other well-heeled guy when she saw the supply was in danger of drying up. How your father was so devastated he didn't even want to have anything to do with his children. She said I was family now, and should know.'

Lifting her slender shoulders in a tiny shrug, she added, 'You're her big brother and she loves you, and she's happy for you, thinking you've finally found a woman you can trust enough to love.' Her voice flattened. 'I didn't prick her bubble—tell her how very wrong she is because you don't trust me at all. And you certainly don't love me.'

But he had done. Once. She was sure of it now. Her heart was hurting, her throat tightening as knowledge of what she'd lost swamped her.

She'd thought of little else since he'd exploded that

bombshell about what had happened the night he'd dumped her, washed his hands of her and walked away. It added up. It was the missing piece of the jigsaw.

He had loved her. When they'd met on Ischia he'd concealed his true identity because he'd wanted to be loved for himself, not his wealth. He had meant every word when he'd said he loved her.

But Dad, with his usual bull-at-a-gate tactics, had killed that love dead as the dodo. He must have recognised his daughter's new boyfriend from the pages of the financial papers he took, and had barged straight in and asked for massive investment in that crazy safari park idea, convinced that everyone would see his latest surefire money-making scheme as the world-beater he alone thought it was.

She was sure it had happened that way, and Francesco's earlier reference to wild animals in his garden clinched it. Didn't it just!

She toyed with her cutlery, not able to eat. And, no, she hadn't broached the subject with her father, insisted he tell her exactly what he'd said to Francesco that evening. Because if he'd confirmed what she already believed she would have blown her top, accused him of ruining her chance of true happiness, causing so much ill-feeling that her approaching wedding day would be even more of an uncomfortable farce than it was going to be.

Besides, she loved her eccentric father uncondition-ally. Creating a real rift between them would be dreadful. What was done was done, the outcome un-changeable. Because of what had happened to him when he was a bewildered, vulnerable small boy Francesco was programmed to suspect any woman who vowed she loved him of having ulterior and mercenary motives.

'I'm sorry. This isn't working.' A slight gesture had the waiter gliding forward with the bill, and Anna watched his eyes frost over, his strong, lean face hard as the transaction was completed.

He stood, every line of his magnificent body tense, his eyes inward-looking, and Anna scrambled to her feet, her legs shaking like an ill-set jelly.

Their cosy date, with him spelling out the slick, totally unreal guidelines for their future, had been blown out of the water because she'd opened her big mouth, told him things he didn't want to hear.

He would never believe she hadn't had a clue as to who he really was when their baby was conceived, and he despised her for trying to tell him otherwise. He was furious because Sophia had spilled the beans about what their mother had done, how their father had behaved towards them as children. It was a period of his life he never talked about, and he obviously resented her knowing.

Had he, like her, come to the conclusion that their marriage was on the rocks before it even happened?

A black cab was already waiting. Francesco handed her in. He had a whole lot of thinking to do. Finding the truth was now imperative—and that included a long overdue talk with her father.

He'd been off his head to have believed he could put a shiny gloss on their future—paste over the fissure-like cracks, pretend they didn't exist.

Insisting on marriage hadn't all been about his son. Anna herself was at the core of it. At last he was honest enough to admit that he still loved her. He wanted to believe she still loved him. But if what came out of his conversation with her father failed to convince, then he was not going to follow in his own father's footsteps and enter a marriage where one partner loved and the other just took.

Initially he'd believed he could make the marriage work for the sake of his son. Rub along, shut out the past, be civilised—with the bonus, of course, of great sex. But now that he'd finally faced up to the fact that no woman had ever been able to affect him as she did, that he loved her, he knew it could never work. It would fail, as his parents' marriage had, leaving him bitter and hurting.

'I'll walk.' He gave the address, passed notes to the driver, turned back to her, his eyes bleak. 'I'll see you at the altar.'

Maybe.

CHAPTER TWELVE

'YOU look so beautiful!' Beatrice Maybury's eyes were misty as Sophia, elegant in a suit of amber-coloured silk, finished fastening the myriad of tiny buttons at the back of the elaborately beaded white satin wedding gown and adjusted the filmy veil.

'Fantastica!' Sophia sighed. 'So romantic—Francesco is a lucky man!'

Anna tried to smile.

Difficult.

There was nothing remotely romantic about this wedding.

Sophia fussing, Cristina preening, proud as a peacock in her lemon-coloured wild silk bridesmaid's dress, hopping from one foot to the other in excitement, demanding, 'Is it nearly time to go yet?' Mum sitting in regal splendour in her blue and gold brocade coat and amazing hat, nursing Sholto and looking dotingly at everything she laid her eyes on, the coming ceremony itself—all this was nothing but an elaborate stage set, with herself as one of the principal actors, playing her part in a fantasy of cruel unreality.

She hadn't seen Francesco since they'd left the restaurant.

'It's bad luck for the groom to see his bride so close to the wedding,' Mum had informed her. 'He's booked into a hotel—you'll see him at the altar!' Too interested in trying to decide which shoes went best with her mother-of-the-bride outfit, she had failed to notice the bleakness in her daughter's eyes.

The strangely chilling mood he'd been in when they'd parted had given her the impression that he'd washed his hands of her. Standing at the altar with her was the very last thing he wanted!

It was a horrible situation, she thought with utter misery, her self-esteem flat on the floor. He was only marrying her for the sake of the tiny son he so obviously adored, and she'd allowed herself to be as good as blackmailed into accepting him. Which would be OK, she supposed glumly, if she really *was* the sneaky money-grubber he believed she was.

But she wasn't! She'd stopped being blinkered and admitted she still loved the brute! And that made everything so very much worse!

She'd made one last desperate attempt to convince him of her integrity, but that had had the effect of changing him from someone who was willing to sweep the past under the carpet, to make the best of a bad job with a semblance of grace, in to someone who gave the impression that he never wanted to set eyes on her again!

'Stop daydreaming!' Sophia chided affectionately, putting a bouquet of white roses into her trembling hands. 'The cars are here.'

And so was her father. Looking good in his hired morning suit, a white carnation in his buttonhole, proud as punch as he took in his daughter's wedding finery.

As soon as they were alone he gave her a gentle hug, being careful not to squash pristine perfection, bringing tears to film her eyes. He was her father, and she loved him, and she knew he loved her, but he had been the cause of Francesco's unshakeable distrust of her.

'Nervous, poppet? Don't be—you'll make Bride Of The Year, and good old Dad's here to make safe passage!'

Too churned up inside to ask him what he was talking about, she found out, to her horror, when they walked through the outer door to face a small army of photographers, pushing, crowding, firing questions. Her head was swimming as Dad, with the help of the uniformed driver, allowed her to gain the sanctuary of the car without too much loss of dignity for the short drive.

There would be more of them waiting at the church she guessed. She supposed with a lurch of her already churning stomach that the marriage of one of the world's most eligible bachelors to a nobody made a story of sorts.

Cinderella!

Her heart wrenched. Without the happy ending!

'Poppet—I'm sorry. It's all my fault,' William Maybury said gruffly as the car purred forward.

'Don't be stupid,' Anna muttered tiredly. The photographers weren't snapping like crazy because of *him*. It was all down to who Francesco was.

'No—listen. I had a long chat with your young man last night. He asked me to go to his hotel. It was late when I got back, and you'd gone to bed, and this morning it's been hectic, so—'

'Dad, I don't want to talk. Not now. Please!' Her face pale and set, she turned her head away.

She simply could not bear to hear yet another paean of praise for the paragon! She couldn't blame her parents for being overwhelmed by the generosity that would enable them to live out their lives in luxury and security—they were practically unable to talk of anything else and she could understand that—but she didn't want to hear any more. Their future security had been bought at a mile-high price to herself!

Doing her best to ignore the photographers, Anna entered the fashionable church on her father's arm and saw Francesco waiting. Tall, achingly handsome, his morning suit clothing the perfection of his lithe body with elegance and style.

So her vague doubts that he'd show at all, that he'd washed his hands of her, had been unfounded. Her steps faltered. In a way it would have been better if he had left her standing at the altar! It would have been a clean break. She would have got over it. Eventually. Living the rest of her life loving him, knowing he thought she was—

'Chin up, poppet.' Her father's hand tightened on her elbow, urging her forward. 'Everything's absolutely fine, I promise!'

What the heck did he know? was her irreverent thought as his hand fell away and she found herself standing at Francesco's side.

He was looking at her, his too attractive features set, his eyes dark with emotion as they raked her pale face and huge haunted eyes. His voice was thick as he murmured, low and emotive, 'I love you Anna. *Love you.*'

The ceremony passed in a blur, Anna's head spinning, asking herself the same questions over and over. Had he really said that? Or had she misheard? A panic-induced, hopeless illusion? And, if he *had* said it, was it because he'd taken one look at her and, fearing she'd take flight, grab her little son and run, said the one thing guaranteed to root her to the spot?

It seemed no time at all before they were in the car to take them to the reception at some fancy hotel or other. The blonde iceberg had told her which one but she hadn't really taken it in.

'Did you mean what you said?' she questioned tightly, her tummy flipping.

He settled his long, elegant frame at her side and the car moved forward. His smouldering eyes moved over her. He took both her trembling hands in his. 'You are unbelievably beautiful. How could I not mean every word? I love you, *cara.*' He lifted her hands to his lips, turning them over to place softly lingering kisses in her palms, and her heart jerked painfully.

Was he just saying that? Using lavish helpings of that devastating charm he could conjure out of thin air just to keep her sweet until the public ordeal of the reception was over? His ego wouldn't stand the humiliation of having his new bride look one iota less than totally ecstatic.

Or did he mean it? How could he?

He raised his head, said something in his own language that sounded like a violent expletive. Then, 'We have arrived. There's no time to say what I must. Anna—' he cupped her face briefly '—trust me. I love you, and I swear I will prove it to you for the rest of my life!'

His avowal threw her off balance. He looked and sounded so sincere. And the way he held her hand and didn't let go until they were seated for the banquet, the focus of two hundred pairs of eyes, almost convinced her that a miracle had happened.

She so wanted to be convinced. And she allowed herself to be as the lavish wedding feast progressed and his eyes rarely left hers. They were the love-drenched eyes of the man she had first fallen in love with on that sun-soaked Italian island almost a year ago, and all doubts fled when, under cover of the applause and laughter at the end of Fabio's best man speech, Francesco reached into an inner pocket and slid a huge sparkling yellow diamond onto her finger above the plain gold band.

'I noticed you don't wear the ring I more or less forced on you—with such gross insensitivity.'

'You were impatient,' she excused, green eyes huge. 'I couldn't make up my mind. In any case.' Her small chin came up. 'I didn't want anything from you that wasn't given with love.'

Smouldering silver eyes met hers, and his voice was thick as he confided, briefly touching the ring that glittered on her finger, 'I chose this for you because the blonde stone reminded me of your lovely hair. It was in my pocket as I drove to Gloucestershire all those months ago. I was going to ask you to be my wife. It was chosen with love.'

He had loved her then, had wanted to marry her. Then everything had gone pear-shaped. Dad had blundered in and ruined everything. The stark reminder of cold reality sent an icy spasm round her heart and her eyes brimmed.

Nothing had changed. Not really. How could it when whenever she tried to convince him that she'd had no idea of who he was when they'd met he as good as accused her of lying? His private opinion of her must still be rock-bottom.

She couldn't fault his efforts to do just what he'd suggested in that restaurant—sweep what had happened under the carpet and put a glossy veneer of togetherness on their marriage. But—

'We have to talk. Properly talk,' she mumbled raggedly, hating the thought of living with a much-loved husband who, deep in the secret places of his heart, believed she was only with him for what she could get out of him. His protestations of love would only be made to ensure their marriage wasn't a battleground, an unfit arena for his son's upbringing.

'Of course.' He took her hand in his. 'Later.' His charismatic smile lit his spectacular features as he stood, drawing her with him. 'We are now expected to lead the dancing.'

Aware of music coming from the ballroom, and the gradual exodus of guests from the lavishly appointed dining room, Anna swallowed a sigh.

The show must go on!

Pinning a smile on her face, she allowed herself to be swept into a slow waltz, melting into the lean, hard strength of his body because she couldn't help herself, willing herself to believe that a miracle could happen, that he really had changed his mind about her, really did love her.

She snapped out of the dreamy state of complete capitulation that being held in his arms always induced when Fabio tapped him on his shoulder and claimed her.

Later, halfway through a dance with someone whose name she couldn't remember, had perhaps never known, she excused herself on the grounds that her feet were killing her, took a glass of champagne from a passing waiter, and went to find somewhere secluded to sit.

As arranged, Peggy and Arnold had taken Sholto home to be fed, changed and put down to sleep, and Francesco had done his duty, dancing with her mother, his sister and his cousin Silvana.

Finding a chair against a far wall, she sat, her eyes homing in on her husband, now dancing up close and personal with the redhead who had been with him on that never-to-be-forgotten weekend when she'd catered for his cousin and her husband.

Sick to her stomach, her emotions all over the place, she swallowed the contents of her glass in one go. The slinky redhead had been his latest squeeze that weekend. Now she was all over him, making a public spectacle of them both. Her face flamed. How dared he invite an ex-lover to his wedding? Or was he planning to reinstate her?

'Dance?'

Anna glanced up, about to refuse, saw Nick looking decidedly gloomy, and said, 'Why not?'

'I'm not much good at this,' he said, 'and proved it by treading on her foot.

'Not to worry.' Avoiding his size twelves would take

her mind off what Francesco was doing with that woman! 'We can just shuffle. Where's Melody?' The invitation had been for both of them.

'She couldn't make it. We were both gutted. We were looking forward to it, and to spending her weekend off here in London—booked a hotel and everything. Dammit—sorry!' he grumped, as he steered her into another couple. Holding her tighter, until she felt she would never be able to breathe again, he explained dourly, 'She's a vet nurse. There's only three in the practice. One's on holiday, and the one who was supposed to be on duty came down with a viral sickness, so poor old Mel had to fill in. So I'm on my tod.'

'Poor you!' Anna sympathised, glancing up and finding Francesco's eyes on her from the far side of the dance floor. He looked furious. No sign of the redhead. Furious because she was dancing with Nick?

Her heart skipped. He had given her ample evidence that he couldn't stand to see her old friend around her. And she'd accused him of being jealous. He'd denied it, of course, but you didn't feel possessive of someone who meant little to you, did you?

'I think I'll give the next dance a miss, Nick.'

She'd grab her brand-new husband and ask him why he'd been in a clinch to music with his one-time lover, inform him that if he thought he could resume his old womanising ways while he was married to her then he could darn well think again!

'Good idea,' Nick responded as he escorted her from the dance floor, heading for a pair of vacant gilded chairs, his arm around her narrow waist. 'Wait here.' His bluntly good-looking face was beaded with sweat. 'I'll fetch us a drink—something long and cold. I'm sweltering.'

The words to tell him not to bother on her account, because she was going to find Francesco, nail him down if necessary, died on her lips as he promptly disappeared in the direction of the bar. Shrugging slightly, she turned and found herself face to face with the redhead.

'I suppose I must give you my congratulations?'

'Thank you.' Anna didn't want to acknowledge the woman, but pride forced her to respond.

'Don't thank me.' The glossy scarlet lips parted on an insincere smile. 'Thank your own forward planning and fertility. Entrapment, I believe they call it.'

'I can't believe you just said that!' Anna was shaking inside with the force of her emotions. Was that how Francesco viewed his situation? Probably, she conceded in utter misery, and was drainingly humiliated when the other woman smoothed the dark green slinky fabric of her daringly low-cut dress over her snake hips and responded.

'No? Everybody thinks it—even though they're sweetness and light to your face. But that's not my style. Call a spade a spade, that's me. Francesco married you because you made sure you got yourself pregnant— why else would he tie himself to a bog-standard cook? But take it from one who knows. He won't be faithful. I got it from the horse's mouth. He invited me to your wedding specifically to tell me.'

CHAPTER THIRTEEN

As Nick appeared with two brimming glasses Francesco arrived, his eyes shooting ice as he said, cold as permafrost, 'My wife won't be needing that. We're leaving.'

The emotional upheaval going on inside her head meant Anna couldn't think straight, never mind resist, as a long-fingered hand clamped around her upper arm and hustled her out into the vast reception area.

He spoke into a mobile phone, clipped, authoritative, then snapped it closed and growled, 'Did you train him to dance attendance?'

'Don't be silly!'

'What was silly,' he countered, his eyes glittering, narrowed, 'was the moony love-lorn look on the guy's face as he trundled you around in a bear-hug—as if he couldn't face letting go of you.'

Looking up into his tension-riven features, Anna felt a reprehensible stab of triumph. He *was* jealous of Nick! That being so, could he really intend continuing his affair with that woman?

Or was it a case of sauce for the gander but not for the goose?

Firmly resisting the urge to string him along—and in the light of what the slinky redhead had said to her and the way they'd been practically seducing each other on the dance floor he deserved it—she informed him coolly, 'Nick was fed-up. Melody—the woman he's crazy about—couldn't be here. They'd planned to stay on for a day or two in London, but she'd had to cancel to cover for a sick colleague. And it wasn't a bear-hug! He was holding on to me because he kept on bumping me into other couples. He's got concrete boots when he's dancing. So don't lump me and Nick into the same league as you and *that woman*!'

'What's that supposed to mean?' Apparently unmollified by her defence of Nick, he was really on his high horse. His waiting silence was like an unscaleable brick wall, but Anna was too enraged to back away.

'The redheaded harpie you were practically seducing on the dance floor just accused me of entrapment and told me you'd invited her to our wedding to tell her that the fact that you were married wouldn't interfere with your affair with her. How sick is that?'

'*Dio mio!*' Francesco uttered grimly. Two hands on her upper arms, he swung her round to face him. 'That is pure poison!' Strain tightened his sensual mouth. 'I swear on our son's precious life that I have never had an affair with that woman. I hardly know her. She is my cousin's friend. Silvana invited her that weekend—she's a hopeless matchmaker, and the two of them obviously hoped something would come of our proximity.' He gave her a tiny shake, silver eyes searching emerald. 'I wasn't interested and I let her know it. I haven't given another woman a single glance since I lost you—I refused to believe it, but I was still in love with you. I never stopped.'

'Oh!' Light-headed with happiness at that unexpect-edly emotional statement, Anna felt her eyes brim.

'She's just out to make trouble,' Francesco delivered fervently. 'It was she who was all over me, and apart from creating an undignified scene on my wedding day there was nothing I could do about it.' A muscle jerked at the side of his strong jaw. 'I can't ask you to trust me. I didn't do you the courtesy of trusting you, and for that I can never apologise enough. But we will confront the wretched woman, wring the truth from her.'

Hell hath no fury like a woman scorned! Those old sayings always hit the nail on the head.

Anna grinned. The man who was always right was actually saying sorry! 'There's no need for that,' she said with conviction. Her eyes were glowing. 'I trust you. You love Sholto. You would never have sworn to something that wasn't the absolute truth on his little life. And while we're about it—' she gave him a look of mock reproof '—you can stop being jealous of Nick. We've been good friends since we were barely out of nappies. Yes, he did ask me to marry him.'

She reached up to stroke the frown of displeasure that now drew his dark brows together. 'Because he was worried about me being a single parent. But, as I pointed out at the time, we weren't in love with each other, and, although I was touched by his offer, I wouldn't have been selfish enough to let him make such a sacrifice, because one day I knew he'd find someone he was crazy about. And now he has. In any case, I was still in love with you. Though, like you, I tried to deny it.'

That charismatic grin transformed his spectacular features as he briefly crushed her to him. 'You still love me?'

'Of course.' She tilted her head back. 'I tried to tell you before, but you wouldn't believe it.'

Francesco gave a driven groan. 'I have been a fool!' Gently, he stroked away a strand of blonde curls from her forehead. 'I will spend the rest of my life making it up to you, I promise, *amore mia*! And now we go!' He swept her up in his arms, the beaded skirts of her wedding dress trailing on the floor, and headed for the service area, past the kitchens and through a narrow door.

'What are you doing?' Not that she cared. Whatever he did was fine with her! Her arms looped around his neck, she didn't know how her body could contain such happiness. He *did* love her!

'Avoiding the photographers—the car is waiting.'

Arnold was waiting by the spacious Lexus, she registered, as Francesco's long stride hit the cobbles of the delivery access. 'Shouldn't we be seen off?' Common sense reasserted itself as her gorgeous husband slid her down his fantastic body. 'I promised to make sure Cristina caught my bouquet. Only…' Her brow creased. 'I've already lost it.'

'Shush.' Smiling lips stopped her words. 'The last I saw of her my niece was waltzing around the dance floor and her partner was your bouquet. I challenge anyone to take it off her! And I don't want to be "seen off", as you put it. I want out of here. Now. With you. We fly to Italy.'

Sholto was fast asleep in the car, securely fastened in his baby seat. Anna slid in beside him and Francesco followed, taking her hands as Arnold, grinning broadly, went round to the driver's seat and eased the big car smoothly away.

'I can't travel in a wedding dress.' Anna just loved the way he lifted her hands to his lips, placed tiny kisses in the palms, along the sensitive skin of her inner wrists.

'There's no law that says you shouldn't.'

'True.'

'I adore seeing you in a bridal gown. I adore having a bride—I will take it from you tonight.'

Such a wealth of promise in that statement of intent. A deliciously convulsive shudder shot through her. 'I can't wear it for the whole of our honeymoon,' she gasped, giggling.

'As our honeymoon will last for the rest of our lives, that would be impractical,' he conceded on a purr. 'Peggy has packed for you and Sholto. Anything missing can be easily rectified. I shall like taking my wife shopping. Spoiling her.'

As his private jet became airborne Francesco undid his seat belt and did the same for Anna. She looked flushed and happy, utterly adorable. His son was asleep in the skycot, his Italian housekeeper was expecting them, and the future promised everything he could hope for. And more.

'If this is entrapment then I'm all for it,' he told her softly, prepared for her immediate objection.

'I didn't deliberately—'

'I know you didn't, *cara mia*. Neither of us acted responsibly that first time. How could we? And I will give thanks for that for the rest of my life,' he stated with startling sincerity. 'If it hadn't been for our son we would never have found such happiness. So if this is a trap it is pure honey, and I gladly wallow in it.'

'Me too,' she sighed blissfully, nestling against him as he put an arm round her shoulder and shutting out the hideous thought that if she hadn't conceived she might have spent the rest of her life telling herself she hated and despised him. 'I'm not being picky, but when did you decide you could trust me? I know why you didn't—you were sort of programmed, I guess. But I would like to know.'

He shifted slightly, holding her eyes with his steady gaze. 'I was a mad fool. After the time we spent together on Ischia I truly believed I'd found true love and trust. Then your father asked me for a large amount of investment and I felt betrayed. Hurt beyond healing.' He dragged in a breath. 'I am so sorry for thinking for one moment that you were even remotely like my mother.'

'What happened to her?' Anna wasn't afraid to broach the taboo subject now. It was good to get him talking.

His face sobered. 'We heard of her death in a car crash with her latest rich lover shortly before Father died. He'd spent the intervening years pining for her, hoping that she'd eventually return to him and her children. When that hope was extinguished, my guess is he just gave up on living.'

As he'd given up on the children who had needed him years before that. 'So when did you start to trust me?' she pressed, to take his mind off such an unhappy track.

'When I started to think with my brain instead of my prejudices,' he confessed rawly. 'At first I put down your vehement refusal to take anything from me—in spite of my acceptance of responsibility for your and our child's welfare—to a plan to get far more from me. I should have been locked up!' he castigated herself bitterly. 'Then when Sholto was born, and I knew I had to be a proper father to my son, I asked you to marry me.'

'Told me!' she murmured, cuddling closer.

'You did not accept with the greedy happiness I was programmed to expect,' he responded drily, drawing her even closer. 'It was only on the night I put my crazy plan for a calm marriage to you in that restaurant that I finally found my sanity and started to put the pieces together. The way you'd refused to accept lavish maintenance payments before the birth; your reluctance to accept the clothes I paid for; the way you spurned the engagement ring I thrust on you which, to my knowledge, you had never worn. I had done you a great injustice. I loathed myself. I booked into a hotel and spent the most miserable hours of my life.

'To rub salt in the wound of my misplaced distrust, and to confirm what I already knew in my heart, I invited your father to meet me last night. It was just as you had said. You'd had no idea who I was or what I was worth. But he did—from reading the financial press. He told me he had never mentioned the episode to you—he was too ashamed of his crass behaviour. He explained that once he got an idea in his head everything else went right out of it. He hadn't thought he had jeopardised what we had between us. He hadn't realised our brief holiday romance—as he saw it—was serious. I can tell you he was totally gutted when I pointed out just what he had done.'

'Oh, goodness!' Anna heaved herself upright. 'Dad tried to tell me on the way to the church. But I told him to button his lip.' When he'd claimed it was his fault she'd thought he was talking about the gaggle of photographers! If only she'd listened to him she wouldn't have spent all that time agonising over whether Francesco had meant what he'd said when he'd told her he loved her at the start of the ceremony.

Her voice earnest, she pressed, 'No more misunderstandings. No more secrets. Promise?'

'Promise.' His voice was a purr of happiness as he lowered his dark head and kissed her.

The *palazzo* was something else—perched on a wooded spur, surrounded by sensationally beautiful gardens, the verdant Tuscan countryside rolled out beneath it.

'It's just perfect,' Anna breathed as Francesco, carrying Sholto, took her hand and led her in to meet Katerina, the housekeeper, and a group comprising daily helps and outdoor staff whose names she promptly forgot.

Beaming at them all, she promised herself she would take pains to remember their names in the future, would get to know them, learn to speak Italian. She stood by, deliriously happy, as Francesco presented the now wakeful wriggling baby to his staff.

The rest of the late afternoon was spent settling Sholto into his perfect nursery, happily arguing over who should bath him, finally doing it together and both getting their wedding finery liberally soaked. When the happy, replete baby lay fast asleep in his fancy crib, and they had agreed that not only was he perfect but completely remarkable, Francesco led her on a voyage of discovery around the magnificent property, her wedding gown trailing.

As they entered the grand salon, with its vaulted and elaborately painted ceiling, cool marble floor, priceless antiques, porcelain bowls of fragrant flowers everywhere and long windows open to the soft warm air, Anna breathed, 'Wow! You live in some style!'

'*We* live in style,' he stressed, his arm tightening around her waist. 'But, remember, if there is anything you want changing it shall be done.'

'Everything's just perfect.'

'I am glad!' His smile warmed her. 'The house and lands have been in my family for generations. Apparently, my mother hated it. She preferred bright lights, city living. This place was unvisited for long years. It became sad and neglected. When I inherited I made sure it was brought back to life.'

Anna melted inside. At last he was talking about the parent who had done him so much damage quite naturally, with no trace of bitterness, just stating facts. The damage was healing. There was one last thing she wanted to know.

Tilting her head to look up into his face, she asked, 'Tell me why—with all this luxury at your disposal— were you living in that stone shack when we met, dressing like a beach bum and wearing a pretend gold chain that left green marks on your skin?'

A wide grin slashed his features. 'Escapism. I love

the sea. I go there to unwind, to pretend I'm not a millionaire with a world-spanning business empire to run. I am incognito, living like a peasant, messing about in a small boat. I am not to be disturbed. But on the day we met one of my senior PAs had broken that rule, had come to me with a problem he believed only I could solve. As punishment I made him accompany me to drop lobster pots while he ran the problem by me! On our return to my private cove I found the most beautiful creature I'd ever seen. And we both know what happened then.'

'We fell in love,' Anna supplied softly. 'But why wear that tacky chain? Wasn't that overkill?' She reached up to draw his head down to hers, green eyes wickedly sparkling as his hands drifted down over her curvy hips.

He eased her forward against the hard cradle of his manhood in one smoothly erotic movement and answered, his breathing unsteady. 'Cristina gave it to me. My sister and her family were staying at my hotel for a couple of days. I had to wear it; she'd bought it with her pocket money. You'll recall I had to show some people around the island? Sophia and her family. You got the impression I was a freelance tour guide, picking up a few euros where I could. I didn't put you right. How could I when the last thing I wanted was for the lovely, sexy young woman I found to know who I was?'

Pressed against the urgency of his powerful body, Anna was melting, boneless, but she found the breath to assure him, 'I loved you when I thought you were a penniless drifter. If you lost everything tomorrow I would still love you, and—'

Claiming her mouth, he stopped her words with a hunger that sent her spinning into orbit, and she was so weak with wanton longing that she was a molten pool of submission as he swept her into strong arms and carried her out, mounting the curving staircase with determined strides, nudging open the opulent bedroom they were to share and setting her on her unsteady feet.

'My bride.' Long fingers deft, he began to undo the tiny buttons at the back of the wedding dress, and the hot ache inside her escalated to almost uncontainable proportions as the bodice fell away from her pouting, sensitised breasts. He smoothed the rest of the costly fabric from her hips, revealing tiny lacy panties, and groaned deep in his throat, telling her with husky intent, 'The moment I turned and saw you enter the church I promised myself I would do this.'

He scooped her up and laid her on the rich satin coverlet of the massive bed...

MEDITERRANEAN BOSS, CONVENIENT MISTRESS

BY
KATHRYN ROSS

Kathryn Ross was born in Zambia, where her parents happened to live at that time. Educated in Ireland and England, she now lives in a village near Blackpool, Lancashire. Kathryn is a professional beauty therapist, but writing is her first love. As a child she wrote adventure stories and at thirteen was editor of her school magazine. Happily, ten writing years later, *Designed With Love* was accepted by Mills & Boon. A romantic Sagittarian, she loves travelling to exotic locations.

CHAPTER ONE

CHARLIE opened her eyes and memories from the night before flashed through her mind with agonising clarity. The date had been a complete disaster.

She hadn't really minded the fact that the man she'd met had turned out to be five feet two instead of six feet two, as he had described himself on his profile, or even the fact that he had been nearer to fifty than thirty…she wasn't ageist and she didn't think that looks were the most important things in life. However, his grey pony-tail had been a bit of a turn-off…as had the fact that they had absolutely nothing in common except that they were both divorced.

After the first fifteen minutes the date had gone rapidly downhill. Maybe internet dating wasn't a good idea. She shouldn't have allowed her friends to talk her into it.

The alarm clock rang and she reached sleepily to switch it off. A few moments later Jack came running into the bedroom. 'Time to get up, Mummy,' he sang in his usual happy tone before bounding into the bed to give her a hug.

'Morning, darling.' She kissed the top of his dark silky hair.

'Nana let me have chocolate and watch TV with her when you went out last night.'

'Did she?' Charlie smiled. 'Nana spoils you to bits.'

If it had been a weekend they would have snuggled down

for a little while and chatted. For a four-year-old Jack was a great conversationalist….probably better than her date last night, she thought with a smile. But this was Friday and there was no time for frivolity.

'Come on, then we'd better get you ready for school.'

The cottage felt cold, Charlie thought, and she put her hand on the radiator as they padded through to the bathroom. The central heating hadn't come on, which meant there was very little hot water.

Once she had dressed Jack she went to investigate the problem, but she couldn't fix it, so it was a job for the plumber again. She dreaded to think how much the repairs were going to cost.

After that there was just time for her to tie her long blonde hair back from her face, grab a piece of toast and flick through the morning post. Bills, bills and more bills…pretty much the norm. The terraced cottage was small but it cost a fortune to maintain.

At the moment Charlie was a PA and worked as a temp for an agency owned by her friend Karen. Her current position working for a doctor of psychology, who was also a best-selling author, was her most profitable assignment to date. But she still found it hard to balance her finances. The truth was that running a house and being a single mum wasn't easy and at the end of the month there wasn't a lot left over for luxuries…let alone boiler repairs!

But she would manage, she told herself firmly as they left the house. She always did.

It was a misty September morning and her old car coughed and spluttered before flaring into life. Then Jack pushed a CD into the player and they sang along with some classic love songs all the way through the rush-hour traffic.

Twenty minutes later, with Jack safely ensconced at school, she pulled back out into the traffic. She turned the volume up and hummed along to the CD as she headed for Oxford and her heart lifted. OK, so her date last night had been dreadful and there had been nothing but bills in the post, but she had the best son in the world and at the moment she was working for a very dishy boss. Just thinking about Marco Delmari gave her a little flip of anticipation.

When she had first started working for him she had instantly been attracted to his sizzling good looks. Then reluctantly her common sense had taken over and told her not to even think about it, because the job was too good to put at risk, and besides, she had priorities, she had Jack. Anyway, she realised she wasn't his type. Marco preferred stick-thin, model-perfect and incredibly glamorous women. She on the other hand was none of those things and, although she had nice hair and skin and large green eyes, unfortunately she had to wear spectacles most of the time at the office; otherwise she couldn't read the computer screen.

So not even by the flicker of an eyelash had she let him guess she thought he was gorgeous. Instead she had made herself indispensable and politely businesslike, with the result that he sang her praises, and told her how pleased he was that she had streamlined his office system and his diary. And in the last few months they had relaxed around each other and formed a repartee that was very enjoyable.

She glanced at the clock on the dashboard. Marco had to go into London to give a radio interview this morning and she wasn't sure if she'd see him before he left the office.

She took a few shortcuts down narrow, leafy lanes and arrived outside her boss's Georgian red-brick house on the outskirts of Oxford ten minutes early. His car was still parked in the courtyard and she felt a flash of exhilaration as she grabbed her briefcase and hurried up the steps to open his front door.

Her footsteps sank into the thick Persian carpets as she

hurried across the wide hallway. The house was a designer's dream, decorated in restful shades of butter-gold and cream, and furnished with stylish antiques to exactly fit the period property. But today there was no time to admire her surroundings and she went straight up the stairs to the office.

'Morning, Marco,' she said breezily as she stepped through the door and tossed her bag down on her desk. 'Beautiful day, isn't it?'

He was standing with his back towards her, looking out of the window.

'Yes, beautiful.' He turned and looked over at her, and as usual she felt a *frisson* of awareness as she met his intensely sexy dark eyes.

OK, she was relaxed around him, but not enough to stop noticing how wildly attractive he was. Marco was Italian with broodingly intense looks. His thick dark hair just brushed the collar of his blue shirt and his face was autocratically strong and handsome. The first time she had seen him was on TV and she remembered being totally taken aback by his appearance. She hadn't expected a doctor of psychology to look like him. For a start he was too young. She had pictured someone older, someone staid. The reality was a man of thirty-seven, tall, dark and powerfully built, wearing chinos and an open-necked shirt. In all honesty he had the kind of looks that a movie star would die for. Not that Marco seemed concerned about his appearance.

As soon as Charlie had started to work for him she realised that the only thing that really mattered to Marco was his work.

He had girlfriends, of course…all extremely beautiful and all crazy about him. In the short time she had worked for him she had watched them come and go, had observed how oblivious he was to their adoring looks. He really didn't have a clue how many hearts he had broken with his casual, laid-back indifference.

Marco smiled at her and a shiver of pleasure ran up her spine. 'So how was your date last night?'

His sudden question caught her off guard. She'd forgotten she'd told him about her date. He'd casually asked about her plans last night as she put her coat on to leave… He'd only been making polite conversation and she could have said what she usually said—'Nothing much'—or she could have invented some parent meeting at Jack's school, but oh, no, she had opened her mouth and before she knew it the truth had popped out.

'It was OK,' she answered airily now, but couldn't quite meet his eye. She hated lying but the truth was far too embarrassing. 'Shouldn't you be getting ready to leave for the radio station?' Swiftly she changed the subject and glanced at her watch. Marco was due to give an interview at the BBC to promote his new book, an analytical study into why love shouldn't be the number-one reason for a partnership. 'If you don't set off soon you'll be late—the traffic going into London will be horrendous. It's Friday morning, remember.'

'Yes, I do realise that, Charlie. I'm waiting for Sarah; she wants to accompany me in and go over a few of the questions she thought they might ask.'

'Oh, I see.' Charlie switched on her computer. Sarah Heart was Marco's agent and publicist, an extremely pushy woman with an excess of confidence. Charlie found her grating. But she was good at her job and that was all that counted, she supposed.

'I don't know where she's got to but if she isn't here within the next five minutes I'll have to leave without her,' Marco muttered. He turned his back towards her again and looked out of the window, down towards the courtyard.

'Do you want me to phone her on her mobile?'

'I've already tried that. I just got her messaging service.'

'She's probably stuck in traffic somewhere.'

'Probably.'

Charlie wondered if it was her imagination or if Marco really was unusually edgy this morning. Maybe he was just concerned about being late for this interview, although he certainly wouldn't be worried about it. Marco was very good at dealing with the media; he was always laid-back and extremely amusing and entertaining.

In fact he was much in demand on radio and TV these days and was fast becoming quite a celebrity. Academically he was brilliant and his books were always well-received, but Charlie suspected that his heightened profile and recent success was more to do with the fact that he was so captivating he even made the subject of psychology seem sexy.

There was a moment's silence as Charlie sat down at her desk and took her reading glasses out of her handbag.

'So Mr *"Dreamboat"* lived up to expectations, then?' Marco asked suddenly.

The question seemed outrageously personal and out of place in the scholarly surroundings of the book-lined office, a place where emotions were only ever discussed in the most analytical and diagnostic of terms.

'Well…' Charlie could feel her skin heating up with embarrassment as he turned and looked at her again. If it had been a mistake telling Marco about her date it had been an even bigger one telling him she'd met the man on the internet. As soon as the words were out she had imagined a hint of derision in his eyes that had made her go on to tell him that internet dating was very 'in', everyone was doing it, and the man she'd arranged to meet seemed very nice…in fact, more than nice—a bit of a dreamboat actually.

She should never have said that, she thought now with annoyance. She felt really foolish.

'Well?' Marco prompted her.

'He was OK…'

'That's good.' He inclined his head. 'I was a bit concerned.'

'You were?' She looked over at him in surprise.

'Yes. Meeting up with a total stranger can be risky.'

'I suppose so.' She was filled with a warm feeling inside. It was a long time since anyone had shown concern about her welfare. 'But I was careful; we met in a crowded restaurant and I didn't give him any of my personal details.'

'Well, I'm glad it worked out for you.'

'Actually it was a bit of a disaster,' she admitted a little awkwardly. 'We had nothing in common.'

'Oh!' Marco looked at her with a raised eyebrow. 'Not a recipe for a second date, then?'

Charlie shook her head. 'It was a struggle getting through one date, never mind two. I couldn't wait to say goodbye to him outside the restaurant.'

Marco looked amused now. 'You didn't give him much of a chance, did you?'

'I didn't need to give him any longer,' Charlie said briskly.

'I suppose not, and it's better to find out you are not compatible sooner rather than later.'

She nodded. 'Trouble was, I knew we weren't compatible within the first fifteen minutes.'

'No, you knew that the chemistry wasn't instantly there,' he corrected her. 'That's something entirely different.'

'Not to me it's not! I know your professional views on this, Marco, and I agree with them to a certain extent. Maybe love can grow if you work at a relationship, but the chemistry has to be there to start with.'

'The chemistry can be a double-edged sword,' Marco said carefully. 'Sometimes it gets in the way of the truth; blinds you to the fact that you are not at all compatible.'

'It still needs to be there to begin with.'

'Not necessarily.'

'Of course it does…I mean, you just know when you meet someone if it's going to be right…don't you?'

Marco smiled. He had a nice smile, she thought; it seemed to warm his eyes to dark golden honey. 'No. You know that you'd enjoy going to bed with them,' he said softly. 'That is an entirely different thing.'

Charlie wondered how they had got on to that subject, and suddenly felt uncomfortably hot. She always tried to keep conversations with Marco inside a safety zone, friendly but businesslike and never too personal.

'But you are right,' he continued smoothly. 'Desire can be a very important part of a relationship. It's central to a good rapport to enjoy each other in bed.'

Charlie could feel herself getting even hotter on the inside now. Marco's Italian accent had a sexy depth to it that was mesmerising, as was the way he was looking at her with those molten dark eyes. Without warning she found herself wondering what it would be like to go to bed with *him*. The question was shocking and yet at the same time wildly exciting. He would probably make a fantastic lover.

'But there is no such thing as love at first sight, if that is what you are driving at,' Marco concluded laconically.

The words drew her back to reality from the strange feelings that had taken hold of her. 'Actually, I think there is,' Charlie said staunchly. 'My parents fell in love at first sight and they were married for thirty-three years.'

Marco shook his head. 'That was lust at first sight.' He noted the look of horror in her eyes and laughed. 'Sorry to disappoint you, Charlie, but your parents would have had to get practical and work at their marriage to make it last thirty-three years.'

'It was still love at first sight,' Charlie maintained stubbornly.

Marco shook his head. 'I take it you are a bit of a romantic.'

'No!' She didn't know why she hotly denied the charge, because she *was* a hopeless romantic. Maybe it had something to do with the sudden derisive tone of his voice.

Marco watched the colour deepen in her creamy skin, saw the way her green eyes sparkled with annoyance, and smiled. 'I think you are,' he said softly. 'In fact, I think that maybe deep down you would like to find the kind of relationship that your parents enjoyed...complete with love at first sight.'

'You mean I'm looking for something you say doesn't exist,' Charlie muttered angrily. 'Any minute now you are going to ask me to lie down on your couch. I don't need to be psychoanalysed, thank you, Marco. I had a disastrous date last night but it hasn't left me scarred. I am quite well-adjusted, thank you.'

Marco laughed.

For some reason that irritated her even further.

Marco watched as she brushed a self-conscious hand over the smoothness of her hair and noticed how she swiftly changed the subject. 'You're going to be late for your interview,' she said crossly.

He smiled to himself. Charlie intrigued him and had done so since the first moment she had walked into his office. There was something about the way she carried herself with a cool dignity that was quite beguiling. Never once during the months she had worked for him had he known her to completely lower the barriers that surrounded her. However, as the weeks had gone by an easy compatibility had sprung up between them and her wary reserve had fallen a little. He noticed in particular that when he asked about her son she came alive with a warmth that was completely captivating.

On the other hand she certainly wasn't at ease talking about her date last night...watching her blush was a whole new revelation, as was the vulnerable glint in her green eyes when he had accused her of being a bit of a romantic. She had thought he'd just wanted to psychoanalyse her, but he didn't need to get her on the couch to know that some man had hurt her badly...

probably her ex-husband. But that wasn't any of his business and he certainly didn't want to pry into her personal life.

One of the things he liked about Charlie was the fact that she was so self-contained. Her practical attitude in the office was a real bonus. It suited him to have someone calm and reliable around, someone who didn't get emotional. His last PA had been a nightmare. She'd been through a series of relationship break-ups, and when he'd offered a word of sympathy she had developed a weird kind of fixation on him that had made work impossible. After that experience he had decided to hire a temp for a while. Charlie was a real blessing. She was always on an even keel, steady and dependable. Charlie never came into the office hung-over or late after a wild night on the tiles. In fact—bizarrely, considering the fact Charlie was in her late twenties and an attractive woman—she didn't appear to have a love life. Maybe he had even started to take that fact for granted… Why else had he been so taken aback when she'd told him about her date last night?

She stood up now to go and get a file from one of the cabinets and he found his eyes following her. He'd probably just been concerned about her. Sometimes, despite her self-possessed manner, he sensed an underlying vulnerability about her….something he was sure she took great trouble to hide.

Yes, that was it…he'd just been concerned for her safety last night. His attention was distracted as she reached up to a high shelf to get a new folder. For a moment he was treated to a clear view of her shapely body. As his eyes drifted down over her curves he wondered, not for the first time, why she always wore clothes that hid her physique so completely. She had a nice hourglass figure which was very desirable, but you could hardly see it in the shapeless black business suit.

Annoyed with himself, he looked away and glanced at his watch. He had more important things to think about. 'Looks like Sarah isn't going to make it. I'll have to leave without her.'

'When she arrives, shall I tell her to follow you to the studio?' Charlie asked as she sat back down at her computer.

Marco watched as she put her spectacles on and concentrated on the screen as if she had dismissed him entirely from her mind.

'No.' Marco shook his head. 'Because you'll have to come with me instead.'

She looked up at him in surprise. 'But I've got research notes to catalogue—'

'You'll have to leave them until later,' Marco said firmly. 'Come on, be quick. I need you to drive because I have notes to read. And, bearing in mind the lateness of the hour…you might have to drop me at the door and park the car for me.'

Charlie took off her spectacles and with reluctance found herself switching off her computer. Then, snatching up her bag, she followed him down the stairs. It was strange but since that conversation about her love life she felt a bit on edge around him somehow. It was as if the professional barriers that she had managed to keep in place around him had suddenly been shifted to one side.

CHAPTER TWO

CHARLIE had to practically run to keep up with Marco as they crossed the courtyard at the side of his house. She scrabbled in her bag for her keys as she stopped next to her car.

'What are you doing?'

She looked up and saw Marco was standing next to his own car.

'You said you wanted me to drive.'

'I do. But I meant in my car.'

Charlie looked over at the brand-new gleaming red sports car and quickly decided she definitely didn't want to drive such perfection through the traffic! 'Do you mind if we take mine?'

Marco glanced sceptically at her old car. 'Do you think it will get us there?'

'Well, it gets me to work every morning!' she said indignantly.

'Fine.' He shrugged and moved towards her vehicle.

Marco was so tall that his legs were crushed up against the dashboard when he got in. He released the seat and moved it backwards as she turned the key in the ignition. As usual the car didn't want to start immediately.

'It's OK—it always does this,' she reassured him hurriedly in case he started to get out.

The engine flared into life at the next turn of the key and at the same time music filled the car and Marco was treated to a rendition of *Love and Marriage* as crooned by Frank Sinatra.

Hurriedly Charlie rushed to switch it off and in her haste turned the volume up. 'Sorry!' she shouted over the sentimental words about how love and marriage went so well together and then switched the CD off. But the music kept on and it was a moment before she realised that it was the radio that was playing.

'That was Frank Sinatra's opinion of love and marriage,' The DJ said cheerfully, 'but in a short time we will be talking to the eminent Dr Marco Delmari about his new book and why he thinks putting love at the top of your list when you get married could spell disaster.'

'Sorry, I thought it was my CD that was playing,' Charlie said uncomfortably as she turned the volume down. Out of the corner of her eye she saw that Marco had found the cover for the CD of love songs and was reading through the track list.

'And you tried to tell me you weren't a romantic.' He looked over at her with wry humour.

'I've also got classical music in the glove compartment and a selection of rock albums.'

Marco smiled. 'Interesting. I wouldn't have had you down as a rock chick. Do you have the leathers and the bike too?'

'But of course,' she lied with a bat of her dark lashes. 'I didn't realise you were analysing me.'

'Of course I am.' He laughed. 'It's what I do.' He slanted her a teasing look. 'And by the way, there is nothing wrong with being a bit of a romantic,' he added softly.

'That's not what it says in your book.'

'No, what I said in my book was that people get carried away by the idea of romance. That they imagine themselves in love too easily, when in fact they are just in lust, which is absolutely fine for a short-term affair, but for a longer-term commitment you need more stability. '

'"Love should not be the only reason for marriage."' Charlie quoted one of the lines from his book.

'Ah… So you have read it, then.'

'Of course I've read it.' She looked over and found that he was still watching her with a light of amusement in his dark eyes. 'I bought a copy before I started to work for you.'

'As a precursor to internet dating?'

'No, as research towards working for you…and actually, just for the record, last night was my first sojourn into the world of internet dating.'

'Will you continue with it?'

'If you'd asked me that question when I got home last night I'd probably have said no….but…' she paused for thought '…I suppose a date like last night's can happen even when you meet someone under more conventional circumstances.'

'So you'll go out again on another date?'

Charlie shrugged. 'Maybe…'

'But not with Mr *Dreamboat*?'

'Definitely not.' She smiled at him.

Marco reached across and turned the radio off. 'So how does this internet dating service work? Do you get to see photos of the people you can date?'

'Yes, not that it helps much. My dates's photo must have been at least ten years out of date.' She glanced over at him teasingly. 'Why? Are you thinking of trying it yourself?'

'Not this week,' he said sardonically and instantly she wished she hadn't made the joke. Of course, Marco wouldn't need to look on the internet for a date—unless he was running an experiment for one of his books! But for Charlie, who didn't go out to socialise a lot—partly because she had to arrange babysitters, and partly because she didn't really like the nightclub or smoky-bars scene—it was a practical solution. 'It's just a bit of fun,' she said with a shrug. But her tone was defensive now.

'Is it?'

'Yes, of course.'

'So you aren't looking for a serious relationship?'

The gently asked question seemed to echo inside her in a very strange way. She had to admit that recently she had been feeling lonely and when she looked around the world suddenly seemed made up of couples. She missed the intimacy of a relationship...not just the sex but the tenderness and warmth and the feeling that someone was there for her.

Not that her ex-husband had ever really been there for her. They had only been married for twelve months when she had fallen pregnant and, although Greg initially seemed to be pleased, she had soon discovered this wasn't the case.

At the time they had been living in an apartment and had decided to look around and buy a house...something, as Greg put it, more 'child-friendly'. They had found what they were looking for pretty quickly, the ideal property; a beautiful old cottage out in the countryside.

Charlie had been ecstatic, full of dreams and plans for the future. But although their offer was accepted she had never got her dream cottage. As soon as their apartment was sold Greg had left her, taking half the money from the sale with him.

The shock had been immense. She had loved Greg and believed that he loved her, and she had never suspected for one moment that he wanted out of the marriage. Left alone and pregnant, she'd known there was no way she could afford to buy the cottage on her own, and the sale had dropped through.

So, no, she couldn't lie to herself—Greg had never been there for her...and he certainly had never bothered with Jack. That hurt more than anything.

She suddenly remembered how the other day she had seen the man next door taking his son out to play football and how for some reason it had made her eyes prickle with tears. But it had just been PMT, she told herself quickly.

She shook her negative thoughts away and answered

Marco's question. 'I don't think I want a serious relationship right now, but if someone special came along in the future that would be nice.' Charlie pulled down the visor of the car to cut the glare of sun that was so low in the sky it was shining straight into her eyes like a light of interrogation. 'Apart from anything, there are times when I think Jack needs a dad.' The words slipped out almost without her being conscious of saying them.

'Doesn't Jack see his father?'

'Not really…an occasional phone call and birthday card…' She glanced over at Marco and suddenly felt completely self-conscious when she found he was watching her with a very serious expression in his eyes. Why was she telling him this? It was none of his business! 'However, he's no great loss,' she added hastily. 'And I like my independence. I'd certainly rather be on my own than in a bad relationship.'

'Very wise,' Marco said with a nod.

'Anyway, I'm distracting you from your work,' she said briskly, trying to change the subject. 'You should be reading your notes.'

'Yes, I suppose I should.'

Silence descended between them. Charlie felt awkward now as he shuffled through papers. She wished she hadn't had that conversation. She had to work with the guy and it was always best to keep personal conversations to a minimum and maintain a cool and businesslike front. The strange thing was that recently she had been finding that more and more difficult. Marco was very easy to talk to…but then he would be, she thought suddenly; he was trained to get people to open up and reveal their innermost feelings.

After a few moments she felt his eyes resting on her again. Why did she feel that he was looking at her with closer attention than usual? She glanced over at him questioningly.

'Sorry, was I staring?' He shook his head. 'I just realised

that you are not wearing your spectacles. Don't you need them for driving?'

'No, it's OK.' She smiled and looked back at the road. 'I'm not going to crash the car. I'm glad to say I only need them in the office for the close paperwork and the computer.'

'You look different without them.'

'I know…they don't suit me, do they?'

'Actually—'

Charlie was glad that the ring of Marco's phone interrupted the conversation at that moment. She didn't want him to politely lie and tell her that her glasses did suit her because in retrospect it sounded as if she had been fishing for compliments, which certainly wasn't the case.

She watched out of the side of her eye as he took the phone from his inside jacket pocket and flipped it open.

'Hi, Sarah; where the heck are you?' he demanded. 'Really?' He smiled. 'No, Charlie was good enough to drive me in. We'll be about twenty minutes.' He listened for a moment to something she had to say. 'I don't think that will be a problem because I've done the research. The facts speak for themselves.' Marco's voice held a dry edge now. He was clearly irritated by something. 'We'll talk about it later…OK?' Then he hung up.

'Problems?' Charlie asked, overcome with curiosity.

'Yes, the problem is that sometimes Sarah can be very irritating,' he said tersely.

Those were Charlie's sentiments exactly, but she wondered what Sarah had said to aggravate Marco. The pair usually seemed to get on so well, sometimes almost sickeningly so. Many times Charlie had watched as Sarah fawned over him, agreeing with his every word, fluttering her eyelashes coyly and then basking in his attention. There was no doubt in Charlie's mind that the woman fancied the pants off him, and Marco had never seemed averse to the attention.

They had left the motorway now and Charlie followed the

signs for the city centre. 'You need to turn left down here,' Marco said as they approached a busy junction.

'Where is Sarah anyway?' Charlie asked as she negotiated the traffic.

'She's had a crisis on her hands. Apparently one of her celebrity clients has confronted her husband's mistress in the lingerie department of Harrods and has been arrested for making a public disturbance.'

'Really?'

Marco nodded. 'Sarah's had to rush down to the police station to get her out before the Press get wind of it.'

'Never a dull moment in her profession.'

'You can say that again. Yesterday she was trying to talk me into getting married, or at least getting into a monogamous long-term relationship.'

Charlie shot him a startled look. She was so surprised she nearly ran a red light and just put the brakes on in time.

'It's her latest business idea apparently.'

'A business idea?' Charlie was nonplussed.

'Yes. As you know, my book is due to be released in America soon and I'm going on tour to promote it. It's already getting a lot of coverage; magazines and chat shows are discussing my ideas. So it should shoot in high in the book charts.'

'That's good. But I still don't see where Sarah's idea fits in with this.'

'Sarah thinks that the fact that I am a bachelor will substantially affect sales. And that I might not make the number-one slot because of it.'

'That's ridiculous. It's a scientific book, not one written from a personal angle. It uses statistics, case studies and research projects.'

'Exactly. I said all this to Sarah last night. But she still thinks that if I were committed to someone it would give the book vital credence. We had quite a disagreement about it.'

'She's unbelievable,' Charlie muttered and at the same time she wondered if there was method in Sarah's madness. Perhaps she had herself in mind to be on the arm of her darling doctor? 'It's just absurd.'

'Well…' Marco shrugged. 'I suppose if I did get together with someone I could prove my research that love isn't the most important prerequisite for a successful relationship. However…' he grinned '…I'm not entirely sure I approve of Sarah's suggestion and I told her that.'

Charlie nodded emphatically and enjoyed picturing the disappointment on Sarah Heart's face as Marco disagreed with her. Sarah was undoubtedly very beautiful but she had all the warmth of the dark side of the moon. It was somehow gratifying to know that the woman didn't get everything she wanted.

Marco directed her down some side-streets and a few seconds later they turned through the gates into the radio station. A security guard raised the barrier and allowed them in. 'Will you park the car, Charlie?' Marco asked as he looked at his watch. 'I should go straight in.'

'Yes, of course.' She pulled to a halt by the front door. 'Do you want me to wait for you out here?'

'No, come in and get a coffee.' He reached for the handle and stepped out of the car. 'I'll tell the receptionist to expect you.'

Charlie noticed how a young woman walking towards the building gave him an admiring look. He said something to her and then held the door so that she could precede him into the building. She looked as if she was going to swoon. It was no wonder, because he really was drop-dead gorgeous, Charlie thought dreamily. Everything about him was sexy, from the way he dressed…to the way he just looked at you as if he could unlock the secrets of your soul. It was little wonder that Sarah Heart had designs on him.

Realising that she was just sitting staring after him, Charlie shook herself out of her contemplation and drove the car around the back of the building to park. Then she collected her bag and walked towards the front entrance.

As she reached the front door a taxi pulled up. The door of the vehicle opened and a pair of high black stiletto boots and long, shapely legs swung out. As Charlie's gaze moved upwards she saw a red skirt, and then as the woman uncurled herself from the car completely a long black cashmere coat swirled around her. It was Sarah Heart and as usual she looked very glamorous, her long brunette hair shimmering with cappuccino highlights in the sun, the perfect proportions of her face flawlessly made-up with a light smudging of gold frosted shadow over her dark eyes and a glossy shimmer of ruby-red on the fullness of her lips.

'Hello, Sarah.' Charlie stood and waited for her.

'Hi.' The woman gave her what could only be described as a look of dismissal before turning to pay the taxi driver. Charlie was tempted to just walk into the studio without her, but she forced herself to wait.

'Did you manage to spring your celeb client from jail?' she asked as the woman turned to walk with her into the building.

'Yes, thank you, although it is a confidential matter that I'd rather Marco hadn't mentioned to you.'

'Well, maybe you shouldn't have told him in the first place then.' Charlie couldn't resist the retort. Really, the woman could be most disagreeable.

Sarah ignored that. 'Is Marco already in the building?' she continued, unperturbed.

'Yes, he went on ahead.'

'Good…well, I suppose there is little point in you hanging around, then, not now that I'm here.'

'Marco has asked me to stay,' Charlie said firmly. She wasn't about to be dismissed in such a manner.

'I thought you might have typing to get on with,' the woman shrugged, 'or some filing perhaps.'

Charlie wondered if Sarah practised that condescending tone or if it just came naturally to her. She decided to ignore the remark and followed her towards the front desk.

Sarah nodded at the receptionist. 'I'm here with Marco Delmari,' she said in a crisply confident tone.

'And your name?' The receptionist looked down at the register in front of her.

'Sarah Heart.' Sarah drummed one well-manicured hand against the desk as she waited.

'I'm sorry, Ms Heart, but I don't appear to have your name on my list.'

'I beg your pardon?' Sarah looked as if she was about to turn an interesting shade of purple.

Before she could launch into a scathing remark Charlie leaned across her. 'Excuse me, but have you got my name on the list? It's Charlotte Hopkirk,' she said quietly.

The woman ran her eyes over the book again. 'Oh, yes, your name is here, Ms Hopkirk.'

'Good, well, this is Dr Delmari's publicist, so she should be down as well.'

'I see.' The girl smiled at Charlie. 'Then I guess it's OK for her to accompany you through. You'll find Dr Delmari in the hospitality suite next door to studio five, the door should be open.'

'Thank you.'

'What on earth are you thanking her for?' Sarah muttered as they moved away from the desk. 'She was clearly incompetent.'

'Your name wasn't down, so it was hardly her fault. Anyway no harm done; it's just a good job that I stayed with you,' Charlie couldn't resist adding.

Sarah slanted her a narrow-eyed look but said nothing.

They found Marco talking to the station manager. He smiled over at Charlie as she walked through the door. Then he turned his attention to his publicist. 'Sarah, this is a surprise! There was no need for you to rush down here.'

'I wanted to, Marco. I'm so sorry I was held up,' she said smoothly. Charlie noticed how her voice had softened now that she was talking to Marco. Then she flashed a winning smile at the station manager. 'Sarah Heart,' she said as she extended her hand. 'Marco's publicist.'

'Pleased to meet you, Ms Heart.'

'Call me Sarah, please,' she practically purred.

'Well, Sarah, we are just waiting for our DJ Sam Richmond to come through and have a word with Marco then we'll go through to the studio.'

'How is Sam?' Sarah gushed. 'It's a while since I saw him.'

'You're a friend?' the station manager asked.

'Oh, yes, Sam and I go way back.'

He was probably ex-husband number three, Charlie thought darkly. According to gossip Sarah had been married and divorced four times, which was no mean feat by the age of thirty-eight. Ex-husband number four had been a top TV executive and a wealthy man. It was through his contacts and money that Sarah had started her business.

The DJ came in at that moment and Sarah made a performance out of greeting him and introducing him to Marco. She probably wouldn't have bothered to include Charlie only Sam Richmond smiled at her and reached to shake her hand.

'Oh, and that's Charlie,' she tagged on, her tone less than gracious. 'She's—'

'My right-hand woman,' Marco finished the sentence smoothly.

Charlie caught Marco's eye and he smiled at her. Something about that smile made her feel warm and special. It was a delicious feeling. She almost had to shake herself to get rid of its dreamy effect.

A few moments later she was left alone in the hospitality suite as Sarah accompanied the men through to the studio. Charlie poured herself a coffee from a pot that was sitting on the sideboard and sat down in one of the comfortable armchairs to wait. She could see the others through the glass partition between her and the studio next door but she couldn't hear what they were saying, she could only hear the record that was being played on air.

She found herself watching Marco, studying him as he talked. She liked the sincerity in his eyes as he listened to people, and she noticed that when he smiled he had a dimple in his cheek. As she glanced away her eyes connected with Sarah's and she knew the other woman had caught her watching her boss. Hastily she looked away feeling guiltily uncomfortable…although for the life of her she couldn't work out why.

She had just got up to replenish her coffee when Sarah joined her. 'I'll have one of those while you're there,' she told Charlie as she sat down. 'White, no sugar.'

Charlie poured her the drink and handed it across. She noticed how Sarah didn't even bother to say thank you. She really was quite rude, Charlie thought with annoyance.

Sarah watched as she sat back down in her chair opposite. 'So…' she murmured idly as she crossed her long legs and smoothed down the silky material of her skirt, 'tell me, Charlie…how long have you been in love with Marco?'

The outrageously personal question was asked with such nonchalance that for a moment Charlie wondered if she had misheard. 'What on earth are you talking about?' She stared at the woman in astonishment.

'I think you know,' Sarah continued smoothly.

'All I know is that you are asking me an absurd question!'

'Am I?' Sarah shrugged. 'From where I'm watching it seems blindingly obvious that you have a thing for him.'

Charlie was so outraged that she could barely find her voice. 'I'm not even going to deign to answer that!' she finally muttered.

'You know you aren't his type, don't you?' Sarah smiled but

her eyes were cold. 'And I'm not just talking about the fact that Marco only seems to date women who look like super-models, I'm talking about the fact that Marco would never fall for a romantic. He's far too practical for that. So I'm afraid that unless you take those rose-coloured glasses off when you look at him…I think you have a problem.'

The sardonic tone grated on Charlie. 'I think the only problem around here is you,' she said succinctly. 'And I'll thank you to keep your weird opinions to yourself.'

Sarah just laughed.

At that moment the music stopped and the radio interview started. Charlie tried to switch off from the preposterous accusations and concentrate on the conversation in the studio but Sarah's words kept echoing around in her mind with disturbing emphasis.

How long have you been in love with Marco?

CHAPTER THREE

'ARE you OK?' Marco's quiet tone cut across the silence in the car.

'Absolutely fine.' Charlie changed gear with a grating sound that exactly mirrored the way she was feeling inside.

'You haven't spoken much since leaving the radio studio.'

Because she couldn't believe the audacity of Sarah Heart—imagine asking a question like that! If anyone was in love with Marco Delmari it was Sarah herself. The woman had been almost sycophantic towards Marco as they were leaving the station. She'd invited him over to her apartment for dinner on Sunday, ostensibly to discuss his American tour, but by the tone of her voice she'd had more in mind than business discussions…and Marco had accepted the invitation quite happily. But maybe the thing that had annoyed her most of all was the way Sarah had looked at her as Marco accepted Sarah's invitation. There had been triumph and disdain in the other woman's eyes, as if to say *you will never hook a man like Marco Delmari.*

'Well, you know me, I'm always quiet,' Charlie murmured as she realised Marco was waiting for a reply. 'The interview went well,' she said, trying to change the direction of her thoughts. She wasn't in love with Marco and it didn't matter what Sarah Heart thought.

'Yes,' Marco frowned. 'Except for the questions about my love life; I didn't think they were relevant.'

'No, they weren't, but I suppose he had to ask. People will be interested in your private life.'

'You are starting to sound like Sarah,' Marco said drily.

'Sorry!' The last thing she wanted was to sound like Sarah Heart!

'That's OK. Maybe on reflection she has a point.'

Charlie glanced over at him in horror. 'No she hasn't!'

Marco smiled. 'From an academic's point of view she hasn't. However, I'm not aiming my book solely at academics. It's for the mass market and I have to give Sarah her due, she is a good businesswoman. She knows how to work the media…knows what sells.'

Charlie wanted to correct him and tell him that Sarah Heart just had her eye on the main chance…that she fancied a sexy doctor as husband number five. But she pulled herself back. 'You're not considering her idea of entering into a relationship as…as some kind of a publicity stunt, are you?' she asked instead, her tone laced with incredulity.

'Well, I'm still not completely convinced. But I suppose having a partner around at the moment wouldn't go amiss.' He shrugged. 'But it would have to be somebody who is on a similar wavelength to me—'

'You mean someone who wouldn't get carried away by it all and imagine herself in love with you?' Charlie guessed wryly.

'No, I mean someone who believes in my ideas,' Marco corrected her pointedly. 'However, as my book tour starts in just a few weeks, I'd have to be quick to find a suitable candidate in that time.'

'Oh, I'm sure you would be able to dig up someone acceptable very quickly,' Charlie murmured. *Sarah Heart* for one, she thought sardonically.

The edge in her voice wasn't lost on Marco. 'The idea of a

relationship without love really offends your sense of romance, doesn't it?'

'No. I just have doubts that it would work out in the long term.'

'What kind of doubts?'

'Well, you know…that it would actually *last*.'

'Of course it will,' Marco said softly. 'I've backed up the hypothesis with exhaustive research studies. If two people are serious about wanting to get married…or about making a long-term commitment…and they follow the steps I've outlined in the book, then the relationship should be successful regardless of whether they are in love or not, the main proviso being both parties are willing to work at the agreement.'

'It doesn't sound very romantic. I always thought that all Italians were incredibly impulsive and passionate,' Charlie murmured thoughtfully. 'But you don't really fit the criteria… do you?'

'What makes you think that? ' Marco gave her a half-smile that made her tingle with sudden awareness of him. 'Being impulsive and passionate with someone is one thing…making a lifelong commitment to them is quite another.'

'Well…yes…obviously…' Charlie was mortified now; she wished she hadn't said that. 'I was just talking about the romantic side of a partnership.'

'But that is my whole point. For a relationship to be successful you're supposed to work at that side of things as well.'

'But if you are both in love to begin with, surely romance follows naturally like night follows day.'

'Nice theory.' Marco smiled at that. 'But unfortunately not true. Very often love is just an illusory feeling…a misleading mirage…and even if it is not you can't rely totally on just that feeling to sustain a relationship over the long term. You need to look deeper than that.'

Charlie looked over at him wryly. 'Maybe you just don't believe in love.' She couldn't resist the comment.

'When making a long-term commitment I think it is an emotion that should be approached with caution.' Marco's voice was dry. 'All too often people confuse making love with being in love…two different things entirely. It's fine to have wild nights of passion and not think too deeply about things. But before you make any promises you should think with your head, not your heart.'

'Sometimes you sound more cynical than sensible.'

'I'm just a realist, Charlie.' He shrugged. 'I believe if you are looking for a successful long-term relationship it's best to be practical, not starry-eyed. And, as bizarre as it sounds, my findings are that if you can disregard love from the equation you can see a relationship more clearly. But maybe the theory wouldn't be successful for someone like you.'

'What do you mean, someone like me?' Charlie pulled the car to a halt in front of his house and turned to look at him.

'Well…' he shrugged in that particular way of his '…you're obviously an incurable romantic.'

'I wish you would stop saying that.' Charlie glared at him.

'Sorry, Ms Hopkirk.' His tone was teasing. 'But that is my considered opinion and the prognosis isn't good, I'm afraid. There's no hope for you.'

Unfortunately Charlie failed to see the humour behind his words. 'Well, that is where you are wrong…*actually.*' She emphasised the word with derision. 'I was cured from my…as you would term…*delusional* state a long time ago. I got divorced and became a single parent. That has a way of grounding the senses, believe me.'

'Hey, I was just making a light-hearted remark!' Marco held up his hands and looked at her with that glint in his eye that she was starting to recognise so well.

'No you weren't, you were being condescending. Well, yes, I do like roses, soft, honeyed words and moonlight…but I'm not so stupid that I would fall in love and get married just because they are applied to a situation. And let me tell you, I'm looking for something much more realistic next time around, believe me.'

'Are you?'

The sudden interest in his tone pulled her up and made her realise that she had just lost her temper, but why she had got so steamed up she didn't know. Maybe because she was still smarting from Sarah's earlier remarks, or maybe it was because she didn't like the idea that Marco seemed to think that she was some kind of dreamer who had completely unrealistic expectations of life and wasn't to be taken seriously. Just because she believed in true love and romance didn't mean she was bewildered. Well, perhaps this was her chance to prove—even if she did have to lie a little bit! 'Of course I want something realistic. I've made one mistake in my life by choosing the wrong partner and I don't want to make another,' she answered him hesitantly. 'Sorry to disappoint you but my days of being starry-eyed are long gone. Deep down I am also a realist.'

'So are you saying that if the terms were right you wouldn't be averse to the idea of a serious relationship based on common sense rather than love?' Marco continued wryly.

'Terms?' Charlie frowned.

'Marriage, or cohabitation, should be treated like a business partnership; you need to know exactly what you want out of it before you enter into it.' Marco noticed the high colour on her cheekbones and smiled. 'You see…you do find the idea too clinical…distasteful even. I rest my case.'

'No! If the terms were right I might consider such an idea.' She raised her head defiantly. She wasn't going to back down.

Marco gave her a sardonic smile. 'Well I don't believe you…I think your heart would be far too soft and emotional to ever be happy with that kind of an arrangement.'

'And what are you basing that opinion on?' Charlie asked dismissively. 'The fact that I listen to romantic music?'

'No…I'm basing it on what you have told me about yourself…about your parents' marriage…about your date last night.'

'You don't know anything about me.' Charlie shrugged. 'But believe what you want! Now…I think we should forget this nonsense and get back to work.' She tried to switch the subject and reached for the door handle, but Marco touched her arm, stopping her from getting out of the car.

'So what *are* you looking for in your next relationship?'

The blunt question took her completely by surprise. She looked back at him and as she met the seriousness of his dark eyes she realised that perhaps this conversation had gone a little too far. 'Well….I….hadn't really thought about it that deeply. I mean…I was only speaking hypothetically.'

He was looking at her very intently as if he could see into her very soul…see the romantic streak lurking beneath the surface. And to her dismay she felt herself blushing wildly. This wasn't fair—he had no right to ask such personal questions!

Marco laughed. 'A word of warning, Charlie; never try and play poker, you wouldn't be much good.'

It was that derisive, cynical laugh that pushed her over the edge. 'Well, OK, then, if you really want to know, next time around I'd want…companionship.' She pulled the word wildly out of mid-air.

'Companionship?' He didn't know whether to believe her or not. She could see the dark light in his eyes was tinged with just a hint of uncertainty.

'Well yes…' She held his dark gaze determinedly. 'What's the matter—isn't that practical enough for you?'

'We're not talking about me…we are talking about you and what *you* would want,' Marco corrected her softly. 'And would companionship really be enough for you?'

She wished those dark eyes of his weren't so intense…

Companionship would be good but she knew deep down it would never be enough for her. She would want a deep and passionate love…nothing less would suffice. She wished she'd never stated this lie now. Charlie glanced away from him. 'Obviously the guy would have to care deeply about Jack and be good with him.' She added the provision hastily. That at least was the truth.

'Obviously.' Marco nodded.

'As you said in your book, it's important not to allow emotions to cloud reality.' She threw the line in for good measure.

'You have been paying attention.' He smiled.

She frowned; was he being facetious? 'No, I've been through a divorce and, as I said before, it has a way of grounding the senses. Why do you think I've chosen internet dating? Let's face it; it is the ultimate practical way to meet someone. You read through a list of a person's attributes and decide from that if you have something in common. There are no hearts and flowers about choosing a partner using that method, I assure you.' She left out the fact that it had been her friend Karen who had talked her into it.

'I guess so.' Marco frowned for a moment. 'Maybe you are a little more practical than I gave you credit for.'

'A *lot* more practical,' she corrected him quickly. Even though she veered towards the romantic, that didn't mean she wasn't sensible.

Marco held up his hands. 'Obviously I was very wrong in my assessment of you.'

'Yes, you were.' She smiled, pleased with the new note of respect in his tone. And now she knew why she had felt so compelled to lie. The label of incurable romantic was not a good one to have around Marco.

His eyes swept over her thoughtfully. He'd always had Charlie down as someone who could never view a relationship in just practical terms, but now that she had convinced him otherwise perhaps she was just what he needed… 'So, now that we have established the fact that we are both on a similar wavelength…so to speak…how about shelving your internet-dating idea for a while and coming out to dinner with me?'

The question was asked so nonchalantly that for a moment Charlie wondered if she had misheard. 'I beg your pardon?'

'I was asking you out for dinner…you know, the meal that comes after lunch and before bed.'

The teasing, provocative words caused Charlie's heart to slam hard against her chest. She didn't know how to take this sudden turn of conversation at all. 'As in…a date?'

'Yes…as in a date,' Marco said softly and suddenly his tone was very serious.

As their eyes met Charlie felt a flare of pure sexual attraction so raw it took her breath away. She couldn't deny that she was wildly attracted to him. Then common sense kicked in as she reminded herself that Marco was not only her boss but also a man who only dated women who looked as if they'd come straight off a catwalk.

She tilted up her chin. 'And why would you do that?'

Marco noted the expression of surprise and consternation in her eyes.

'Why not?' he countered quietly.

'Well, for one thing, you're my boss and it's not good to mix business with pleasure.' She decided to concentrate on practicalities, with her words stiff and formal.

'I didn't realise you were so conventional.' His mouth slanted in a half-smile.

'I was being sensible.'

'Well, as you know, I'm all for being sensible.' He regarded her with a wry, teasing gleam in his eye. 'But you've intrigued me now and I want to find out more about this deeply practical side of your nature and what you are searching for in your next relationship.'

'I'm not really searching for anything!' Charlie said hurriedly.

'That's not what you just said.'

'I was just speaking hypothetically….just…you know… proving that my poker skills are better than yours.'

'But you told me that you were specifically looking for a realistic type of relationship.' Marco murmured the words silkily, knowing how she would react. 'I kind of got the impression that you might have been sussing me out…testing the water…finding out if I was up for the idea.'

'I certainly was not!' Charlie was furious. 'How could you think such a thing?'

'Very easily when you are laying out your requirements in such an open and honest way.'

'Oh, for heaven's sake…' Charlie trailed off as she suddenly noticed the glint of devilment in his dark eyes. 'Are you winding me up?' she asked suspiciously.

'Just a little…' He smiled and his eyes moved over her countenance thoughtfully.

Something about the way he was looking at her made her feel extremely self-conscious. 'Well, I think the joke has gone far enough.' She glanced away from him, feeling foolish now. 'We should get back to work—'

'Hey, not so fast.' He put a hand on her arm as she made to turn away from him again. 'You still haven't given me your answer. Will you have dinner with me?'

She turned back and regarded him with a frown. 'I told you the joke has gone far enough, Marco.'

'I wasn't joking about dinner,' he said quietly.

He watched the scepticism flicking through her eyes. 'Of course I was serious,' he added gently. 'I told you…you've intrigued me.'

She noticed how his gaze moved over her with leisurely appraisal. There was something in its warmth that touched her defences for a second. 'And why is that?' she asked huskily before she could stop herself.

'Well, for one thing, it's very rare that I meet a woman who views relationships in my level-headed terms.'

The matter-of-fact answer snapped her quickly back to reality. 'Let me guess. You want to get inside my brain to research a woman's take on practicality.' She tried to sound flippant, but deep down she was aware of an irrational curl of hurt. She knew he wasn't asking her out for her beauty, but did he have to be so blunt about it?

'I wouldn't have worded it quite like that,' he contradicted her softly. For a moment his eyes drifted down over the soft curves of her body.

In fact, whom was he kidding? he thought drily. He wouldn't put it like that at all. Perhaps the reason he had been so concerned about her internet dating last night was more complex than he'd first thought. He was a man who had a healthy sexual appetite and during the last couple of days he had been surprised to find that there was something about the way she looked at him sometimes…the way she moved…that turned him on. But, as she so rightly had pointed out a few moments ago, business and pleasure did not mix.

He had mockingly accused her of being conventional for having such sentiments, but in truth weren't they part of the reason he had felt so at ease around Charlie these last few months? After the uncomfortable atmosphere his last PA had generated it had been great to be around someone who thought like him and wanted to keep the working environment strictly complication-free. In fact he had been so at ease with Charlie that he had enjoyed trying to draw her out from behind those reserved barriers of hers, and now somehow he had managed to become interested in her sexually. Being interested in her in that way was not the prudent and practical thing to do. But…now he was starting to revise that opinion.

The clinical part of his mind had clicked on when she had talked about finding something more realistic for her next relationship. Maybe there was an opportunity for business and pleasure to mix very well indeed here… Maybe it would be OK to pursue Charlie…maybe…in practical terms she was just what he needed right now.

'Perhaps we should try each other out for size.' His eyes drifted back towards her face.

The sudden change of tack took her by surprise. There was something almost hypnotic about the smoothly sensual Italian tones. 'Now you are just being…' Charlie struggled to find the right word. She could hardly think straight when he looked at her like that '…outrageous.'

'Am I?' He smiled. 'You were talking earlier this morning about chemistry… There is more than a *frisson* of that between us…don't you think?'

'No!' She cut across him abruptly. He was moving into dangerous territory now that she didn't want to analyse.

Her eyes were drawn to his lips…they were curved in a derisive smile…but they were also sexily inviting. Was it her imagination or was he very close? She could smell the tang of his aftershave, fresh and very inviting.

She noticed that his eyes were on her lips. Unconsciously she moistened them with the tip of her tongue. A strong feeling of desire suddenly laced the air between them. It was so heavy that Charlie could feel it thundering through her, making her heart race, twisting a latent need into life with shocking force.

In that instant she wanted him to kiss her—no, more than that, she wanted him to take her into his arms and make passionate love to her…

The knowledge rang alarm bells inside her but she couldn't stem the feelings, they were flowing through her with the most amazing force. She couldn't remember the last time a man had turned her on so completely like this without even touching her!

'How about I pick you up tonight about seven?'

The smooth words were more of an order than a suggestion. He really was insufferably sure of himself, Charlie thought hazily, and really she should tell him right now that she had other plans.

But for some reason the words just wouldn't come out. She swallowed hard as he reached out a hand and touched the side of her face; although his fingers were a whisper-soft caress against her skin, she felt them with such a pleasurable, forceful intensity that involuntarily she closed her eyes.

Charlie wanted that caress to go on and on, it was as if she were falling into a very deep, spiralling trap with nowhere to go except towards the light of desire and need. She had never felt like this before, it was as if she wasn't in control of her own senses…it was scary and yet it was wonderful at the same time.

Then Marco pulled back, leaving her shaking and breathless.

'So I'll see you tonight, yes?'

His voice was so arrogantly cool and calm that it brought her back to her senses as sharply as if he had slapped her. Shocked by the intensity of her disappointment because he hadn't kissed her, she struggled to pull herself together.

'We've got to work together, Marco,' she murmured reprovingly.

'Yes.' He nodded and then grinned. 'Have I ever told you that I like that prim and proper attitude of yours? It's very refreshing.'

'It's not supposed to be refreshing, it's supposed to be sensible.'

He smiled. 'You're talking my language again.' He glanced at his watch. 'And yes, I agree there are things we need to discuss…sensibly. Unfortunately there is no time now. It will have to wait until tonight.'

She shook her head…mesmerised by his determined

attitude. 'I couldn't get someone to look after Jack tonight. It's too short notice—'

'OK, lunch tomorrow.' He cut across her nonchalantly. 'I'll pick you up at about twelve-thirty.'

'Marco…' But she didn't have time to say anything else because he had turned and opened the car door to step out into the bright afternoon sunlight.

This really was preposterous, Charlie thought as she grabbed for the door handle and stepped out after him. 'I am not going on a date with you, Marco!'

'Why not?'

Why not indeed? As Charlie looked across at his tall handsome physique she was asking herself the same question and weakness started to invade. With determination she raised her chin and forced herself to be level-headed. She couldn't go out with him because he was her boss, she reminded herself sharply. Business and pleasure didn't go together. And added to that he was only interested in her now because she had lied to him about the type of person she was. He had admitted earlier that it would help endorse his theories and his book to have a girlfriend around for a while who thought the same way he did. Well, that position definitely wouldn't suit her! 'Because…it wouldn't work out,' she told him firmly.

'I told you earlier, Charlie, in order to find out if something will be successful you have to give it a chance.' He shrugged. 'However, you can relax, there are a few work-related issues I'd like to discuss with you anyway. So tomorrow would be a good chance to do that.'

'What kind of work issues?'

'We'll discuss that tomorrow.' He glanced at his watch. 'I've got to get over to St Agnes Hospital now to deal with two referrals.'

He sounded very calm and assured and it was light-years

away from how she was feeling. She was utterly confused. Had tomorrow's lunch date just been relegated to a business meeting?

'So let me get this right; you told your boss that you weren't averse to having an intimate relationship with him based on compatibility alone and he suddenly asked you out?' Karen was sitting at the kitchen table analysing the story.

'I didn't mention the word intimate,' Charlie corrected her quickly. 'And I wasn't talking about having a relationship with *him,* I was just talking hypothetically! He took my words out of context.'

'Hmm.' Karen looked at her with a raised eyebrow.

'I was just trying to convince him that I'm not a hopeless romantic.' Charlie tried to make light of the subject.

She had phoned her friend Karen as soon as she got home from work because she had felt she needed to talk about what had happened. Karen had then come straight around to her house to go over it all again, and Charlie wished now she hadn't mentioned it; it was all too uncomfortable.

'Because Sarah Heart accused you of being in love with him?'

'Well, that was part of it, the other part was that Marco can be quite condescending when it comes to people who are…emotional rather than practical.' She put a pot of tea down on the kitchen table between them and sat down again. 'Anyway, let's just forget about it, shall we? It's all rubbish. I've no intention of going out with Marco on a date.'

'Why not?' Karen leaned back in her chair. 'Going by what I've seen of him on TV, he is quite a dish.'

'Yes, he's very good-looking.' Charlie shrugged. 'But he's my boss and…well, for a start, we think differently; he doesn't believe that love is the most important thing in a relationship and I do.'

'So you lied…so what?' Karen shrugged. 'It's a mere formality anyway.'

'Not to Marco it's not. I told you he's very serious about viewing a relationship in a purely practical way.'

'Well, if I were in your shoes I'd just continue to pretend that I was Ms Practicality. He doesn't need to know that your favourite film is *Sleepless in Seattle*…does he?'

Charlie laughed.

'And he's only your boss for another month—then your contract is finished,' Karen reminded her succinctly. She raked a hand through her short brown hair. 'You could risk a short involvement with him to see how things go.'

'And let him think that I was propositioning him when I said I'd consider a relationship based on practicalities…because that is what he thinks, you know. The guy is pretty big-headed.' Charlie shook her head. 'Anyway, I've already turned him down so it's too late for all that. If we go out tomorrow it will be to discuss work. He's quite happy with that. His interest in me is businesslike anyway. '

'You're just frightened of getting hurt again, aren't you?' Karen observed suddenly. 'You can't keep hiding yourself away like this, Charlie. You've been doing that since your divorce. You've got to get out there again.'

'I know.' Charlie reached out and poured the tea. 'But I don't think Marco is the right person for me. Now, let's change the subject. I don't want to think about him a moment longer. How are things at the agency?'

To Charlie's relief Karen let it drop. 'Actually they are a bit chaotic.'

Charlie was on the books of Karen's employment agency and knew only too well that things were manic in there. From time to time in between contracts she went in to help her friend run the place and it was an arrangement that suited them both. Karen got extra help from someone she could trust implicitly, which meant she could take some time off to be with her children, and Charlie got a job to fill some of the gaps between her temping contracts.

'It's peaks and troughs, it will calm down next week probably,' Charlie said soothingly.

'Maybe.' Karen put her cup down. 'But I'm seriously considering selling the place, Charlie. You know I told you I'd had a take-over bid from a rival agency?'

Charlie nodded. Her friend had been stressed for a while trying to balance her home life with work and had talked about selling last month, but hadn't been offered enough money.

'Well, they've upped the offer.'

'That's really good, Karen!'

'Yes, except for one thing: I think they will close my office here. They are a big company and basically they are just interested in squeezing out the competition and covering contracts with their own people.'

'I see.' Charlie felt a pang of apprehension as she realised this probably wasn't going to bode well for her future work. Then, seeing the worried expression on her friend's face, she quickly pulled herself together. 'Karen you must do what is right for you,' she said sincerely.

'I just hate the thought that this isn't going to work well for my staff,' Karen said with a shrug. 'And then there is you. You've always been so brilliant at bailing me out in the office—'

'Karen, nothing stays the same in life, and I'm probably lucky to have got away with temping for as long as I have.' Charlie smiled and topped up her tea. 'Whatever you decide, I'll be behind you,' she said firmly. 'Don't worry about me. I'm a survivor.'

CHAPTER FOUR

CHARLIE had the strangest dream that night. She dreamt that Marco Delmari was making love to her. She could feel his hands on her body…his lips on her lips…demanding, ruthless yet so erotic that she woke up breathless, her heart pounding.

'Foolish in the extreme,' she berated herself as she lay looking up at the ceiling. Perhaps she had been so long without sex that her brain was turning to mush.

Karen was right, she thought. She really needed to get back out into the world of relationships again. Although she'd had a few dates since her divorce none of the men had been attractive to her. The problem was that she couldn't have sex with just anybody…she had to have feelings for a man before she could sleep with him. Consequentially the last person she had slept with was her husband four and a half years ago.

Even Karen didn't know that! The fact was that she hadn't had feelings for a man in such a long time that she had started to think maybe she would never be aroused again. And now this! It was bizarre.

Her thoughts would be better occupied thinking about what she was going to do if Karen sold her agency, she told herself firmly as she got up and reached for her dressing gown. Maybe she needed to start job-hunting for something permanent now, as there were only a few weeks left on her contract with Marco.

The phone rang next to the bed and sleepily she reached to answer it. Marco's smoothly sexy Italian tones took her by surprise.

'My apologies for ringing so early, and don't worry, I'm not cancelling our lunch—I just thought I'd catch you before I head over to the hospital to check on some patients.'

'I wasn't worried,' Charlie corrected him firmly. Really, he could be very arrogant! 'Actually I'd forgotten about lunch,' she lied swiftly. 'I thought you were the plumber, ringing to arrange a time to fix my central heating.'

'Ah, I see.' Marco laughed. He had a lovely laugh…it was just as sexy as his voice. 'It must be cold in your house. Do you want me to come earlier, see if I can warm you up?'

The question made her pulses quicken. She imagined him warming her up the way he had in her dreams last night and the thought of it made her sizzle. She pulled her dressing gown around her as if by holding it firmly across her body she could shut out the crazy images. 'No, it's OK thank you.' Her voice sounded very prim even to her own ears.

'OK, but I'm not bad at fixing things,' he continued. 'It comes from being brought up in a century-old farmhouse in Tuscany. Anyway, getting back to our arrangements for this afternoon…'

Instantly she could feel butterflies in her stomach. 'You said you wanted to discuss something about work?'

'There are a number of things I want to discuss,' he said smoothly. 'But they can wait until later. I thought we could go to the Summer House. They have an excellent menu.'

'So I've heard.' Charlie had never been to that restaurant but she knew it was one of the most exclusive in the area with sweeping views out across the River Thames.

A picture rose in her mind of somewhere formal and stiff where people were elegantly dressed. What on earth would she wear to go there? She found herself doing a mental trawl through her wardrobe and not coming up with anything very suitable.

'So I'll pick you up at twelve-thirty.'

'Marco!' She cut across him abruptly. 'Do you think we could go somewhere else?'

'Yes, of course.' Marco sounded unfazed by the request. 'We can go anywhere you would like. Have you got somewhere in mind?'

Charlie thought fast. 'There is a country pub in the next village called The Waterhouse.'

'OK, we'll eat there instead. I've got to go Charlie, see you later.'

The line went dead. Charlie replaced the receiver and realised that instead of fobbing Marco off as she had intended she had capitulated very easily.

It was just one outing…she reassured herself. Moreover Marco was probably only going to talk about work. Not much to worry about really.

Charlie had hoped that by the time Marco arrived to pick her up she would be organised and ready.

The reality was that the plumber arrived to fix her heating and held her back. So everything was done in a last-minute rush. She had just stepped into a pair of black jeans and a white blouse when Marco pulled up outside.

She looked at herself in the mirror. Her hair was tied back from her face in its usual severe style and she wondered suddenly if she should try and look different today.

On impulse she pulled the tie out, allowing the golden strands to fall around her shoulders. Then instantly she regretted it. She didn't want to look as if she was trying to be glamorous, because this wasn't a real date and anyway she knew she could never compete with the women Marco usually liked on his arm.

The shrill ring of the doorbell shattered the silence of the house. It was too late to tie it back again now!

Feeling nervous, she went down to open the front door.

And as she came face to face with Marco her heart seemed to miss a beat.

'Hi.' He smiled at her and all she could think about was how handsome he was. He was wearing casual clothes, but he looked incredible in them. Chinos, a thick cable sweater and a suede jacket that emphasised the breadth of his shoulders all added up to his look of pure, sexy Italian style. And when she met those dark eyes of his she just wanted to melt.

'I am ready, but come in while I get my bag.' She moved back and held the door for him.

'You look lovely.' He didn't take his eyes off her as he stepped into the hallway.

'Thank you.' Charlie smiled self-consciously.

'You should leave your hair like that more often. It makes you look very…alluring.' He reached out a hand and touched the golden strands, running it through his fingers like liquid silk.

The gesture was nonchalant and yet it felt like such an intimate thing to do that she was aware of her heartbeats increasing and was more than aware of the *frisson* of sensuality that suddenly sprang up between them.

She took a step away and didn't know what to say to that, she felt completely out of her depth. For the past few months she had been trying to pretend that she wasn't sexually aware of Marco and now suddenly there was no hiding from it. Now there was more awareness between them than she knew how to deal with.

Marco was just a charmer, she reminded herself firmly. It didn't mean anything.

She was glad when Jack came racing downstairs at that moment, followed at a more sedate pace by her mother.

'Marco, this is my mother, Helen, and my son, Jack,' Charlie introduced them.

'Pleased to meet you.' Marco smiled at the older woman.

'And hello, Jack.' He crouched down so that he was at eye-level with the child. 'I'm pleased to meet you too. I've heard lots about you.'

Jack smiled shyly. 'Is that red car outside yours?' he asked suddenly.

'Yes, it is.'

'Wow!' Jack's dark eyes lit up.

'So you have a passion for beautiful cars…you are like a true Italian.' Marco ruffled the child's dark hair playfully.

Charlie smiled and reached for her handbag. 'We won't be long, Mum. Thanks for looking after him.'

As it was a sunny day, Marco had the top down on his car. As they zoomed along the narrow country lanes the breeze caught Charlie's hair, whipping it around her face in wild disarray.

Marco glanced over at her as he pulled the car to a standstill in the pub car park and watched as she tried to smooth the golden strands back into place.

'I should have tied it back,' she murmured as she caught his eye.

'I don't think so.' He seemed to look at her with deep concentration and Charlie felt herself growing hot inside. Then he reached across and brushed a strand of hair back into place. 'There—perfect again.'

The light touch of his fingers against her skin made Charlie's heart contract.

'I'm pleased you changed your mind about lunch today.'

'Well, you wanted to talk about work.' She tried to think sensibly but she felt that she was drowning in his sexy eyes.

'Yes, I did.' He gave her a teasing look. 'Amongst other things.'

'As I was saying yesterday, I do think it's important that we keep a close boundary line between work and anything personal.' Was she rambling? she wondered hazily. She was trying so hard to be level-headed. But he seemed to be very close to her, she could smell the tang of his cologne, warm and evocative. She remembered how he had touched her yesterday and a wave of longing suddenly swept through her. What would it be like to be held in his arms, feel his hands move slowly and intimately over her body? The sudden unbidden thought reverberated through her, making her temperature rise dramatically. She tried to dismiss it but the sensual picture refused to move from her mind.

'Actually I have a notion that, where you and I are concerned, business and pleasure could fit together very nicely.' He murmured the words huskily, his eyes on her lips.

'I don't see how…'

Marco smiled. 'Well, as you are such a practical person and so am I…boundaries will always be in place.' He reached and brushed his fingers lightly down over her cheek. 'Therefore the problem ceases to exist…don't you think?' His hand lingered at her chin, tipping her face upwards so that he could look at her.

The intensity of his eyes and the touch of his hand against her skin set her heart slamming against her chest. She felt her body tense as he moved even closer. She wanted him to kiss her…wanted it so badly that every nerve-ending in her body seemed to be yearning for him…and yet at the same time she was willing herself to move away, telling herself that this situation was a mistake and that she could get badly burnt. The trouble was that the need to risk the fire was overwhelming…

'Anyway, I think talk of work can wait until later…' he brushed a finger across the smoothness of her lips '…whereas this…can't.' His hands gently cupped her face as his head lowered towards hers. The touch of his lips against hers and the way he held her as he kissed her felt incredibly sensual and possessive. It was no gentle kiss either, it was powerfully masterful, very dominant. Charlie's senses swam with desire and before she could think better of it she was kissing him back with a hungry response. She was aware that his fingers moved to lace through her hair, controlling her as he thoroughly explored the sweetness of her mouth.

Charlie's emotions were all over the place as he pulled away. A part of her wanted to go back into his arms, wanted him to continue kissing her. The other part was mortified by how easily she had just capitulated to his caress, by how wantonly she had returned his kisses. *He was her boss, for heaven's sake! This could only lead to disaster.*

'What on earth are we doing?' she murmured breathlessly.

He smiled at that. 'I think it's known as enjoying ourselves,' he murmured with lazy amusement.

She felt a flare of annoyance at his casual rejoinder, but whether it was at herself for kissing him back so passionately, or him for being so nonchalant about it she wasn't sure. 'You're just a flirt, Marco…' She tried to sound dismissive but there was a revealing huskiness about her tone that she didn't like.

He smiled. 'But just for the record I really do want to discuss work with you.' He turned to get out of the car. 'Come on, let's see what the food is like in this pub of yours.'

Hurriedly she stepped out after him and tried to gather herself together. Obviously he wasn't even giving that kiss a second thought, so she needed to be as cool and urbane about it as he was. The trouble was, she couldn't think of anything cool or urbane to say.

They continued on down to the pub in silence. The Waterhouse was an old coaching house nestled in the curve of the River Thames. Behind it there was a small beer garden where people could sit on a sunny day and admire the view. Today, however, only the hardiest of souls were sitting outside in the autumn sun and it was a pleasure to walk into the warmth of the slightly dark old-world interior.

Marco stood back to allow Charlie to enter the building first and as he did so he noted the way her long hair swung silkily around her back, noted the long length of her legs, the lovely curve of her bottom in the tight-fitting jeans.

She really was quite sexy; he'd been blown away when she opened the door to him earlier, her face flushed, and her hair tumbling around her shoulders. He'd often watched her in the office and wondered what she would be like when she let her barriers down and relaxed. He had suspected that behind that prim and proper demeanour there was a hidden sensuality, and he had been right. The way she had kissed him had proved that without a doubt.

Now he found himself wanting to tear down the rest of her barriers and take her to bed.

They found a table next to a roaring log fire and Marco pulled out a chair for her to sit down. 'What can I get you to drink?'

'A glass of white wine would be nice, thank you.'

As Marco waited for the barmaid to get their drinks he glanced back at the table. Charlie was taking off her jacket now to hang it over the back of her chair. His gaze flicked over her contemplatively. Usually the women he dated were dressed in more obviously seductive apparel, yet there was something very appealing about the plain white blouse that Charlie wore. It was fitted in at her small waist and it emphasised in a subtle way the full curve of her breasts.

She glanced over and caught him watching her and he smiled before turning back to the bar.

She really was quite lovely; in fact she even brought out a protective streak in him that he hadn't felt for a while. It was something to do with the way she could look quite vulnerable at times…like just now when she'd caught him watching her…and the way she had looked at him yesterday with that defensive sparkle in her eyes as she talked about her classic love-songs CD and her parents falling in love at first sight.

He had to admit, when she had told him that she would consider a relationship that was based on realism rather than a starry-eyed premise he had been sceptical to begin with. He had already judged her and in emotional terms he had placed her in the high-maintenance bracket.

It wasn't that Marco was against the idea of love…he just didn't believe that it conquered all, and he didn't want to get involved in a relationship with someone who believed that it did. He had learnt at first hand how unrealistic expectations could tear people apart. He had watched his own parents destroy each other; it had been painful and messy and he certainly didn't want to get involved in a relationship like that. In fact he didn't really want a serious relationship in his life at all… The girls he usually went out with were fine for short-term flings, but they didn't understand his theories regarding long-term relationships at all. However, a liaison with someone of a like mind…someone who wasn't emotionally driven… well, that was a different matter.

Until yesterday he had never suspected for one moment that Charlie might be that like-minded individual. But any woman who could say she was looking for companionship had to have relegated love to a secondary position in her life. And he had realised that maybe she wasn't looking for that all-consuming love, maybe she had been hurt so much in her first marriage that she was looking now for more practical and realistic relationships.

He shouldn't have been so surprised to discover this about her but he still was—surprised and genuinely pleased because not only did it leave him free to pursue her, but it also meant that she could be quite an asset to him professionally.

The fact was that right at this moment Marco was getting very tired of giving interviews that suddenly veered off to dwell on his own personal life. It didn't seem to matter that he had produced the evidence for his theories already—people still wanted to know about his romantic circumstances. And as Sarah had pointed out, the problem wasn't going to go away. In fact when he went on his book tour to America it would probably get worse.

So having someone like Charlie around, someone who thought in the same way he did, was great. Having her in the background right now just might help play down all those annoying little questions about how his personal life compared with his theories.

The fact that he also wanted to get her into bed was simply a bonus. He hadn't planned to kiss her in the car, but the temptation had been too strong to resist and had taken him a little by surprise. As had her hungry response to him.

He returned to the table and put the drinks down.

'Thanks.' She smiled and tried not to notice that there was a group of women in the corner who were looking over at Marco with undisguised admiration.

He didn't seem to notice them at all. 'It's very pleasant in here,' he said as he took the seat opposite to her and sat with his back to them.

'Yes…kind of quaint…' She took a sip of her drink.

'So how do you usually spend your Saturdays?' he asked suddenly.

'Mostly my weekends are taken up by spending time with Jack and catching up on housework.' She shrugged. 'I'm sure your weekends are very different!'

'It must be difficult working full-time and looking after a house and a child.'

'Sometimes, but I have a child-minder and good back-up from my mother. My dad died a few years ago so in a way Jack has been company for Mum, and helped focus her attention away from her grief.'

'It's good to have family support.'

Charlie nodded. 'But I try not to put on Mum too much. She

has a busy life. That's why I decided to work for a temping agency; it's been great while Jack's been small because it's given me flexibility.' Charlie raked a hand through her hair. It looked as though all that was going to finish if Karen sold the agency, she thought distractedly.

'And Jack's dad doesn't help out at all in this arrangement?'

Charlie focused on him again and shook her head. 'Greg is a pilot and he is based in America now, he has an apartment in LA.'

'He doesn't see his son at all?'

Charlie could hear the note of disbelief in Marco's voice. 'Greg's life is busy. And, although he does fly into London, he's on a tight turn-around schedule—well, that's the excuse I give Jack, anyway.'

'I see.'

As she met his steady gaze Charlie wondered if Marco was thinking how reprehensible it was for her to lie about why Jack's father didn't see him.

She knew Greg would actually have plenty of time to see his son in between flying around the world. But how could you tell a four-year-old that his father wasn't interested in him?

Marco looked at the bright blaze in her eyes as she looked across at him, and noticed the way she raised her chin slightly. Obviously the mere mention of Jack's father still had the power to touch Charlie on an emotional level.

'Anyway, enough about that.' She changed the subject swiftly. 'You wanted to talk about work, not listen to me rambling on...'

Marco noticed that once more the shutters had come down over her expression. 'You weren't rambling on and I was interested,' he said softly. 'Your ex still has the power to upset you, doesn't he?'

She didn't like the observation. 'What makes you think that?'

'I don't know...it could be something to do with the expression in your eyes whenever he's mentioned.'

'I'm not upset about Greg.' There was a hint of steel in her tone suddenly. 'I'm just upset for Jack. I feel for him and the fact that he doesn't see his dad.'

'That's understandable.'

'Well, that's all it is. Apart from the fact that I have his son, Greg is history.' She angled her chin up even more. 'So…let's get back to why we are here. You wanted to discuss work.'

Marco hesitated. He wanted to delve deeper, but if he wanted to get closer to her he was going to have to break down her defences and get her to open up to him. Maybe now wasn't the time.

He drummed his fingers on the table for a moment before making a decision. For now he would drop the personal questions and concentrate on things from the safety zone of work. He was going to have to take things slowly.

'OK…' Marco looked up and fixed her with a dark, penetrating look that made her insides tighten '…as you know, your contract with me is coming to an end soon. But I'd like you to consider extending it, staying on.'

She hadn't been expecting this! 'How long were you thinking?' she asked swiftly.

Marco shrugged. 'Another twelve months, possibly longer, we'll see how we go from there.'

Charlie felt a dart of pleasure mixed with relief. 'That would be great.' She smiled at him. 'To be honest, the offer couldn't have come at a better time. I think the agency I work for will be sold soon and I was wondering what I should do after that.'

'It will suit us both, then.' Marco sat back in his chair, feeling pleased. He had been planning to offer Charlie a permanent job regardless of his personal interest in her. He really didn't want to lose her from the office. Things had never run as smoothly as they did now. The added advantage that this would make it easier to get closer made the agreement very sweet. 'Shall we say the same hours?' he said nonchalantly. 'I know it's not easy working full-time having a young child, but I can be flexible.'

'Thanks, I'd appreciate that.' She looked over at him gratefully. 'It can be a nightmare sometimes if Jack's ill.'

'I understand.' Marco nodded. 'The only thing is I'll need you to accompany me on a few trips now and then, seminars…that kind of thing.'

Charlie hesitated before answering him, and he could see her weighing up the fact that she didn't want to leave her child alongside the fact that she wanted this job.

'It will be mainly over the next few months but after that things should settle back to normal,' Marco told her gently.

She nodded. 'Well, it shouldn't be a problem, then.'

'Great. As you know, I've got a very busy period coming up with this book tour so I'm delighted to sort that out.'

She smiled at him, feeling a surge of happiness. Twelve months working with Marco sounded like bliss. She really did like him, Charlie thought suddenly. Maybe she even liked him too much. The thought distracted her from what he was saying, and her gaze started to drift over the rugged, handsome contours of his features. She found herself lingering for a moment on his lips as she remembered how sensational his kiss had been.

'So you are OK with all of that?' He fixed her with that intently sexy look of his and she felt her heart starting to slam against her chest again.

Was she OK with all of this? The exuberant feeling of relief she had experienced when he'd asked her to stay on began to fade a little. How was she going to maintain a professional relationship with a man who made her feel like this?

'Charlie?'

Aware that he was waiting for an answer, she quickly pulled herself together. She had a pile of bills waiting on the sideboard and a house that desperately needed even more money spent on it. According to the plumber this morning, she was probably going to need a whole new central-heating system. She couldn't afford to allow irrational feelings to mess up a job opportunity.

'Yes, perfectly.'

'Good.' He smiled at her and for a moment his eyes drifted lazily over her. 'Well, now the main business is out of the way, we should relax and order something to eat.'

Charlie picked up the menu from the table. Relaxing around Marco was probably not a good idea, because that was when these feelings of attraction started to strike. Things would be OK once they got back into the office, she reassured herself firmly. They were always so busy; there would be no time for anything personal.

'I have to go to Tuscany at the weekend,' Marco said suddenly.

'Oh?' She looked over at him with interest. 'You were telling me on the phone that you grew up there. What was it you said—a century-old farmhouse? It sounded lovely.'

'Yes, it is. Have you ever been to Italy?'

Charlie shook her head.

'Well, the villa is set in a very beautiful area. In the summer the meadows are alight with the gold of sunflowers…just hectare after hectare of them under a blazing blue sky. And right now there will be a mellow warmth in the air and they will be harvesting the vines.'

'How did you ever bear to leave a place as beautiful as that?'

'Very easily actually.' He smiled ruefully. 'I'm not the sentimental type.'

'Of course.' Charlie forgot herself for a moment and looked at him teasingly. 'Because that could go under the heading of being romantic…and you wouldn't want that.'

'Definitely not.' Marco smiled.

As their eyes met that feeling of awareness and intimacy

suddenly sprang forcefully to life between them again. Charlie could feel it twisting in the air like a living entity ready to coil around her and draw her deeper and deeper under its spell.

Desperately she tried to ignore it. 'So are your parents still at the farmhouse?' She moved the conversation on.

'Unfortunately my parents died in a car crash five years ago.'

'I'm so sorry, Marco. That's awful!'

'Yes.' He met her eyes candidly. 'I've come to terms with it now. But it was a traumatic time.'

She nodded.

'I still own the farmhouse and sometimes my sisters bring their children there for holidays, but apart from that the place lies empty.'

'That's a shame.'

'I suppose it is.' Marco shrugged. 'Anyway, I'll be there for the weekend. It's a business trip but it will give me the opportunity to check on the place. And the reason I've mentioned it is that, now you have agreed to work for me permanently, I want you to accompany me.'

The invitation was tagged on so casually that Charlie wasn't sure how to take it. She looked across at him and her heart started its rapid tattoo again. 'You mean on business, of course?'

'Of course.'

Charlie cringed and wished now she hadn't sought clarification!

'There will be time for us to get to know each other along more personal lines as well,' he added softly.

As their eyes met her emotions seemed to race with peculiar intensity, pleasure…panic and a large helping of desire all seemed to merge and flutter. A weekend in romantic Tuscany getting to know Marco Delmari would probably be better than all her wildest fantasies put together.

Stop it, Charlie, she warned herself furiously. *This is dangerous territory.*

Marco watched the uncertainty chasing across the shadows of her green eyes and smiled. 'I was thinking a trip to Florence and dinner,' he said teasingly. 'Sharing a bedroom is optional.'

The provocative words made her skin flare a bright crimson. 'You know, Marco, I think you like to make outrageous statements just to ruffle my equilibrium and get a rise out of me.' With difficulty she kept her tone light.

She noticed the gleam in his dark eyes. 'You're probably right,' he said. 'You do look very attractive when you blush. And it's such a rare attribute these days.'

Charlie tried as hard as she could to remain impassive to that remark. She was damned if she was going to give him the satisfaction of getting another response. 'Just for the record, I wasn't worried about the sleeping arrangements.'

'Good.' He smiled at her and she felt her insides starting to heat up again.

And that was when she knew for certain that she was lying. The knowledge curled uncomfortably inside her.

She wasn't worried that Marco would pressurise her into sleeping with him—she knew instinctively he wasn't that kind of man. Apart from anything else, there was any number of women who would willingly do that. And, despite the way he had kissed her and his teasing comments, she was sure Marco's priorities where she was concerned were mainly businesslike. The only thing that had changed between them was that he now believed she was on his wavelength emotionally, which meant he viewed her as fair game for a casual fling...

What concerned her were her reactions to him. The way she had found herself responding to his kisses scared her a little. She hadn't been turned on like that in such a long time and now she wondered what would happen if he touched her or kissed her when they were alone together in Italy.

Would she be able to pull back from the situation?

She felt a swirl of deep anxiety. If anything happened

between her and Marco and things went wrong she could ultimately lose her job. Going away with him could be a big
mistake.

But how could she avoid it? She bit down on her lip and tried
to think sensibly. This was business…and Marco had made it
clear that he expected her to accompany him on a few trips. It
was hardly an unreasonable request, given the salary he was
paying. And. although it was fairly short notice, she knew her
mother would be only too happy to have her grandson with her
for a whole weekend.

'So what exactly is involved work-wise?' she asked cau-
tiously.

'It's fairly straightforward.' He shrugged. 'I'm giving an
interview for Italian TV to promote my book. That will take
up a lot of time on Sunday and I have a stack of notes in my
office at the villa that need to be catalogued ready for a meeting
later that evening back in London with Professor Hunt.'

It sounded reasonable enough. And if she couldn't handle
her emotions around him she was going to mess this opportunity up before it started. 'Fine,' she said calmly. 'It's only one
weekend it shouldn't be a problem.'

Was it her imagination or was there a gleam of triumph in
his dark gaze now?

Charlie hurriedly dismissed the thought. This was business
and she needed the job.

CHAPTER FIVE

WHAT was she doing, Charlie wondered in agitation as the fasten-seatbelt sign came on and the pilot told them to prepare for landing. She should never have agreed to this…it was madness!

As she looked up her eyes connected with Marco's. 'Not long now and we'll be on the ground.'

Charlie forced herself to smile at him.

The sudden panic had hit her mid-flight out of nowhere, which was strange because during the week she had managed to convince herself that she wasn't in the slightest bit concerned about this trip. She supposed the fact that it had been extremely busy in the office had helped.

Marco had been his usual friendly self but the familiarity that had flared over last weekend had seemingly been forgotten. In fact as soon as he had dropped her off at home after lunch last Saturday it had been forgotten, although maybe not entirely by her. Sometimes when she had glanced up and caught his eye the memory of that kiss had been there, but it had been a fleeting thing and it hadn't encroached on work.

But now, sitting next to him on the plane, she felt all those dangerous feelings of desire flooding back in force. Suddenly she was aware of everything about him. The scent of his cologne, even the way his arm brushed lightly against hers as he moved made her tingle with consciousness.

It was only because they were out of their usual environment, she told herself soothingly. As soon as they started to work at his office in the villa things would be fine again, common sense would snap back into place and these silly feelings would go.

'You've forgotten to fasten your seat belt,' Marco reminded her.

She made to reach for it, but he had already found it and was leaning across to slip it into place.

For a second he was so close that she could feel the strength of his hard-muscled arms through the light material of her blouse. She tensed at the fleeting touch of his hands against her waist, her senses pounding.

'There.' He smiled at her and her gaze drifted from his intensely sexy eyes to the firm, sensual curve of his lips.

'Better safe than sorry—isn't that what they say?' he said lightly as he sat back.

That saying should be branded on her consciousness for the entire weekend, Charlie thought wryly, because if she didn't get a grip she was going to be in deep water.

'Thanks.' She smiled politely and then turned to look out of the window into the darkness of the night.

She hoped he didn't know what kind of an effect he was having on her because that would be too embarrassing. He would be totally amused.

A picture of the kind of amusement he could find flicked through her mind in a searing, red-hot vision of them entwined in a double bed.

Stop it, Charlie! If you value your job you won't even think about that.

She clenched her hands at her sides and reminded herself in severe terms of just how important this job was. Karen was in the process of selling the agency…they had talked a few days ago and it seemed the deal would go through pretty quickly.

If she didn't stay on with Marco she could be in financial limbo for a while. She had no doubt that she would find another job but it could take time and she would be lucky to find something as well-paid.

The plane touched down and there was a screech of brakes.

Don't let yourself think about anything that isn't related to business, she told herself briskly. It was Friday night now, and their flight home was booked for late Sunday afternoon. All she had to do was hold her nerve and keep her distance for two short days.

As the plane came to a halt Marco stood up and collected the hand luggage from the overhead compartment.

He put an arm around her as they stepped out into the mellow warmth of the night air. 'Welcome to Italy…' He murmured the words against her ear, making her senses sizzle.

It didn't mean anything…he was just being Italian, she assured herself. But even so, it was enough to bring her panic racing back. Yes, it was only two days *and two nights…with Marco*…a man who could turn her on with a mere whisper.

'Thanks…' She tried very hard to sound businesslike. 'Maybe one day I'll come here for pleasure rather than business.'

'I think we can make some time for pleasure,' Marco said with amusement.

Would sharing a bed come under that remit? she wondered suddenly. The question pulsated through her along with the touch of his hand and the knowledge that she was aching to be even closer!

With difficulty she broke the contact and stepped away from him. 'Well, we'll see. But we have a lot of work to do,' she said briskly.

He smiled. 'I knew we would make a good team. With you by my side I need never fall behind with work again.'

She wasn't sure if he was being facetious or serious. There

was a gleam in his eye that was very disconcerting. 'I'd better go collect my luggage…'

Marco watched her walk away, a look of contemplation in his eyes. She was as jumpy as a skittish colt. This weekend in Italy was just what they needed. He would break through her barriers, he told himself firmly. He was determined about that. When he wanted something he usually got it.

Marco didn't have any luggage to collect, as everything he needed was already at the villa, so he went to see about their hire car while Charlie waited by the carousel for her case.

They met in the arrivals hall a little while later, and within a few minutes Charlie was installed in the passenger seat of a Mercedes and they were heading away from the town of Pisa into the countryside.

Charlie switched on her mobile phone and checked to see if there were any messages from her mother. There was nothing, which probably meant that everything was fine and Jack was in bed.

Marco glanced over and noticed the phone. 'Are you going to give Jack a ring?'

'He goes to bed at seven-thirty, so he'll be asleep now. I like to keep him in a routine.'

Marco nodded. 'Kids like routine. It makes them feel safe.'

Routine could also make adults feel safe, Charlie thought as she watched the powerful headlights slicing through the darkness of the narrow lanes. Usually at this time on a Friday after she had read Jack his bedtime story and tucked him in, she would catch up on chores around the house before settling down to watch TV. If she was honest she had to admit that she had been hiding away behind her routine for the last few years. She had preferred it and she hadn't wanted a relationship. The bottom line was, if you didn't open up to people then you didn't get hurt. But, as Karen said, she couldn't hide forever and it was time she started dating again.

But not with Marco, she reminded herself firmly. She needed this job too badly to risk any involvement with him…he was out of bounds.

'This is the first time I've left him overnight.' She snapped her phone closed again.

'It must feel a bit strange, then.'

'Yes…a bit.' She smiled over at him. 'Although not quite as strange as dropping him off at school for the first time at the beginning of this month, he looked so grown-up in his uniform.'

'At least he likes school. My sister's youngest child cried every morning when she was dropped off. It broke Julia's heart.'

'How distressing for her.' Charlie glanced over at him curiously. 'Where does your sister live?'

'Julia is in Ireland. She's married and has four children. My sister Tess is in France working as an interpreter for a law firm. Then my sister Maggie lives in Norway with her partner and they have three children.'

'How lovely to have sisters. Have you any brothers?'

'No, there was just me.' He grinned. 'I'm the eldest. The one who bosses them around.'

'And looks out for them,' Charlie guessed. She had heard the warmth in his tone. 'It must be nice to be part of a big family,' she said wistfully.

'You don't have any siblings?'

'No, I was an only child.' She glanced over at him curiously. 'So what was it like growing up in a predominantly female household?'

'Put it this way, I was very glad when we had some *en suites* fitted, because before that I seemed to spend years queuing outside bathroom doors.'

Charlie laughed.

'That's better.' Marco glanced over at her and smiled. 'You seem more relaxed now. You were a bit tense earlier.'

'Was I?' Charlie cringed; she'd hoped he hadn't noticed! 'Sorry I was a bit distracted.'

He looked over at her questioningly.

'Thinking about the office…' she improvised hastily.

'Really?' His voice was dry. He didn't sound as if he believed her.

He flicked an amused glance over at her and she felt herself blush. It did sound unbelievable that she would be thinking about the office on a Friday evening in Tuscany!

Marco smiled. 'Do you want to know what I was thinking?'

She *really* hoped he wasn't going to make some glib comment that would make her embarrassed. It would be just like him to tease her about the sleeping arrangements right now.

'I was wondering if we should stop off at a little *trattoria* I know for something to eat or if we should head straight to the villa and I'll cook.'

'Oh!' She relaxed and smiled.

'You know, I've never met anyone who thought about work more than me.' He continued on in a jovial tone, 'It's a whole new experience.'

'Well, you know what they say,' she said lightly; 'if something is worth doing, it's worth doing well… So, getting back to your thoughts…' swiftly she changed the subject, '…can you cook?'

'Of course; why do you sound so surprised?'

'Maybe because you are always so immersed in work I didn't think you'd have time to spend in the kitchen.'

'Oh, I make time for food.' Marco laughed. 'After all, I'm Italian. Food is one of our passions.'

Charlie smiled and tried not to allow her mind to race towards what his other passions might be.

Marco paused the car at a junction. 'So, are we eating out tonight or shall I cook for us?'

Somehow whatever option she chose sounded perilously cosy! 'When do you want to get down to doing some work?' she countered instead.

'You've already got the job, Charlie; you don't need to try and impress me with your dedication a moment longer.' He grinned.

'I wasn't trying to impress you, I was being—'

'Practical,' he finished for her wryly. 'And I really like that about you. But you know what, Charlie? Let's give practicality a rest for now. It is Friday night. We can think about the office tomorrow.'

'Fine…'

What else could she say? Charlie wondered frantically.

'Tell you what, I'll cook…it will give us a chance to talk without being interrupted. We can go out tomorrow.' The decision made, Marco put the car into gear again and moved away from the junction.

Talk about what? It was all sounding a little too intimate for her peace of mind Charlie thought warily. 'Well, maybe that's best,' she murmured. 'After all, we are both a bit tired and we might want an early night.' She made the statement thinking it might be a good escape route for later, but as soon as the words were out she realised they sounded riskily provocative.

'We might indeed.' He smiled at her and as their eyes met she felt a tug of sexual attraction that was so fierce it was almost palpable.

Hurriedly she looked away. 'So, do we need to stop off and get some groceries?'

'No, Rita, my housekeeper, will have done all that.'

Her spirits lifted a little. Maybe they wouldn't be entirely alone after all. 'I didn't realise you had a housekeeper. Does she live in?'

'No, but she will have done the shopping, made up the bed and the fires will be lit. So the place should be aired and warm.'

He'd said *bed*, she noticed. Shouldn't he have said *beds?* Maybe it was just a slip of the tongue…maybe it was his accent and he had said beds but she hadn't heard him correctly. Or maybe he was taking it for granted that she would fall into his arms and his bed. Let's face it, she thought, there couldn't be many women who would turn him down…

Don't even think about it, Charlie, she told herself heatedly.

The road was winding up out of the valley now. Charlie could see the dark shapes of cypress trees against the clear midnight-blue of the sky. A few houses were dotted along the way, throwing golden light into the lonely darkness.

Marco turned the car up into a driveway, gravel crunching beneath the tyres as they drove higher then rounded a corner and came to a halt in front of a large stone building.

'Here we are.' He switched the engine off and they both stepped out of the car. They were high up and probably by day there was a spectacular view out over the valley, but all she could see was the clearness of the night sky ablaze with stars against the shadowy darkness of the landscape. There was silence except for the sound of cicadas and the air was fragrant with blossom.

Marco handed Charlie the keys of the front door. 'You open up and I'll get your case.'

The front door opened into a large flagged hallway. There was a vase of fresh lilies on the table and their perfume filled the air. Through an open doorway Charlie could see a lounge with a stone fireplace at one end where a log fire was blazing. A few lamps had been left on, throwing a subdued glow over the polished maple floor and the white furniture.

Marco came in behind her.

'Your house is lovely.'

'Thanks. Come on, I'll show you upstairs.'

As he led the way up the curving staircase Charlie tried not to think about how intimate this was. They turned onto the landing and Marco opened up a door then stood back to allow her to enter the room first.

The first thing she noticed was the huge double bed, its crisp white covers folded back invitingly. A log fire crackled inside a wood-burning stove and there were some pine logs and cones in a basket beside it, which probably accounted for the fresh scent in the room.

'This is lovely. Thank you.' She watched as he put down her case. Then he straightened and looked over at her.

They were standing inches apart and for a while there was silence between them, the only sound the crackle of the fire and the drum of her heartbeat.

He really was far too handsome for any woman's peace of mind, she thought distractedly. She wanted to take a step backwards from him…and at the same time perversely she wanted to reach out and run her hands up and along the broad contours of his shoulders, until her fingers found the dark thickness of his hair.

Marco watched the way she put her hands behind her back and stepped away, and noted the guarded expression in her green eyes.

'In case you are wondering, I've given you the room directly across the corridor from mine.'

'Oh…I wasn't wondering,' she said lightly.

He smiled and she could tell he knew she was lying.

'Of course, you don't necessarily need to stay in here.' There was that teasing sound in his deep voice again. 'There are six bedrooms along this landing. You can have any one of them you want.'

'I'll bear that in mind.'

Marco was watching her as if she was the most entertaining of creatures. 'Well, now we have that sorted out I'll go and get dinner underway. I'll see you downstairs when you are ready.'

'Thanks.'

As soon as the door closed behind him Charlie sank down onto the bed. He obviously just enjoyed bantering with her but she felt so emotionally drained it was as if it had taken every last ounce of strength just to keep the situation light and keep her distance from him.

Across the room she caught a glimpse of her reflection in the cheval mirror. She had travelled in jeans and a blue silk blouse and her hair was tied back from her face in the usual style she wore for work. She looked smartly casual but nowhere near as glamorous as the women Marco dated.

For all his teasing remarks, he wasn't really interested in her, she reminded herself. She wasn't his type. Of course, the fact that he now believed she was in tune with his theories on romance meant he was more interested in her than he had been before. And no doubt, given any encouragement, he would sleep with her…but it would just be light entertainment to him, something to fill a gap.

Knowing all these things as she did, why was she having such difficulty switching off her feelings of attraction for him? It made her angry. She had promised herself when Greg left her that no man would ever take her for a fool again. So why was she even tempted to play with fire now?

With renewed vigour she stood up and opened her case to take out a change of clothing. She wasn't going to allow stupid feelings of a short-lived desire to ruin her working relationship with Marco. She would have dinner with him and she would laugh and joke with him but *she would keep him at arm's length.*

Twenty minutes later she went back downstairs, her mood focused and determined.

She found Marco in the kitchen at the back of the house.

He turned as she walked in and his gaze moved slowly over her, taking in the black dress cinched in at her small waist with a wide leather belt, before moving down to her high-heeled suede boots.

Charlie tried very hard not to allow her new-found self-assurance slip. There was something very Italian about the way he didn't try to hide the fact that he was looking at her with purely sexual interest.

'You look great,' he said softly. 'And I know I've said it before but you should wear your hair loose like that all the time.'

'It would get in the way at work.'

'It might.' He nodded, a spark of devilment in his dark eyes now. 'But not for the reasons you mean.'

The warmth of his tone made her pulses quicken, made her very aware of the flare of attraction between them. Their eyes held each other's gaze for a moment too long…before she quickly pulled her senses together.

'Do you need any help with dinner?'

He smiled as he noted how abruptly she changed the subject. 'No; everything is under control. Take a seat.' He nodded towards one of the high stools at the breakfast bar. 'I'll pour you a glass of wine.'

'Thanks.' She did as he asked and watched as he uncorked a bottle of red.

'This comes from the vineyard next door.'

Charlie took the glass he offered and tasted the drink; it had rich, fruity undertones. 'I'm not a connoisseur by any means but this is very good.'

'Most of the Italian wines are,' he said matter-of-factly.

'Not that you are biased or anything,' she added with a smile.

'Heavens, no! Whatever gave you that idea?'

She grinned and raised her glass towards his. 'Here's to Italy,' she said.

He touched his glass against hers. 'No, here's to your first visit to Italy. May it be the first of many.'

Charlie tried not to be distracted by the warmth of those words. Her gaze moved from him towards the rustic charm of the kitchen with its maple cupboards and dark flagged floors. There was an enormous wine rack at one side, completely full of bottles. 'Were your family in the wine-making business as well?'

'No, my grandfather grew flowers, hence the name…La Casa del Fiori…house of flowers.'

'If you don't mind my saying, that sounds very romantic.' Charlie looked over at him mischievously and he laughed.

'It might sound that way, but I assure you it wasn't. The flowers were grown for purely commercial purposes. When my grandfather died he left the place to my father and we moved here from Milan. My father was an architect so the flower business was not to his liking. He rented the land off and worked in the town near-by.'

Charlie watched as he chopped some herbs. He looked totally at home in this kitchen and more relaxed than she had ever seen him. She noticed that he had changed out of the clothes he had travelled in and was now wearing a chunky black sweater teamed with a pair of black jeans. His hair gleamed dark under the overhead light.

'Do you feel as if you've come home when you come here?' she asked curiously.

'Not really. This hasn't been my home for a very long time. After I left to go to university I didn't come back here….except for visits, of course.'

'And you haven't been tempted to sell it?'

'The thought has crossed my mind, but it's been in the family for generations; I just couldn't bring myself to do it.'

'So it must hold happy memories for you.'

'Some…' Marco shrugged. 'But in truth this house never rang with much happiness. My mother hated it, she was a city person, born and brought up in Milan. To her the countryside was great for a day out, nothing more…she felt trapped here.'

'And yet it is so beautiful.'

'You can get used to beautiful scenery…and so bored after a while that you don't even notice it any more.'

'I can't imagine ever being that bored,' Charlie murmured. 'It sounds sad.'

'Yes, I suppose it is.' Marco looked over at her contemplatively. 'But unfortunately one man's paradise can be another's prison. There has to be more substance to a situation than just what you can see. My father was a countryman at heart and he couldn't understand why my mother wouldn't settle here. He thought that if she loved him she would be happy.'

'But love wasn't enough to keep her happy?' Charlie guessed wryly.

'That's about it in a nutshell. I think my father would have moved back to Milan for her, but unfortunately by the time he realised just how much she hated this place his finances were already tied up. He had bought into a business partnership and it's not so easy to walk away from your own business, even if you want to.'

'So what happened—did the marriage end in divorce?'

'No, my father didn't believe in divorce. My mother got herself a job in Milan and lived most of the time there under the guise of work…then came home at weekends. We all knew she had another man in her life but it was never spoken about.'

Charlie looked over at him with sympathy. 'That must have been a difficult situation for everyone.'

'It wasn't a picnic.'

Charlie sensed that the flippant reply hid a rawness that probably was still with him to this day.

'Do you think your belief that love isn't enough to sustain a relationship stems from what happened between your parents?' She asked the question impulsively.

Marco looked over at her and laughed. 'Are you trying to analyse me, Charlie?'

'Maybe.' She blushed a little.

'Well, I don't think I'm particularly scarred by what happened, but when you watch two people you love destroy each other I suppose it has an effect. And we are all products of our past.' One sardonic eyebrow lifted as he fixed her with that probing look of his.

'Yes, I suppose we are.'

'So now we've discussed my hang-ups, shall we have a turn at dissecting yours?'

For some reason the quietly asked question hit on a sensitive nerve. 'I don't have any hang-ups.'

Suddenly his eyes were completely serious. 'What about those great steel barriers that come down as soon as anyone starts to try and get close to you?'

'I don't know what you are talking about,' she said quickly.

The expression in Marco's eyes was so intensely perceptive that she found herself dropping her gaze. 'So…is dinner nearly ready, because I don't mind telling you that I'm ravenous?'

For a moment she thought he wasn't going to let her move the subject so easily, but after a brief pause, he went along with her. 'Yes, antipasti is ready to be served,' he said light-heartedly, 'so if you will follow me through to the dining room…'

He moved to open a sliding door beside him and Charlie found herself looking through into a dining room where a table was laid for two.

The setting was one of seduction. A table was laid with white linen and silverware, and there were candles flickering along the sideboard and on the table, reflecting over polished surfaces.

'All Rita's handiwork,' Marco admitted as he saw her look of surprise. 'She always has everything perfect for me.'

'I see.' As Charlie moved further into the room she felt a flare of annoyance mixed with trepidation. Obviously Rita was well-used to him bringing his conquests here. 'You forgot to tell your housekeeper that I'm just your employee, not your girlfriend.'

'I haven't forgotten anything, Charlie,' he said quietly. He caught hold of her arm as she made to move past him. 'We both know that there is a connection between us that is deeper than that…'

As she looked up at him the memory of their kiss swirled inside her with vivid intensity. She pushed it back with difficulty. *It meant nothing.* 'You mean the fact that we both view romance with a sceptical eye?'

'I view romance with a rational eye,' he corrected her firmly. 'And I was talking about the fact that we've been drawn to each other recently but we've been sidestepping the feeling.'

'I haven't noticed anything.' The lie dropped quickly from her lips.

'Of course you have. You know it and I know it.' His hand moved to touch her cheek; it was the lightest of caresses yet it burnt against her senses like an iron brand.

And suddenly her breath felt as if it was painful to draw. She wanted him to kiss her again…wanted him so badly it hurt. The knowledge terrified her.

'Marco, don't.' Her voice was filled with a sudden panic.

'Don't what?'

Her eyes seemed too large for her small face. Marco saw the way they clouded with desire, but he also noted the way she almost flinched away from him.

'Don't assume that I am just another one of your conquests, because I'm not,' she told him angrily. 'It doesn't matter how many candles you light or how many lies you generate—'

'Charlie!' he cut across her firmly. 'I wasn't thinking of telling you any lies.' He sounded mildly surprised by the accusation. 'Generally speaking, I think I'm an honest person. And believe it or not I wanted to spend time getting to know you this evening because I like you…' He looked at her pointedly. 'I know you find that hard to believe but it's true.'

The gentle sincerity in his tone totally disarmed her for a second.

'And I have no intention of pouncing on you,' he added. 'It's not my style.'

'I know that,' she said swiftly.

'Well, at least that's something.' He raked a hand through the thick darkness of his hair. 'Because the way you flinched a moment ago, I was concerned that was what you were thinking.'

'Of course not!' She felt guilty now! Her fear had been directed inwardly at her own reactions towards him…never the other way round. 'Look, I don't know why I said those things,' she admitted huskily. 'I just felt a bit…'

'Tense?' He supplied the word with a mocking smile. 'Yes, I have noticed.'

Feeling acutely embarrassed, Charlie moved to sit down at the table. 'I'm just worried we will mess up our working relationship,' she said lightly.

'That is only part of what is bothering you.' Marco pulled up a chair and sat down beside her. 'This goes deeper than just being worried about your job.'

She stared at him for a moment, her heart thundering against her chest. Of course, he was right. This did go deeper. Yes, she was concerned about her work…she really needed this job. But there was more to her fears than that.

'I think the truth is something much closer to your heart—'

'Just leave it, Marco,' she warned him unsteadily.

He ignored her. 'I think you've been hurt so badly in the past that you tend to run in the opposite direction from any emotional contact.'

When she didn't answer him immediately he reached out a

hand and brushed her hair back from her face so that he could see her expression. The gesture was tenderly provocative and it was that rather than his words that caused the feelings which had been locked away deep inside her to reverberate with violent force.

She looked up and met his eyes.

'I'm right, aren't I?'

'Maybe…' She admitted the truth huskily. The touch of his hand against her skin sent little shivers of need racing through her.

He let his hand drop and sat back with a smile. 'So now that we are being completely honest with each other…no barriers whatsoever, I do have a confession to make too.'

'What's that?' She looked over at him with a frown.

'The idea of trying to get you into my bed has crossed my mind…' He spread his hands and looked at her with a glint of devilment in his dark eyes. 'Of course it has…what can I say…? I'm Italian…a red-blooded male. And I find you attractive.'

'You are also my boss, which makes it a conflict of interest.' She found the strength to rally herself from the feelings of desire that were flooding through her in mutinous waves.

'Maybe.' He shrugged. 'But why don't we forget about conflicts of interest for one evening? In fact, why don't we forget about everything, put all our preconceived ideas about each other to one side, and just enjoy having dinner together and getting to know each other?'

When she didn't answer him immediately he smiled.

'Or does that sound a little too dangerous?'

The challenge in that question sounded so absurd that Charlie laughed. 'No, it doesn't sound dangerous.'

'Good. Then that is what we will do.'

Charlie met his gaze and felt a flow of warmth around the frozen loneliness of a heart she had been trying so fiercely to protect.

Where was the harm in relaxing and enjoying herself with a man she felt attracted to?

She leaned back in her chair and smiled at him, his soothing words obscuring the fear that she had just made a fatal mistake by lowering her defences.

CHAPTER SIX

To SAY that Marco was a charismatic dinner companion was putting it mildly. She couldn't remember a more enjoyable evening.

When she thought about it later she realised they hadn't really talked about anything of particular depth over the meal, just amusing anecdotes from their past. But Marco was incredibly funny. He made her laugh and he held her enthralled with his stories...he also listened as if he was interested in every last detail of what she had to say.

It was a long time since anyone had made her feel the way he did—as if she was the most interesting and the most beautiful woman in the world. Of course, she realised this was probably the effect he had on every woman he spent time with. She wasn't naïve enough to believe otherwise...but it was so nice to relax with him. She hadn't realised until now how much she had missed male company...how much she had missed just being herself around someone who made her feel special.

'That was a fabulous meal,' Charlie said honestly as he got up to clear the table. 'You're a great cook.'

'Comes with living on my own for so long,' he said with a shrug. 'When you've no one to share the domestic chores with it makes you sharper.'

'Well, I've been on my own for a number of years now and my domestic skills haven't improved to that standard.'

Marco went over to the sideboard and poured them both a coffee. 'How long have you been on your own?' he asked over his shoulder.

'Four and a half years.'

'That long!' He returned to the table and put the cup and saucer down in front of her with a frown. 'But Jack is only four!'

'Greg left when I was pregnant.'

Charlie's matter-of-fact tone didn't fool Marco for a moment.

'That must have been difficult to cope with,' he reflected quietly.

'It wasn't easy. I had to deal with my father's death, my pregnancy, a divorce and finding somewhere to live all at the same time.'

'Couldn't you have stayed in the house you had?'

She shook her head. 'We'd sold it already to find something more child-friendly.'

'And then your husband left before you could make the next purchase?'

She heard the distaste in his voice.

'He'd met someone else.' She shrugged. 'Anyway, I don't know why I just told you all that. I coped without him, so it doesn't matter now.'

No wonder he sometimes glimpsed that look of distrust in her eyes…that raw vulnerability. 'I'm glad you did tell me.' He put his other hand over hers and squeezed it gently. 'It makes me admire you all the more.'

'You admire me?' For a moment amusement chased the shadows in her eyes away.

She had such expressive eyes, he thought. And, despite everything, laughter came so easily to them.

'Well, yes, I do. I admire the way you've coped so well on

your own; I admire the fact that you have a great spirit. You are quite remarkable.'

Charlie laughed. 'And, of course, indispensable in the office.'

'Goes without saying.' He smiled, enjoying the sparkle of fun that danced between them.

She glanced down at his hand, so large against hers, and was aware that what had started out as a gesture of sympathy had changed into something else.

His fingers caressed slowly over her skin, and the touch was intoxicating; it sent shivers of desire racing through her in delicious little waves. Like a taster of the pleasure he could bring her given full reign.

As soon as the thought flicked through her mind she forced herself to pull away from him. That was exactly what she shouldn't be thinking about, she told herself firmly!

'I suppose we should call it a night,' she said briskly. 'We've got to get to work in the morning.'

'It shouldn't take too long with both of us going through the files.' If he noticed how abruptly she withdrew from him Marco didn't show it. 'But I suppose you are right—we should turn in.'

Charlie watched as he blew out the candles on the table and perversely she felt a stab of disappointment that the warmth that had enveloped them all evening had to come to an end.

She was being silly, she told herself. It had been a lovely evening but it was time for them to say goodnight. Otherwise... She looked over and met the darkness of his eyes and her senses wavered alarmingly. *Otherwise things could get complicated.*

Hurriedly she reached to pick up the coffee cups. 'I'll help you clear away the last of the dishes.'

'Leave everything, Charlie. I'll see to it.'

'No, honestly, it's the least I can do after you've gone to so much trouble.' She headed into the kitchen and put the crockery in the sink.

'Charlie?' His voice was very close behind her.

He put a hand on her shoulder, turning her around to face him. They were just inches apart.

'Everything in the kitchen is under control,' he said softly.

Not everything, she thought wryly. For one thing, her emotions were pounding in a way she had no control over at all.

'I've really enjoyed this evening.' His eyes moved over her with a deep contemplation that made her burn inside.

'Yes, me too,' she murmured huskily.

Charlie noticed his eyes were on her lips and she felt her heart bounce crazily against her chest. She really wanted him to kiss her. What harm would it do to have one goodnight kiss? a little voice was whispering provocatively inside her.

'Marco…' She murmured his name, hardly aware of what she wanted to say…all she could think about was the way he made her feel.

He leaned closer and suddenly his lips touched hers. The feeling was heavenly; she felt floodgates open inside her as she melted against the caress and kissed him back.

She couldn't remember the last man she had enjoyed kissing as much as this. It was certainly a long time since any other man had stirred up this rush of excitement, this dizzy feeling as adrenalin rushed through her veins. She reached up and put her hands on his shoulders.

By contrast, Marco's hands did not leave his sides. Even though she ached for him to touch her, he didn't, instead his kisses intensified, his mouth plundering hers with an expertise in seduction that was mind-blowing.

When he finally pulled away from her she was left throbbing with pure frustration.

'I meant it when I said there were no strings attached to dinner this evening. So unless you want to take this further I suggest we stop.'

Although he sounded firmly in control, one look into the

blaze of his dark eyes made her realise that he was holding on to his restraint by a thread.

She tried to think sensibly but it was difficult. 'Yes…of course. We have to work together and it would be madness to take things too far…'

'But an enjoyable kind of madness all the same,' he said teasingly. He stroked one hand softly down over the side of her face. The caress sent butterflies darting wildly inside her.

He lowered his head and kissed her again. 'I can't tell you how much I want you.' He murmured the words huskily against her mouth.

'I want you too.'

She heard herself say the words and yet felt no rush of panic, which was strange, considering how much deliberation she had been giving to this matter. In fact, all she felt as she looked into his eyes was an overwhelming sense that this was just *right*.

Marco smiled. 'Well, in that case…wouldn't it be madness *not* to take things further?' He kissed her again, this time with such a forceful, hungry passion that she was breathless as he pulled back.

'I think you're right,' she agreed tremulously. Then she looked up at him, a spark of mischief in the intense green of her eyes. 'But maybe you'd better kiss me again just so I can double-check…'

He laughed. 'You are a minx, Ms Charlotte Hopkirk, and you are driving me wild with desire…'

'That's good,' she smiled and pressed her lips to his, 'because you are having a similar effect on me…'

The next moment he had swung her up into his arms and was carrying her in a fireman's lift out of the room.

'Marco, put me down!' She was laughing breathlessly as he carried her up the stairs and into the bedroom opposite to hers.

'With pleasure.' He placed her down on the bed with a

playful thud. But as she looked up at him suddenly the laughter was gone and the atmosphere was very serious.

For a moment his gaze raked over her, taking in the soft fullness of her parted lips, the creamy flush on her high cheek-bones, the sparkle in her eyes and the way her hair was spread out around her on the bed in wild, golden profusion.

Then his gaze moved lower towards the buttons on her dress.

'I've wanted you in my bed for some time, Charlie…' His voice held a husky rasp that she hadn't heard before; it sent tingles of awareness rushing through her.

Her heart thundered unsteadily. If they stepped over this line where would their relationship go from here?

Marco regarded her steadily. 'Are you having second thoughts?'

'No. I'm not having second thoughts. I'm just…' She struggled to express her feelings. She was scared, yet she couldn't stop things now.

'It's a while since you've done this, isn't it?' he said gently. 'Let me guess…it was with your husband just before he left?'

He saw the creaminess of her skin heat up and felt a dart of a fiercely protective emotion mingle with the animal desire that was eating him inside.

'Hey, it will be OK.' He bent over her and kissed her softly.

His velvet Italian tone seeped into her consciousness making her forget the momentary pangs of apprehension. Yes, it would be all right, she told herself as desire once more took her over. She wound her arms around his neck, and kissed him back with a sweet tenderness that seared into him.

His hands were on her body now, caressing her through the silky material of her dress. He felt her breasts tighten and harden beneath his touch, felt her acquiescence in every trem-bling, passionate kiss.

Pulling back from her, he peeled off his jumper and cast it

to one side. Underneath he was wearing a short-sleeved white T-shirt and it showed off the hard-muscled perfection of his broad shoulders and arms.

Hell but he had a fabulous body. She watched as his hand moved to unfasten the buckle on his leather belt.

Leaning up on one elbow, she took off her own belt and then kicked off her shoes. Then she started to unbutton her dress.

Marco had stopped undressing and was watching her now. She glanced up and saw the intense desire in his dark eyes and her heart thumped as if she had been running in a race. Suddenly her attempts to undress were slowed by hands that weren't at all steady or coordinated.

Marco smiled and reached out a hand to pull her up from the bed. 'Here, let me help.'

She allowed him to unfasten the last of the buttons and then stood silently in front of him as he pulled the dress from her shoulders and let it drop to the floor. Then his eyes moved with slow and thorough contemplation over the curves of her breasts in her black lacy bra before moving lower over her body and down across her stomach to the matching black knickers.

For a moment she felt acutely self-conscious as she suddenly wondered if he was comparing her voluptuous curves with the petite, perfect women he usually took to bed.

'You have a wonderful figure, Charlie,' he murmured. As he spoke he reached out a hand and trailed it lightly over the outline of her bra and she shivered with need.

She longed for him to really touch her, to caress her and kiss her, but instead he reached behind her and unfastened her bra, taking it from her with a slow deliberation that was tortuously provocative.

Apart from her lacy knickers she was naked now, whilst he was still almost fully dressed.

'Exquisitely sexy…' he murmured, his fingers trailing over

the side of her neck before moving lower to softly glide over the full, up-tilted firmness of her breasts.

Charlie closed her eyes on a wave of ecstasy as his lips started to follow the teasing, provocative trail down over the side of her neck and then lower until his lips found the hard, rosy peak of her nipple.

She drew in her breath on a gasp of pleasure and her hands moved upwards to rest against his shoulders. She could feel the warmth of his skin through the T-shirt and the tautness of his muscles.

He drew back from her for a moment and said something in Italian. But before she had a chance to ask what he had said he was pulling her underwear down, his hand lingering over the curves of her hips. Then, reaching behind her, he threw back the covers on the bed and gently pulled her down against the crisp white linen.

Lying sideways across the width of the bed, she watched as he pulled his T-shirt over his head. His skin was a deep golden bronze and smooth. Her eyes moved hungrily over the powerful torso and then lower towards his narrow hips. He was unzipping his jeans now.

Her heart was thundering fast and uneven against her chest. She wanted him so much…

'Hurry.' She breathed the word almost feverishly and he smiled.

'Patience, Charlotte,' he whispered teasingly.

'I don't want to be patient,' she complained huskily and he laughed. Leaving his jeans on, he straddled her. She could feel the coarse denim material against the soft flesh of her hips as he raised himself up, looking for something in his back pocket.

'Marco, really…' She writhed just a little beneath him, her senses on fire with longing. It felt as if there were a live volcano inside her and if he didn't get to it soon it was going to surely erupt without him. *'Hurry!'*

He brought out a foil packet and she realised that she had been so turned on that she had almost forgotten about contraception. He however, was very much in control. He was also *extremely* aroused, she noted as she watched him quickly remove his jeans and boxer shorts before deftly putting on the condom.

A moment later he leaned closer and found her lips. Then he kissed her in a way she had never been kissed before. It was hungry and passionate and so deeply arousing that it made her tingle deep inside her very core.

Murmuring words in Italian, he then kissed her face, trailing his heated, passionate lips down over her neck, whilst his hands possessively caressed her breasts.

Just when she thought that she couldn't wait another moment longer he entered her. The feeling was exquisite and the volcano of need inside her rose closer to the surface. She tried desperately to have some control over it so she could make the sensation go on and on for ever.

He stroked his hands over the soft roundness of her breasts, playing with her nipples and teasing their hardness with exquisite little butterfly kisses before taking them in his mouth. That was when she couldn't stand it any longer and she exploded in a million shattering, fantastic pieces.

She moaned a little and found herself gasping, then his lips moved to capture hers as if drinking in her shudders of ecstasy.

He held her close for a while, his hands tenderly soothing now as they moved over the silky softness of her skin.

She could smell the scent of his aftershave mixed with the clean smell of the linen. Nestling closer into the crook of his arm, she smiled sleepily.

'That was wonderful.' He growled the words against her ear and watched how her smile curved even more. 'You were worth waiting for.'

She cuddled closer and allowed her fingers to run over the powerful contours of his shoulder and his arm. It was blissful being held close like this. 'You certainly know how to please a woman,' she murmured sleepily.

He laughed. 'Well…what was it you said? If something is worth doing, it is worth doing well.'

She smiled and pressed her lips against his chest in a teasing kiss.

They lay entwined in each other's arms for a few moments more and then suddenly Marco pulled away from her.

'Where are you going?'

'I've just remembered that I forgot to put out the rest of the candles in the dining room. They have probably burnt out but I'd better go check.'

He stood up and pulled on his jeans.

'Hopefully the house isn't burning down.' He grinned over at her. 'I've already put out one fire today.'

She tossed one of the pillows from the bed over at him and he laughed as he disappeared.

Charlie repositioned herself in the bed and pulled the sheet over her. She had forgotten how lovely sex was…in fact, now she came to think about it, it really had never been as good as this with Greg.

Feeling sleepy and intoxicated with the afterglow of their lovemaking, she glanced around the room and saw the soft lamplight reflected over the bronze satin covers of the bed. Like her room across the corridor, there was a wood-burning stove in the corner and she could see the glow of flames flickering in the shadows. It felt cosy in here and blissfully quiet.

She closed her eyes and rested for a moment.

When Marco returned Charlie was fast asleep. He took off his clothes and slipped back into the bed beside her and for a while he watched as she slept.

There was an air of fragility about her, he thought. It was there in the softness of her smile and the way her hair was tousled in golden curls on the pillow around her head. Her eyelashes were dark and glossy against the smooth perfection of her skin. He reached out and trailed a finger over the silky smoothness of her shoulder. She stirred slightly and her lips curved into even more of a smile.

He was overwhelmed with a longing to take her again; it swept over him with a fierce intensity, taking him totally by surprise. Dipping his head, he trailed his lips along her shoulder and then upwards along her neck, breathing in the familiar scent of her perfume.

She smiled and murmured something sleepily.

'Hey, gorgeous…wake up!' His hand moved beneath the covers and slid over the satin of her skin. 'I want you…'

Her eyes flickered open and for a second their gazes held.

She was aware of a feeling inside her that was very strange. She felt as though she belonged here with him and that she wanted him to hold her against him and never let her go.

He kissed her gently, his lips sweetly provocative.

'The house hadn't burnt down, then?' she murmured sleepily.

'Not yet.' With a smile he pulled her closer, his hands coaxing and caressing her with slow deliberation, his kisses heated and yet tender.

The passion that flared between them was so intense and so pleasurable that she felt she couldn't get close enough to him. She just couldn't get enough of him.

A shiver stirred deep inside her. Emotions that were this intense were bound to have reverberations. The notion was fleeting though and was quickly taken away by the aching need that he stirred inside her with such ease.

Nothing mattered except this….

CHAPTER SEVEN

THE valley was shrouded in mist. It hung in the air like a mystical presence revealing only the faint gleam of the oyster-pink morning sky and the top of the lush green cypress trees on the hillside.

Somewhere a bell was chiming.

Charlie wrapped her silk dressing gown further around her body and on impulse opened the kitchen door and stepped onto the terrace. The morning air was cool and so fresh that she leaned against the stone parapet and took deep, revitalising breaths.

Behind her she could hear the bubble of water in the kettle on the stove. It was the only sound in the stillness of the morning.

As the sun rose from behind the mountain the oyster-pink of the sky turned flamingo and tinted the white mist with its brilliance. A hint of warmth stole across the day like the breath of summer.

Upstairs Marco was still sleeping in the warmth of the double bed. It had been an incredible night. Charlie had never known such passion. And lying wrapped in his arms afterwards had made her feel safe and contented and cherished… The thought made her frown. Of course, it was passion without love, she reminded herself firmly. So those feelings weren't correct.

It had just been sex—but the knowledge tore through her, causing an alarming feeling of pain.

Impatiently she raked a hand through the thickness of her blonde hair. This was what people in the real world did—they went to bed with someone they wanted and didn't analyse it afterwards…they just enjoyed the moment. So why couldn't she? Why were all these fragile emotions ricocheting through her?

Why had she woken up this morning and been filled with an aching void of need?

All she knew now was that she should never have gone to bed with him! It had been a mistake—a wonderful and very enjoyable mistake, but a mistake nonetheless. She should never have lowered her guard and allowed her weakness for him to get the better of her. All it had done was to leave her wanting more from him on a deeper emotional level and that was one thing she knew Marco would never be able to give.

A sound from behind made her turn around. Marco was in the doorway, watching her. Their eyes met and held and for a few breathless moments the memory of what had happened lay between them with a sensual heat.

His dark hair was still tousled from sleep and he was wearing a pair of black pyjama bottoms and nothing else. How was it that he looked even sexier when he was disheveled? she wondered. She longed to go over and kiss him, and smooth his hair back from his face with tender fingers. But actions like that were not for the cool light of morning. In fact, she couldn't ever allow herself to act like that around him again, she told herself fiercely.

How was she going to work with him now? she wondered in anguish. How would she ever get back to a place of safety where she could pretend indifference?

'*Buon giorno, Charlie.*'

The velvety Italian tones made her want to melt. Hell, but this was no good! She was going to have to pull herself together.

'How are you feeling this morning?' he enquired with a lift of one eyebrow.

'Fine…I slept really well.' She tried very hard to match his casual, laid-back manner.

'You got up very early.'

'I couldn't wait to have a look outside at the view,' she lied. In truth she had made herself leave the warmth of his arms because she had liked being there too much, and she couldn't bear the fact that he might wake and see that in her eyes.

'Would you like a coffee?' she asked now trying to be cool and collected.

'*Si.*' Marco watched as she made her way carefully around him and went back into the kitchen.

His eyes flicked over her, taking in her bare feet before moving upwards over the curvy silhouette of her figure. Then they lingered on her face. He noticed not for the first time that she didn't need make-up. Her skin was fresh and clear and had a kind of luminous quality. Her lips were a soft peach and her hair tumbled in a sexy cascade over her shoulders. He remembered how she had felt beneath his touch, the silk of her skin, the heat of her passion. He had enjoyed every moment of last night and she had left him wanting more.

Charlie was acutely conscious of the fact that his dark eyes were moving over her with that boldly assessing gaze of his. She wished she had brushed her hair before coming downstairs…because she was sure the dishevelled look didn't do her any favours, unlike him.

She raised her chin a little as she looked over at him. 'You are making me a bit nervous,' she admitted suddenly.

'Am I?' He looked at her with amusement. 'Why is that?'

'Because you are looking at me with such concentration! And it's too early in the morning for that. I need at least an hour getting ready before I can pass such scrutiny!'

Marco laughed. 'You are very amusing, Charlie!'

She shot him an impatient look. She didn't want to be amusing! She wanted to be gorgeous and beautiful and all the things that drove him wild…the way he drove her wild. The thought made her angry with herself. Why should she care what he thought? She needed to get real. Last night was about sex and nothing more.

'What's with that look?' he asked softly.

'What look?' She put his coffee down on the counter beside him.

'That *I'm not taking any of your nonsense* look.'

Despite herself, Charlie laughed, she couldn't help herself. 'And you say I'm amusing!'

'Do you regret last night?'

The question caught her off guard. She couldn't look at him now. 'No, it was…fun.' She tried very hard to sound unruffled. 'I just think we need to concentrate on more important things now.' It took every last ounce of strength to make herself look up at him. 'We have work to do this morning.'

She noted an edge of approval now in the dark, steady gaze that held hers and she realised that she had unwittingly reinforced the idea that she was in tune with his theories…that practicality had to come above emotion. She was obviously a better actress than she had imagined, she thought sardonically.

'You're right, of course.' He reached out and trailed a finger softly over the side of her face, tracing its contours as if committing them to memory. And suddenly she just wanted to forget any pretence and go back into his arms again, and to hell with practicality.

'But after a night like last night we really should say good morning properly.'

The provocative note in his voice and the way he was looking at her sent darts of awareness and need instantly racing through her. She tried desperately to ignore them but they didn't want to leave. 'You mean…*buon giorno?*' She tried to make light of his words and copied his Italian with a smile.

'That's very good,' he murmured, tracing one finger over the softness of her lips. 'I could make an Italian out of you yet. But I was thinking more along the lines of actions speaking louder than words…'

Then he bent his head and kissed her. It was the most fabulous sensation—possessive and sensual and spine-tingling all at the same time. For a moment she found herself kissing him back, then reality started to seep in and she realised that this was a mistake. This shouldn't happen again. She couldn't allow herself to get pulled further into a situation she couldn't cope with.

Because the fact was that she was a million miles away from ever being in tune with Marco's theories and his cool, carefree attitude towards love and sex would just annihilate an old-fashioned hearts-and-flowers girl like her.

Hastily she pulled away from him. 'We need to draw a line under this now, Marco, and get back to how things should be.'

'Of course.' He agreed with her immediately, and she noticed that, unlike her, he was completely relaxed. He glanced at his watch. 'I'll go shower and get dressed and we'll meet downstairs in my office in, say, half an hour. How does that sound?'

'Fine.' She swallowed hard. In reality she wanted to go upstairs and lock herself away for the rest of the weekend. She really didn't know how she was going to maintain a professional distance after this. Hurriedly she picked up her coffee and turned away.

Marco watched her go with a look of deep contemplation in his eyes. He was well aware that she wanted to pull up her barriers now and close him out but, while he was content to allow her to do that for the business side of their relationship, he had no intention of allowing her to retreat from him completely. He had worked too hard to reach her for that. He had other plans for Charlie.

* * *

'Will you take a copy of these notes?' Marco put a stack of papers down in front of her. 'Oh, and try and get Professor Hunt on the phone. I could do with talking to him about our meeting on Sunday.'

'I'll get on to it straight away.' Charlie reached for the desk diary. This was really weird, she thought as she leafed through the pages to find the professor's number. Somehow their professional barriers were in place…somehow they had been working alongside each other all morning as if nothing had happened last night.

Charlie couldn't quite figure out how they were managing it. Maybe it was the fact that they were in a room that was very reminiscent of Marco's office in London. Or maybe it was just the way Marco could totally tune in to his work with a single-minded absorption, something that had always fascinated her about him.

She put his call through, then got up to switch on the scanner. Marco's velvet tones resonated through the book-lined room as he talked to his colleague. She glanced over at him, momentarily distracted from what she was doing. Even when he was talking about business he sounded sexy.

As if sensing her gaze he glanced up and their eyes collided. The impact made her stomach contract with a sudden need that hit her out of nowhere. Hurriedly she looked away and tried to concentrate on what she was doing as he finished his conversation.

'I think we are just about finished here,' Marco said a few moments later as he replaced the receiver. 'The rest of it can wait until we get back to London.'

Charlie collected the copies that were churning out from the machine. He was right—they had managed to sail through everything in a relatively short space of time. The trouble was, she didn't want to step out from behind the screen of work. 'You've got to sign the letters on your desk,' she reminded him.

'I will do it later.' He stood up and glanced at his watch. 'Time to go out.'

She frowned. 'Actually, Marco—'

'It's a beautiful day and I did promise you that there would be time for sightseeing.' He cut across her as if she hadn't spoken. 'And you can't come all the way to Tuscany and not see Florence. It would be a sin.'

The matter-of-fact tone dented her reservations. She really would like to see Florence. And at least if they were in a city they would be surrounded by other people, so it was hardly high-risk for seduction!

'OK...but do you mind if I phone home first? I'd like to check everything is all right with Jack.'

'Sure.' He smiled. 'Use the landline.'

They left the villa half an hour later. The sun was shimmering down from a clear blue sky and a heat haze danced over the winding roads. Charlie was glad that she had taken the time to change out of her trouser suit into a dress. She felt summery in the feminine blue and white creation.

Relaxing back in the comfortable leather seat, she watched as the countryside passed by and told herself that she was only going to think about the scenery...nothing else.

In the distance a mountain village dazzled the senses with shimmering gold turrets amidst a profusion of terracotta roofs. Vineyards criss-crossed the land in geometric patterns, the grapes incandescent and heavy, ripened by long months of sunshine.

They stopped for coffee before heading on towards Florence, the Tuscany capital. And instead of the mood between them being tense or uncertain there was a surprising light-hearted feeling of exhilaration. They found themselves laughing over the most trivial of things, and suddenly just enjoying the moment was all that seemed to matter.

Charlie didn't think she would ever forget that day, strolling around in the heat of the sun, marvelling at the architecture, the medieval churches, the art and history of the city blending so easily together. They ate lunch outside at a pavement café and then lingered over a glass of Chianti as they watched the people go by.

After lunch Charlie shopped for some presents to bring home. Marco watched as she deliberated carefully over what to buy Jack.

'Which do you think I should get?' She held up a shiny red remote-control car and a boxed game.

'I think the car,' he said firmly. 'Jack loves cars.'

'Yes…but the game is educational, it will teach him something about Italy. Plus it looks fun.'

'Then you should get both.' Marco smiled.

'Just what I was thinking.' She put the toys in the shopping basket, a gleam of enjoyment in her eyes. 'He'll be really thrilled.'

There was something very…endearing about Charlie, Marco thought as he followed her further around the shop. He noticed she'd caught the sun today and had a sprinkling of freckles over her nose now. She really was very attractive. Not magazine-model beautiful but seductively alluring in a much warmer and interesting way.

He liked the lively glint in her eyes that spoke of intelligence and good humour…and the way her lips curved upwards; so soft and sensual. He even liked the way she was taking so much trouble over choosing the perfect presents for Jack.

Things were really working out quite well. She was great in bed, plus she was very businesslike—a wonderful combination.

He tried to pay for her purchases at the till but she wouldn't hear of it.

'I didn't realise you could be quite so bossy,' he said as they stepped back outside onto the pavement.

'I didn't mean to be. It was kind of you to offer to pay but I don't know why you did—'

'Because I *wanted* to.' He reached to carry her bags for her and grinned teasingly. 'Truth is, I quite fancied the car myself. I'd have given my right arm for that when I was a boy.'

She laughed. 'Well, you can come around and play any time.' She knew she shouldn't be flirting with him like this...but the spark of mischief in her felt good.

'Now, there's a promise and a half!' He looked at her with a raised eyebrow and she felt a thrill of emotion deep inside.

As they strolled back towards the car he casually reached to take her hand in his.

It was a nonchalant, relaxed gesture but to Charlie the possessive touch was deliciously intoxicating and it made her heart warm with pleasure. It was a long time since she had felt like this around someone.

As they paused by the kerb a motorbike suddenly pulled up in front of them and two men jumped off with cameras in their hands.

'Marco...' They called to him, and said something in Italian.

Charlie looked over in astonishment as they started to take rapid pictures of them crossing the road. 'What on earth are they playing at?'

'It's the paparazzi.' Marco squeezed her hand. 'Don't worry about it,' he said easily. 'We are nearly back at the car now. I suggest we head out of the city and get away from them.'

She nodded wordlessly.

'Sorry, I should have warned you about the photographers,' Marco said casually as they left the heat and noise of Florence behind and drove out in the direction of Sienna. 'That kind of thing is happening quite a lot recently.'

'Yes...I suppose it is.' Charlie frowned. Marco was so down-to-earth that she had forgotten that she was with a celebrity.

He looked over at her. 'You're not bothered by it, are you?'

'No. I just hope they snapped my good side,' she added flippantly.

Marco laughed. 'Well, as you don't have a bad side, I think you're safe.'

The country roads they took were through the majesty of winding hills with olive groves, old cottages and castles. Cypress trees stood guard against the fierce blue skyline.

They stopped the car to allow a shepherd to herd his goats out across the road and Marco glanced in the rear-view mirror. 'You can relax now, we seem to have lost them.'

'I was relaxed,' she murmured. 'It would take more than a few photographers to ruin such a lovely day.'

'You're right.' Marco glanced over at her, a gleam of approbation in his dark eyes. 'You know, asking you to come to Italy with me was a great idea,' he said softly.

She looked over at him and tried not to be carried away by the depth of sincerity in his gaze. 'Well, we managed to get through all that work this morning quite quickly.'

'I was thinking about more than just the work we got through.'

For a moment their eyes held. And suddenly the atmosphere seemed to change from teasing warmth to something else…something much more serious.

She felt her heart thudding so hard against her chest it felt as if it were going to explode. This was the point when she should move back, she told herself. But when he leaned across towards her she didn't do any such thing, instead she allowed him to take her into his arms and kiss her with a passion that was overwhelming.

This was how she wanted life to be, Charlie thought hazily. Nights of love in Marco's arms and snatched moments like this. Maybe she should stop fighting it and just enjoy an affair with him.

The idea sizzled through her, causing immediate consternation. What on earth was she thinking about? An affair was all very well…but it wouldn't last for more than a few weeks. She had seen for herself how quickly Marco lost interest in women. And even if the affair lasted months instead of weeks she wouldn't be able to cope with Marco's cool take on emotions. It would tear her apart. Plus it would put a strain on her job. Allowing herself to believe otherwise was just inviting heartache.

She pulled away from him abruptly. 'Listen, Marco…last night was great but—'

'But I had better curtail my animal passions…hmm?' He drawled the words softly.

'I think it's for the best.' Her voice was distracted. 'I don't think we should let it happen again.'

He reached out and touched her face. 'I'm not so sure about that.'

The words sent little quivering darts of pleasure racing right through her body.

And as she looked into his eyes she realised exactly why she couldn't have an affair with him. The truth was, it would never be enough because she was falling in love with him.

The knowledge hit her out of nowhere and it sent shock waves pulsating through her entire system.

Maybe Marco had been right all along, she thought in panic…maybe when sex came into play you couldn't trust emotions…couldn't trust feelings to be correct, because surely she couldn't be this foolish?

She knew Marco's feelings on this subject! He wasn't looking for emotional involvement…. In fact that was the last thing he wanted.

And she didn't want it either. She knew how painful love could be when it all went wrong…and it could never work with Marco. They might be sexually suited but in emotional terms they were poles apart.

She was supposed to be Ms Practicality, she reminded herself scornfully. To Marco last night was just a fling—a bit of fun—and he believed she had the same ethos. If he even guessed what was running through her mind now he would be horrified.

'Charlie, are you OK?'

He was looking at her with questioning eyes.

'Yes, of course I'm OK,' she made herself reply cheerfully.

A car horn blared behind them and Marco glanced abruptly away. He saw that the road was now clear and he was now holding up a line of cars behind him.

He quickly put the engine into gear and the powerful car moved forward. 'Anyway we'll talk more over dinner. There is a *trattoria* further along this road. We'll stop there.'

Charlie made no reply; she was too busy listening to her heart telling her she was completely out of her depth here.

CHAPTER EIGHT

As THEY pulled up outside a rustic *trattoria* the sun was starting to dip down behind the mountains, sending long shadows over the rolling plains. And with the setting sun there was a sudden coolness in the air.

Charlie shivered a little as she stepped out of the car but she wasn't sure if it was from the evening air…or her thoughts. She really needed to pull herself together, she thought crossly.

It was a relief to be greeted by a lively, buzzing atmosphere inside the restaurant. At least if she was a little quieter than usual Marco might not notice.

A waiter hurried over to greet them, talking rapidly in Italian.

Charlie listened as Marco answered in a slower, more measured tone. She loved the sound of his voice when he spoke in English but when he spoke in his own language it was an incredible turn-on.

She remembered how he had spoken in Italian to her as they made love last night…whispering the hot words in her ear as he took her higher and higher into spasms of pleasure.

Desperately she tried to shut those memories away.

The waiter led them to a secluded alcove with views out of the window towards the setting sun.

'I take it you are a regular here when you're home?' Charlie tried to keep the light tone in her voice as she sat down opposite to him.

'Yes. It's convenient for the villa and the food is excellent.'

'I love Italian food.' She flicked open the menu and pretended to study it with every shred of her concentration. But in truth she couldn't concentrate or even see very well. The lighting was low and she really needed to put her glasses on…something she was loath to do around him.

'Yes, Italian food does rate high on the list of life's pleasures,' Marco agreed easily. 'Along with good company and passionate interludes; all of which have made this trip perfect.'

She glanced over and as their eyes held Charlie tried very hard to rationalise all the feelings that suddenly flowed through her with vivid intensity.

It would be very easy to read all the wrong signals from that intense gaze. Just as it would be easy to imagine that what had transpired between them in the bedroom was serious.

But it wasn't.

He had just referred to last night as *a passionate interlude.* She needed to take heed of what was real and what was imagined. He'd probably brought numerous women for such interludes to his house, and here to this restaurant, she reminded herself. The thought twisted unpleasantly inside her.

'Yes, it's been fun while it's lasted,' she said coolly.

Hurriedly she looked away from him and tried to focus on the noisy bustle and repartee of the waiters, and the roaring open wood-fired ovens where the chef was baking bread.

Marco wondered why Charlie was suddenly so tense and withdrawn. For a while this afternoon he had really thought he had won her around again, as she had been so relaxed and open.

He watched as she opened her handbag and put her reading-glasses on. She looked very cute in them and he liked the way her nose wrinkled a little as she concentrated. He was suddenly filled with an almost irresistible urge to reach out and touch her, to smooth the little frown lines away. He forced himself to pull back, sensing that if he didn't handle this right she could withdraw completely.

She glanced over and caught him watching her.

'You look good in your glasses,' he said smoothly.

'I've been told that they make me look too serious.' She glanced back towards the menu. She didn't want him to start lying to her. One of the things she liked about Marco was his honesty.

'Really? Who told you that?'

She shrugged. It was her ex-husband but she didn't want to tell him that. 'I can't remember. Does it matter?'

'No, except I wouldn't take any fashion tips from whoever it was. Because you look lovely…incredibly sexy, in fact.'

His voice held a husky honesty that tore at her defences.

'You are just a charmer, Marco,' she managed to say primly and switched the subject. 'Now, although I can now see the menu, I can't understand it…'

He smiled and leaned a little closer. She could smell the scent of his cologne, intoxicating and warmly provocative. It made her remember what is was like to be held in his arms.

Somehow she managed to make herself concentrate on the blithe conversation and laugh with Marco as he helped her to translate some of the dishes.

They placed their orders and Marco reached to pour her a glass of wine. Outside darkness stole over the countryside and the flicker of candlelight lit the room.

'So are you all prepared for your TV interview tomorrow?' Charlie asked, taking the lead in the conversation. She was determined not to let things slip towards anything personal.

'Just about…' He paused for a second and then to Charlie's relief followed her lead. And suddenly they were back on safe ground again, talking about work.

'Of course, when you join me in America for the interviews there it will be pretty hectic. Not much time for sight-seeing, I'm afraid.'

The line was thrown casually into the conversation but it caused an immense wave of consternation inside her. 'You want me to go to America with you?'

'Well, I'll need you to join me for a few days in New York. Nothing more than that.'

'Oh!' Her heart was thumping wildly again and the feeling that she was out of her depth resurfaced with violent intensity.

'I did tell you that I would need you to accompany me on a few business trips.' He looked over at her with a frown.

'Yes…but I assumed you might need me at the conference in Edinburgh for a day…that kind of thing.'

'No, I'll be relying on you to run the office while I'm in Edinburgh. I'm expecting some important files around that time and you'll need to categorise them.' He looked at her very seriously now. 'But after that I want you to fly to New York and join me for three, maybe four days. I take it that won't be a problem?'

The light in his eyes and the no-nonsense tone suddenly reminded her in no uncertain terms that this was her boss. They might have enjoyed a fling last night but he certainly didn't expect it to get in the way of work. He wouldn't be impressed about her crossing the line and letting him down.

'Of course not,' she said quickly. This was business, she reminded herself as she fought down the feelings of apprehension. She had already agreed to a few trips and there was no way she could lose this job.

'Good.' He smiled at her and the fleeting steel-like mood was gone, replaced with a warm gleam of approval. 'Because our working arrangements are going very well, I think.'

'Yes…' She frowned. If only she could get past these personal feelings they would be perfect.

They talked for a while longer about work. She relaxed back. Everything would be fine, she told herself staunchly.

Marco was right about the food—the antipasto was mouth-wateringly good.

'Why is it that pasta doesn't taste as good as this at home?' she asked as the waiter cleared away their empty plates to put their main course down.

'Probably because it's made fresh here.' Marco shrugged. 'But, of course, you can find good pasta in England…if you know where to go.'

'And where is that?' She glanced over at him with interest.

'Around to my place for dinner, naturally,' he said with a smile.

She wished she didn't feel that instant flare of warmth at that suggestion. 'That's what I like about you—you're so modest,' she murmured, but she couldn't help but smile over at him.

'So shall we call that a provisional date some time?' Marco reached and took a sip of his drink.

'Maybe…' She tried to match his casual tone. He was just teasing, she told herself. 'If we can find a space in the diary.'

He smiled. 'And that's what I like about you…'

'What's that?' She glanced over at him warily.

'The fact that you always have your feet on the ground and are so totally practical, of course.'

Although it was just a light-hearted remark, there was a serious edge to it. Charlie knew that…

'Of course.' She avoided his gaze and pretended to concentrate on her meal.

And his belief that she was so practical in all areas of her life was why a relationship between them wouldn't work out.

'The fact that you are still very sexy without the glasses is also quite a draw,' he added with a spark of devilment.

She looked over at him and wished she were the person he imagined…an ultra-modern career girl who didn't allow herself to be ruled by emotions. She wished she really could just view sex as a recreational enjoyment instead of something serious. She wished she could go back to bed with him tonight and not worry about where it was leading.

'Have you ever been in love, Marco?' She asked the question impulsively.

He regarded her quizzically for a moment. 'Why do you ask?'

'I don't know… I guess I'm just curious.' She shrugged and felt suddenly self-conscious. She probably shouldn't have asked him that!

'I lived with someone once,' he answered slowly. 'We met at university and shared an apartment for two years.'

Charlie looked at him in surprise. 'Really?'

'Yes. We considered marriage and then we realised that we weren't suited, that we both wanted different things out of life.'

'You didn't want to make the commitment to her?' Charlie guessed.

'It was a mutual decision.'

Somehow Charlie didn't believe that.

'Some people just aren't cut out for marriage,' he said with a shrug. 'And it's all too easy to get swept along by passion and emotion and forget that. Fortunately we didn't and because of that we have managed to remain good friends.'

'That takes some doing!'

'Not really.' Marco frowned. 'We are very much on an academic wavelength. So usually when we meet up it is to discuss our work.'

Charlie was surprised to find a flicker of jealousy curl inside her and she hastily pushed the feeling away. She wasn't the jealous type and she wasn't going to start now. 'It's surprising the relationship didn't work out…when you had so much in common,' she said lightly.

'Well, it didn't.' He looked over at her steadily.

Charlie told herself to leave the subject alone. It was none of her business, but somehow she just couldn't. 'So why do you think that was?'

For a moment he didn't answer her.

'I guess you broke her heart,' she added flippantly.

Marco laughed at that, but the sound held none of his usual warmth. 'Well, then, you would be wrong. The relationship broke down when I was away on business. Maria went out with friends one evening and met up with an old flame. She had a one-night fling with him.'

Charlie was totally taken aback, not just by the fact that any woman would want to cheat on someone as gorgeous as Marco but also by a glimpse of some stark emotion in his eyes—an emotion she had never seen there before.

'So how did you find out about it?' she asked curiously.

Marco shrugged. 'She felt guilty and told me.'

'So it really was just a one-night fling?'

'Yes.' Marco held her gaze impassively. 'But if the relationship had been right she wouldn't have felt tempted to stray. Obviously there were flaws that needed to be addressed, and when we looked into it we realised that the flaws were too deep to continue with the relationship.'

'I see…' Charlie watched him across the table and saw the flicker of darkness in his expression. Betrayal was something he couldn't handle. The realisation flashed in her mind and suddenly she understood Marco's wariness where commitment was concerned. Obviously watching his parents tearing each other apart had made him cautious and then Maria had reinforced that.

This was why he was so determined not to get emotionally involved.

Unexpectedly the insight lit a small ray of hope inside her. *Maybe if Marco found someone he could trust he would allow himself to fall in love and he would start to change his views about emotional commitment. Maybe he would start to believe in its power for the good.* The thought brushed through Charlie's mind. *Maybe he just hadn't found the right person.*

She liked the idea…but then again, she would, she thought drily. She was a romantic.

'Now…do you think we could leave the past alone?' He reached across and took hold of her hand. 'Because I've got other more pressing interests right now, and I'm not talking about work either.'

The touch of his hand on hers sent little darts of desire racing through her from nowhere. But for once she didn't feel the need to pull away from him. In fact she actually felt a tentative need to respond to him. Like her, Marco had been hurt, and maybe if she could prove to him that he could rely on her and trust her then maybe one day he might open up to her the way she had to him.

She knew it was a risky strategy. Marco didn't allow himself to get involved with anyone for long. But by virtue of working with him, she was closer to him than anyone had been in a while. Maybe it would give her a slight edge.

'Do you know what I would like right at this moment?' he murmured huskily.

'What's that?'

'I'd like to take you home…undress you very, very slowly and then kiss you all over…' As he was speaking his thumb traced little circles over the inside curve of her arm. It was a deliciously erotic feeling.

The last of her reservations fell away.

'I think I'd like that too,' she admitted softly.

When Charlie woke the next morning she was curled up in the protective warmth of Marco's arms. The sun was slanting in through the open curtains and the only sound was the sweet trill of birdsong in the morning air.

She smiled and buried herself deeper into Marco's arms. She loved being here with him like this. Languid memories of their lovemaking flicked through her mind. They had barely made it home from the restaurant before they had started to tear each other's clothes off. If she looked up from the pillow she knew she would see a trail of clothing leading from the door.

Their lovemaking had been intensely passionate and unlike anything Charlie had ever experienced in her marriage. Marco could arouse her with such ease.

The first night she had tried to tell herself that the intensity of pleasure she had experienced was because she hadn't made love for so long. But now she knew that this was just the way Marco was able to make her feel. It was incredible and addictive and the more she thought about it…the more she wanted him all over again.

She tilted her head and studied him as he slept, her eyes moving over the aristocratically handsome face and taking in every detail.

Even in sleep he looked powerful…like a sleeping tiger. But she knew the truth, she thought with a zing of pleasure. Marco wasn't as cool and composed as he liked to pretend. He had a vulnerable edge. Like her, he had just built up his own set of defences to hide the fact. How to find a way around those defences was the question that was occupying her this morning.

He opened his eyes suddenly and caught her watching him. She noticed the golden flecks in their dark depths.

'Buon giorno.' She whispered the words softly, her voice shy.

He smiled sleepily and, brushing a hand through her long hair he reached and kissed her tenderly on the lips.

Her naked body was crushed against his and she could feel his arousal. He rolled her over, pressing her down against the softness of the mattress as he kissed the side of her face, her neck, before his lips moved lower…

Her hands raked through the darkness of his hair. And she closed her eyes on a wave of pleasure as once more he made love to her with a thorough passion that made her dizzy and made her gasp his name…

As always Marco was totally in control, steadying her, soothing her, kissing her senseless until she was almost begging for release. He smiled as he took her to climax... raking hungry, possessive hands over her body, claiming her and making her totally his.

Then as she collapsed weakly against him, clinging to him, her body damp, her senses swimming, he suddenly pulled away and looked at the clock on the bedside table.

'Is that the correct time?'

Charlie could hardly think coherently, never mind look at the time. She glanced blearily at her watch. 'I think it's eight-thirty.'

'Damn! I'd better get moving.' He threw the covers back and got out of bed. 'I've got to be at the TV station for my interview in less than an hour!'

She snuggled back down against the pillows, watching as he threw a robe around his shoulders.

'Hey, don't get too comfortable!' He threw her a smile. 'I want you to come with me.'

Charlie groaned. 'I feel like staying in bed. You've worn me out.'

He laughed. 'Sorry, but we've got a plane to catch...and we'll have to leave straight from the TV station.'

Back to reality... The unwelcome thought crept in. What was going to happen when they got home? Would she be able to hold on to this tentatively wonderful feeling that was spiralling between them?

He sat down on the side of the bed suddenly and looked at her. 'By the way,' he drawled lazily, 'just in case I forget to tell you, I've enjoyed every minute of this weekend with you.' He punctuated the sentence with a lingering softly sensual kiss.

'I've enjoyed it too.' She felt her heart thumping loudly against her chest. There were no sentimental words of love and she didn't for one moment expect that. But telling her how much he enjoyed every minute was the next best thing…wasn't it? At least he was honest and she respected him for that.

She wound her arms around his neck and kissed him back. Maybe she could handle this situation. She'd have to do a great job of acting when she got home…pretend that she wasn't head-over-heels in love and that she was in tune with his thinking on romance. It would be worth it though, she thought dreamily…if Marco opened up to her and allowed her into his life.

He pulled away from her. 'Right, come on…' He tugged the sheet. 'My public awaits…'

She laughed breathlessly. 'If they could see you now!'

'It might do wonders for my profile,' he teased as he went through towards the dressing room and the *en suite* bathroom. 'It would certainly please Sarah…which reminds me, I promised to phone her this morning.'

The very name of Sarah Heart encroaching in on the day was enough to send shadows over it.

She heard Marco turning on the shower in the next room and at the same time the phone beside the bed rang.

'I bet that's her!' Marco shouted. 'Answer it, will you, Charlie? Tell her I'm in the shower and I'll phone her back later.'

Pulling a face, she rolled over and lifted the receiver.

Marco was right; it was Sarah, and her breathy, cheerful voice was just as grating as ever. 'Hi, Marco; how's it going?' she gushed. 'Hope everything is on track for a really great inter-view this morning.'

'Actually, Sarah, it's Charlie,' she answered. 'Marco's in the shower, can he ring you back?'

There was a slight pause before Sarah continued in the same cheerful tone. 'Oh, hello, Charlie. How is your weekend going?'

'It's going fine, thank you.' Charlie frowned. It was unlike Sarah to try and make polite conversation.

'Having a nice *romantic* time?'

Was it her imagination or was there a definite sarcastic edge to Sarah's voice now?

'Well, we've been working…but we are *both* having a wonderful time,' she answered coolly.

'Well, you certainly look like a real couple…and as I said to Marco, that's what really counts. It's all about getting the right spin on a situation, and he's certainly doing that with lots of hand-holding and smouldering glances…great.'

A cold feeling was starting to churn inside Charlie now. 'What on earth are you talking about?'

'Sorry, Charlie, I'm rambling, aren't I? I'm looking at the photograph of you and Marco strolling hand in hand through the streets of Florence. It's in the morning papers. And I'm just so pleased. It's great publicity.'

'Well, I'm *so* glad you're pleased.' Charlie tried to keep her voice on an even keel but her brain was racing frantically and anger was starting to rise. Words like *spin* and *great publicity* were whirring around like instruments of torture. 'But I can assure you we were just enjoying ourselves.'

'Well, that's a relief, because when I set up the photo and suggested this I was a bit hesitant. I mean, you never really know how these things will work out, do you? And Marco was very reluctant to follow my ideas at first…well, you know what he's like, so stubborn…and didn't like the idea of getting tied into a romantic involvement even as a publicity stunt.'

Charlie felt her heart go into freefall. 'Yes, I know what he's like,' she said numbly. Had Marco known the photographers were going to snap them yesterday? Had he got her to Italy on false pretences? Seduced her and used her as some kind of publicity stunt to promote his book?

'Anyway, I just knew that you would be the perfect foil for him,' Sarah continued merrily. 'Especially when he mentioned that he felt comfortable around you and that you were on a similar wavelength, that's why we decided that a short

weekend in Italy would be a good starting point for you both—
you know, just to test the waters.'

We decided? The words ricocheted through Charlie. Marco
had discussed her with Sarah…had invited her here *on Sarah's
suggestion?*

'Has he asked you to go to America with him yet?' Sarah
asked suddenly. 'Seeing it's going so well, I'm sure he will.
And that would be brilliant, Charlie…it will really help having
you in the background just to overset these awkward questions
about his personal life.'

Charlie felt sick. Where the hell had her brain been these
last few days? All these years of playing things safe and now
it looked as if she had walked straight into a damn set-up…she
had allowed herself to be used. *She had fallen in love with a
man who thought nothing of her…a man who had discussed
her and probably laughed about her behind her back.*

'Charlie, are you still there?' Sarah asked with a smile in
her voice. 'You've gone awfully quiet.'

Fury was starting to take over from heartache. She had
always known that Sarah Heart was a complete bitch—she was
enjoying this! She was also probably totally eaten up with
jealousy, Charlie reminded herself. Maybe this wasn't even
true. Maybe Marco knew nothing about Sarah's plans for the
photographers to catch them!

'Yes…I'm here…to be honest with you I'm falling
asleep.' Charlie managed to fake a yawn, a yawn that felt
achingly as if it wanted to turn into tears. 'Marco and I have
been enjoying a weekend of wild passion…in fact things have
progressed out of all control between us. It's been absolutely fantastic.'

'That's great.'

Charlie felt a little better as she heard Sarah's voice drop a
decibel of cheer.

'Yes, it has been great…so *if* you've suggested this then

thank you so much from both of us. Anyway, better go now. *Marco needs me....* He'll phone you if he gets time.'

She slammed down the phone and just lay there, her heart thundering with fury and hurt.

What was the truth behind this situation? Was Sarah making things up?

Marco had told her up front about Sarah's publicity ideas for his book. What was it he had said that day in the car? *'Having a suitable partner around at the moment wouldn't go amiss.'* He'd even gone so far as to tell her that as his book tour started in five weeks, he probably wouldn't be able to find a suitable candidate in time.

And what had she had said? *'Oh, I'm sure you will be able to dig up someone acceptable very quickly.'*

Charlie cringed. God, it looked as though Sarah was telling the truth...and she had walked right into it with her lies about being on his wavelength!

She remembered her first instinct regarding involvement with Marco had been wariness. She had known it would suit his purposes to have someone like her around, but somewhere along the line she had let go of those concerns and she had honestly thought that he'd invited her here just in her capacity as PA. And that night when he'd made dinner for her and they had relaxed together she had imagined that there was a genuine connection between them.

But now little things that he had said to her over the last few weeks started to trickle with chilling emphasis through her mind.

When he had taken her out for lunch on that first day, he'd said, *'Where you and I are concerned, business and pleasure could fit together very nicely.'*

And yesterday when he'd mentioned her joining him in America he'd looked implacable, as if the trip was all-important. What was it he had said? *'Our working arrangements are going very well, I think.'*

And to think that deep down she had imagined he really was attracted to her! How stupid was she? The truth had been staring her in the face and she hadn't chosen to see it…why hadn't she chosen to ask herself why someone like Marco would suddenly want to spend time with her?

Instead she had naïvely been fooling herself into thinking a relationship with him might stand a chance!

As Marco returned to the room Charlie snatched up her dressing gown and wrapped it around her body with shaking fingers.

He was wearing a dark suit that sat perfectly on his broad-shouldered frame, making him look dangerously attractive and powerfully compelling. She felt her stomach flip over.

Marco could have his pick of the most glamorous and beautiful women but he had chosen her because he deemed her safe and *comfortable*. He thought she was Ms Practicality, who wouldn't get carried away by emotion or expect more from him than he wanted to give.

'Was that Sarah on the phone?' he asked as he strolled across to the wardrobe to flick through a rack of ties.

'Yes; I said you'd ring her back.'

'Thanks.' He selected a silver tie and started to put it on. 'Hurry up, Charlie.' He slanted a wry look over as she made no attempt to leave the room. 'You haven't got long to get ready!'

'I'm aware of that.' Her voice wasn't entirely steady. 'Marco, did you know those photographers were going to be around yesterday?' She had to hear the truth from him so she could know for sure if what Sarah had told her was correct.

He didn't appear to miss a beat, just continued to fasten his tie. 'Why are you asking me that now? I told you…they are always around these days.'

'Yes, but did you specifically arrange with Sarah for that photograph to be taken yesterday?'

Marco looked at her now. 'She did mention something about it…' His voice was casually indifferent. 'But I told you, didn't I, that she wants to spice up my profile romantically?'

Fury lashed through her at that casual admission. 'Yes, you did. I just didn't realise that I was the spice in question.' Her voice was laced with sarcasm.

To her annoyance Marco merely looked amused by the accusation. He met her clear green gaze and then shook his head. 'I thought you didn't mind about the photographs? When I asked, you said it didn't matter.'

'It didn't matter when it was an unforeseen incident…it matters a hell of a lot more when you deliberately set me up for it!' Her eyes were blazing into his now.

'I didn't set you up for it!' he said calmly.

'Oh, sorry…let's get this right. *Both* of you set me up for it. In fact…you only asked me to come to Italy with you in the first place to test the waters…ready for the big PR exercise in America.'

A sudden look of anger passed over Marco's dark features. 'Did Sarah say that?'

'Yes, she damn well did!' Charlie wished that her voice hadn't faltered at that moment. 'Not that I care or anything.' She lifted her chin defiantly. 'But you should have been more honest with me…'

'Charlie, I was honest with you…you are being silly.' Marco walked towards her and she backed away. She couldn't bear for him to touch her now. It was too raw…too painful to bear. 'Sarah had no right to say those things.'

'Has she spoilt your fun?' She flung the words at him bitterly.

'Charlie, stop it!' He reached out and caught her arm as she made to swing away from him.

'She had no right to say those things because they are not true.' He pulled her around and put a hand under her chin, forcing her to look up at him. 'I asked you to come to Italy with me because I needed your help in the office and I also thought we could have fun together. I wanted to spend time with you. I'll be honest that I was aware that the timing was convenient as far as a PR exercise is concerned…but that was just a bonus.'

Her heart was thundering painfully against her chest now and as he pulled her even closer she felt sure he would be able to feel it.

The words seemed to mock her…*have fun…convenient timing…PR bonus.*

'Just let me go, Marco…'

He ignored her. 'And we have had fun…haven't we?' His eyes were on her lips now.

Her heart twisted with painful need. And she hated herself for it.

With a supreme effort of will she wrenched herself away from him. 'Yes, it's been fun, Marco…but this is where it ends. From now on you'll have to find some other PR puppet to play games with.'

CHAPTER NINE

THEY were sitting side-by-side thirty-five thousand miles up in the air and they weren't talking.

It had been like this since they had left the villa to go to the TV station. Marco had tried to reason with her at first but she was in no mood to listen and somehow his words just seemed to make everything worse.

'You know you are being ridiculous,' he had muttered in the car. 'I don't know why you are blowing a conversation with Sarah Heart up out of all proportion.'

'Am I?'

She had seethed with hurt and anger.

'Yes, you are. I told you about Sarah's ideas up front.'

'You didn't tell me you were planning a PR exercise involving me behind my back!'

'It wasn't a PR exercise, it was a working weekend that was also supposed to be fun. And I didn't plan things behind your back. I made a passing remark to Sarah over dinner about how well we get on in the office and how you seem to be very in tune with my theories…and that's true…isn't it?'

The question was still causing unpleasant little ripples to spread throughout her body… She was accusing Marco of not being completely honest with her about his motivations this weekend—but she hadn't been completely honest with him either.

And there lay the crux of their problem. She was emotionally torn because she was in love with him. And he couldn't understand why she was so upset…because hey…it had just been a bit of fun anyway.

Charlie wondered if he had mentioned her at all during his interview on TV. She had sat waiting for him in the hospitality suite and had watched him on the monitor, but she hadn't understood a word because it was all in Italian. When the inevitable question about his personal life had arisen—what had he said?

Probably something along the lines of yes I'm dating my secretary. I feel very *comfortable* around her.

She glanced over at Marco, who had been flicking through the in-flight magazine, but he put it down now. He glanced over at her and their eyes met.

He looked so cool and collected and so damned handsome that instantly the raw pain of earlier sprang into ferocious life again. Being emotionally detached was too hard, she thought wretchedly. But she was going to have to try. And at the same time she hoped that he wasn't feeling quite so damn comfortable around her now.

'Have you calmed down now?' he asked quietly.

The cool enquiry just made her feel a hundred times worse. He was so damn cavalier!

When she thought about how she had opened up to him this weekend…tentatively trusted him…luxuriated in his warm embrace—and even dared hope he might return her feelings one day—it just made her want to either hit him or cry at her own stupidity.

'No, I haven't calmed down, Marco.' She was really pleased by how composed she sounded. There was no hint of turmoil in her voice. 'I don't appreciate being used in some cheap stunt.'

'Well, that certainly wasn't my intention!'

When she made no reply to that he frowned. 'Come on, Charlie, let's put this behind us and be friends again…hmm?'

Friends…the word grated mockingly inside her.

'I wouldn't have minded if you'd been honest with me,' she muttered, trying to ignore the little voice that was calling her a liar. 'I would have played the PR part to perfection…I mean, I understand the score, for heaven's sake.' She took a deep breath and forced herself to add, 'We were having a bit of light-hearted fun!'

'Exactly.' He looked at her with that teasing gleam in his eye that she knew so well. 'Look, I genuinely didn't think twice about Sarah's plans with the paparazzi. And I'm sorry you feel that I misled you. Let's just forget about it…hmm? And we can have lots more fun.'

He reached to take hold of her hand but she pulled away. If he touched her she didn't think she could maintain this air of indifference.

He was so arrogantly sure of himself! 'Yes, OK, we'll just forget about it,' she said stiffly. 'After all, we have to work together, don't we?' She swallowed hard and looked away from him out of the window.

If he wanted Ms Practicality, well, then, he could damn well have Ms Practicality in spades, she thought angrily. But she didn't want any more *fun* with him. It hurt too much.

The pilot announced that they would shortly be landing. Marco frowned and settled back in his seat. Obviously Charlie hadn't forgiven him! She was blowing the whole thing out of proportion…and he felt annoyed by the way she was being so cold towards him now. It wasn't a reaction he was used to where women were concerned.

He told himself to just forget about it. He'd apologised for any hurt feelings that he hadn't intended to cause. The weekend had been casual and the PR stunt had been Sarah's damn project, not his.

So why was he even thinking about it now? He had a meeting with Professor Hunt lined up for seven forty-five. And there were some extra notes he needed to deal with before then.

But he was furious with Sarah and his anger encroached on the businesslike thoughts. He had only just succeeded in getting Charlie to relax around him and now Sarah had ruined everything. How dared she say something so damn insensitive?

The last thing he wanted was to hurt Charlie… He glanced over at her. She was watching the TV screen on the seat in front of her, but he had the feeling she wasn't giving it her full attention. She looked so vulnerable sometimes that he wanted to reach out and touch her, take her into his arms and feel her melt against him in that incredible warm way of hers. She had been wonderful to be around…she was passionate, with a great sense of humour and she was great in bed. He was going to miss her tonight, in fact…

The plane touched down on the runway.

Marco pulled his attention away from Charlie and unfastened his seat belt. Outside the London afternoon looked grey and miserable, and there was a fine drizzle—the type that drenched you through without you realising it was happening.

As the aircraft came to a halt Marco stood up to get his briefcase and Charlie's hand luggage. 'Would you like to come back to my place for a coffee?' he asked casually as they walked together out into the terminal.

'No, thank you; I want to get home to Jack.' She smiled lightly.

'OK, well…you get your luggage and I'll go get the car and I'll see you outside in, say…twenty minutes?'

Charlie shook her head. 'I'll get a taxi, Marco. You may as well just go. There's no point you waiting around here when you have no luggage to collect.'

He frowned and for a moment his eyes raked over her face. She looked so young suddenly. 'But I want to see you home,' he insisted.

She desperately wanted to go with him and to forget the hurt that was insistently flowing through her. She longed to just lean in against him and kiss him…

But there was only so much pretence that she could handle and she had her pride. 'There's no point, Marco. You have an appointment, and don't forget, those notes you need are in a new file—'

'To hell with the files and the damn meeting, Charlie!' He sounded suddenly annoyed. 'Look, we've had a lovely weekend—why spoil it now?'

'I wasn't aware that I was spoiling anything.' She remained cool. 'Yes, it's been a nice weekend but we both have other commitments to get back to.'

What exactly was happening here? Marco wondered in agitation. He was usually the one making comments like this when a woman was coming on too strong!

He met her deep green guileless gaze. 'Yes, I suppose you are right…Professor Hunt is a bit of a stickler for time.' He forced himself to say the words and to sound positive and practical, but somehow for once in his life the feelings about work felt false.

Actually he couldn't have given a damn about Professor Hunt! He frowned. 'Are you sure I can't give you a lift?'

There was a moment's pause. Marco was barely aware of the crowds flowing around them as he looked at her. He wanted her to change her mind. He hated this sudden feeling between them that they were just strangers who had slept together…the warmth and passion of the weekend were too strong in his mind for him to be happy with that.

'Quite sure.'

'OK.' When she made no attempt to weaken he leaned closer…and then he saw her expression change. He saw a flicker of emotional intensity for just a moment. He smiled and then his lips crushed against hers in a passionately possessive way.

He felt a moment's resistance and then she kissed him back, her lips sweetly submissive and tantalising.

'See you in the office tomorrow,' he said with a smile as he stepped back.

She would forgive him, he thought with pleasure as he walked away.

This time tomorrow they would be working out the dates for her to join him in America.

Charlie opened her eyes and blinked against the early-morning sunlight. For just a moment she imagined that she was back in Italy with Marco and the feeling was joyous…then she stretched a hand out into the cool, empty side of the bed and the dark clouds of memory closed around her heart.

She groaned and buried her head in against the pillow. Sleep had been elusive last night, her mind going around in tortuous circles over her feelings for Marco. It hadn't solved anything because she still loved him and hated herself for the stupidity. How could you love someone when it was clear that they would never return your feelings?

The thought of facing him in the office today was unbearable and yet bitter-sweet all at the same time. How she was going to maintain a cool, professional distance she just didn't know.

Jack came running into the room. 'Morning, Mummy!' He leapt in beside her and she smiled and drew him close.

She had a little boy to take care of and responsibilities. She couldn't afford the time to be heartbroken, she told herself firmly. She needed this job with Marco and even if she could just stick it out for twelve months it would give her enough money to get herself back on track financially, pay for the things that needed doing around the house, pay her bills off…and then she could find some other position.

The sensible thought galvanised her into action and she

pushed back the bedcovers. She was just going to have to forget her feelings for Marco.

It was the usual Monday-morning rush to get out of the house. Once they were in the car Jack put her CD of love songs into the player and turned up the volume.

'I don't think I'm in the mood for that today, Jack.' She reached over and turned it off.

It was probably listening to music like that that had got her heart in this mess in the first place, she told herself fiercely. Marco was right about one thing: love *was* a dangerous emotion.

She dropped Jack off at school and headed for Marco's house with a heavy heart. It was the first time she had felt like this since she had started working for him. Usually she felt happy at the thought of spending the day with him…happy and excited. She had enjoyed being around him, enjoyed the little smiles he sent her way every now and then or the casual touch of his hand as it brushed against hers… Heck! Why hadn't she seen the fact that she was falling in love with him? she wondered in despair. It seemed so obvious now.

She parked her car next to Marco's and checked her appearance in the vanity mirror. Her hair was drawn back from her face and secured neatly in a pony-tail. Her make-up was applied with a careful skill to hide the shadows under her eyes and she had put a brighter shade of lipstick on today to cheer herself up. She would pass, she thought irately as she flicked the mirror shut. And she couldn't put this off any longer.

Taking a deep breath, she hurried into the house and up to the office. She could handle this, she told herself. She would be cool and practical and distant…

Her confidence dipped, however, as soon as she walked in. Marco was perched on the edge of her desk, flicking through the work calendar. It didn't help that he looked so handsome in a dark grey suit.

'Morning, Marco.' She tried to make her voice sound breezily indifferent.

He looked up and smiled at her and her heart missed a beat. Suddenly she was thinking about those mornings in Italy when he had wished her *buon giorno* and kissed her with steamy passion… Hastily she looked away and hung her jacket on the stand next to the door.

'So how are you today?' Marco asked quietly, his eyes following her movements.

'Fine, thanks; did your meeting with the professor go well?' It was the only thing she could think of to say that would help maintain a businesslike atmosphere. But inside she felt as if she was dying.

'Yes, thanks.'

To her consternation he made no attempt to move out of her way as she walked over towards her desk. Instead his eyes seemed to rake over her with sharp intensity.

'How was Jack last night?' he asked. 'I bet he was pleased to see you.'

'Yes, he was.' For a moment she remembered Jack hurtling across the room to hug her fiercely. She had wanted to cry as she had held him close. She wanted to cry again now. Her emotions were all over the place. She hadn't felt this level of hurt since the day her ex-husband walked out. And that angered her. She had promised herself that no man would ever make her feel like this again.

'Did he like his presents?'

'He loved them…especially the car, of course.' She tried not to think about that day in Florence and how they had laughed as they bought those toys together and then walked hand in hand. Which was all a damn set-up for the paparazzi, she reminded herself fiercely. Marco should mean nothing to her now, she thought severely…nothing. So why did she feel so broken inside when she looked over and met his eyes?

'Anyway, back to reality.' She smiled at him coolly and moved to go past so that she could sit at her desk.

He caught hold of her arm to stop her and the touch of his skin against hers made her senses instantly swim with desire. She flinched away, hating herself for the weakness.

Marco noticed and frowned. 'Listen, I was thinking we could have lunch together today,' he suggested softly. 'I've got to go over to St Agnes Hospital to give a second opinion on two referrals but I should be back around twelve.'

'I don't think lunch is a good idea, Marco.' Although her voice was calm, inside there were thunderous emotions racing…a big part of her wanted to say OK…that would be nice…

But she had to be strong, she thought. Because the more time she spent around Marco, the harder it would be to extract herself and switch off her emotions.

'Why not?' he asked calmly.

'Because…you know how I feel about mixing business with pleasure, it just doesn't work.'

'It worked when we were in Italy.'

The calm reply lashed at her emotions. 'No it didn't. And that was different, anyway; it was a…one-night stand.' She forced herself to say the words. That was all it had been, she reminded herself.

'As I recall, it was a little more than that.' He pulled her closer. She could smell the familiar tang of his cologne—evocative and warmly tantalising.

She still wanted him so much! The realisation killed her. How could she be so weak?

She pulled away. 'You and Sarah aren't cooking up another little photograph opportunity, are you?' she asked archly.

'No.' He frowned. 'I thought we'd agreed to put that behind us?'

'Yes…of course we have.' She chastised herself. Making

barbed comments wasn't a good idea. If Marco guessed how emotionally involved she was he would be horrified…maybe he would even tell Sarah Heart about it and the two of them would sit and discuss her and Sarah would smirk….

She switched her thoughts away from that. She was being ridiculous. Marco didn't know how she felt…and he never would. So her pride was intact, if nothing else.

'But we have a lot of work today, and I have letters to type.'

'Try to finish them by twelve o'clock. And then…' he leaned a little closer '…we could have some quality time…lunch and lovemaking….not necessarily in that order.' He whispered the words against her ear, his breath tickling against the sensitive area. 'I missed you last night.'

Her stomach flipped over with longing. She had missed him too…so much.

'I can't, Marco…really.' It took all her strength to keep her voice from trembling. Hastily she moved another step away.

'Why not?' He looked at her with a raised eyebrow. 'I've checked the calendar and both of our schedules this afternoon could be sidelined until tomorrow…'

'And then I'll be even further behind with things!' She went over to the filing cabinet to take some folders out. 'I want to keep things on a strictly business footing from now on.'

'As you know, I've no objection to keeping things business-like,' he said evenly, 'but today we could organise our time a little better and enjoy ourselves as well.'

'I don't think so.' Charlie shut the filing cabinet and went to sit behind her desk.

'You're still annoyed with me I take it?' Marco's tone was sardonic.

'No, of course not.' She found her reading-glasses and put them firmly on her nose. When he still didn't move and just continued to sit there with a wry look of sardonic disbelief in his eyes, she met his gaze firmly.

'Marco, I really enjoyed our weekend, but I don't think we should take things further. We've had our fun. I think it's time to move on.'

She could see the surprise in his dark eyes and felt wretched.

'You *are* still hung up about this PR business!'

'No I'm not!' She looked over at him calmly. 'I was mad at the time because you didn't tell me what your plans were up front. But now I'm just thinking in practical terms. And an affair with you is not what I need in my life right now.'

'So what do you need in your life right now?' he asked with a directness that made her frown.

'I have a four-year-old son, Marco. Stability is my main priority. Don't get me wrong, if I weren't a single mum I'd enjoy continuing our casual fling and playing a part in your PR plans. But under the circumstances I feel I need to be more circumspect about these things.'

'Well…I can understand that.' Although his voice was relaxed, he was looking at her through eyes that were slightly narrowed.

She was really relieved when the phone rang on her desk. 'Excuse me a moment.' She snatched it up as if it were a lifeline.

'Good morning, Professor Hunt,' she greeted Marco's colleague with cheerful enthusiasm. 'Yes, you've just caught him. Hold on.' She covered the mouthpiece. 'Shall I put him through to your private line?'

After a brief hesitation Marco nodded.

She returned to the phone with a false smile. 'I'm putting you through now, Professor,' she said, flicking a switch.

For a moment Marco didn't make any attempt to move and she thought he was going to ignore the call. Then suddenly he stood up. 'We'll continue our conversation later, Charlie.'

'I really have nothing more to say on the subject.'

She was pleased how together she sounded; weird really, when inside she was falling apart.

'Professor Hunt is waiting,' she reminded him firmly.

'Yes…I know.' His voice was dry. 'OK, Charlie, have it your way. I will, of course, still expect you to join me in America.'

Charlie felt a flicker of uncertainty. It was one thing keeping Marco at arms' length in the office but, as she knew from experience when they were away together, things got complicated. 'I told you to find someone else for your PR exercise.'

'And shall I find someone else as my PA as well?' he countered coolly. 'I thought we had agreed not to allow emotional issues to come before work?'

He watched her face flare with colour and for a moment he hated himself for pulling rank. But he wasn't about to let her slip away from him without a fight. 'The trip is purely business, Charlie,' he added more gently. 'But, as I said, we'll discuss this later.'

Charlie watched him head towards the inner office and close the door. Her heart was thundering out of control.

He was right, of course; she had just allowed personal feelings to come in the way of her job. But the simple truth was she couldn't go to America with him now even if it was strictly for business. Because, even knowing that she meant nothing to him, she still wanted him.

She bit down on her lip and despised herself for being so pathetic. Financially this job was a godsend and she was ruining it for herself.

Desperately she tried to think straight. But, no matter how calm and businesslike she tried to be, the mere thought of being alone with Marco in New York made her blood start to pound, confusing her senses with desire and trepidation.

The only solution was to get away from Marco as soon as possible. She was going to have to start job-hunting and fast.

CHAPTER TEN

CHARLIE had just stepped out of the shower when the front doorbell rang. She hurriedly reached for a towel and wrapped it around her wet hair before pulling a bath sheet around her. Karen had said she might call this morning if she had time. But by midday her friend still hadn't arrived, so Charlie had finished her housework and had started to get ready to go shopping.

'Jack, could you answer the door, please?' she called as she stepped out onto the landing.

There was no reply; Jack was playing with toys in the lounge.

Holding the towel tightly around her, she walked towards the stairs. She wanted to see Karen. They had spoken last week when Charlie had asked if she could find her another placement before the sale of her agency went through, which she had. But the downside was that the job was short-term and paid less.

She couldn't afford to drop her wages, so she'd had to refuse the offer.

Karen was coming to talk to her about it, and she hoped she wouldn't have to go into detail as to why she wanted to quit her job with Marco, as she found it too emotionally exhausting to explain. It had been hard enough working with him this week. The atmosphere in the office had been tense and she had been relieved to get out of there last night.

As Charlie started to go downstairs the doorbell rang again and Jack suddenly shot out of the lounge. 'I'll get it, Mum!' he said cheerily as he ran along the hallway.

'Oh, hi!' Charlie heard his cheerful greeting as he opened the door, and smiled. Jack was always pleased to see Karen. 'Mum's just got out of the shower.'

'Well, that was a bit of good timing.'

Charlie froze. It wasn't Karen—it was Marco's dulcet tones she could hear. And before she could stop him Jack was swinging the door wider to let him into the house. She looked down at herself in horror. All week she had maintained a well-groomed image with not a hair out of place. Somehow it had helped to know that at least she didn't look as if she was falling apart, even if she felt like it. Now Marco was going to catch her in a bath sheet with her hair in a towel!

'Actually, now isn't a good time,' she found herself calling out, trying to back up the stairs. 'I'm too busy to see anyone.'

He must have heard her, but he appeared at the bottom of the stairs anyway. She noticed the way his dark eyes swept boldly up over the long length of her legs and the curve of her figure. 'You look good in that towel.'

'Very funny,' she murmured. 'But, as you can see, I'm not in a fit state for visitors.'

The fact that he was his usual handsome and stylishly groomed self in a pair of chinos and a pale tan shirt didn't help her equilibrium at all.

'Don't worry about me. I like the turban look, by the way, it suits you—very exotic.'

She tried to ignore the seductive, teasing light in his eye, and fought to remain cool and reserved, but the truth was that her emotions were see-sawing wildly. There was a part of her that was so glad to see him…and she hated that. 'Was there something in particular you wanted, Marco?' She kept her tone cool.

'Yes, there is.' He folded his arms and leaned against the end of the banister rail. 'Are you coming down or shall I come up?'

'Neither,' she answered him quickly, her voice slightly unsteady. 'We're all right as we are.'

'You know that's not true.'

Something about the softness of his reply made her heart miss a beat.

'Which is why we need to talk,' he continued swiftly. 'And you can start by telling me exactly why you are job-hunting, because I think I have a right to know.'

Shock flooded through her. 'What makes you think I'm job-hunting?'

'Well, catching you looking through the situations-vacant column yesterday was a bit of a give-away,' he grated derisively.

She bit down on her lip, she'd only had a five-minute scan through the pages in her lunch break and he'd chosen that very moment to appear behind her with some papers he wanted her to file. She'd hoped he hadn't noticed, but she should have known better. Marco missed very little. 'I was just browsing,' she said defensively.

Marco was momentarily distracted by the fact that in her agitation she had allowed her towel to slip an inch, treating him to a provocative glimpse of her shapely curves. How was it that she could even look sexy in a bath towel? he wondered.

'So I take it you haven't found another job, then?' He forced himself to concentrate on the conversation.

'If I had, you would be the first to know.'

He raked a hand through the darkness of his hair. 'We really need to discuss this situation, Charlie.' His voice was reasoned. 'Go and get dressed and I'll take you to lunch.'

'No I will not!' She felt a flare of anger. 'You've no right to come barging around here on a Saturday, ordering me about.'

'You're right.' He held up his hands and his voice was gentle. 'But we need to sort this out, Charlie…and we haven't had a minute all week. I just feel that if we don't talk now you are going to walk away and I'm going to lose you.'

The words made her senses thunder unsteadily. Of course, he was only bothered about losing her in the office, she reminded herself fiercely and she hated herself for allowing that to hurt. 'Well, I wouldn't worry about it,' she retorted flippantly, 'because if I did leave you would no doubt find someone suitable to replace me very quickly.'

'But I don't want someone else.'

The quiet words wrenched at her emotions. So she was good at her job…but she wanted so much for him to need her on more than a business level. She looked away from him hurriedly as he suddenly swam in a mist before her eyes. Furious with herself, she blinked the tears back. She was being irrational.

Marco always thought in practical terms. That was part of who he was.

'Let me take you to lunch,' Marco said softly.

With determination she pulled herself together and looked back at him. 'I can't and anyway, I've no one to look after Jack.'

'That's OK—Jack is invited too.'

Charlie's eyes narrowed on him.

'There's a place down the road that is child-friendly apparently.'

'And why would you want to go somewhere like that?'

He looked at her with a serious light in his dark eyes. 'Because I think you'd like it.'

'Marco, I haven't found another job so there's really no need for you to take me out to lunch or be nice to my son. The crisis is averted…you still have your PA. And I really don't want to play games like that with you.'

'I think the time for games is over,' he cut across her firmly. 'And that's what I want to talk to you about.'

She frowned. What was he up to? she wondered.

'Just give me a few hours of your time, OK?' To her dismay he started to advance slowly up the stairs towards her.

She felt completely at a disadvantage and her heart was thundering at the purposeful glint in his eye.

Although he stopped on the stair beneath her, he was still a good head taller. 'By the way, your towel is slipping.' He reached and pulled it up a little for her.

She refused to blush. She didn't want to let him know how the touch of his hand made her long to go into his arms, and ache with a need that tore her in two.

Instead she held his gaze with determined green eyes, trying to ignore the prickles of awareness that were shooting through her. 'I don't think anything can be gained by us going out for lunch, Marco.'

'You know I think a lot of you, Charlie,' he said lightly. 'But on the negative side you do have a dreadful stubborn streak that can be very irritating.'

'You only think I'm stubborn because you can't twist me around your little finger.'

'And that's the other thing I like about you.' His fingers traced slowly over the side of her face. His eyes seemed to be on her lips. 'That no-nonsense attitude is very refreshing. You have the most incredibly lively mind.'

She stepped back from him. She didn't want to hear about how he admired her lively mind whilst he was caressing her like that—not when his touch was opening up a need inside her as wide as the Atlantic Ocean. 'Why don't you just say what it is you want to say, Marco? And then you can go.'

'Why would I do that and mess up a perfectly good opportunity for us to have lunch together…hmm?' He smiled. 'Plus I'm sure Jack would enjoy a trip out.'

'No he wouldn't…'

'Would we go in your car?' Jack's little voice from downstairs made them both look around in surprise. Charlie had thought he had gone back to playing with his toys once he had let Marco in.

He was standing quietly, watching them with avid interest.

'Yes, we'll go in my car, Jack.' Marco walked back downstairs and crouched down to speak to him. 'Would you like that?'

'That would be cool!' The little boy's eyes were alive with excitement now. 'Can we go, Mum? It would be great.'

Marco turned and looked at Charlie with a mocking gleam in his dark eyes.

Charlie tried not to be swayed by the fact that both of them were watching her closely.

'Please, Mum…please,' Jack said again.

Her eyes went from her son towards Marco.

'You know what they call this, don't you?' she told him wryly.

'No, what?' He straightened up.

'Emotional blackmail.'

'I'll take that as a yes, then,' he murmured with a smile.

It took Charlie ten minutes to dry her hair and throw jeans and a T-shirt on. She'd made no effort to try and look glamorous, and instead just tied back her hair and applied some lip-gloss.

Now she was sitting in the front seat of Marco's car, listening as her son chatted happily with him. Jack was asking about the car and Marco was giving him all the facts about it as if he were an adult. Charlie tried to relax back in the comfortable leather seat. She probably shouldn't have agreed to this but it did feel good being out with him again.

She watched the competent way he handled the powerful sports car through the country lanes. And for a moment her mind flicked back to that day in Italy when they had driven out towards Sienna and he had stopped the car and kissed her. Her eyes moved over his profile, remembering the tenderness and the steamy passion, and her heart missed a violent beat.

He looked over at her and caught her watching him and instantly she looked away. She shouldn't be thinking about things like that, she told herself furiously, because it didn't help and it didn't change anything. Marco's only concern was his work. He needed her around at the moment both in a PA capacity and a PR one, and he thought he could sweet-talk her into shelving any plans of leaving.

They turned through some high gateposts with the name Fogle Farm over them and pulled up outside an old country manor house.

'I think you'll like it here, Jack,' Marco said nonchalantly. 'They have a playground in the back and a pets' corner.'

Charlie glanced over at him as they stepped out of the car. 'So how did you find this place?'

'The internet recommends it as a place to bring children.'

Marco had obviously done some homework on this outing! 'You were very confident we were going to come out with you.'

'Quietly confident,' he corrected with a grin.

'Not really your kind of place, though, is it?' she couldn't resist adding as they walked around the side of the building and the sound of children shouting and laughing grew louder.

'Why do you say that?'

'Come on, Marco! Listen to it. It's not your sophisticated bachelor scene, is it?'

'You can get bored with sophisticated bachelor-type places.'

'Really?' She looked over at him sceptically.

'Yes, really.' There was a humorous spark in his dark eyes as they met hers. 'It's good to have variation in life.'

Marco took hold of Jack's hand as the child jumped up to walk along the edge of a low wall. 'We are going to have fun, aren't we, Jack?'

Jack nodded happily and Charlie noticed how he kept hold of Marco's hand as they followed the path around the house.

There was a huge play area around the back where a multitude of children were enjoying themselves, and before long Jack was dashing about, joining in the fun.

Although the sun was shining it was bitterly cold. Charlie huddled further into her jacket.

'You OK?' Marco came to stand back beside her.

'Yes.' She waved at Jack, who was on a merry-go-round now. 'Jack is having a lovely time.'

'I told you he'd enjoy it.'

'Hmm.' Charlie looked up at him wryly. 'The paparazzi aren't going to pounce out from behind a hedge at any moment, are they?'

The note of humour in her voice didn't fool Marco; he knew she was still bothered by Sarah's meddling. 'Is that why you are looking for a new job?'

'I was just idly glancing through the paper.'

'I don't believe that.'

'Well, as I said, you don't need to worry; I'm not going anywhere…not for a while anyway.' She shivered suddenly.

'You're cold!' Before she could stop him Marco had taken hold of her hands. He held them in the warmth of his for a moment and the touch of his skin against hers was electric. She swallowed hard as she looked up into his eyes. She wished with all her heart that she could switch off the intensity of her feelings for him, because it was so foolish…and it hurt so much.

'Why don't you go and sit inside?' He let her go and nodded towards the conservatory. 'There's a fire in there and you can watch Jack from the warmth. I'll stay out here to make sure he's OK.'

Charlie hesitated and then nodded. 'All right, thanks.'

Marco turned to watch Jack as he played. But his mind was still on Charlie.

When she had told him she wanted to keep their relationship on a strictly business footing he'd decided he would give her some space and then talk her around when they got to New York. It had been a shock to find her looking through the jobs column in the paper yesterday. He'd wanted to confront her immediately but had stopped himself.

Then he'd spent all last night mulling over it.

He couldn't let her go, and he didn't like that feeling. A long time ago he had prided himself on never making the same mistakes as his father.

But of course his need for Charlie was more pragmatic than illogical, he reassured himself firmly. Yes, he wanted her body…but she linked in with work…linked into all the ideas he had espoused in his book.

Jack ran over towards him. His coat had come unbuttoned and he was flushed with excitement. 'Can we go and see the animals now?'

'Yes, but I think you should do up that coat first.' Marco crouched down beside the child and fastened the buttons. 'That's better.'

To his surprise the child put his arms around his neck and gave him a quick hug. 'Thanks, Marco,' he said matter-of-factly before running off again.

As Marco watched him go he was suddenly reminded of days spent with his nieces and nephews. He'd thought of himself as a family man at heart once and had used to think that he wanted his own children one day, but somehow over the years other things had intervened and he'd lost sight of that part of himself.

Charlie was sitting in a booth by the warmth of the fire when Marco arrived back carrying Jack high on his shoulders. They were laughing, and both of them were glowing from the cold air outside.

She felt a jolt of surprise as she looked up at them. Marco seemed to be getting on very well with her son! But then anyone could get on with a child for a short space of time she assured herself as she watched him put Jack down. It didn't mean anything special.

'Mum, I saw some black potbelly pigs.'

'Did you, darling? That's wonderful. What else did you do?'

'Marco pushed me really high on the swings.'

'Did he? That's great.' Charlie reached to help Jack take his coat off.

She noticed that Marco only had to glance in the waitress's direction and she came over to take their order. What was it about him that had everyone instantly running to please him? she wondered. It irritated her, and it irritated her even more that she felt warm inside as she met his eyes.

Why couldn't she shut out these feelings for him? she wondered frantically.

'Mum, can I go over there?' Jack pointed towards the next room, where other children were in an indoor play area.

Charlie hesitated. 'OK, but you've got to come back as soon as your lunch arrives.'

'He's a great kid,' Marco said with a smile as he watched him run off. 'His dad is missing out, not seeing him.'

The words prickled through Charlie's emotions. 'What are you playing at, Marco?' she asked quietly. 'I know you don't want to lose me as your PA but taking me out and pretending to have an interest in Jack—'

'I'm not pretending anything!' He met her eyes steadily. 'I meant every word.'

He sounded so sincere that he made her feel almost guilty for daring to say such a thing. Then he smiled at her across the table and she felt her defences start to melt away.

Hurriedly she glanced away from him and tried to compose herself. Marco was a charmer with an eye to the main chance, she reminded herself.

'I've been thinking about what you said when you ended things between us the other day,' he said suddenly.

She glanced back at him with a frown.

'About how you have to consider the effect a casual relationship could have on Jack,' he continued smoothly. 'And how you have to give him stability. I admire you for that. It must be hard bearing all the responsibility for bringing up a child single-handedly.'

'I manage very well.' She met his gaze steadily. 'Why are you trying to charm me?'

'Do you have to be so suspicious? Look, before you say anything more, just hear me out. Of course I don't want to lose you as my PA but this goes deeper.' His voice lowered and was suddenly very emphatic. 'The thing is, I've realised since coming back from Italy that I don't want to lose you *at all*. I like having you in my life.'

Charlie felt her heart starting to thump painfully against her chest. She had wanted desperately to hear him say something like this but now that it was actually happening she couldn't quite believe it.

He noticed the guarded light in her green eyes.

'I know you've been through a painful divorce and you are cautious about relationships. And I can understand where you are coming from. As you know, I'm wary myself.'

'I had noticed,' she said lightly and he smiled.

'And that's one of the reasons I think we are good together. Neither of us are taken in by glib, meaningless words. We are both very down-to-earth with our expectations and are on a certain wavelength.'

Charlie felt herself starting to tense up; any minute now he was going to tell her he felt *comfortable* around her! 'I don't know if we are *that* similar, Marco…' she murmured uneasily.

'Of course we are. Didn't you tell me once when you were internet-dating that you were looking to meet someone who would fulfil a certain criteria as a good partner?'

'Companionship.' Charlie said the word numbly. 'I think

that was the word I used.' She remembered the conversation clearly and recalled her lie with excruciating intensity.

'You were very realistic.' Marco nodded. 'And the more I think about it the more I realise what a good team you and I would make.'

'A good team?' Her voice didn't sound as if it belonged to her. She felt slightly dazed by all of this. 'What exactly do you mean by that?'

He looked over at her with a serious expression in his dark eyes. 'I mean that instead of ending our relationship we should allow it to develop into something more serious. I am talking about a partnership.' He leaned a little closer across the table. 'I want you to move in with me, Charlie.'

Charlie stared at him in shock. Silence stretched in a long, tense moment. She wasn't aware that her hands were clenched and her nails were cutting into her skin until Marco reached across to take both hands in his. He smoothed out her fingers and held them gently.

'So what do you say?' he asked softly.

Charlie pulled away from him abruptly. She couldn't allow herself to be swayed by the feelings that his touch generated and she couldn't afford to ignore the facts. Marco had asked her to move in with him and that was exciting and wonderful and her heart had leapt for a moment when he said the words. But there was one little word missing from the equation. And that was love.

But of course he hadn't mentioned that word because he wasn't in love with her, she reminded herself drily. You only had to listen to his reasoning to know that to him the emotion was of little importance, and much more vital was the fact that he thought they were suited in practical terms, that they would make *a good team*.

'I realise I've sprung this on you and it is a big step…but I'm confident that it will work,' Marco continued when she said nothing.

How could it work when love would never be of secondary importance to her? The knowledge swept through her painfully.

'Well, I'm sorry, Marco, but I'm not.' She swallowed hard on a knot that was forming in her throat. 'The answer has to be no.'

He looked rattled for a moment. 'Charlie, think about it! You and I get on brilliantly. For a start we work well together and that says a lot for a relationship's chances—'

'You are starting to sound like your book.' She cut across him derisively. She didn't want to hear all the calm, practical reasons why they would be good together—he was asking her to move in with him, for heaven's sake! At the very least she wanted *some* sentiment, although the fact that she was being totally unrealistic even thinking like that made her all the more angry with herself and him. 'Next you will be telling me not to allow emotion to influence my decision,' she muttered.

'Not a bad piece of advice,' he said calmly. 'You should always allow facts to influence decisions…nothing else.'

'And what about the fact that this could be another one of your damn publicity stunts?' she flared.

'Is that why you are saying no?' He relaxed suddenly and his expression softened. 'Hell, Charlie…I admit you are a tremendous plus point when it comes to handling questions from the media but asking you to move in is no mere stunt. I wouldn't do that!'

The gentleness of his tone made her reactions swing wildly from angry to tearful. She forced herself not to give in to that weakness, and instead to remember how he had discussed her in cool, clinical terms with Sarah Heart. 'Wouldn't you?' She raised her chin a little higher. 'I'm not so sure.'

'Well, I assure you that is not the case,' he said firmly. 'I am who I am, Charlie. And if I sound like my book it's because I believe in the theories. And I'm asking you to move in because I think that you and I will work.'

'So I'm a kind of test case now?' she observed mockingly. 'How romantic!' She couldn't help the sudden emotional outburst.

'Charlie!' He frowned. 'You are being ridiculous now! The fact is that we get on. We enjoyed Italy, didn't we? It was steamy and passionate. We are sexually compatible.' The huskily compelling tone of his voice made her senses blur. 'There is no doubt about that.'

He was right, there was no doubt about that. But to him it was just sex and to her it meant a hell of a lot more.

'Why don't we just give things a try?' he continued smoothly. 'Move in with me and we'll test the waters. What's the worst that can happen?'

She took a deep breath and sat back. The worst that could happen was that she would get her fragile heart well and truly smashed to pieces. And she knew what that was like all too well.

'I can't, Marco.' The reminder served to make her voice calm and steady now. 'I have my son to consider. I can't just move in and casually test things out with you. My responsibilities won't allow for that—'

'I think you are hiding behind your responsibilities.'

'I'm not hiding behind anything,' she said firmly. 'And may I remind you that a few moments ago you were admiring me for taking my responsibilities so seriously?'

'I do admire you for that, but right at this moment you are hiding behind them.'

The obdurate certainty in his tone annoyed her. 'Have you stopped to consider for one moment what it would be like having a four-year-old around? You are a confirmed bachelor, for heaven's sake!'

'Of course I've considered it! You and Jack are a package deal and that is not a problem because I like Jack.'

'You don't even know Jack!'

'I know that he is a lovely little boy who could benefit from having a father figure around.'

'Don't you dare bring that into the equation!' She glared at him and felt tears suddenly prickling behind her eyelashes. Angrily she blinked them away.

'It's true though, isn't it?' He held her gaze steadily. 'You told me that yourself.'

'I meant it would be nice to have someone who will be around for him. Not someone who has decided he wants to play at fatherhood on a whim.'

'This isn't a whim, Charlie. I would have thought you knew me better than that. I would like to be there for you and Jack. I'm offering you a stable, secure environment for your child. All I ask in return is that you are there for me—'

'That I share your bed, you mean.'

'But of course.' He smiled and his eyes held hers with bold emphasis. 'I'll want you on a regular basis. That goes without saying.'

She tried to ignore the sudden flare of heat inside her at those teasingly provocative words and cut across him coolly. 'So that you can prove your theory that love is unnecessary for a successful relationship.'

'So that I can prove that I'm right and we are compatible for a long-term partnership,' he corrected her with a frown.

The door opened behind them and a blast of cold air rushed into the conservatory as a crowd of people came in.

Charlie was glad of the distraction and the opportunity to compose herself. She watched the fire flicker dangerously low as the draught caught it and then flame into roaring life again as the door closed. A bit like her emotions, she thought sardonically.

'It's getting busy in here,' Marco reflected. 'Hardly the best place for this conversation.' He looked back at her, taking in the pallor of her skin and the steel-like determination as she raised her chin and met his gaze.

He hadn't meant to talk to her about all this in here; he'd been going to wait until later. And he now had a feeling he had pressed her too hard. If he wasn't careful she might rebel and go in the opposite direction. He needed to take a more softly-softly approach or he was going to lose her.

'Just give the idea some thought…OK?' he asked calmly. 'We can discuss it more when we get back to your place.'

'Actually I've got my friend Karen coming round,' Charlie said dismissively, 'so that won't be possible.'

He looked at her with a raised eyebrow. 'But you will give it some thought?'

For a few heartbeats she didn't answer. She *couldn't* answer, because she knew the correct response should still have been no.

How could she move in with Marco and share his bed—share his life—knowing that the whole relationship was based on the premise of a lie…*her lie*. Not only that, but she'd always have the knowledge that he didn't love her…maybe would never love her.

Could she really live with that?

CHAPTER ELEVEN

'Is Charlie going to go to America with you next week?' Sarah Heart asked, popping the question casually into the conversation as Marco stood up to leave her office.

'I don't know yet.' Marco's reply was terse. He glanced across at Sarah and could see she was dying to ask further questions but didn't dare. Probably because he had told her in no uncertain terms that he didn't like the way she had spoken to Charlie on the phone in Italy. And it was now a raw subject.

'Time is moving on, Marco,' she said instead, her tone cautious.

'Yes, I'm well aware of that.' Marco picked up his briefcase from her desk. It was just over a week since he had asked Charlie to move in with him and she still hadn't given him her answer.

'You've got two tickets for the literary dinner at the Plaza Pendinia in New York. Do you think she will join you there?'

'I've told you, I don't know. Just leave the subject alone, Sarah.'

She shrugged and looked momentarily annoyed. 'I'm just trying to do my job. But…you know your own business, I suppose.'

He met her gaze firmly. Sarah was seriously starting to irritate him. He'd been tempted to fire her after the debacle of the way she had spoken to Charlie in Italy. Only the fact that his tour in America was imminent and the timing was wrong had held him back. 'Yes, I do. And don't forget that!' There was an underlying steel-like warning in the words. 'You work for me, not the other way around, Sarah.'

'Yes, of course!' Sarah backed down immediately. 'Don't let's fall out. You know I only have your best interests at heart!'

'Just don't overstep the line, OK?' he said heavily.

'Scouts' honour!' she said with a gleam of mischief in her eyes.

He smiled. 'You are impossible.'

'I know!' She batted long, dark eyelashes and looked at him coyly. 'Look, I have a few meetings set up in NY for next week and I'll probably attend the dinner at the Plaza myself. So if you want I can accompany you that evening. I don't mind playing the part of your lover for a while. I can create some great spin out of it for you.'

'Thanks for the offer, Sarah!' Marco laughed. 'But I don't think it's such a good idea.'

'I don't see why. I think we'd be quite believable as a couple. You can use me in your interviews…' She lowered her voice huskily. 'In fact, you can use me any way you want,' she added playfully.

'You are my agent, Sarah. Let's keep it that way.' Marco shook his head and turned away towards the door. 'Besides my name is already linked with Charlie.'

'That's in the European papers—'

'Sarah, I've said no.'

'You are losing your sense of humour these days,' she muttered in annoyance and then hurried after him as he walked towards the lift.

She was probably right, Marco acknowledged drily. He knew he was on a short fuse. It was all this waiting around for an answer from Charlie. He was trying to take things slowly but he wasn't a patient man at the best of times. He'd tried a little old-fashioned courtship, by sending her flowers, and he'd behaved like a total gentleman…but it was getting him precisely nowhere. The only plus point was that he was getting to know and like Jack a lot. Which was just as well because every time he called at Charlie's house he had ended up spending more time with him than he had alone with her.

He wasn't used to being fobbed off where a woman was concerned. The suspense was killing him; and yet at the same time he was firmly convinced that she was worth waiting for. He wondered suddenly if she had been deliberately testing him to see how he got on with her son…?

'Marco?'

As they stepped out of the lift he realised Sarah was speaking about an interview in LA that she was still setting up.

'Sorry. I've got things on my mind at the moment, Sarah,' he told her distractedly. 'I'll phone you to get the last-minute details. I'm flying to Edinburgh for a conference later tonight. I'll be there for five days.'

Sarah frowned. 'Yes, I'd forgotten.'

Marco turned to look at her. 'I know this tour in the States is important, Sarah. But the most important thing to me is my work.'

'I know that, Marco.'

'Good; well, just keep that in mind when you are handling the PR, OK?'

'Don't worry.' She smiled and then stood on tiptoe to kiss him on the cheek. 'I'm here to assist you in any way I can.'

'That's good to know,' he said wryly as he turned away.

'And don't forget my offer to be the ideal prototype partner in the US is always open.'

'I'm hoping the position is already filled.' He looked back at her. 'And on the subject of Charlie, try to use some discretion.'

As he stepped out onto the street Marco hailed a taxi and climbed in. He was glad Sarah had no inkling that he had asked Charlie to move in with him. If she had she would be working out a spin on it for the papers already.

He supposed that was what made her so good at her job. But he didn't like it. He just hoped he hadn't made a mistake in not firing her.

The traffic going out of London was gridlocked. Marco glanced at his watch. Charlie would have shut the office and gone home if this didn't clear soon. Damn! He had been hoping he would catch her before she left. He intended to get an answer from her before he set off for Edinburgh. The time for playing this softly-softly game with her was over.

Flicking open his phone, he dialled the office number. She answered after the first ring.

'Dr Delmari's office.'

Her breezy, efficient tone made him smile. 'Hi, it's me,' he said, settling back against the seat. 'How are things with you?'

He listened as she started to give him a run-down on the office. He'd hardly been in today but by the sounds of things she had kept everything running smoothly.

'How did your meetings go?' she asked when she had run out of the day's events.

'Fine. All finished. I'm caught up in traffic. I'll be at least another hour.'

'OK; well, don't worry—I'll lock up here—'

'No, you are going to have to wait for me,' he cut across her firmly. 'We have things to sort out before I go to Edinburgh.'

'Can it wait?'

Her brisk tone had gone now and he could hear the caution creeping in.

'No, Charlie, it can't.' He hung up.

Charlie went down to Marco's kitchen and switched the kettle on. There wasn't much else to do. She had finished all the filing and had even made a start on tomorrow's jobs.

As she waited she glanced around at the kitchen with new eyes. Although she had been in here a hundred times before, she had never paid much attention to her surroundings other than to admire the expensive fittings, the pale ash cupboards and the black granite worktops. Now she was looking at it all with new eyes.

She was trying to picture herself and Jack here and it was surprisingly easy. If she said yes to Marco they would sit as a family at the kitchen table, laughing and talking… She could even see Marco and Jack playing football in the garden and racing the remote-control cars out on the patio. There was no doubt that the two liked each other. She had watched them together over these last couple of weeks and there was an easy rapport between them that couldn't be faked.

In fact, Marco's patience with Jack had completely surprised her. For an inveterate bachelor he was remarkably good with children.

Not that that should make any difference to her answer. It was a definite plus that Jack and Marco got on but she couldn't say yes just because of that.

But there were other positive points in favour of saying yes, a little voice reminded her unequivocally. For a start there was the fact that she wanted to go back into Marco's arms. Every night she lay in bed and she ached for him.

She had felt lonely after Greg had left her—in fact, she had thought she was heartbroken, but it was nothing to the gaping great chasm she had inside her now.

It didn't matter how many times she told herself that she should have more self-respect than to love a man who didn't return the feelings. She still wanted him, and she still loved him.

And that was why her answer had to be no, she reminded herself fiercely as she spooned some coffee into a pot. She couldn't live a lie, pretending to be emotionally detached, pretending she didn't care that Marco saw her in terms of practicalities rather than love. She should never have weakened and said she'd think about it. Because when she did get the strength to say no again he'd probably think she had been stringing him along. But she hadn't, she just couldn't bring herself to say the word and make the sensible choice.

She could tell recently that he was becoming impatient. And by the tone of his voice on the phone just now it sounded as if they had reached crunch point. She could have tried to stall him by telling him she had to get home for Jack, but the truth was that Jack was sleeping over at Karen's house tonight, as it was her son's birthday party. And anyway she couldn't in all conscience put this off any longer.

The sound of the front door opening jarred on her senses like a starter gun. This was it; there was no more room for prevarication. Sorry, Marco…she practised the words in her head. The answer is still no…

'I'm in the kitchen, Marco,' she called out as she heard him cross the hall. She heard his footsteps change direction and stop in the doorway. She could feel his eyes on her back.

'I'd finished everything upstairs so I thought I'd make a drink. Would you like one?' So much for not prevaricating, she thought deprecatingly.

'No, thanks.' His voice was brusque.

She didn't look around, and just continued to pour the boiling water over the coffee grains. The rich aroma suddenly reminded her of mornings in Italy and the heat of their passion. *Don't think about that,* she warned herself sternly.

He walked towards her and then reached across to put an envelope down on the counter beside her.

'What's that?' she asked warily.

'Air tickets: I booked you a flight from Heathrow to JFK on the 20th of the month.'

She looked down at the envelope and made no attempt to pick it up or to move.

'I want you there in your capacity as my PA. But I also want you there as my partner.'

He put a hand on her shoulder and turned her firmly to face him. And suddenly she was very close to him...too close, in fact. His body was just a whisper from hers.

She looked up at him and wanted to drown in the darkness of his eyes.

'I've waited long enough for your answer. I need to know now.' He reached and touched her face. The whisper-soft caress made her senses soar. 'Will you move in with me?'

'I think it's too big a step...too great a risk.' She tried to focus on the practicalities of the situation, just as he had advised. 'I've worked very hard to be independent and if I sell my house and things go wrong with you—'

'Don't sell it.' He cut across her decisively. 'Hold on to it and rent it out.'

'So if it doesn't work out between us I just move back in as if nothing has happened?' Her voice held an edge of derision.

'It's just a security net.' Marco shrugged. 'I'm confident you won't need it. Things will work out,' he said calmly.

'I don't know how you can be so sure. You lived with someone once before...and that didn't work out did it—'

'That was different,' he said dismissively.

'How was it different?' She looked up at him and willed him to give her one shred of evidence that he might learn to love her the way she loved him. All this businesslike discussion when he was so close was just tearing her apart. She longed for some emotion...some wild declaration of feelings.

'Some relationships aren't meant to progress beyond an affair. But you and I have something real...something solid to build on.' His eyes moved over her countenance searchingly.

It should have been enough but it wasn't. She took a deep, shuddering breath. 'Marco—'

'I want you, Charlie...' he murmured huskily.

Her heart bounced unsteadily against her chest at the sudden words.

God, she wanted him too. Did it really matter that he was talking in practicalities to her? Greg had given her all the words of love in the world and they hadn't meant a thing in the end.

Tears prickled behind her eyes.

'OK, I'll join you in the States but—' She had been going to say that they could talk after that about moving in together.

His lips on hers abruptly silenced the words. At first the kiss was gently searching, and then suddenly it became hungrily possessive, plundering her softness with brutal, forceful intensity.

'No more prevarication, Charlie…you'll join me in the States on my terms and then on my return you will join me here in this house and in my bed.'

His mood was dangerously forceful, but the really frightening part was that she started to yield to him instantly.

'Maybe…we could give things a try…' Her arms wound up and around his neck.

'That's better…' There was a smug satisfaction in his tone at her acquiescence. 'I don't know how I've waited this long for you…' He murmured the words huskily against her lips. 'You've been playing a very dangerous game with me, Charlie…'

'I don't play games.' She felt almost delirious with need as he trailed fiercely heated kisses down her neck. 'I've made one mistake in my life and I'm just scared of making another.'

He pulled away from her a little and looked into her eyes. 'I know you've been badly hurt in the past. And perhaps deep down you believe that you are still a little in love with your ex.' He put a finger on her lips, silencing her protests. 'It doesn't matter…your ex-husband is in the past, Charlie, and I know you are sensible enough to realise those feelings aren't reliable. What we have is real…it's sensible and it will work.'

The word *sensible* might have jarred on her except for the

way he was looking at her and the tone of his voice. She was
aware that his hands were high around her waist and that his
thumbs were stroking the edge of her bra.

'Now…' his hands moved and he swiftly started to unfasten
the buttons on her blouse '…I've got four hours to kill before
heading to the airport. Let's seal the deal and go to bed.'

'You are totally outrageous, Marco…' She trailed off as he
leaned forward and kissed her with a slow, seductive passion
that rocked her world completely.

'Outrageously hungry for you…' He growled the words
close to her ear.

The jacket of her suit fell to the floor and then her skirt
was being unzipped before it joined her jacket. Her bra was
quickly removed as she felt his hot lips move down towards
her soft curves.

Charlie raked her fingers through the darkness of his hair.
She was beyond any reasonable, sensible thoughts now. All she
could do was give in wholeheartedly to the feelings of desire
that were suddenly raging out of control inside her.

Sex with Marco was incredibly enjoyable and satisfying but
also completely exhausting, Charlie thought with a smile as she
lay in his arms.

She remembered how things had got completely out of
control between them in the kitchen. He had ripped her clothes
off whilst kissing her and touching her with an expertise in seduction that blew her mind. The very memory made her blush.
She had pictured many things in that kitchen but she hadn't
pictured herself naked, with Marco taking pleasure in her
against the counter-tops!

It had been crazy and wild and wonderful and then he had
brought her upstairs to his bedroom and had taken her all over
again. She was still breathless and still gathering her senses.

'I'm going to have to go. I haven't packed and I've got to

be at the airport in an hour.' He gave her a swift kiss on the forehead before pulling away from her.

She watched as he walked over towards his wardrobes and opened them. He was completely unselfconscious about his nakedness, she noticed. Although it was no wonder really because he had an incredibly perfect body. It made her marvel all over again that Marco wanted her. *He really wanted her.* It didn't matter to him that her body wasn't perfect or that she wasn't a model-like beauty. He liked her the way she was.

The knowledge made her glow inside or maybe that was just the after-effects of some very stimulating lovemaking, she thought with a smile.

Marco took out a suit and hung it on the side of the door. Then he went into the *en suite* bathroom.

Charlie took the opportunity to get out of bed and retrieve her clothes that were scattered on the floor. She had just put on her underwear when he appeared back in the room, a towel wrapped around his waist.

She felt shy suddenly as his eyes swept over her figure, which was absurd, given the circumstances.

'Do you have to go and pick up Jack?' he asked casually.

'No, he's at my friend's house for the night.' She reached for her blouse and quickly put it on.

'So we could have had the night together if I wasn't rushing off?'

She nodded.

'That's unfortunate.' He shook his head. 'This conference couldn't have come at a worse time.'

'Never mind, we will see each other when you get back.'

'Unfortunately I'll be on a tight schedule when I get back. I have a meeting with Dr Sinclair at the hospital to hand over my list of patients for the two months I'm away. And after that I've got to catch a midnight flight to LA.'

Charlie felt a flicker of disappointment, as she hadn't

realised he was leaving for the States so soon. 'I thought you were leaving a few days after you got back from Edinburgh?'

'Sarah has changed the schedule to fit in an extra interview on the Ed Johnson show.'

'That's a very popular programme.' Charlie reached for her skirt and stepped into it.

'Yes, prime-time stuff, so a great start to the tour. Sarah can be irritating but she knows what she's doing.'

Charlie didn't even want to think about Sarah, never mind talk about her.

'But it means I'm going to need you to reschedule a lot of my appointments for the extra days I'm away,' Marco continued lightly.

'Don't worry, I'll sort things out.' She looked away from him. All this talk of business straight after their lovemaking was disconcerting. 'We'll catch up when I join you in New York,' she added softly.

'I'm so glad I asked you to move in with me.' He smiled. 'Because you and I are going to get along just fine, Charlie…do you know that?'

'I hope so.' There it was again…that practical tone in his voice that flayed at her emotions. She tried not to think about it too deeply and instead started to tidy her hair, brushing it back from her face with her fingers.

'I know so…' he walked back towards her '…because you are just what I need. Reliable, uncomplicated and perfect in every way.'

That sounded like an endorsement for the perfect PA, not a live-in lover.

For a moment she couldn't bear to look up at him because the ache inside her was suddenly heavy and deep. She loved him so much and longed for him to return her feelings.

The need was so intense that it flayed her and that in turn made her angry.

What did she expect? she asked herself furiously. This was Marco. He was a warm and passionate lover but not one for flowery sentiment. Practicalities came first; she would have to accept that if she wanted to make their relationship work.

He put a hand under her chin and tipped her face upwards, his eyes moving searchingly over her countenance.

She tried to veil her feelings and look at him with self-assurance. He smiled as he noted the proud way she held his gaze. Then he bent and kissed her softly on the lips, making the ache intensify, tinged with sweet, searing desire.

She was very glad that he didn't look into her eyes again as he pulled away…because she was sure he would have seen a glimpse of her pain and that would have been too much to bear.

He turned to open a bedside drawer. 'I've got a spare front-door key in here somewhere…ah, yes, here it is. You may as well start moving some of your belongings in whilst I'm away.'

Marco held the key out towards her.

She didn't take it immediately. 'What about work?' she asked uncertainly.

'What about it?' He looked at her wryly. 'I was hoping we'd continue as we are…for now anyway. But don't worry I'll be a very flexible boss,' he added teasingly.

When she still didn't take the key he reached out for her hand and pressed it into her palm. 'Now…that's enough talk about work. We can sort details like that out at any time.'

'Yes…I suppose we can.' Her hand closed over the key. She was going to do this. Because she wanted Marco…wanted him with all her heart. And maybe one day he would return her feelings. Maybe he just needed to learn how to trust her, and if she was patient everything would come right…

He smiled. 'So how about going back to bed?'

The sudden huskily sexual request took her by surprise. 'What about your flight?'

'I'll take a later one.' He leaned closer and kissed her and it was so incredibly possessive that she instantly melted against him. 'We've got some more catching up to do before I go anywhere,' he growled.

CHAPTER TWELVE

THE stretched limousine turned on to Fifth Avenue and Charlie looked out at the familiar names…the Rockefeller Centre, Saks, Tiffany's, Cartier. She felt as if she had been beamed down into a film set and that this wasn't real somehow.

The lights of the city glittered diamond-bright against the velvet darkness of the night and the whole place seemed to pulsate with life and energy.

Excitement curled inside her. She was finally here in New York and Marco was waiting for her at the hotel.

He hadn't been able to meet her at the airport because of a book-signing session, and although she had told him she would take a cab into the city he had insisted on sending a limo for her.

Charlie couldn't wait to see him. It was two long weeks since he had left London and she hadn't thought it was possible to miss someone this much. Just the sound of his voice on the phone had made her throb inside. She longed to be held in his arms.

The limousine pulled to a halt in front of an impressive hotel. A doorman hurried down the red-carpeted steps and opened her door.

She stepped out onto the street and was immediately engulfed by noise. The sound of the traffic and the urgent blare of a siren seemed to reverberate between the tall buildings.

By contrast the inside of the hotel was tranquil, with a pianist in the centre of the lobby playing classical music on a gold baby-grand piano. Fresh flowers perfumed the air and the blue and gold décor was elegantly sophisticated.

She walked across the thickly carpeted foyer towards the reception area.

'Ah, Ms Hopkirk, Dr Delmari has left a message for you.' The receptionist handed her an envelope from one of the pigeonholes as she signed the register. 'You are in suite 200 on the top floor. I'll arrange for someone to bring your luggage up. Have a pleasant stay.' He slid a key card across to her.

Charlie opened the envelope as she walked towards the lifts. Inside there was a short note in Marco's flowing handwriting.

Hi Darling,

I'm going to be longer than I thought. It's a damn nuisance but it can't be helped. Don't forget we are to attend the literary dinner at the Plaza Pendinia tonight and we have to be there by eight. Hope you feel up to it after your long flight.

Looking forward to seeing you,

Marco

Charlie felt a dart of disappointment. She knew that they would only have a few short hours alone together before having to go to this dinner and she had hoped to spend every spare minute in his arms. It looked as though that wasn't going to happen. She crumpled the note and tossed it into a waste bin. It couldn't be helped, she told herself firmly, and at least it would give her a chance to freshen up and make herself more presentable before seeing him.

The lift doors opened on the top floor and she walked down towards the suite. It was spectacularly elegant inside. There was a lounge area and then the biggest double bed Charlie had ever seen in her life. There was also a magnificent bouquet of flowers for her on the table, and next to it Marco had scribbled on a gift tag, *I've missed you.*

Charlie smiled. Marco may not believe in romance but he was very thoughtful. She just wished he had put the word *love* somewhere on the card. Though as soon as the thought crossed her mind she dismissed it. She had told herself she wasn't going to dwell on things like that. It was enough that Marco wanted her, and maybe one day his feelings would deepen.

He had certainly phoned her enough times during the fortnight he'd been away. And, although a lot of the conversation had centred on business-related issues, a fair amount had also centred on the fact that she was going to move into his house. It had been exciting talking about it; Marco had given her free rein to arrange things and had told her to choose whatever room she wanted for Jack. She hadn't moved any of her belongings in yet, though, it hadn't seemed right with him not being there. But at least he had made it clear that he wanted her to treat his house as home, and just wanted her to be happy.

That solicitous, caring manner was enough for now, she assured herself. Plus there was the fact that, sexually-speaking, their relationship was so hot it was on fire. She wished he would hurry and get back from this damn book-signing…

The porter arrived with her luggage and she tipped him and then unpacked. She had bought a new dress for tonight and she hung it up in the *en suite* bathroom so that the steam from her shower would get rid of any creases.

Then she stripped off and turned on the shower. She didn't feel too bad after her journey because Marco had booked her a first-class air ticket and she had been pampered all the way. But it was lovely to stand under the hot, refreshing jet of water and get rid of the stale feeling of travel.

She dried her hair and left it loose in soft waves around her face. Then she glanced at her watch. There was less than an hour now before they had to be at the dinner. So she started to put on her make-up and get ready.

Charlie was sitting in the lounge, flicking through the TV stations, when she heard the front door open and Marco walked in.

Her heart caught in her chest as she saw him. He looked so dynamically handsome that it was hard to believe he was her lover, or that this was for real. She felt suddenly shy, as she had gone to a lot of trouble with her appearance for tonight and she hoped he liked the way she looked.

'Sorry, honey—that was more of a marathon than I could ever have imagined.' He tossed the key card down on the side and walked towards her. 'Did you have a good flight?'

He stopped in his tracks as she stood up. 'God, you look amazing!' His eyes moved over her appraisingly.

His wolf-whistle and the way he was almost undressing her with his dark eyes made her blush. 'Thanks,' she smiled at him. She knew the dress was fantastic. The material was pale blue silk and its cut flattered her figure to perfection, emphasising her slender waist and her curves before falling to the floor in straight, sophisticated lines.

'You said to get something special to wear so I did. I hope it's suitable.'

'It's more than suitable! The only problem is I don't want to take you out now, I want to take you to bed,' he said huskily as he came a little closer.

'Well, unfortunately we don't have time for that.'

He trailed one finger down over the smooth, creamy perfection of her face, his eyes on the softness of her lips. 'I've missed you…'

'I missed you too.' Her heart missed several beats as he took her into his arms and kissed her.

At first the kiss was tenderly sensual but it quickly turned intensely possessive. She felt his hands on her body in a firm caress and sexual hunger tore through her like a searing, white-hot heat.

The phone on the table rang and he pulled back from her with a smile of regret. 'Do you mind if I get that? It might be important.'

'No…of course not.' She sat back down to wait for him. It didn't matter, she told herself. They would have all night together after this dinner and then three whole days and nights before she had to fly home again.

It was a call about a seminar in Seattle that Marco had said he would attend. Charlie tuned out after the first few minutes.

He put the phone down and raked one hand through the darkness of his hair. 'Sorry about that,' he said distractedly.

She shrugged. 'You'd better hurry and get ready if we are to be on time for dinner.'

'Yes.' He glanced at his watch. 'I'll have a quick shower. I won't be long. How's Jack, by the way?'

'He's fine. He's staying at Karen's because Mum is away for a few days with some friends.'

'Is he OK about moving?'

'I haven't told him yet.'

She saw his eyebrows rise. 'I'll tell him when I get home,' she added quickly.

He nodded and moved through towards the bedroom. Marco was right to look surprised, she supposed. She probably should have told Jack about her plans last week. But something had stopped her.

Charlie flicked through the TV channels and tried not to think too deeply about some of the doubts that had beset her last week. Every relationship was a risk. Even if Marco had declared undying love, moving in with him would still be a risk. The fact that he hadn't shouldn't really have mattered. Marco had said in his book that love would grow if you worked at it. And maybe that was what would happen between them.

She suddenly noticed with a start of surprise that she was looking at Marco on the TV screen. He looked fantastic, like a movie star about to discuss his latest part.

'You're on TV,' she called out.

'It will be a re-run of the Ed Johnson chat show. They keep showing it,' Marco called back as he disappeared through to the bathroom.

Charlie listened to the interview with interest. Ed Johnson was good at what he did and the show was intelligent as well as light-hearted. They touched on Marco's roots in Italy, his education and his past books, before dwelling more intently on his current book that was swiftly climbing the American charts. Marco was fantastic, entertaining, funny, very charismatic. He gave an account of his theories in a way that was serious yet very engaging. It was no wonder he was so much in demand and had achieved celebrity status.

'So basically what you are telling us is that the old saying about love being blind is true?' Ed Johnson asked.

'That's exactly right,' Marco agreed smoothly. 'You have to discount the feeling when looking for serious commitment. Of course, it's great to be in love, we all know that, and if the passion is there between you that's fantastic. But the feeling of love itself can be an illusion…you can think yourself in love or imagine that feeling is there because you really want it to be. And sometimes by the time you realise the mistake it's too late and you are heading for the divorce courts. That's why when you are looking for a long-term relationship you've got to look deeper than just emotional feelings. In fact, it's preferable to be best friends rather than to be deeply in love…'

'So where does your relationship fit with your theories?' Ed asked suddenly. 'Because I believe you have a new girlfriend in your life, and that the relationship is serious.'

'That's right. Charlie has been my PA for nearly six months now and we have been steadily getting closer over that time.'

She had heard Marco discussing his theories many times but it was really strange listening to him discussing their relationship. Even though she tried to tell herself that this was just a light TV programme, Charlie started to feel oddly vulnerable as she listened.

'So how close are you planning to get?' Ed asked.

'We're planning to move in together when I get back to England.'

The audience applauded wildly.

'And how does your relationship with Charlie compare to your theories?' Ed asked suddenly. 'Is this a love match or are you practising what you preach, so to speak?'

Charlie found herself moving forward on the sofa, her breath catching in her throat as she waited for the answer.

'Charlie and I work together well and we have a bond that is incredibly strong. In practical terms as a couple we tick all the right boxes.'

'So is this a love match?' Ed pressed for his answer.

'This is a match where neither of us have unrealistic expectations, we are on the same wavelength. We are willing to compromise. We're great friends and that's better than any unrealistic love match.'

Charlie felt suddenly sick. It was one thing telling herself that she could live without wild declarations of love, it was another thing entirely hearing the man she adored, the man she was about to move in with and dedicate her life to, describe her as merely his friend!

The phone rang, distracting her. 'Can you get that, Charlie?' Marco shouted from the other room.

She stood up and switched off the TV. She had heard enough.

She couldn't say that she was surprised by what she had

heard, because she had always known that was the truth. As far as Marco was concerned, they worked well together and 'they ticked all the right boxes'. They had passion, they had friendship but as for 'love'—well, apparently that was something you worked at…and maybe it was even an unnecessary emotion.

She hadn't expected anything more. And yet…the ache of disappointment and hurt was incredibly intense.

What if Marco *never* felt the same intensity of emotion for her as she did for him? She could wait and wait and it might never happen. The thought brought a chill deep inside.

'Charlie, are you going to get that phone?' Marco called again.

She picked it up impatiently. It was the chauffeur, who was waiting for them in the lobby, ready to take them for dinner.

'It's our driver,' she told Marco as he came through from the bedroom. He looked so handsome in his dark dinner suit and white shirt that she felt the lump in her throat grow.

'Right.' Marco looked at his watch. 'I suppose we will have to leave now.'

The last thing Charlie wanted was to go and have dinner with a room full of strangers, especially of people who had probably watched that interview. She was sure they would look at her and know the truth, know that her handsome lover didn't love her at all and that it was just a relationship of convenience.

With difficulty she forced herself to bury her smarting and crushed emotions. She had known the score when she had made her agreement with Marco. She couldn't start backing out of their agreement at this stage. For one thing, Marco was depending on her for the positive PR spin on his book. And for another, what could she say? Marco had never lied to her…he had never promised her love…and he didn't deserve for her to let him down now!

But could she really carry on with this and move in with

him? Did she really know what she was doing? The question pierced through her.

The large ballroom was filled with hundreds of people. The glitter of chandeliers dazzled over the diamonds and finery that the women wore. Charlie was very glad that she had splashed out on her sophisticated new evening dress.

She was horrified to find that Sarah Heart was attending the dinner. As soon as she and Marco stepped into the room Charlie saw her standing by the door, talking to a group of people. The woman looked stunning in a long red dress, her dark hair woven back from her face into a style that showed her classical bone structure and long neck to perfection.

'You didn't tell me that she was going to be here!' Charlie said in a low tone.

'Didn't I?' Marco shrugged. 'Sarah also represents Karina Kaplinski, so she's over here to do some promotional work for her as well.'

Charlie swallowed down a feeling of distaste. She may have disliked Sarah Heart intensely but she had very high-profile clients. Karina Kaplinski was a high-flying actress who had just written a sizzling autobiography that had taken the media by storm.

'That's Karina over there.' Marco nodded towards a beautiful, flame-haired woman in a long black dress.

As if sensing Marco's eyes on her, the woman turned and smiled at him and then blew him a kiss.

'Another one of your fans, I see,' Charlie remarked with a smile.

Marco laughed. 'We were on the same chat show last week. She's very theatrical.'

It wasn't long before Sarah was winging her way across the room towards them. 'Darling, how lovely to see you,' she gushed as she reached to kiss him on each cheek. 'And Charlie...' She turned to look towards her and seemed to do a double take as she took in her appearance. 'It's great you could make it.'

The welcome held a slight edge of insincerity, but then Charlie was surprised Sarah even acknowledged her. Usually she totally ignored her as if she didn't exist.

'Did you have a good journey?' Sarah asked solicitously.

This was even weirder, Charlie thought. Sarah rarely if ever tried to make any polite conversation with her. 'Yes, thank you.'

'Wonderful. Well, shall we take our seats for dinner?' Sarah smiled at Marco. 'As luck would have it we are sitting next to each other, Marco.'

Some things never changed, Charlie thought wryly.

They were seated at a table towards the front of the ballroom. Charlie found herself placed opposite Marco's editor, Jeffery Green, a tall, rather distinguished-looking man in his late fifties who had a thick head of grey hair and a twinkle in his blue eyes.

Karina Kaplinski was also at the table. She didn't so much make conversation but hold court over the long table. In particular she kept trying to get Marco's opinion on everything from the weather to the state of the nation and it didn't seem to matter to her that Charlie was sitting next to him because she flirted outrageously with him.

Marco took it all in his stride and just seemed lazily amused by her.

Jeffery smiled over at Charlie as Karina paused to draw breath. 'Great news about Marco's book.'

'What news is that?' Charlie asked.

'Oh, hasn't he told you? It made number one in the American bestseller charts two days ago.'

'Really? That's wonderful.' Charlie looked over at Marco and wondered why he hadn't told her when they had spoken on the phone. 'Congratulations.'

He smiled at her. 'Thanks.'

'I can't believe you didn't tell Charlie that!' She could hear Sarah's low whisper to Marco as the lights in the room suddenly started to lower, signalling that the meal had come to a close and the speeches were ready to begin. 'Don't forget, she's supposed to be your partner.'

Supposed to be your partner. The mocking words echoed inside Charlie as the music from the stage area started to blare, drowning out whatever Marco's reply had been. Then the compère for the evening walked out towards the podium.

She saw Karina lean across the table towards Marco and say something. She was probably propositioning him, safe in the knowledge that his *supposed partner* was no real competition.

Charlie didn't think for one minute that Marco was sexually interested in Karina or, for that matter, in Sarah. But what would happen when a woman came along who did interest him?

The question reverberated painfully through her mind.

It was all very well having this practical relationship based on friendship, but what happened when some woman really blew Marco and all his logical theories away? It was bound to happen one day because he was like a walking magnet for women. One day that special someone would come along and then where would their comfortable, practical relationship be?

She suddenly found herself remembering the last painful stages of her marriage when Greg told her he was leaving her and that he loved someone else.

She couldn't bear to go through something like that again.

Marco leaned closer and she could smell his cologne, which was tantalisingly provocative.

'Are you OK?' His voice was a whisper close against her ear.

'Yes.' She forced herself to smile. 'It's great news about your book.'

'Yes; thanks for your help with the PR side of things.' He kissed the side of her face. The casual kiss made her hurt inside as if someone had put a tight band around her heart and was squeezing it hard.

She could put up with Sarah's jibes…she could even put up with Marco speaking about their relationship in cool, business-like terms, but what she couldn't live with was the knowledge that one day Marco would leave her just the way Greg had, without so much as a backward glance.

She should never have weakened and said she'd move in with him. It had been a terrible mistake. The realisation hit her like a physical blow.

'And now a man who needs no introduction from me other than to say we have an eminent doctor in the house.' The loud tones of the compère rang through the auditorium. 'Ladies and gentlemen, please put your hands together for Dr Marco Delmari.'

Charlie watched as Marco walked up towards the stage. She listened to the thunderous applause and saw the way he handled it with that relaxed charm of his.

As he made a speech and then moved on towards handing out some award, Sarah moved into his empty seat and leaned across to speak to her. 'He's incredible, isn't he?' she said with a smile. 'This tour is going so well.'

'Yes, so it seems,' Charlie answered, wishing Sarah would move away. The last thing she needed right now was snide comments from her.

'Sorry if you were upset by what I said to you in Italy,' Sarah whispered suddenly.

'You didn't upset me.'

'Really? Marco thinks I did. But how was I supposed to know that he was going to carry this loveless-relationship idea to such lengths? Anyway, no hard feelings and I hope it works out for you.'

She moved back to her own seat as Marco started to leave the stage.

Charlie bit down on her lip. Sarah was such a horrible person, she'd just had to rub it in about their relationship being a sham. Although there wasn't much she could have replied to that because what Sarah had said was true.

Marco returned to his seat as the lights came on in the room. An orchestra started to play and a few couples went out onto the floor to dance to a smoothly romantic melody.

'Great speech, Marco,' Karina said silkily.

'Thanks.'

'Would you like to dance?' she invited softly.

'Sorry, not right now—I've got some catching up to do with Charlie.' He softened the refusal with a smile. 'Maybe later.'

'I'll hold you to that,' she practically purred and then turned to talk to a crowd of people who had come over to speak to her.

Marco turned back towards Charlie. 'I don't know about you but I could do with getting out of here,' he muttered.

'Yes, me too.'

'There are some people I have to see…' he looked around the room '…but once I've had a few words we'll escape.' He looked back at her. 'Do you want a dance first?'

'No, thanks, Marco, I'm a bit tired.' She didn't think she could handle going into his arms right now. She felt as if she had been on enough of an emotional roller coaster for one evening.

'Sorry! I keep forgetting you've had such a long journey today.' Marco glanced at his watch. 'What was Sarah saying to you, by the way?' he asked as he looked up.

The sudden question took her by surprise. 'Nothing much.'

'Well, she was saying something. I hope she wasn't stirring it again.'

'No…well, unless you count wishing us well in our loveless

relationship.' She tried to sound as if she was merely amused but the tone of her voice was more brittle than she had wanted.

Marco looked annoyed. 'She can't shut up, can she?'

'She was only speaking the truth. Neither of us have a right to be annoyed about that, have we?'

There was an uncomfortable silence between them for a moment.

'Charlie, I—'

'Let's not talk about it now, OK?' she cut across him breathlessly and her eyes blazed suddenly with unshed tears. If he said one word to defend their 'practical' relationship right now she knew she would break down.

He frowned. 'You're having second thoughts about us, aren't you?'

'Let's just get through this charade first, shall we?' Her voice was stiff. She really wanted to cry and she couldn't bear to do that here in front of him and all these people.

Someone stopped by the table to talk to Marco and as soon as he was distracted she took the opportunity to get up and move away. The room was packed and it was an effort to make her way towards the ladies'. Then she saw an exit door and headed for that instead.

What she needed was some fresh air and some space to clear her head.

After the crowded heat of the ballroom it was a relief when she got outside onto the pavement.

She took deep gulps of the cold night air. And then she tried to get things in perspective. She had done a lot of travelling today and she was probably over-tired and over-emotional.

Crowds swirled around her and, although she was outside in a flimsy evening dress, no one paid her any attention. It was as if she wasn't there.

A couple walked by, wrapped in each other's arms. The guy was looking at his girlfriend with rapt attention. That was what she wanted, she thought suddenly, someone who would look at her with that level of adoration…someone who really loved her.

She realised with a rush that she wasn't merely over-tired and that she was thinking more clearly than she had in weeks. She couldn't play this game of pretence with Marco. It hurt too much.

Before she could stop to analyse her actions she stepped forward. There was a yellow cab coming up the street and she flagged it down.

CHAPTER THIRTEEN

ONCE she was in the taxi she tried to phone Marco on his mobile but it was switched off and she just got his messaging service.

'Hi, it's me.' She tried to sound composed but there was such a fierce pain inside her chest from the weight of emotion she carried that it was hard to even speak. 'Look, I realise by rushing off like this that I'm behaving very badly and…probably erratically. I'm sorry,' she drew in her breath, 'but I can't go through with this, Marco. I realised tonight that it just wouldn't work between us. I'm heading back to the hotel and I'm going to pack my stuff and check out. I think it's for the best. I hope you'll forgive me.'

She hung up and put the phone back in her bag.

The words rang hollow inside her but she knew despite the pain that she had done the right thing. Better to end things now than to let them get too far out of hand.

She had learnt her lesson with Greg. She couldn't go through that again. And it could be even worse with Marco…she was so head-over-heels in love with him it was crazy.

The cab pulled up outside her hotel and she paid the driver and hurried inside. She needed to pack and get out of this hotel before Marco got back. If he started to try and persuade her to stay she knew she would get emotional and say things she didn't want to say.

At least if she got away now she would have time to pull herself together and when she did speak to him again she could try and exit from his life with some scrap of dignity.

As soon as she got back into their suite she took out her suitcase and opened it on the bed. Then she took off her dress and put on her jeans and a T-shirt before throwing everything else into the case.

The trouble with not taking the time to fold things was that the case then refused to close. After the fourth attempt she finally got the locks closed and picked it up. And that was when she heard the door open.

Her heart thundered erratically as she turned and came face to face with Marco.

'What the hell are you playing at?' His dark gaze moved from her towards the suitcase.

She took a deep breath. 'I'm really sorry, Marco. Did you get my message?'

He tossed his mobile phone down on the table. 'Yes, and it made about as much sense as seeing you standing there with your suitcase. Where do you think you are going?'

'I'm going to check into another hotel.'

'Why?'

She shrugged helplessly. 'I told you on the phone. I realise I've made a mistake. I can't move in with you, Marco. So I think it's best I leave.'

He watched the way she held her head high, the spark of defiance in her eye.

'You don't really need me here now anyway. I've done what you needed. Plus your book is number one in the charts, so it's OK.'

'No, it's not OK,' he cut across her firmly. 'Look, you are over-tired, you've had a long day and now you've just got a classic case of cold feet.'

'Well, thanks for the diagnosis, Doctor, but you're wrong.'

His calm manner irritated her. 'You talked me into moving in with you but I was never sure it was the right thing…and now I know it's not.'

'Really?' He crossed his arms. 'Because of some outrageous comment from Sarah Heart?'

'It wasn't an outrageous comment.' Her voice trembled slightly. 'It was true and you know it.'

He didn't say anything to that and she suddenly felt tears welling up inside her. 'I'm not leaving just because of Sarah's comments, it's more complicated than that.'

'What's that supposed to mean?'

When she made no reply he muttered fiercely, 'I think I deserve more of an explanation than that. Don't you?'

'Well, for a start, there was your TV interview.' She shrugged helplessly.

'What about it?'

The calm question made her temper flare. The hurt feelings that she had been trying so hard to rein in since she had listened to that interview started to spill out. 'You mean apart from the fact that you told the whole world that you and I are just some kind of experiment in relationship terms?'

'Don't be absurd!'

'That's what you said more or less. That you are with me to prove your point about love not being necessary.' She put her hand on her hip. 'Well, I've decided that you can go and prove your point with someone else.'

'Charlie, I haven't asked you to move in with me to prove a point.' His voice softened.

'Well, you could have fooled me!'

'You are being totally irrational,' he said with a frown.

'Am I?' She glared at him. 'Well, I did try to warn you that we are not as compatible as you thought,' she blazed furiously, 'because the fact is that I can be wildly illogical when I want to be.'

'Really?' Instead of looking annoyed he seemed briefly amused.

'Just move out of my way, Marco—I want to leave.' She took a few steps forward towards the door but he made no attempt to move out of her way and he looked very serious now.

'I'm sorry, Charlie, but there is no way I am allowing you to leave,' he said softly. 'Not until I know exactly what the hell you are talking about.'

'Well, let me make it clear, Marco: I really thought I could live a life with you that didn't involve love but I just can't.'

'Love will grow between us,' he said gently. 'I know it will.'

She shook her head and tears threatened to spill now. 'I can't take that chance, Marco. It hurts too much when everything goes wrong.'

He moved across to her and took her suitcase from unresisting fingers. Then he pulled her close and held her.

For a moment she allowed herself to lean against him and the feeling was blissful.

'Everything won't go wrong between us.' His voice was low and reassuring. 'We are good together. You know that deep down.'

'But it's not enough.' She pulled away from him. It felt so good to be in his arms but she couldn't allow herself to be swayed by emotions that weren't real. That was what always happened when she was around him and it was a dangerous distraction.

'But you said you wanted companionship and stability and we can have all that—'

'It's not enough, Marco,' she cut across him with raw emphasis. 'And I'm sorry I led you to believe otherwise.' She swallowed hard. 'You once told me I was too emotional to ever be happy with that kind of arrangement and you were right. You should have gone with your first analysis of me.'

When he didn't say anything to that she looked up at him with shimmering eyes. 'It's not that I don't believe in your theories about working at a relationship, because I do.' Her voice became a mere whisper. 'But, you see, for me love is the building block, the starting point, and without it there's really *no* point.' She bit down on her lip.

'So you couldn't learn to love me, then?' he asked quietly.

The husky words made her heart suddenly miss several beats. She wanted to tell him that she already did love him, but pride made the words stick in her throat.

She couldn't meet his eye now. 'I think it's just best that I go and we call it a day. Don't worry, we can keep it quiet from the media—'

'To hell with the media, Charlie, I really couldn't care less about it,' he grated angrily.

She frowned. 'Well, of course you care. Your book and your work is all-important to you.'

'Not as important as you.'

Charlie had been in the process of turning away but she paused in her tracks.

'Don't go, Charlie…please.'

Her heart stopped for a second at that husky, uncertain tone that was so unlike him.

'Do you know why I didn't tell you that my book was number one in the American chart?' he asked abruptly. 'Because it meant that in practical terms I didn't need you here…the book was doing well and I was doing fine without a partner by my side.'

She frowned, not following what he meant.

'I didn't want to tell you because I thought it would give you an excuse not to come,' he continued bluntly. 'And the truth was that I needed you…'

'You did?'

He nodded. 'I missed you so much that it hurt. I love you, Charlie.'

The admission made her whirl around to face him, her eyes wide.

'Is this some sort of game?' she whispered.

'Yes, it's called the truth game.' Marco's lips twisted derisively. 'Look, I've tried to take things slowly so as not to scare you off. But I can't let you go.'

She took a tentative step towards him. 'Say that again,' she whispered.

'I can't let you go.' He reached out and touched her face. 'Because I love you.'

She could hardly believe what he was saying to her.

'In fact, I love everything about you,' he added softly. 'The way you wear your hair—whether it is tied up or left loose,' he added. 'With or without glasses…in evening dress or even wrapped in a towel.' He gave a helpless kind of shrug.

She stared at him in a sense of wonderment. 'I thought I was just a "friend" who ticked all the right boxes?'

'A friend who I fell in love with,' he corrected softly. 'Look, I know you don't feel the same but it will grow…I know it will, because that's what happened to me. When I came back from Italy I realised how deeply I felt for you and that I just couldn't live without you. The debacle with the photographers in Florence made me recognize that I never wanted any hurt to come to you ever again. I tried to deny the feelings but…' he shrugged helplessly '…some things just can't be denied. And if you just give me a chance to prove myself to you I know I can make you happy.

'Charlie, don't cry!' He looked appalled as he saw huge tears spilling down her face and pulled her into his arms. 'God, it tears me apart, seeing you like this.'

'I'm OK,' she murmured huskily.

'No, you're not, and it's my fault. I tried to rush you into moving in with me because I couldn't bear not to have you in my life. But I should have taken things slower, given you time to get used to the idea, time to think about us as a family—'

'I don't need more time…not now—'

'Just give things a little longer,' he cut across her earnestly. 'We'll take things slow. I'll do whatever it takes—'

'Marco, I don't need to take things slowly.' She looked up at him. 'Because I already love you; I always have.'

She saw the look of surprise in his expression. And then suddenly she was in his arms and he was kissing her with a passion that made her breathless. She clung to him and melted into him, her body tingling with happiness and exhilaration.

'Charlie, when you told me you couldn't live without love I honestly thought you were going to walk out. I've always prided myself on the fact that I look at situations in a rational way…but God, I couldn't bear to lose you.'

The rawness in his eyes made her realise how completely she had broken through his defences. 'I meant I couldn't live without your love for me,' she corrected him softly.

A smile started to curve Marco's lips.

He reached out and touched the side of her face, a look of perplexity in his eyes. 'I've always sensed such wariness in you. In fact, I thought that you might not be over your ex-husband.'

'I was over Greg a long time ago. If I was wary it was because I don't want to go through the heartache of another break-up.'

He nodded. 'I can understand that. But I have to admit, when you talked about just wanting companionship and practicalities for your next relationship…I thought it meant he was still in your heart.'

'The only person in my heart was you, Marco.' She swallowed hard. 'I lied about all that anyway. And I think I did it because I've always been in love with you…and I didn't think you would ever feel the same way about me. Even when you asked me to move in with you I thought it was for purely practical reasons, because I'm good in the office, because we get on well…'

'Well, that last bit is true, of course,' Marco said teasingly.

'Marco!' She looked up at him reproachfully and he kissed her. It was a kiss that was so sweetly full of emotion she could feel his love like a tangible force inside her.

'I would have thought kisses like that might have told you something else,' he murmured as he pulled back.

'I thought you were just good at passion because you are Italian,' she said with a smile.

He laughed at that.

'I've never kissed anyone the way I've kissed you.' He looked deep into her eyes. 'And I'm not talking about the fact that we are good in bed together…which we most definitely are. I'm talking about the way you make me feel in here.' He put a hand on his chest. 'You've touched my heart the way no one has ever done.'

'Do you realise that is the most romantic thing anyone has ever said to me?' she said teasingly. 'And this from the man who shuns sentimentality of any sort.'

'It just happens to be true. So it's not sentimental slush!'

She smiled at him. 'God, I love you, Marco…'

'Does that mean you will move in with me?'

'Of course it does.'

For a long while they didn't speak and just kissed. They were the most blissfully happy moments of Charlie's life.

'When you move in it's for keeps, Charlie,' he told her firmly as he pulled away. 'In sickness and health, for richer or poorer…all of that.'

'All of that,' she agreed softly. 'So what's happened to the inveterate bachelor…the guy who wasn't cut out for commitment?' she asked with a smile.

'He just found the right woman.'

Marco's lips crushed against hers in a kiss of such tenderness that it took her breath away.

'And who would have thought that the woman in question was an incurable romantic?' she murmured as she wound her arms up and around his neck. 'Did I tell you that I fell in love with you at first sight, by the way?'

'Sorry to disappoint you, but that was just lust, Charlie,' Marco laughed, and picked her up to carry her back towards the bed.

She didn't argue…but she knew he was wrong about that.

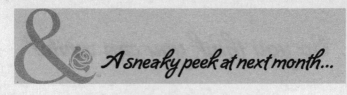

Have Your Say

You've just finished your book.
So what did you think?

We'd love to hear your thoughts on our
'Have your say' online panel
www.millsandboon.co.uk/haveyoursay

- Easy to use
- Short questionnaire
- Chance to win Mills & Boon® goodies